PIASA

PIASA

Third Edition

Michael Kott

For
My Grandchildren
Jessica, Felicia, Nicholas, Jason, Jake and Zoe

And
Great-Grandchildren
Asher and ?

It all Began with:

PIASA

The Native American legend:

In 1673, while voyaging down the Mississippi River, French explorers Marquette and Joliet, came across the painting of a strange creature up on the bluffs, high above the river near the area of Alton, Illinois. The beast, a conglomeration of bird, animal, reptile and fish characteristics, was sketched in Marquette's diary. The Native American tribe who lived there, the Illini, told them they had no idea who painted it; in fact it had always been there. The Illini called the creature the Piasa, which in their language meant, "the bird that devoured men." While the original painting was later destroyed by early settlers, the town has continued to paint the above image of the Piasa on the bluffs along the river down to the present day. There have been all kinds of theories as to who painted the original and why, but the truth is: no one really knows.

AUTHOR'S NOTE . . .

If you've already read this novel (a few people have) you're probably wondering, *What the?*

Let me explain the reasoning. My original story was written long before the initial publishing date. It was copyrighted in 2004, but I had worked on it since 1998. I came across the legend when my daughter and I were working on another story and met in Alton, which happened to be about midway between the Chicago area, where I lived, and Memphis, where she was living at the time. In fact, I used a rough description of Jackson House, where we stayed, in my novel. Jackson House has since closed down. *Piasa* was originally first published in 2010 (the book said 2011 but it was actually December of 2010) by the now-defunct Two Moon Press in Marshall Michigan. While Marshall Press promised the moon to authors, they delivered nothing and eventually were sued by other authors, many who never even received any copies of their books. A year later, the Marshall Police were pursuing a complaint and asked me for a statement, which I gave them, but I never heard any more about it. One of the things promised was a professional edit, which they never did. In fact, if anything, they undid editing and the book, while readable, was riddled with errors. In fact, they initially formatted it all wrong and it was unreadable. So, they said they'd destroy that initial printing. Did they? Well, I actually saw one advertised on-line from a bookstore in the south. How do I know it was one of those? They used the name Mike Kott on the cover instead of how it was submitted, Michael Kott. My apologies if you "bought" one.

In 2017, trying to correct the errors, I re-edited the novel and re-released it. While better, I am a poor excuse for an editor, and yet it still got me compliments with the caveat it could be way better if properly edited. So, I contacted my current editor (yes, I now have a terrific editor who has worked on my last three published books and several that I am in progress of writing) to take a shot at it. She did so, while pointing out parts she thought could stand improvement. I have made most of the changes she called for, and this is that republished story under the same book title but with a new cover, ISBN number, and a publishing date of 2020. The main story remains basically the same. Well, slightly different.

While I am aware of new theories, formulated and published since my initial research from 1998 to 2002, as to how the petroglyph of the Piasa came to appear on the bluffs overlooking the Mississippi River just north of Alton, Illinois, I do not share them. Since the original petroglyph is gone and with it the people who lived then, we'll never know positively who created it. Any theory is based on speculation. I still prefer the answer the native Americans gave Father Marquette when he asked who created it. They said, "It had always been there." Regardless, my story remains a YA fictional adventure and is not to be construed as truth. The story of the Piasa, as presented in the novel, is based on what I found in the early 2000s, and I have not embraced any new speculations.

Will I also redo the follow-on novel, *Cryptid*? Thinking about it, but I have projects galore, so it'll be hard to fit in.

Michael Kott
April, 2020

CHAPTER 1

Chicago, Illinois
Last Day of February...

"Move, you skinny doofus."

That's what Brett Kovar said, just before he shoved me into the row of lockers. Not that I was in his way. It was just plain meanness, meant to embarrass me. He relished doing things like that when I was with my friends. I was an easy target because I just no longer fought back. Not physically or verbally. Whenever anyone got upset with their life, I'm sure they thought, 'Where's that little dweeb, Sara Williams? I need to hit someone.'

"Stop being a doormat, Sara," Gina said. "Why do you let the lowlifes push you around?"

"I guess I'm always in someone's way," I pleaded.

"No, you're not," Stacy said. "You need to get a backbone and stand up to those bullies. You can start with that stepdad of yours."

I used to have a comeback for everything. All the girls flocked to be my friend because they thought I would be the one to lead the in-crowd in high school. Then, two years ago, my dad, a Marine, was killed by a roadside bomb in Iraq. I was just thirteen. My world disintegrated, and I haven't been the same since. Now, I was left with my small group of four friends.

"You mean like you're doing now, Stacy?" Emily interrupted. "Stop being so hurtful." Emily was always leaping to my defense; even now she signaled her support by lightly gripping my elbow. I wanted to say something to them, but didn't want to make things worse, so I held back. I had so few friends left. I couldn't afford to lose any by arguing with them.

"I'm not the one physically abusing her," Stacy lamented, then looked at me. "Why'd your mom have to marry that creep, anyway?"

"I'm sorry, guys, you know my situation," I said. Spring break time had come to us in the northeastern part of Chicago, but as usual, I was the one throwing a flag on the plans. It had come as a big disappointment to them when I announced I was unable to go on our scheduled trip.

* * *

My mom, desperate to support the two of us, had recently remarried. Rod, now my stepfather, and I just didn't get along. He hated that I refused to acknowledge my mom had actually married him and that I still went by

Williams, my father's last name. I couldn't blame Mom, she was trying to do the best for both of us. She just couldn't see what my friends and I saw— Rod hated that girls had minds of their own. Mom fed his ego by doing everything she was told so she was exempt from his anti-female rantings. Plain and simple? He was a bozo who just detested the opposite sex. What exacerbated the situation was he had Peter, his sixteen-year-old son from his previous marriage. And the apple hadn't fallen far from the tree. Like father, like son.

Peter had buddies like Brett, who never resisted the opportunity to inflict pain on me. They shoved me all the time, stole stuff from me, and called me every name in the book. They kept escalating the embarrassing things they did to me.

I couldn't help I was only five feet tall and about ninety pounds. And that's dressed, with shoes. Between the boys in school and Rod and Peter, I saw no good in the male sex. I steered clear of male friends because of how they treated me, except for my real father. I hated them all.

Last week, they trapped me after school in the girl's locker room. I had cross country practice and was the last one in. I had showered and just gotten dressed when they found me. I tried to run, but Brett grabbed me. When I tried to get away, he held me while Glenn Butler slapped my face. Glenn said he needed to "smack a little sense into me." I knew, though, that Peter was behind this. The three were best friends. Of course, Peter, the little coward, didn't want to show himself.

They called me awful names, and then Glenn stuffed me in a locker. Before they closed the door, Brett said. "You tell anyone we did this and next time we won't be so nice." It was so humiliating when the custodian found me and let me out. Of course, I had to say I never got a look at who did it, they grabbed me from behind.

* * *

"Hey, guys," Amanda cut into my nightmares of mortification. "Spring break is in two weeks. We need to decide what we're doing . . . now. Picking on Sara isn't helping. She can't go, so let's just plan it without her, okay?"

I winced inwardly as I stood there while the rest made their plans. Did they really need to do this in front of me?

Inundated with these terrible memories and knowing tears were seconds away, I grabbed my books from my locker and headed for the exit doors.

"Sara? Where are you going?" Emily asked. I caught her words to the others as I hurried away. "We could have made these plans another time, Amanda. You know what her home life has become. Why do you have to add to her suffering? Leave her alone."

PIASA

Once outside, I just stood on the sidewalk and waited for the tears to flow. *Why did Mom have to pick my spring break to visit her sister in southern Illinois anyway?* During the past week, there had been a small earthquake in Alton, way down in southern Illinois where Aunt Claire, my mom's younger sister, lived. Even though Auntie said all was fine, Mom insisted we go down to see if she needed any help. My spring break, and I had to go to Hicksville, USA. I loved and was worried about Aunt Claire, but this trip couldn't have come at a worse time.

However, Mom and I had a deal, and I had to honor it. She was hoping some of the animosity between Rod, Peter—his vile little horror of an offspring—and me would ease. Fat chance of that, but I couldn't rain on Mom's parade. She was all I had, so I was forced to grin and bear it. Emily almost saved the day for me by volunteering to go with us to Auntie's, but Rod wouldn't hear of it. Emily was loyal to me, so she wouldn't even talk to Peter and his friends. The only people Peter disliked more than me were my friends, especially Emily.

Emily caught up with me where I now stood on the sidewalk, tears flooding my eyes. We had been close since first grade, and she would go along with whatever I said. But the rest of our tiny posse was always trying to break into a higher strata of the cliques at Magnolia High School, and having the class wimp for a friend wasn't conducive to that goal.

"You'll ruin your makeup," she said, slipping an arm around my meager shoulders.

"You know I don't wear makeup, Emily."

"Yeah, but what else could I say? You'd smear your freckles?" She paused and rubbed my back in sympathy. "Ignore those ignoramuses. I wish I could go with you. I'd kick that smart aleck brother of yours right . . . where it would hurt the most."

"Me too," I said with a shake of my thick red curls. "Wish you could go, that is."

She pulled out a tissue and handed it to me. "You better dry those freckles. I hear tears make them multiply."

"Thanks, Emily, for sticking by me . . . again."

3

Chapter 2

Southwestern Illinois
Early March...

"Peter, stop!" I yelled as my stepbrother's slimy hand snaked across the seat once again and pinched my leg. This time I reflexively swung my hand across the seat, smacking him on the side of his face.

The faker immediately let out a cry of pain. I knew this trip wasn't going to work, why couldn't mom see that? It was bad enough riding with him on errands around the city. A trip of some two hundred and fifty miles was pure agony.

Rod turned around and yelled at me, "Sara Williams! Stay on your own side and stop pestering your brother."

Me? Brother? I had never accepted that snot as a relation of mine. However, I tried to explain. "But I didn't—"

"You're supposed to be mature," he interrupted. "When are you going to show some signs of adulthood?" As usual, it was me in the wrong.

When you do, bozo. "That cry was so phony. Besides, he—"

"Quiet! Why are you so jealous of him? You should . . ."

I tuned out the rest as he continued to rant. I should have stayed home. Once he called me by my surname, there was no reasoning with him. I squirmed around uncomfortably, trying to stay out of range of Peter's roaming fingers. When I glanced up, I met his idiotic grin on the other side of the rear seat. His stupid grimace said it all.

In an effort to block out his repulsive face, I turned one-eighty and watched the snow whipping past our speeding car. After calming down, I tried to nap, while outside, the white flakes continued to cascade down. I noticed that in spots it was starting to stick.

* * *

"Rod!"

The sound of Mom's voice woke me an hour later. My head was crushed up against the rear window and a line of drool extended down into the door.

"Rod, slow down. It's snowing and you're driving like a maniac." Mom's plea had once again fallen on deaf ears. As usual, he slowed down briefly and then resumed his over-the-limit speed. I pushed back the urge to echo Mom's words. After all, I had every right to live, and he didn't seem to care about anyone in the back seat. Well, me anyway.

Mom turned, and seeing me fidgeting nervously around, said to me, "Why don't you get some rest, dear? It'll be a while before we get to Aunt Claire's."

"I'll be okay. It's just so cramped back here." I used my head to silently point to Peter, not wanting Rod to come to his defense. Mom would know what I meant.

"Why don't you get more comfortable?" Mom suggested. "Listen to your CDs." With that, she turned back and once again shouted, "Rod, slow down, for heaven's sake!"

In disgust, I glared at the back of Rod's head, then refocused on Peter. I saw he was facing his door and was lightly snoring. Thank God he had finally fallen asleep, and for a change, on his side of the car.

An idea quickly took form in my head. I slipped my sandals off and put my size five feet up on the seat, wriggling the stiffness out of my toes. I reached down and manually fanned them with my hand. A problem with a nerve between my toes had at times caused me a lot of pain. The doctor said it was from the pressure of footwear that was too small. Having small feet made it difficult to find well-fitting shoes. Whenever I could, I solved the problem by going barefoot.

After glancing over at Peter, sprawled out on the other side of the seat, I propped my pillow behind my back, loosened my seat belt a little, then leaned back against the door and put my feet up on his back. He slept on oblivious, like I knew he would. When that useless carcass of leftover manure slept, an atom bomb couldn't wake him up. *If he knew what I was doing, he would throw a fit. Not that there's anything wrong with my feet. It's not like they smell or anything. Not like his.*

I closed my eyes, but the mental anguish that had troubled me for months now crept into my thoughts. My dad had been everything to me. I just couldn't adjust to his being gone. Now, my friends had already begun to talk about college and life after high school, but I was clueless. Here we were, going to be sophomores next year, and they already had their futures carefully planned out. For me there was only bewilderment. It was useless to look into colleges if you didn't know what you wanted to do with your life. Where was my dad when I needed him? Life was so unfair. Besides all of this, Rod used paying for college as a weapon.

"I'm not paying for college for some kid who doesn't even have my name. Change your name or we're not paying for school." And thus far, as I was in a public high school, I have refused. Somewhere, I thought, there has to be a college I could afford. Because of him, and those nasty guys at school,

I needed to find an all-girl school. Or, at the very least, one where the girls outnumbered the guys. Otherwise it would be difficult to make friends.

Right now, I needed to calm down and get all these troubling thoughts out of my head. Finally, I picked up my CD player—*Rod* told me I couldn't get an iPod—put the earpiece in and turned it on. What he didn't realize was I didn't want one. While everyone made fun of me with my 'old-fashioned ways,' I actually preferred my CDs. There was something about handling the discs as opposed to just electronic music that I liked. Feeling immensely better now that I was virtually alone in the back seat, I studied the plastic case. The cover picture of Alanis Morissette and the album title, *Now is the Time,* stared back at me. Thanks to Emily, I had secretly, and successfully, bid on eBay for the Canadian singer's second album, recorded and released only in Canada before she became a household name. Wriggling my toes once more, I mouthed along as a younger version of Alanis began singing like she knew I was alone.

From up front, I heard Mom once more say, "Please, Rod. Slow down!"

* * *

What was that? I had been having a nightmare that I was in a dark place and something terrible was pursuing me. I had been struggling to escape. It seemed to be closing in on me, so I silently kicked out, then awoke with a start. Luckily, I had been kicking the air above Peter's back, so he continued to snore peacefully. This latest nap of mine had to have gotten us closer to the end of this nightmarish journey.

When I looked out on my right, there was the dark, moving water of the Mississippi River sliding silently along. Framed by dark-gray, snow-spitting skies, the river looked menacing in the late afternoon hours. However, it appeared we had moved out from under the main part of the clipper system, whose snow was blanketing the north and central parts of the state, and into the area north of Alton and St. Louis. Sporadic snow showers still burst out without warning, but then quickly dispersed.

As the radio station began to break up, Mom twisted the dial to locate another. Suddenly, I recognized WLS, a powerful Chicago station, that blared out:

"This just in to WLS News. There has been a multi-car pileup on the westbound Eisenhower Expressway, just east of Harlem Avenue. Police ask you to avoid traveling on it for the next couple of hours."

Mom turned to Rod. "If we were still around Chicago, that would probably be you. You drive too fast. How far are we from Alton?"

"About ten miles," he grumbled, another reminder that he was nowhere near the man my father had been. "We just zipped through Grafton, but we're still north of Godfrey. We should get to your sister's shortly. Are they still sleeping?"

I quickly closed my eyes, but not before Mom turned around and looked at me, my feet still up on Peter's back. I winked at her and she smiled.

"Yep, like babies," Mom said. "Wish they were always this quiet," she gave me a wink back. "Their constant bickering wears me down."

Not wanting to take any chances he would turn around and look, I silently pulled my feet back and fastened my seat belt. Unknowingly, I was saving my life.

"Here's an update on that accident just into WLS News. There appears to have been two fatalities in the collision, a young mother and her daughter. Police refuse to confirm this, but ask you continue to avoid the artery, now backed up for several miles."

My eyes widened as a big pocket of snow suddenly enveloped the car.

"Slow down, Rod," mom cautioned. "How can you see?"

The sudden burst of wind-driven snow obviously impaired Rod's vision, because our Mercury crossed lanes and drifted into the northbound lane of the roadway. Suddenly, as quickly as it came, the snow dissipated. Staring through the windshield, I was alarmed when I saw a large delivery truck looming on a collision course right in front of us.

I screamed as our car swerved to the right to avoid the truck and began to slide sideways down the slippery highway. The seat belt bit into my stomach, and I was pulled toward Peter's side of the car. We avoided the truck, but when I again looked through the front windshield, I saw a car now headed straight for us.

The SUV struck us broadside on the passenger side. My body had initially pitched forward, but the force of the collision slammed me into the door. The door flew open and I was yanked by centrifugal force into the yawning opening. The seatbelt kept me in place, though, while Peter, who had removed his, was hurled across the seat and into me, crushing me and smashing my face into the window. The door had swung back, but pinned my left arm and leg, causing me to scream in pain. As the demolished car spun on the snow-covered road, the forces hurled Peter back toward the other side. Looking up in horror, I watched as he was flung out through the exploded window. Our car, shoved back into the southbound lanes, flipped over and tumbled down the banks of the river.

Items from the car, seemingly in slow-motion, flew out the shattered windows and were strewn about the river banks. Amazingly, through the now windowless door, I could see my Alanis plastic CD case bounce down among the rocks and, last I saw, end up close to the river.

The car came to rest right side up with the passenger side against a large boulder. Something wet ran into my eye as I again screamed out in pain. Although I was barely conscious, my mind told me to undo my seat belt and crawl out, but my arms and legs refused to function. I wiped at what was running into my eye and saw that it was red. Drifting in and out of consciousness, I was suddenly aware that the front of the car had burst into flames.

CHAPTER 3

Alton, Illinois
March…

When I awoke, it was two days later. Aunt Claire was in the hospital room with me. She gradually broke the terrible news to me—my stepdad and brother were killed in the accident.

"What about my mom?" I asked. "How is she?"

Auntie bowed her head and shielded her eyes. "You need to hold onto something, Sara," she said. "My sister . . . your mom . . ." Aunt Claire started to cry while all I could do, with my one free hand, was rip at the bedsheets in hopelessness.

I knew it then. I was the only survivor of the accident.

Aunt Claire came every day for the next week, but I was inconsolable at the loss of my mom. Mom was all I had left in the world. What would I do without her? For the first few days, I didn't even consider that I now was an orphan. Devastated, I just cried for my mom. I would have done anything to get her back.

Gradually the realities of the outside world started to creep in.

Aunt Claire ran a bed and breakfast by herself. So, after a week of daily visits, and with a fusillade of apologies, she told me she had to return to taking care of her business, but my cousin, Pamela Sweet, would come by shortly.

"Pamela's an Alton police officer," Aunt Claire said. "She was the one who contacted me after the accident. She also rode with you inside the ambulance to the hospital."

Shortly after she left, I began to think about the hopelessness of my situation. With my parents gone, where would I live? Would they let me live by myself at our home in Chicago? I decided they probably wouldn't, as I had no way to pay bills and such. How could I ever hope to make it back to my high school? The more I thought, the more hopeless things seemed.

In the midst of my pondering, there was a sudden knock on the door. I managed to partially quell the tears that had been flowing and called out, "Yes?"

The door opened and a head peeked in. All I saw was this mass of long red ringlets of hair. I heard a voice speak out from them. "Sara? It's Pamela, your cousin."

When I focused on the rest of her, I was unprepared for the changes in my cousin. The sight of her had at least momentarily caused me to forget I was now an orphan. We didn't get down to Alton very much, but I very vaguely remembered Pamela from my dad's Remembrance Service Mom did in Alton two years ago. She had been in and out because of work. I recalled a thin wisp of a girl, much like me, who hung in the background at family affairs. Since her high school graduation, I'd had little contact with her before and not seen her since. Here and now though, I saw how much she had changed. I recalled thinking she was pretty back at the service, but what I didn't realize was—my cousin had graduated to beautiful. She was still of average height, but now she was curvy like a magazine model. In short, she was now everything I wanted to be.

"Can I come in?" she asked as I stared at her.

I nodded.

She came in like a bomb burst, talking like she had a few seconds to give me the story of her life. "I'm so sorry for you, Sara. I'll get you through this, I promise." At the same time, she made it her life's mission to see that I was comfortable. She came over and tried to make the bed with me in it, fluffing the pillows and pulling at the sheets. Awkwardly, because of my casts, she sat on the bed next to me and tried to hug me. Somehow in the process, I popped her in the head with my plastered arm.

"Owww," came out of a smiling Pamela. "I think you just gave me a concussion."

"I'm so sorry—"

"Oh, that's okay," she said. "It gives me an excuse to stay with you."

"Huh?" I asked.

Pamela just shook her head and told me that she and her partner, Chester, were first on the scene of my accident. "By the time we reached the hospital," she explained, "you had lost a lot of blood, so you now have some of mine. Even though you had several nasty cuts, a broken left arm and wrist, a broken left leg and a bad concussion, I took one peek at that hair and knew we were related."

Once she got that out, she seemed determined to change the subject. Get me off thinking about my situation, I guess. "I haven't seen you in over two years," she said.

I sniffled and touched the bandage above my eye. "My mom kept your high school graduation picture on our piano. But you sure have changed."

"Yeah, that picture was like so years ago," she said. "Before I grew up. You know that little cut above your eye will go away, Sara. You'll be as good as new in a few months."

I tried to ignore her trivializing my wounds. "I used to stare at that picture and pray I turned out at least half as pretty as you were back when it was taken. Look at you now." Then I broke down and started to cry.

"Hey, looks aren't everything, Sara. Mine didn't start until I was in college. Damn, you're only fifteen. When you get to college, you'll have to fight the guys off."

College? Me? I doubt it. I sniffled again and tried to talk without crying. "I—"

"We need to change the subject. I refuse to let you pity yourself."

"I can't help it," I moaned. "I'm just so angry that I didn't say something to Rod when Mom complained about his driving."

"Would that have helped?" Pamela asked.

"No, but maybe he would have stopped, threw my butt out of the car— and then they wouldn't have been in the wrong place at the wrong time. I might be camping along the side of the Mississippi, but at least then I'd still have my mom."

She gave me a tissue and said, "You're talking like a crazy person. Now I know we're related. I never met your stepdad, but Claire told me he was a . . . Sorry, I shouldn't speak ill of the dead. Of course, I'd have dumped that guy after one date."

She fingered my red curls. "Look, Sara. You've already got the hair." She then swooshed hers around her head. "Guys will see those gorgeous locks of yours and not even notice that little scar above your eye. You just need to let it grow out. Why do you have it chopped so short? You look like Little Orphan Annie."

She then facepalmed dramatically. "Oh, great, Pamela, that was stupid. Sorry, Sara."

I had to smile at her embarrassment. "It's okay. I am an orphan now. You've helped me forget the accident for a few minutes and think about other things. I needed that."

She then smiled down at me, realizing that little she could say would upset me. "Seriously. About the hair," she pointed out. "Whoever said blondes have more fun apparently never met a redhead. We rock."

Pamela, I realized, was amazing at moving me off the details of the accident by getting me immersed in less volatile subjects. After she was satisfied she had gotten me thinking about other things, she'd allow herself to switch back to that fatal day. That way, I didn't have to deal with it in one big mind-crushing chunk of information.

Gradually, she told me what she knew of the accident. After the collision, the driver of the truck stopped and came back to our car, which had caught fire. He pulled me out, but could not save the others. Learning this, I cried more uncontrollably, and she just held me.

"I know you're angry," she said. "I want you to let some of that anger out. You need to punch somebody. That's what I do when I really get upset."

"I don't have anyone to hit."

"Yes, you do. Punch me," she said.

I made it a point to look at the cast on my left leg, then the cast on my left arm, which went from wrist to shoulder. I gave her an exaggerated pout and said, "Any ideas how I'm supposed to do that?"

We both laughed.

"Who do you punch?" I asked. "Your boyfriend?"

"Boyfriend? Naw, there isn't a dateable guy within five miles of this dinky town. Except Chester, of course, my partner. Chester is good people, but he's happily married. However, he does let me punch him."

I looked over at her while she kidded and joked with me, her long red hair whipping around as she pantomimed out some of her stories. She'd talk about the accident then change to some lighter subject, incidents from her time in high school or college. I learned a lot about my wild cousin. It kept me from dwelling on the bad things.

On the evening of that first day with me, a nurse came in and told her visiting hours were over.

"I'm not visiting," Pamela said. "I'm Sara's guardian angel and it's my job to watch over her. I'm not leaving. Besides, I think I may have a concussion. Sara accidentally hit me in the head with that cast." I couldn't believe she delivered that with a straight face.

"Come on, Pamela, you'll get me in trouble," the nurse said. "I've got enough trouble with the law as it is."

"What kind of trouble are you in, Marjorie?" Pamela asked. I guess she knew everybody.

"I got a speeding ticket last weekend, twenty-five over the limit. I don't have to tell you how desolate 100 is after midnight. I thought, what's the harm in going a little faster? Now my dad's gonna kill me."

"Tell you what, Marjorie. I stay, your ticket goes."

"You can do that?"

"I'm the law. I can do anything."

A big grin spread over Marjorie's face. "Would you like a cot or something, Pamela? Something for that concussion? How about something to eat or drink?"

For the next three days, except for quick runs to her apartment to shower and change, Pamela stayed with me night and day. She kept up my spirits with her jokes and encouragement. If it wasn't for Pamela, I think I would have just died in the hospital. Given up on life. Of course, that wasn't really possible because, after the first day, my injuries were no longer life-threatening. Unless I hit myself in the head with my plaster arm. I never thought to try that.

I saw Aunt Claire sparingly, but I knew she had her business to run. I remember once she tried to talk to me, but admitted she couldn't really relate to what I was going through. Chester, Pamela's partner, came frequently, bringing us food and laughs. Chester, I found, was really nice.

When I was being discharged, the doctor said the cast could come off in another three weeks. Even now, I can still vividly recall the pain of my arm and leg being caught in that door. My doctor said I would fully recover from my physical wounds, but as we were checking out, I overheard her tell Pamela she was concerned for my mental scars.

I, however, was more concerned with the visible scars. The bone in my leg had torn through the skin and left a jagged mark on my thigh. I had a deep cut on my arm and a three-inch cut above my left eye. I think that was caused by Peter smashing into me and my head being shoved through the car window. The doctor told me not to worry about them, but that didn't stop me from obsessing.

After my three weeks in the hospital, Pamela brought me to Aunt Claire's bed and breakfast. Aunt Claire gave me her back room, behind the kitchen, while she moved upstairs into one of her rental rooms. That way I wouldn't have to constantly maneuver up the stairs on crutches. I felt terrible intruding on her business. However, Auntie waved off my objections.

"Spring is a slow time, my dear, and I never have need of my rental rooms. Not to worry, things will work out," she said. There were three rental rooms upstairs in the house and two small cottages out back. One of the cottages was actually dug into the side of a small hill, and she called it *the Cavern*. I thought it was the neatest place. I secretly wished I could stay there, but I knew its uniqueness made it her highest-priced rental.

Aunt Claire was usually too busy with her work, so I didn't see too much of her over the next month. Instead, I spent a lot of time alone, listening to Alanis and staring out the back window at the empty Cavern, wondering what would become of me. After my casts were removed, I was grateful to be able to walk normally again and use that arm. However, when they came off, a lot of the dead skin also sloughed off my arm and leg. That added to my obsessing about my looks.

Emily called me several times, and we both wished we could see each other. Despite the distance, we made hopeful plans for the summer. I didn't want to bother Auntie with my hopes, so I kept those wishes to myself. On occasion, Pamela and Chester would stop by, and we would sit out on the porch and talk. That became my focal point of the week. Pamela was great at getting me to forget my troubles, if only for a little while.

End of April...

By the end of April it got real dreary, and it rained heavily for several days. The Mississippi and Missouri rivers overflowed their banks in a number of areas, and the newspaper—I missed having my computer—said there was massive flooding all the way down to St Louis. It was surprising how quickly I adapted to a newspaper, something older people took for granted years ago. Aunt Claire said in some areas it was worse than the great floods they had in 1993. According to the news, to the south of Alton, the Missouri River had swelled as it flowed eastward toward the Mississippi. I had a lot of free time, and I kind of liked the printed paper, so I kept abreast of the latest news, something I never did back home. There was not much else to do.

I began to once again think about my mom. I knew I would eventually heal physically, Doctor Smart assured me of that. But my poor mom had met nothing but tragedy in her life, and now she was gone. While at first I was all, "Woe is me," now I was brooding over how fate had treated her so unfairly. First it took my dad, who she said was the love of her life, then it introduced her to Rod, who got her killed. I knew those thoughts, which had consumed me for days, were not going to help my recovery.

When I clicked on the TV, the news pulled me out of my meanderings. It showed video of floodwaters surging around a place called Cora Island, a few miles to the southwest. Then it showed the river spreading north out into the floodplain. It seemed to encircle and swallow everything in its path. I watched video of the water tumbling under the Lewis Bridge and Highway 67, rushing past Littles Island in the Missouri River and spreading out into the lowlands. I knew the names of these places thanks to the map that Auntie gave out to her tenants.

Pamela got to ride in a news chopper reporting on the floods and told me there were numerous caverns in the bluffs along both rivers. She said she had watched as the floodwaters drained into them and ended up who knows where. She imagined that the water would first flow in a slow stream like sand through an hourglass. Then in a torrent, as if going over a spill gate, it would spray down and swirl around in the caverns that had probably not seen the light of day for hundreds of years.

When the rains finally abated and the water receded, I wished I could go out there and take some pictures. Photography was what had kept my life back in Chicago from getting too boring. Only my camera was lost in the car fire, and I didn't have the heart to tell Aunt Claire. She would want to replace it, and I thought she had sacrificed enough for me.

16

PIASA

She made just enough money from the bed and breakfast to cover her bills and living expenses; she didn't need a teenage girl to support. She had mentioned starting me at Alton High School in a couple of weeks, and that upset me more than I let on. I had hoped to somehow return to Chicago, my own high school and all of my friends. However, with each passing day, down deep I had come to accept those as pipe dreams. I began to get resigned to my fate.

CHAPTER 4

Alton, Illinois
Mid May…

Then, one day in mid-May—two and a half months after the accident—everything changed. It all started with Pamela and Chester stopping over for lunch. The three of us sat out on the porch, which by now had become my favorite place to be. The massive old structure, painted bright white, was dotted with soft-yellow wicker furniture and a suspended swing. It also contained two multicolored Adirondack chairs, several small tables, and various potted plants in Native American planters, including several large potted oleander trees. I loved to sit out on the old porch and enjoy the serenity of this scene. It was Aunt Claire's pride and joy.

I had helped Auntie prepare sandwiches for the event because I so looked forward to their visits. I sat in one of the multicolored Adirondack chairs—each of the wooden slats was painted a different bright color—and Chester, as usual, sat in the wicker chair that had an oversized arm on which he would balance his plate. Pamela, dressed in a white and navy horizontally-striped top and very short white shorts that showed off her perfect legs, lounged on her favorite, the swing. These were our usual positions. The sun warmed me and I temporarily forgot about the painful turn my life had taken a few short months ago.

Pamela kicked off her sandals, pulled her legs up under her and winked in my direction. I knew Chester was about to suffer from her unique sense of humor. Chester was the sweetest guy. He was just slightly taller than Pamela's five and a half feet and had this hair that was shades of brown with black. He was also in great shape and worked out a lot. Pamela and Chet had an unusual relationship; they were like brother and sister. She just loved embarrassing him, though, which was hard to do because he was so easygoing.

"Chet," she started out. "What was that call you went on yesterday?" She had purposely waited until he bit into his ham sandwich. I found it hard to believe he hadn't caught onto Pamela's tricks of trying to get him riled.

Chester held up a hand to signify he was chewing as he attempted to hurriedly swallow the mouthful of food. "Another of those strange animal stories," he finally said. "You know, the ones we've been getting inundated with since the flood."

"What strange animals?" I asked, slightly intrigued. I thought I recalled some headline in the paper about it, but I had probably chosen to ignore that story.

"I went out to this guy's house south of town." Chester looked at me while he talked between bites and swallows. "His name's Lenny Webster. Pamela and I know him from high school."

Pamela winked a green eye over at me again while Chester continued to feast. Chester had a special relationship with food. Once he had his portion, he would focus all of his attention on eating. You could talk to him, and he'd answer, but his eyes usually never left his plate.

"Lenny's as squirrely as they come," Pamela interjected. "I don't know why you listen to that guy."

Chester ignored her observation, his eyes fixated on his sandwich.

"Tell me more about what he saw," I asked.

Chester nodded repeatedly to me and continued. "Lenny told me that he and his partner, Carl, saw this large creature with a mouth full of teeth. Sharp ones. Claimed it was at least six feet long and had the biggest eyes. He said they were hunting and just about to walk around a large rock when its head popped up over the top of it."

I thought it remarkable that Chester talked without looking up.

"They probably saw a chipmunk," Pamela smirked. "Lenny used to always exaggerate everything in school."

I ignored her because my interest was piqued.

"I asked what they did then," Chester continued after a slug of iced tea. He held up his glass, finally looked at us and said, "My next question was going to be, 'Were you two drinking?'"

"That's like asking, 'Are you breathing?' to a normal person." Pamela nodded at me. "Those two always have been lushes." I could tell Pamela was already bored with the story, but I wanted to hear more.

"According to Lenny," Chester continued. "Carl pointed his rifle at it, but the creature raised this thing up on the top of its head; said it looked like a rack or something. Well, that movement scared the two of them and they turned to run. When they heard a clatter on the rocks, they looked, and whatever it was was heading through the brush, down toward the river."

"Wait a minute," I said. "Are you two making this up? Chester, is this all to make fun of me being so naive? I know I'm gullible, but—"

"No," Chester said. "I filed this in a report, it's a matter of public record." He said that so seriously, I knew it had to be true.

"I wouldn't let him make fun of you, Sara," Pamela said, and looked over at Chester. "What did the two great hunters do then? Wet their pants?"

"I asked if they followed the thing, and Lenny said, 'And get eaten? No, thanks.' So, I again asked the sixty-four thousand dollar question, 'You boys drink your lunch?'"

His sandwich now gone, Chester leaned back in his chair, smiled at the two of us and began stuffing chips in his mouth.

Pamela was smirking.

I couldn't tell if she was doing so at Chester or his tale. "Pamela," I said. "This is not funny. Someone could have gotten hurt. Continue, Chester."

When I looked to Chester, he was grinning.

"Lenny said, 'No, sir, officer. We saw what we saw and we were sober.'" Chester finally noticed Pamela's smirk and appeared to catch on to her trick. He threw a chip at a grinning Pamela, then continued his tale while focused on me. "So, I asked them to better describe it for me, tell me what it looked like, compare it to something."

Chester paused and shook his head at Pamela, who was chuckling, then continued. "Lenny said, 'It was about a foot wide at the widest part, had lots of teeth, and a raised area on the top of its head like a crocodile. Hey, maybe that's what it was.'"

"What a crock," Pamela said, then laughed at her choice of word.

Chester continued unfazed. "I asked Lenny, 'How would a croc get to Alton, Illinois?'"

"That's easy," Pamela interrupted. "Same way a bull shark did back in the thirties."

"There are sharks in the river?" I asked. *Unbelievable. Maybe I am naive.*

"A shark," Pamela answered. "As in one. It was caught in 1937 by two local fishermen. It was assumed that it swam up the Mississippi from the Gulf. That was back before they constructed dams downriver. That's a story for another time, though. Continue, Chester, what did Len say about how a croc could get to Alton?"

Chester shook his head and resumed. "Actually, it was Carl. He said, 'We didn't see this thing in Alton.' Well, that did it. You're right, I should have known those two were wasting my time. I shut my report book, looked at them and asked where they actually saw it. 'By those new bluffs around the bridge at Littles Island,' Len said."

"You see!" Pamela, eyes ablaze, said to Chester. "That's why you should never go on one of those calls without me. I've always told you those two loony bins should be locked up. Why were they bothering you with this?"

I was lost here. I didn't know what Chester had done wrong.

Pamela saw my questioning, dense look and said, "That's on the Missouri River, in *Missouri*. It's a little out of our jurisdiction, Sara." She looked back at Chester. "Did they have a reason for calling the Alton *Illinois* Police Department?"

Chester scratched at his unshaven face. "They heard about all the missing cats and dogs in this area and—"

"Missing cats and dogs?" I asked.

Chester nodded to me. "We've been getting a lot of calls, not only about pets, but people also claim there hasn't been much to hunt across the river. There are normally a lot of rabbits and pheasants." He turned to Pamela. "Anyway, they thought they were helping us out. I told them to call Russell Samuels and the Missouri Highway Patrol. His jurisdiction."

I knew that last little bit was for my benefit.

"Darn straight. Russ will put those goofs in their place," she snapped at him, then softened. "Maybe it was one of them big snakes like they got in the Everglades," she pointed out with a smirk, then threw a chip back at him.

She just loved to needle poor Chester. They seemed to have such a fun relationship. Sharks in the Mississippi and big snakes in the Everglades were news to me, but they already thought I was clueless and sheltered, so I refused to ask them to explain.

Instead, I asked, "Wasn't that area covered by water during the flood back in April?"

"Yeah," Chester answered while nodding. "Halfway up the bluffs. When the water receded, it left them high and dry."

"Maybe this thing came out of the bluffs," I pointed out. "We've had an earthquake and the heavy rains and floods, why not? Maybe—"

"Have you been listening, Sara?" Pamela asked. "Those two jokesters are always seeing things. But Chet, who should know better, actually listens to them. Drives me bonkers."

"I'm sorry," I said, even though I wasn't. I guess I looked hurt, because Pamela instantly jumped off the swing and was kneeling by my chair.

"No, I'm sorry. Chet knows I'm just yankin' his chain. You're not used to my odd ways yet."

"I'm not upset. I love you just the way you are, Pamela," I said. "You and Chester have made my last few weeks bearable—"

"Hey," Pamela said as she ran her long, tanned fingers through my hair. "Don't get all mushy on me, I can't handle that kind of stuff." Then she hugged me. Pulling away, she said, "Just don't give credence to Chester's speculations. Do you want to ruin the only part of my job that's fun?"

"Well," I said. "I think Chester's on to something. What's next?"

PIASA

At that moment, Aunt Claire walked out onto the porch and began collecting plates. "Next, we've got to clean this place up," Aunt Claire said as she walked about. "I've got a special guest coming in from some big museum in Chicago, and he's been booked for a week or two. I can sure use the money. Thank the Lord for the earthquake. It seems to have opened up some caverns in the bluffs just to the north of town, and he's coming in to accompany Professor Moirés in exploring them."

"What for?" asked Pamela.

"Professor Moirés thinks the caves might have something to do with the Piasa. He has an old friend at the Chicago museum who has agreed to fund an expedition. Heaven knows our museum couldn't afford to pay for anything like that."

"Who's Professor Moirés? What's a Peeassa?" I asked.

"Professor Moirés is this great old guy who operates our tiny museum," Pamela answered. "I'll take you to meet him later and let him tell you about the Piasa. I don't think I can do it without laughing. By the way, it's pronounced pie-a-saw."

"Pamela, you are so bad." Aunt Claire scolded. "You make light of all of our town's old mysteries. But taking Sara over to introduce her to Winston is a good idea. He's been asking to meet her. That'll get you all out of my hair so I can tidy the place up and get the Cavern ready for this man coming down."

CHAPTER 5

Alton Museum
Thursday Morning...

As it turned out, the small museum was on University Avenue, just down the street from Aunt Claire's B&B. When Pamela returned after her shift was over, we walked over to the small building. She told me the buildings on both sides of the avenue were once a small thriving college that had gradually faded into history. Southern Illinois University had bought the abandoned college buildings, and a number of them now functioned as outlying storage and research offices for the main university, which was located elsewhere. The Alton Museum, a two-story building facing University Avenue, was actually one of the old school buildings left over from the now-defunct college.

Pamela asked the young woman at the reception desk for Winston. The girl nodded and hurried up a set of stairs on our right. Pamela pulled out her cell phone, excused herself, said she had to make a call, and stepped back outside for a few minutes. While I waited, I glanced past the stairs and was drawn to a small hallway directly in front of me. In it, I had caught sight of a picture showing a large eagle-like bird hovering above a group of Native Americans.

As I studied the painting, a male voice behind me said, "Are you Sara?"

"Yes. Professor Moirés?" I turned around to a small, graying black man who Pamela had told me was in his fifties.

He surprised me by sticking out his hand, so we proceeded to shake hands.

"Pleasure, Sara, but please, just call me Winston. Claire described you to a tee."

Pamela stuck her head in from the outside door and shouted, "Hi, Professor! Hey Sara, could you walk back alone? I've got to go on a call."

"No problem," I waved back. I had hoped to talk to Pamela alone about my high school dilemma, but it would have to wait for another time.

After she left, Winston nodded toward the picture I was looking at. "The exhibit once was much larger and spread out in the back room, but the Piasa is not a big draw anymore. So, we relegated the best part of it here in the hallway and stored the rest. I have an inventory of it somewhere..."

Winston shook his head, seemingly drifting off, then recovering. "We're still searching for an exhibit that'll draw some people in here. Anyway, I understand you were questioning what the Piasa was."

"Yes, I never heard of it—"

"Professor," the assistant called to him. "You have a call from Professor Wiggins in Chicago."

"I've got to take this, Sara. Just look around, okay? I'll be right back and tell you all about it."

The professor hurried up the stairs to his office as the front door opened and a big man entered. He looked a lot like the movie star, Bruce Willis. A young Bruce Willis, that is. My mom used to love this show on TV called *Moonlighting* that he starred in when he was very young. Anyway, that's who this guy reminded me of. He reminded me of my dad, too—maybe that's why my mom liked the show.

He smiled to the assistant and leaned down to ask a question I couldn't hear. She smiled and pointed upstairs. I assumed he was looking for Professor Moirés.

"Thanks," the man said and walked over to where I was by the exhibit. He smiled and nodded at me, then studied one of the paintings. I walked closer to the center of the hallway, and saw a series of 5 x 7 note cards done in calligraphy, titled *The Legend of the Piasa*. Before I could read them, Winston was back at my side and immediately started his story.

"This creature supposedly menaced the Illini Indians living here along the river before the early explorers came to America. The Indian chief, Ouatoga, felt helpless to protect his people because the creature was pretty crafty . . ."

While I listened to Winston, I couldn't help stealing a peek at the man who intently studied the picture of the huge eagle-like creature hovering above the Indians. I then returned my attention to Winston, who continued.

". . . No matter what kind of a trap they set for the Piasa, it always seemed to be one step ahead of them. The chief finally went through a dream ritual in which he prayed to the gods for a plan on how he could kill the beast. He had a vision in which a group of his braves hid in the bluff foliage, and when the bird appeared, they shot poisoned arrows at a vulnerable spot on its lower chest . . ."

Winston continued his tale, while I kept an eye on the big man who was glancing from one of the artist's conceptions to the next.

". . . To guarantee the creature would appear in the specific location, and at the right time, the chief used himself as bait," Winston said. "With his braves hiding in the brush, the chief stood on an outcrop of the bluffs and sang loudly to the gods. When the Piasa came and attacked him, the braves fired their arrows. One hit its vulnerable spot, and the bird tumbled down the bluffs and into the Mississippi River, never to be seen again. Ouatoga survived, and the Indians celebrated their victory for all to see by painting a large picture of the Piasa on the cliffs just north of Alton."

As the professor finished the story, the Bruce Willis look-alike glanced at him, walked to a spot close to us, smiled, and asked, "Tell me, Professor, do you really believe that poppycock?"

Speechless, Winston turned and stared at him.

The man kept his eyes on the paintings, while using his peripheral vision to observe Winston, who continued to silently look his way.

I too was at a loss for words. Who was this man, and why did he make light of the professor's story?

The man pointed at one of the paintings. "This bird, while attractively painted, doesn't resemble the legendary creature you described at all, now does it? It looks more like a condor crossed with an eagle or something. Much more believable as an actual creature than what the legend described. It's probably a good guess at the likeness of what the tribes of Native America called the thunderbird. And here, someone painted that as the Piasa. Interesting, don't you think, *Professor Moirés?*"

Suddenly, a smile spread across Winston's face. "You must be Mike Kellogg," he said.

The big man smiled. "Guilty as charged," he said, and stuck out a hand that engulfed the professor's normal-sized one. "Sorry to interrupt and cast dispersions on your story." He then stared over at me for the first time. "A thousand pardons, young lady."

"This is Sara Williams," the professor said. "Her aunt operates the bed and breakfast I told Paul about. I booked you in there as you requested."

"Thanks, Professor. I'm very pleased to meet you, Sara."

I just nodded. I was taken aback by his size, and I was not used to strangers talking to me.

Winston slipped over by Mike's side. "So, I assume you know the rest of the story of the Piasa."

"It's been a while, Professor," Mike said.

"Then maybe I can enlighten you both," Winston said. "When Father Marquette and Louis Jolliet explored the Mississippi in the late 1600s"— Winston ignored Mike's skeptical look—"Marquette made extensive notes and drawings of the tribes and attractions along the river. He was the first explorer to sight the bluff painting and sketch it in his journal. Other explorers and settlers who came later also saw the mural, and some captured it in words or drawings."

"Did the Native Americans—Illini Tribe, if I remember correctly—actually say they had created the image?" Mike asked.

Winston's face wrinkled in a frown. "Uh, no. Well . . . actually, the Illini said it was there when they first came to the land around here. The Ouatoga story, which you referred to as 'poppycock,' appeared in an early newspaper; it was put forth by an early settler. So I guess that technically makes you right. It probably is poppycock."

I thought poppycock was a great substitute for a swear word.

"So, who did they say *actually* painted the image?" Mike asked.

Winston again paused. "They said they had no idea. It had always been there."

I couldn't imagine why who said what, when and where was so important.

"My understanding of the rock image, from early descriptions," Mike interrupted, "is that it was not merely a pictograph painted on the rock, but a petroglyph carved into it at some depth."

"Just so I understand," I heard myself saying. "A pictograph is a painting and a petroglyph is a carving, correct?"

"Bingo," Mike pointed at me.

Winston's smile had faded. He snapped, "You really do know your legend, don't you, Michael? I thought you . . ."

I felt out of place. Professor Moirés was supposed to be the expert on this Piasa thing, but it seemed like Mike knew a lot more than he let on. Kind of embarrassed, I stared straight ahead at the hallway exhibit and listened to their exchange.

"I'm sorry, Professor," Mike said. "Yes, I do know the legend, I just wanted to hear your version. But in my job, I deal in facts, not fiction. We both know the popular story of the Piasa is most likely a figment of some early settler's imagination."

"Well, yes," Professor Moirés nodded. "But that doesn't negate the fact the petroglyph did exist at one time and was reputed to have been here for a long time before the Illini came to this area."

Mike smiled. "Exactly. I do believe that, I really do. Tell me, though, what is your opinion regarding the possibility that there were multiple creatures?"

Winston narrowed his eyes and thought a minute. "Yes, some believe there was more than the one painting. They supposedly existed at different spots up and down the river from Wisconsin to Missouri."

Mike leaned back against the wall and listened. I kept stealing glances at him. He reminded me so much of my real dad, and also reminded me of how much I still missed him.

PIASA

"There was said to be a painting in every place the creature frequented." Winston stopped momentarily, then continued. "It's been argued the Alton painting was not done to celebrate the killing of the Piasa, but as a warning such a creature hunted in those places. Hence the multiple paintings. However, I understand none was as elaborate as the one here. I—"

"No," Mike said quietly. "By multiple, I meant the original petroglyph depicted not one but two creatures. Marquette and others wrote of two petroglyphs, either side by side or relatively close to one another. That little fact always seems to be forgotten."

"Ah, you're alluding to the Lewis print and other voyager narratives. Yes, some highly educated travelers to the area in the early 1800s described an avian creature that looked like a large eagle. In contrast, Marquette, though he mentioned two, only described the creature usually depicted in popular retellings of the myth. What we now call the Piasa."

I was just amazed these two men knew all of this. How did they get all of these facts? From a bunch of old books?

"Marquette hinted at a second petroglyph, but he wasn't specific," Winston continued. "Henry Lewis's print clearly showed the carving of a large avian creature closely resembling a gigantic eagle. In the bottom right-hand corner of the image is the head of a second creature. The rest of the second creature appears to be missing. From his print, it's been deduced that sometime between Marquette's voyage of discovery and Lewis's trip in the 1840s, the cliff face came down partially."

"Have you seen the Henry Lewis print?" he asked Mike.

"I have it on a wall in my office in Chicago," Mike answered. "That's the petroglyph I'm interested in, the original one portraying two creatures. Personally, I think it partially came down in the great earthquake of 1812. However, on his voyage, Marquette had to have seen the entire carving."

Winston paused, then replied, "I'm sure you know early settlers building in this area destroyed what was left of it. I agree part of the original one described by Marquette was destroyed naturally, perhaps in a big storm, or, as you believe, the massive New Madrid earthquake. Marquette or Jolliet may have ignored the carving of what looked like an ordinary eagle, however enormous, content to describe the other carving they thought was a fearsome new creature."

"Now we're thinking alike," Mike nodded.

I struggled to keep up in this back and forth story trade-off.

Winston stared thoughtfully at the floor, as Mike once again studied the exhibit. Then Winston tapped on the glass covering the exhibit. "I'm curious, Michael. Are you saying you actually think there were two creatures? They really existed?"

29

Mike slowly smiled. "I was just throwing that out there. It's a possibility, right? Or this whole thing could be a figment of someone's imagination." Silence descended on the small hallway. Then, Mike asked, "You're acquainted with the Native American legend of the *tlanuhwa* and the *uhktena*?"

Winston's eyes narrowed. "The thunderbird and the water panther? Yes, yes, of course. You think *they* were actually real creatures?"

Mike seemed to quickly gather his thoughts, then spoke. "I'm sure you're aware of the popular myth telling where thunderbirds stole Indian babies and hid them in the bluffs with their eggs."

"Yes, yes," Winston interrupted. "When the Indians rescued their babies, they threw the thunderbird eggs into the river so water panthers would eat them."

"That's not what I'm asking you to believe as fact, Professor," Mike said softly. "No, I'm talking about the existence of two creatures, one that lived in lakes and rivers and occasionally preyed on Native Americans. The one the tales referred to as the *uhktena*, but has been translated as a water panther.

"The other creature, the one they called the *tlanuhwa*, was far larger than any ordinary bird. I think it was in fact the thunderbird. These two creatures come up throughout Native American myth and culture. I believe there is some basis in fact for them. Especially for the thunderbird."

Winston was quiet.

I stared at the painting Mike had spent so much time studying. The one of the large eagle-like bird poised above a group of Native Americans.

"However," Mike continued, "while these were strong beliefs of mine when I first studied the Piasa, I'm slightly older and wiser now. I guess you'd say I'm a little more skeptical."

Again, a short silence settled over the hallway while Winston seemed to consider Mike's words. I was really feeling out of place, for while I was learning all of this local legend, I didn't think it was of any use to me.

"They were Native American legends," Winston finally said. "What makes you think they actually existed?"

"Why do you believe the Piasa existed?" Mike shot back. "Back in high school, I could point to countless reports, sightings of huge birds, river and lake creatures to support my beliefs. Other than that picture people keep painting on the bluffs, there are zero reports of anything resembling the Piasa."

Back in high school he was looking into these things? What kind of high school did he go to?

"Of course, no one believes it exists today," Winston said. "I can only point to the text an early settler wrote. I know his son later said he made it up, but I think the son's denial of his father's story is the actual falsehood. I think the son denied the father's story because he thought his father foolish, and it embarrassed him.

"I trust the popular story of one creature, although later denied by the Indians and the settler's son, is actually based on fact. Furthermore, I think the cave of bones exists, and I intend to find it." After apparently waxing off into his private thoughts for an instant, Winston continued in a low voice, "If I knew the exact location of the original petroglyph, I could be certain of the cave's approximate position. However, these new cave openings appear to be in the right general area."

Cave of bones? What the heck did Aunt Claire get me into?

Winston suddenly appeared to realize he was mumbling more to himself and quieted, then looked back at Mike. "Uh . . . some years, vegetation seemed to hide some of the drawings and paintings on the rocks. Or so the settlers said. If there were other images, by now they have probably washed away with age."

Mike nodded. "Sorry, I never really bought into that cave of bones story."

"Yes." Winston smiled and, seeing my look of confusion, said to me, "There were some early accounts of a cave, filled with the bones of the Piasa's victims, located high in the bluffs north of town. An early settler claimed to have seen it, but no one else could ever find it. Some place the location close to the original painting, and speculate the early settlers dynamited it away when they built the road. I don't believe that. There surely would have been a huge outcry had they come across such a cave."

I fidgeted in place but listened politely. Winston turned his attention to Mike.

"The settler who actually visited it said there were almost invisible indentations in the cliff face, which he had to use to reach it. Of course, the bluffs have gone through a lot of change since the settler's time. Not to mention the monster earthquake in the early 1800s, which you seem to think brought down part of the petroglyph that Marquette sketched. The one you put so much stock in as proof of your early beliefs. I think somehow the cave got sealed off and is now unrecognizable as such."

After a silent moment, Mike asked, "What do you really think, Winston? The Piasa—legend or past reality?"

"I take everything with a grain of salt, Michael." Winston paused. "I'll leave you to examine the rest of this in peace. Till tomorrow." Winston smiled, turned and, having apparently forgotten me, disappeared up the stairs.

Mike glanced after the professor, then turned to me. "I hope I didn't upset him. I'm sorry I interrupted your tour."

"It's okay," I said. "I think I've heard more than enough."

"Well, lead on," he said. "I've seen enough, too."

"Lead on?" I asked.

"Weren't you here to escort me to your aunt's place?"

Chapter 6

The Cavern...
Thursday Noon...

"No! My aunt sent me over here because I asked what the Piasa was."

"Sorry," he replied. "And I interrupted . . . Look, if our discussion bored you . . ."

"No, it was kind of interesting."

"Speaking of your aunt, that's my next stop. Can I give you a ride home in exchange for some directions?"

"I'm not supposed to accept rides from older men I don't know."

"I've already introduced myself, Mike Kellogg, cryptozoologist, Chicago Museum of Cryptozoology. And you are Sara Williams, your aunt's name is Claire. Did I miss anything?"

I couldn't help myself, I broke out in a smile. "It's only a short distance away. How about you just follow me while I walk?"

"Are you sure? I don't want you to break any rules . . ."

"Stop," I said and laughed despite myself. "Okay, okay. I said it's only a block or so. Just watch what way I head, then you can even pass me up. You can't miss our B&B, honest."

I'm usually very put off by males of any age. Rod and Peter were my main gauge of the species, and they had not impressed me. Then, you add some of the weirdoes from my high school in Chicago and who could blame me? This guy was different, though. I was awed by him right from the get-go. He was very confident, but he didn't seem to try and astound anyone. But he did impress me with his quiet knowledge. I had a favorite teacher my freshman year in high school. He taught math, but he could tell you the capital of any state or country in the world. He didn't brag about it, we found out about it by accident one day. Mike seemed to espouse knowledge like that.

I followed him outside and he walked around to his car, a Ford Taurus like my friend Amanda's dad drove. I directed him to drive straight out and down Lilac Drive to Aunt Claire's. True to his word, he followed along behind me at a distance, driving very slowly. From about halfway there, you could see the sign for the B&B, which I stopped and pointed out to him. He drove ahead and pulled into the driveway, then stopped abreast of the porch.

As I walked past his car on the passenger side, I saw he was gathering stuff off the passenger seat. I leaned on the door and said, through the open window. "What's a cryptozoologist and why is there a museum for it?"

He got out of the car, walked around and opened the front passenger side door. With a sweep of his hand, he motioned me in. No one had ever done that for me, and it made me feel like a princess. I knew instantly it was not done to impress me. Rather, it seemed like his normal behavior. I had this feeling he wasn't trying to lure me in for some reason or make some kind of an impact on me; he was just plain polite. Besides, I could always bail out or yell for Aunt Claire should he try something weird. I was still hesitant, though, years of beware of strangers training, so I said I'd prefer to stand outside.

From the car speakers came the sound of Elvis Presley singing, "*Don't cry, Daddy . . . Daddy, please don't cry . . .*" Mike leaned in and pressed the skip button, and it went to the next song, "Kentucky Rain." Elvis was my mom's favorite, so I knew him almost as well as I knew my Alanis.

"You know," he said as if nothing had happened, "a zoologist studies animals."

I nodded.

"Well, there are some animals that people claim have existed or they've seen for which science has no physical evidence."

"You mean like Bigfoot?"

He rolled his eyes. "Yes, if that paints your picture. Some of us follow these mysterious animals. Crypto means strange."

"So cryptozoology is the study of strange animals?"

"Right. Now—"

He was staring back at the road, so I turned around and saw an Alton Police car turn into the B&B and pull right up on his bumper.

One look told me it was Pamela, and she looked plenty mad.

"Sara Anne Williams! What the heck do you think you're doing?" Pamela yelled as she got out of the car. "Accepting rides from strange men?"

"Hey . . ." Mike started to say.

"Button it!" Pamela said to him. He smiled in response to the finger she had pointed in his direction, and that seemed to noticeably irritate her even more.

"Pamela, that's poppycock. He's staying at our B&B," I said. "He's the man Aunt Claire was expecting. He came to the museum and I just guided him here. I didn't ride in his car." I could see Pamela visibly relax, while Mike just kept smiling at her.

"Sorry, sheriff," Mike said. "I didn't know it was against the law to offer someone a ride in this town."

"I'm not a sheriff," Pamela said. She looked over at me. "Well, you are standing near his car and it's still running."

"My bad," Mike said, and he leaned in and turned the car off. "I didn't know the law in this town was to immediately shut down your car when you parked."

"It's just common sense," she said to him, then turned back to me. "Don't get too close, and watch who you accept rides from, Sara. I've got to go on call." She then gave Mike a final glare, got back in her patrol car, backed out of the drive and left.

I was instantly glad I had been cautious and not accepted to either ride in the car or get in. I'm sure Pamela would have gone in and blabbed that to Aunt Claire.

"Wow," Mike said. "I'd normally say that girl could use a chill pill, but I realize she was just trying to protect you. You know her?"

"That's Pamela. She's my cousin, and she is kind of protective of me since my accident."

"What accident?" he asked.

"I was in an auto accident awhile back." I pointed up to above my eye. "One of my many reminders."

"I hardly noticed," he said. "You okay with it?"

I nodded. "Yeah, I think so. I lost my mom. My stepdad and brother were also killed. I was close to my mom but not them. I'm the only survivor. I guess that makes me an orphan." It surprised me I could now say that matter-of-factly. It probably sounded wrong to kind of separate their loss. However, no way were they close to equal.

He seemed to wince, like I had somehow hit home. He was quiet, then nodded. "Sorry to hear that, Sara. Must be tough, losing your whole family."

I really didn't want to go there, so I focused on the grass. "Come on, I'll introduce you to Aunt Claire."

"Before we go," he said. "What's with the poppycock?"

"I heard you say it and liked it. My mom used to say I had a potty mouth and she hated when I swore. Product of my school, I guess. Anyway, in her memory, I was looking for a substitute swear word. Poppycock is perfect."

"Get your own non-swear substitute," he said, "you're too smart to be a copycat."

As we walked toward the house, I couldn't help notice how his eyes seemed to take everything in, like he was storing it for future recall. My dad was like that, too. Mike looked at the tall and stately old trees dotting the grounds, and at the sparse grass and flowers growing haphazardly in different areas. His eyes shifted to the large white porch to the right of the front door. The one I so loved to sit out on with Pamela and Chester.

"I hope use of that porch comes with the room," he said. "There's nothing better than an Adirondack chair to sit in and enjoy the great outdoors." Mike looked briefly at the sign on the door instructing visitors to ring the bell, which he did. After a couple of seconds, the door opened, and Aunt Claire greeted him.

"You must be Mister Kellogg."

"No, Mister Kellogg is my dad. I'm Mike." He smiled and held out his hand, which Auntie lightly shook.

"Please come in, Mike, I'm Claire Dahlgren. I see you already met my Sara. I'm on the phone, but I'll be right back." He smiled and nodded while Aunt Claire hurried off toward the back. "Feel free to check things out," she called over her shoulder.

As we stood in the combination reception and living room, Mike glanced around and seemed to approve. I don't know why his approval was important to me, but it was. Auntie had taken great pains in decorating it with a mixture of antiques and newer furniture. She wanted it to look antiquish, but more comfortable. I knew from where he stood, he could see into the dining area. Off to his left, a staircase went to the second floor and the three upstairs rental rooms, one of which was mine now. As soon as the cast came off and the crutches disappeared, Auntie had moved me up there. I knew that she was going to put him in the Cavern so he'd have more privacy.

"Is it okay?" I asked. "Can I get you anything?"

Mike smiled over at me. "Do I like it? Yes, I do. I travel a lot, so I hate modern-day motel or hotel type rooms. They're sterile and lifeless. Whenever I travel, I prefer the folksy charm of the bed and breakfast. People are so much friendlier, and with their help, I can find places and things much quicker."

I don't know why, but I beamed back at him. It was so unlike me to be so friendly with anyone, especially an adult. *Why was I talking so much?* Something about this strange man made me throw caution to the wind, and I instantly liked him.

"Nothing better than sitting down to breakfast with your host and gaining knowledge of the area," he said as Aunt Claire returned.

"I hope Sara was able to answer your questions, Mister—"

"Mike!" he interrupted. "Please call me Mike. Sara is utterly charming."

I smiled even brighter. Me? Charming? No one had ever complimented me in those words.

Auntie continued, "I am so glad I was able to accommodate you on such short notice. You're lucky the Cavern was available. Since the quake, I've had a lot of cancellations and—"

"The Cavern?" Mike asked.

"Oh, didn't Winston tell you? I'm sorry. It's one of the two cottages in back." Mike immediately took on a surprised look.

"Since you're a researcher, I thought you would like your privacy. I took the liberty of putting you there rather than here in the house."

I could tell he was a little displeased at that, after he had told me about his fondness of being close to the host. But to her, anyway, Mike successfully masked his disappointment while he listened.

"I have the Cavern and the Grotto outside and three rooms upstairs. Sara is currently staying in one, a retired couple in the other, and one's on hold. I could move Sara to one of the cottages, but I'd lose on the rental income from that. Plus I'd worry about her out there by herself."

I knew I was costing her money she needed. Somehow I had to get Pamela to help me. She was my only hope for a normal life once again.

"I wouldn't think of relegating her to being alone out in a cabin," Mike echoed with a glance my way.

"Besides," Auntie continued. "I thought you'd appreciate peace and quiet. The Cavern has a large bedroom and bath, a small kitchen/dining area and a living room with its own patio."

"Kitchen?" said Mike.

Oh boy. I recalled what he had said about having breakfast with his host.

"Even though it has its own kitchen," Auntie continued, "I expect you'll want breakfast here in the house, although I can bring it to you if you desire. I'm sure you'll find it quite suitable."

"No, please don't bother to bring me breakfast. I'd much prefer to eat in here." Mike brightened. "It gives me the best of both worlds," he said. "Company for breakfast and a place to spread out and work. Perfect. The Cavern sounds perfect."

"Mike likes the porch," I said to Auntie.

"He does? Well, feel free to use it anytime, Mike. You might have to chase Sara off it, though. She seems to spend a lot of time out there."

I was a little surprised that she had observed me.

"We'll share," he said with a grin my way. I instantly thought ahead to the first time Pamela would come for lunch and find Mike there. After their run-in earlier, I was sure there would be fireworks. I hoped that Chester would referee. I was not sure why, but I assumed he and Mike would get along.

"I'm glad to see the quake spared your place," Mike continued. "I guess you're used to small quakes, living near the Wabash Valley Fault."

"Wabash Valley Fault? No, we're not close to it. That's further to the east and a part of the New Madrid System. They're not sure what caused our quake. We're really west of any of the known fault lines. They think it might be connected to last fall's floods or a fault system connected to the Carbondale Fault. Anyway, not a lot of damage occurred around here. Most of the action centered along the river, the surrounding bluffs and across the river to the west into Missouri. We're farther from the river here, and we're pretty much untouched. Let me show you around the house first, then we'll go around back."

I followed along as Aunt Claire led Mike into the dining area. "Winston said you're a researcher?" Auntie asked.

He smiled over at us both. "Well, I work for the Museum of Cryptozoology in Chicago. My job at the museum is to develop new exhibits. I like to delve into old legends and mysteries and come up with plausible theories as to their validity. Then, I create an exhibit about it, and the museum puts it together."

"How fascinating," Auntie remarked. "So you're not here because of the quake. What legend brings you to Alton? The haunted houses? You realize people call Alton one of the most haunted places in America."

Wow, no one had told me that. Emily, my best friend in high school, would go wild. She loved horror stories, although they scared her silly. I once put on a black robe and my brother's Michael Myers Halloween mask and scared her so bad she wet her pants.

"Haunted? Really?" Mike laughed. "No, I wasn't even aware of that. But, it might be better than the actual one. I deal in strange animals, in this case, the Piasa. The quake opened up some caves along the river and I'm accompanying Professor Moirés's team exploring them. He hopes to find some evidence such a creature might have actually existed. Personally, I think it's a fool's errand and all I'll get out of this is a couple of weeks off."

"How exciting," Auntie said. "However, I take it you don't believe in our legend."

Mike laughed. "No, I think it's just one of those nice little myths with little basis in fact. Oh, maybe a vulture or condor strayed into the area back in those long-ago times, and they saw it was larger than an eagle, so the story started."

"Hmmm," Auntie replied. "Funny you should say that. Recently, the paper reprinted the stories about the big bird that visited this area in 1948. Not quite so long ago. Of course, then some people reported seeing what looked like an enormous eagle, but no evidence of it was found. I think they wrote it off as a little too much celebrating."

"I'm sure that's how the Piasa started among the Indians," said Mike. "An Indian reported a big bird and bingo, the myth of the Piasa came into being."

"That's what they said back in 1948, when the big bird made an appearance."

"You remember 1948?"

"I was five. My father saw it and told me about it. I never actually saw it, but my dad never lied to me. I believe he witnessed something."

Why had no one ever told me about this? That was my grandfather.

"Maybe a small plane," Mike offered.

"He told me that's what he thought at first. Until it flapped its wings."

Mike shook his head. "Maybe a trick of the sun or something."

"My dad spent time in the Army Air Force and was an excellent observer. I know it troubled him for a long time. He seemed to play it over and over in his head like a short movie. I guess some things can't be explained."

For a short time, quiet settled over the room. I was hesitant to ask a question or say anything.

"Well, there is some semblance of sightings to support larger than normal birds, but your town's Piasa is another matter," Mike said lightly.

"Please don't prove him a myth. It would ruin what little tourism we have left," Aunt Claire pleaded. They both chuckled and I smiled politely.

"Okay, lead on," Mike said. "I think we're boring Sara."

"No," I said. "I'm finding out all these things about Auntie and Alton I never knew."

"I never thought you'd be interested, dear," Aunt Claire said to me. She then led Mike through to the dining area. "Can I get you something to drink?" she asked.

"I could use a cup of coffee," Mike replied.

"That's easy," she smiled. "Sara?"

"I think I'd like to try a cup of coffee too," I said.

Aunt Claire kind of rolled her eyes at this, but she pulled out three mugs. I knew she'd have tea, though.

* * *

I loved my first ever cup of coffee. Following that, and some friendly banter, Aunt Claire and I led Mike outside and over to the back. We waited as he pulled his car into the parking area between the two cottages and retrieved a well-worn suitcase from the trunk.

"Sara," Aunt Claire said while she and I stood there. "You've been asking to help out, so I was wondering if you would mind taking care of Mr. Kellogg while he stays here. You know, check with him every now and then and see if there is anything he needs?"

"Sure, Aunt Claire. Mike seems nice. He doesn't treat me like a little kid."

I watched as Mike scanned the surrounding area just as he had when he first got here. He noticed the private patio in front of the Cavern, separated by an area of bushes surrounded by flowers.

"The Cavern," Claire said. She pointed at the unit on the right. Mike looked over at the front that consisted primarily of glass. Two all-glass doors on the left led in, while a large picture window dominated most of the right side.

I saw his look again take in the patio with a table and four chairs. They faced a drop-off to the wooded area. The trees below extended out in both directions as far as could be seen. The L-shaped concrete patio extended to the right around the far side of the Cavern to a sliding door, which led into the bedroom. In front of the patio, where we stood, an area, landscaped with a mixture of rocks, shrubs and flowers, fronted some young trees. From there, a rather steep drop-off plunged to the wooded area below.

Auntie opened the door of the Cavern, but for a moment Mike hung back and seemed to admire the setting.

We waited quietly, then I pointed to the other cottage. "That's the Grotto. No one is staying in it right now, but there might be guests checking into it before next weekend. Isn't that right, Aunt Claire?"

"Sara, I told you to just call me plain Claire. You make me feel like an old spinster calling me Aunt all the time."

"But—"

"Are you not calling Mr. Kellogg Mike?"

"Yes, ma'am, err . . . Claire."

"That's better. Now to answer your question, yes, the Grotto is rented. That is, if they don't cancel. That quake has everyone on edge. They keep asking if we expect some more aftershocks, but I'm not Houdini. I just tell them we're well removed from the area that had the earthquake. Enough of that nonsense, though. Let's show you inside the Cavern, Mike."

Once again, Claire opened the door on the right and handed Mike the key. He examined the inside, decorated in Native American motif. It consisted of a living room, small dining area, and a bedroom with an oversized bathroom. A large whirlpool tub was prominent in one corner of the bathroom. In the living area, a gas fireplace dominated the outside wall. I thought it looked rather cozy. If I was to stay in Alton, maybe Aunt Claire would let me move in here when it was not rented. After Mike left, of course.

I watched as Mike took it all in. "Wow, this place is great. I'm going to hate to leave."

"You just got here; let's not think of leaving just yet," Claire smiled at Mike. "Now, Sara is to be your helper while you are here, so just let her know if there is anything you need, like directions or tips on restaurants around town. She hasn't been with me long, so I'm usually always available, though, if she can't answer your questions."

"Thanks," Mike replied. "Where to stop for lunch would be a good start. I drove straight through and skipped breakfast."

"Uhh . . ." I hunched my shoulders, as I didn't really know any place to eat around town. When Aunt Claire told me to check on him, I didn't consider I'd be some source of information.

"Stop in the house when you're ready to leave," Claire laughed. "I'll give you a map and directions." With a little wave, she left, and I, unsure of what I was supposed to do now, stood by the fireplace while Mike silently took in the room and began to unpack. The first thing he took out was a picture he put on the table.

"Do you need anything right now, Mike? Uh . . . should I leave?"

"Leave? Aren't you going to lunch with me?" he asked.

"Did you want me to?" *Huh?*

"Of course. Claire designated you as my helper. You don't want me to eat alone, do you?"

I shook my head, then nodded.

"Is that a yes or a no?" he asked.

"Yes," I answered. "To going with you. I don't like to eat alone, either." If anyone else had invited me to lunch, I'd have said no immediately. But with him I was curious.

CHAPTER 7

Piasa Restaurant
Thursday Afternoon…

Claire—yes, I'm now calling her Claire—recommended the Piasa Restaurant, a small cozy place located along the river just south of the downtown area. She said it had fallen on hard times, but it was good food and friendly service. As we drove over, more Elvis tunes came from the CD player. I wanted to ask if Elvis was all he listened to, but he still intimidated me a little. Truth be told, I was afraid he'd toss me out of his car if I complained about his choice of music. After all, it was his car.

We parked across the street and waited to cross. My first impression was that the small restaurant was not particularly attractive on the outside. It was badly in need of repainting, but when we walked in, it made up for it on the inside. Encompassing the entire back wall was a large mural of this Piasa thing, very colorfully done in blazing colors of red, yellow, orange, tan, green and black. Just like the description at the museum, it had a head similar to a bear, a body covered in scales like a fish, horns like a deer, a long snakelike tail and large reptilian wings. A young girl handed us menus and nodded when Mike indicated a table under the painting. As he led me over, he said he wanted to put me in the right mood. For what, I didn't have a clue. This whole Piasa thing scared me. It didn't help that now, when I turned my head, I was under the thing's mouth.

Seeing my discomfort caused a big grin to paint Mike's face while his eyes, in that unique way of his, took in the restaurant. I knew that, if I asked, he could tell me everything there was to know about the place.

"Ah," he finally said, looking at me. "Clean and homey, definitely my kind of place. It has 'greasy spoon' written all over it."

"You like greasy spoons?" I asked, struggling to keep my voice normal.

"Yes," he said loudly. "Yes, I do."

In the beginning of our relationship, he both scared and fascinated me. At that moment, he scared me. And . . . fascinated me.

A waitress walked up to us while I studied the menu. She looked hardly older than me.

Looking up at her, Mike grinned and pointed to the mural. "One of your loyal customers?"

"Why? Do you want to be on the menu?" she shot back while staring at her notepad.

"Not today, thanks," Mike ignored her apparent sullenness. "So, what's good?"

"Are you insinuating we'd serve something bad?" she spat back.

What a pasta pazoole, I thought. Yeah, since Mike nixed poppycock, I'm using that word for anything not good. I made it up. My own private 'this is not right' word.

"No. I just thought you'd have a recommendation for someone who just blew into town." I could sense Mike's inward struggle to keep his good mood.

"Isn't that what the menu is for?" she answered, finally looking up.

He slapped the menu down on the table and suddenly asked, "Do you know why I came in here?"

She bent down and stared out the window. "Well, it's not raining, so you didn't come in to get out of the rain."

Even though I was impressed that she was able to trade remarks with him so easily, the waitress, I had decided, was a total pasta pazoole. At this point, I thought he would have given her a tongue lashing and walked out.

He just leaned back in his chair and said, "I favor this type of restaurant everywhere I go, and what I normally like best is the waitresses always seem to be friendly and cordial. But here . . ."

Mike stared up at her and finally finished. "I'm sorry. Look, this place was recommended to us. I assumed friendliness was part of the service. It should be. Maybe we should go elsewhere, Sara."

I thought that was a nice way of saying she was full of poppycock and got ready to give her my best litany of bad words.

Mike started to rise, but was stopped by her hand on his shoulder. "No, I'm sorry," she said. "Please stay. Sometimes I unknowingly allow my personal problems to carry over into my job. Please forgive me. I really need this job. The tuna sandwich is my favorite, unless you don't like fish, then—"

"The tuna will be fine. Thank you, uhh . . ." Mike prompted her for a name as he sat back down.

"Rachel," she replied and smiled. "Rachel Franklin. And you're welcome."

"I'm Mike, and this is Sara," Mike said. "What'll you have, Sara?"

"BLT and a coke?" I asked. I was totally amazed at their change in demeanor.

"With fries, Sara?" she asked.

I nodded, and she left with a parting, "Please forgive my rudeness."

I guess I was staring at Mike, because he looked over and asked, "What?"

"Everything with you is an adventure," I said.

After we ate, he actually made the waitress—oops, Rachel, we were now all friends—sit down with us. "I want your story," he told her. "Why are you so moody?"

Honest, that's what he said. And she eagerly apologized again to us both while she explained. It turned out she had moved here with her mom from somewhere in Minnesota, knew no one, and had problems making friends. All she had was her cat, and that morning it had run away. She was worried sick over the feline. I guess he liked cats too, because he asked her all kinds of questions about it. Things I'm sure only a cat lover would know. He told her we'd—I assume he included me—keep our eyes open around town.

I initially thought he was a little strange, but eventually chalked it up to my sheltered upbringing, mean stepfather, and the so-called boys that tormented me in high school. I decided he wasn't strange. I just never really knew a grown man could care about things like other people's problems and cats. He had an upbeat way that was simply infectious; you couldn't not smile over some of his antics.

When we got back, he said he needed to ask Claire about something, and we went inside the house. While Mike went over to talk to her, I ran upstairs to change.

When I came back down, I went into the dining room and watched as Mike, without looking, reached over to where Claire had set down a fresh pot of coffee and proceeded to fill his cup. *Cool how he does that,* I thought. *It's like he's already memorized where everything was in the room.*

I then heard the front door opening, and someone entered. Claire went to the door and muffled voices drifted back.

He is different, I thought as I slid into a seat. Others always waited for Claire to come back, or sometimes they asked me to fill their coffee cups. What did they think? That I was a waitress? They acted like their arms were broken or something. Mike made himself right at home.

He suddenly glanced up and caught my eye. Giving me a little grin, he took a sip from his cup. I couldn't stop my mouth from forming an answering smile, just as Pamela entered the room with Aunt Claire. I watched as Mike and Pamela's eyes met, and each offered quick smiles to the other. Apparently, the fireworks from this morning were forgotten.

Pamela was my Uncle Dave's daughter, and the resemblance to me was startling. I already mentioned that Pamela was beautiful in a way I could only hope to be one day. Long red hair, with a curvy but thin figure, Claire told me she was always the center of attention. I had imagined the guys in this town would speed just to be stopped by her. And she treated me like a little sister. When I complained about my looks, she told me not to worry, she had been short and willowy until her second year in college. Her delayed growth was something of a family trait. She had rapidly become my favorite person.

Claire formally introduced them, then looked at Mike. "I had hoped Pamela could be the assistant we just talked about,"

He needed an assistant? Why?

"But I was unaware our sleepy little town had gotten quite so busy over the last couple of weeks," Claire continued. "She tells me she's working extra shifts."

"Yeah, I'm sorry," Pamela said. "It has nothing to do with our little tiff earlier. We've been having all these strange happenings and . . . Well, if you had been here two weeks ago, when I was completely bored out of my skull, I'd have said yes."

"I don't understand," said Mike. "What is it you do when you're not the sheriff?"

"I'm a cop," Pamela answered. "Not a sheriff, not a deputy, not a marshal, not Wyatt Earp. Okay?"

Mike smiled and nodded.

"Usually it's quiet around here," Pamela continued. "I would love to take off and do something interesting, especially if it somehow relates to archeology, but lately it's been quite hectic."

Pamela then apparently noticed me quietly sitting there.

"Hello, Sara, how *you* doin'?"

I looked up at her and gushed, "Hi, Pamela."

"Tell me, exactly what does this assistant's job entail?" Pamela said, returning her attention to Mike. "I might recommend someone else who'd take the job."

"I need someone to take notes and enter them into a computer file for the museum. It helps if they know the area and can bring me up to date on the legend. Oh, and hopefully take some pictures."

WHAT?

Pamela frowned, glancing down, then up. "What legend? You mean the Piasa?"

Mike nodded.

Pamela's mood apparently brightened. "You're looking for the Piasa?"

Mike laughed. "No, what do you take me for? A loon?"

I watched as Pamela raised an eyebrow. I thought it was Rachel all over again.

Mike continued, "The quake opened up a vast network of caverns under the bluffs. Your museum here wants to explore that labyrinth for evidence the creature existed. I'm going along for the ride. Do you know anyone who might be interested in basically getting dirty while crawling around in some cave?"

Pamela's smile began to slowly fade as she started to shake her head, then stopped. She looked over at me and grinned. "Yeah, I think I do know someone, and I know she's available. She's a great photographer, and I'm sure she can take notes. She's a little computer geek, too."

"Great," said Mike, brightening. "Who is she? When can you get her over here?"

"She's already here."

I took a glance in the direction of the door. Had someone come with Pamela?

Mike frowned. "I don't under—" He looked across, into my eyes.

Me? Embarrassed, I leaned back from the table, trying to avoid Mike's gaze. I wasn't born yesterday. I now realized Pamela was talking about me. Then, while staring from one to the other, I mumbled, "I don't know anything about the Piasa ... I ... uh ..." My voice trailed off as I shifted into mental mode.

I wish I knew more about this Piasa thing. It sure would be good to get out of the house for a time. Even crawling around in some dirty cave was better than doing nothing. Besides, taking pictures is one of the few things I enjoy doing. But he probably wouldn't want a skinny little fifteen-year-old.

"What about it, Sara? You game?" Mike asked, still looking me in the eye.

"Me? Seriously? You'd really take me?" I blurted out. "Yes, I'd love to do it. Please, Mike, don't tease me. Are you kidding me?"

Claire and Pamela looked to me, apparently surprised that I was so willing. It surely was so unlike me.

"But Sara, you know nothing about Alton. You—" Claire stopped after seeing Mike's upraised hand.

Mike glanced over at Claire, then turned to me. "Do you know anything about this town? The Piasa?"

"No," I said. "But I can take pictures, I'm good with computers, and I can write. My English teacher back home used to compliment my word choice. I really don't mind getting dirty. And ... I learn fast." I stopped before I really started to babble.

As Mike looked over at me, Claire asked, "Will this be dangerous?"

"No," Mike said. "Actually, it should be pretty boring. But you're her guardian. What do you think, Claire?"

Claire slowly nodded her head. "Are you sure it's okay, Mike? I think she'd be safe with you."

47

Mike smiled down at me. "Sure, what the heck. I love someone who's honest about their lack of qualifications. I'll gladly take responsibility for her. I've actually been here in the area before, so I really don't need a guide, and Piasa knowledge is not exactly a prerequisite. Sara is exactly the kind of assistant I need."

Pamela added, "I'll keep an eye out when I can, Claire."

"In that case, I'll be glad to get her out of the house for a few days," Claire said with a smile for me, and then retreated to the kitchen.

"Can we sit on the porch?" Mike asked Pamela and me.

We retreated to the outside porch. I sat in my favorite Adirondack chair while Pamela sat on the wicker swing. Mike faced us, leaning against the railing that separated the porch from the front walk.

"What do you know about the Piasa?" Mike asked Pamela.

Pamela looked up at him while she shaded one eye from the sun. "Let's see. Its picture is painted on the cliffs north of town. The high school team's mascot is the Piasa. Parents use it to scare their kids, saying things like, 'If you don't behave, the Piasa will get you.' Lastly, every call I get lately, where some dog or cat has disappeared, they ask, 'Do you think the Piasa got 'em?' Idiots."

I giggled. Pamela had that great sense of humor.

"Do you think it once existed?" Mike pressed, apparently choosing to ignore her pasta pazoole attitude.

Pamela looked down fleetingly, then back at Mike. "Between you and me?"

Mike nodded toward me.

"Of course I include Sara in that. She and I are related." Pamela brushed her long, red hair off her face then squinted in the sun as she paused before answering. "Yeah, I do."

"Let me get this straight, you believe the legend?" Mike smiled.

Pamela hesitated again, but said, "I think it was as real as you and me."

Mike looked at Pamela deadpan. "I'll be honest here. I don't put much stock in your legend as it's normally presented. You know, the Chief Ouatoga and his people thing." When he said Chief Ouatoga, Mike waved his fingers in the air like it was a scary mystery. "I believe your Piasa was a mythical creature, like the unicorn. I'm sorry if that bursts your bubble."

She reached over and pulled on my arm. "Sit by me," she commanded. I jumped out of my chair and settled in next to her on the wicker swing.

Pamela leaned in close to me and whispered into my ear, "Did I do right by recommending you for this job?"

I nodded enthusiastically, and she wrapped an arm around me, pulled me close and squeezed me, then brushed her fingers through my shorter red hair while she returned her attention to Mike.

"Well, if I thought you were all-knowing"—Pamela flashed him wide eyes—"it might cause me some seconds of doubt. I know you're a big-time explorer who has been about everywhere—yeah, I looked you up—but personally, I don't think you are qualified to comment about our little town and its beliefs one way or the other."

Mike winced as if in pain, then chuckled, "Ouch! I guess you told me."

"I'm sorry, you asked me what I thought," she said with a put-on pout. "Look on the bright side, though. I found you a highly qualified assistant. What she lacks in local knowledge, she makes up big time in enthusiasm and willingness to please. And she takes great pictures."

I resisted the urge to plant a kiss on her. I didn't deserve that buildup, but I inwardly vowed to live up to it.

Mike nodded. "Yes, I did and you did. Anyway, I'm not qualified in regards to your myth. Maybe you can help make up for her lack of local knowledge by bringing me up to date on what's been going on around here in your spare time. Do you live close by?"

Pamela laughed, "Are you asking me for a date?"

Mike reddened. "No, uh . . . I just thought—"

I was surprised this big rugged guy was like putty in Pamela's hands. I so wished I was like her. Guys never took me seriously, nor could I ever say something like that to a guy.

Pamela tilted her head back and laughed. "Relax, I was just teasing. Actually, I live up in Grafton, and my time's pretty full working extra shifts."

Mike got up and stretched. "That's okay, I think your Piasa is nothing but a wild goose chase anyway. I really don't expect to find anything to prove it existed. Otherwise, I wouldn't have volunteered to take Sara."

"If you think this is a wild goose chase, then why are you here?" Pamela asked as she got up, pulling me with her. "No, don't answer that. If you come to your senses and leave, then Sara will be out of a job." She squeezed me as she said that, then released her hold on me. "I better get back to work."

Pamela waved and jumped down off the porch. She ducked as a downy woodpecker brazenly flew past, within inches of her head.

I watched as Mike stared after her while she walked toward her car. Stopping at the door, she reached up and pulled her long red hair into a single mass, tying it with something seemingly pulled out of nowhere. As Pamela got into her jeep and left, Mike got up and silently walked back toward the Cavern.

* * *

49

PIASA

Later that night, it was actually after midnight, I sat in the darkened, enclosed porch behind my room, which was in the back of the house affording me a view of the Cavern. The ledges of the wraparound back windows were very wide. Aunt Claire said the previous owner had several cats, and she'd had this bedroom modified for them so they could lay on the ledges and look out on the creatures of the woods. With her blessing, I had pulled my bed onto the porch and positioned it at a ninety-degree angle to the windows so I could kind of pull myself up out of bed onto the ledge and look out like the cats once had.

I'd had difficulty sleeping since the accident, so I leaned back against the window and turned my head to watch as Mike walked out the Cavern door and seemed to stare down into the woods. They were not very deep. Through them, in the light of the three-quarter moon, I could make out a house off to the right and a well-manicured lawn over to the left. In the daytime, the woods stretched to the right and left as far as one could see.

Mike seemed to gaze intently into the wooded area that sloped down to a depth of maybe fifteen feet away from the patio. The woods then started back up on the other side for a short distance before giving way to scattered houses. After several minutes, Mike turned back and, beer in hand, he walked over to the table and sat down.

Nestled in my little spy perch, cord dangling down from my ear to the CD player, I stretched my legs out in front of me on the bed. As I watched, I wondered what Mike was doing up so late. Why was he drinking by himself? And why did he wander around outside after midnight? *For that matter, what was I doing sitting up in the wee hours of the morning watching him? It reminded me of the last time my real dad was home on leave. I was ten then, and I recall getting up to go to the bathroom one night and seeing him sitting all alone at the kitchen table. Now I wish I had gone to him and kept him company.*

Finally, I looked down at my unpainted toes and bare feet. Back in my old life, before the accident, I had always kept my finger and toenails brightly and meticulously painted. Time to start again. I wriggled my toes as if they were agreeing with me.

My old life. Was it gone to me? I closed my eyes and mentally recalled the plans of my high school friends in Chicago. Stacy planned on commuting to U of I Circle campus and being a nurse. Emily had chosen Indiana, where she hoped to get into some kind of pre-law program. Amanda wanted to be a teacher like her mom and even wanted to go to the same school, Eastern Illinois. Gina had dreams of being an actor, and with a name like Gina Diamond, she wouldn't even need to change it. My plans? Unknown, but I still had three years of high school, plenty of time to decide things like that. My only question now was, where would it be?

PIASA

Hearing a noise outside, I turned and saw Mike get up and walk back toward the Cavern. When he stopped and appeared to stare into the trees, I decided that, like me, he was just mulling things over.

Returning to my thoughts of school, I realized there had always been this blank wall when I thought of my future. I could never see myself doing any of the jobs my friends desired. Why did high school have to end? To my friends' repetitive questions like "Where are you going to college?" or "What are you gonna do after graduation?" I had always given my usual answer of, "I'm still weighing my options." Now, I only wish I had options to weigh.

I glanced down at the eight-inch long scar on my thigh while I fingered the one above my eye. Forget acting or modeling.

I recalled that Mom had been even harder to deal with than my friends. In addition to constantly reminding me the present was the ideal time to begin researching colleges and universities, she had pushed me to make decisions every chance she got. None interested me. I had reacted by going to my room and hiding in the corner behind the bed. That one spot had always been my safe haven. The place where I looked through pictures taken from various trips, and tried to chart a course to follow during what I thought was the most difficult time in my life. Back then, I never imagined what life really had in store for me. Now, Mom was gone. Who could I turn to for help in deciding the course of my life? Now, when I really needed direction.

I shrugged off those unsettling thoughts and returned my attention to the music. In my ear, Alanis sang about being alone late at night and not able to sleep. Like me.

I silently pulled my feet up under me and planted them side by side on the windowsill as I wiped at my eyes. It was the first time since the accident I had seriously thought about friends and high school. *Why do I feel so alone?* I pressed my back against the glass as tears rolled in earnest down my cheeks.

CHAPTER 8

Ride-Along...
Friday Morning...

Sitting out on the front porch the following morning, I looked up as an Alton police car pulled into the driveway. It was Chester, Pamela's partner. At times she would meet him here, like when she planned on visiting me that day. I jumped up and ran to the side of his vehicle.

"Pamela get here yet?" Chester asked as he undid the seat belt.

I shook my head. "She should have been here about ten minutes ago. I think she might have left late."

"I told her to get here early, we're supposed to cover an early call. Maybe I can catch her on her cell phone." Chester picked up his phone and punched a couple of buttons. When Pamela apparently answered, he told her where he was and told her to hurry up, reminding her they had an early call.

"She's on her way," Chester said to me and got out of the car. We walked back over to the porch and sat down.

"What kind of call do you have, Chester?" I asked.

"Some guy fishing in the Mississippi thinks he saw a giant snake very early this morning," he smirked. "Crazy, I know, but we have to respond."

I giggled. I mean, how ridiculous was that?

Chester chuckled. "I know," he said. "Sometimes it's hard to keep a straight face. I hear strange stories all the time, especially now, lately, since the big floods and the earthquake. Then there's listening to Pamela and her dream."

"Her dream?" I asked. "Tell me, Chester."

Chester looked around, then over at me like he had said something out loud he shouldn't have.

"Please?" I whispered.

"Don't you tell her I told you," he said. "You know she'll never let it rest. She'll skin me alive. The other day, after we stopped a car for speeding, she told me she has this reoccurring dream in which she's on patrol alone and stops a car for speeding. When she walks over to the offender's vehicle and looks down at the driver, his face blurs and she hears the Wedding March in her head. She figures it's the guy she's supposed to marry. I think she's a little wacky."

53

PIASA

The sound of a horn told us Pamela had arrived. She pulled her Jeep around Chester's police car and parked back next to Mike's car by the Cavern. I assumed he was still asleep after his late night. As she ran into the B&B, I hurried after her. I had a favor to ask of her, and I knew she'd use my room to change as she always did. I took the stairs two at a time after her.

As I slipped into the room, she was already shedding her clothes. "Is this going to be dangerous?" I asked.

"What? Me changing?"

"No, the call you're going on with Chester."

"No," she laughed. "We just have to talk to this guy who was out fishing. He works at the bank."

"Can I go with?"

"Police business, Sara."

"You told me last week you'd take me with sometime to ease my boredom. Please?"

Pamela stopped after pulling her shirt on and buttoning a couple of buttons. "Why? You've got a job now with that Mike character. That should keep you from getting bored."

"Yes, but he expects me to be his right-hand person and he's an investigator. I thought I could pick up some tips from my favorite cousin, who also happens to be the best cop in Alton."

"Boy, you read me like a book. You know I'm a sucker for compliments, even if they're coming from a fifteen-year-old girl. Okay. Sure, you can come. Don't interrupt, though. Just hang back and listen."

"Thanks. I'll be as meek as a lamb. You won't even know I'm there."

Chester never even asked as I climbed into the back seat of the patrol car.

Great River Bank in Alton

"Charlie Lowenstein?" Pamela asked. I stood behind her and Chester.

"Yeah," he said with a glance over at me.

"She's a ride-along," Chester said. "Don't worry, she knows whatever you tell us is not to be repeated to anyone."

"Mr. Lowenstein," Pamela said. "You called the Police Department about something you've seen in the river?"

"Yeah, I had planned for several weeks to take Scott, my son, on a fishing trip on the Mississippi. After the quake and flooding, I would have preferred to cancel the jaunt, but I knew Scott would not understand. So, since I don't start here until nine, I took him very early this morning."

What is it with boys and fishing? Sitting in a boat on a river or lake? It sounded so boring.

"We were cruising south on the river," he continued. "Just north of where it joins the Missouri. I let a line troll out behind the boat; it's a trick I learned from my dad years ago. 'Never know what'll take the line,' my dad used to say.

"As the boat passed the spot where the rivers meet, I noticed a strange sight on the water about a hundred feet away. Something seemed to be zipping along on the surface. From my position, and judging by the wake behind it, I thought it had to be at least ten feet long, but I couldn't be sure of that or its girth. The only fish in the Mississippi that big is a sturgeon, but they're bottom feeders. This was almost . . . snake-like. Far too big to be a real snake—"

"Maybe a log?" Chester asked.

"No, I'm sure it moved on its own. It was going against the current. Not many logs do that, and it was making sinuous waves."

Pamela's eyes meandered around the bank as he talked. I knew she was not taking this seriously. Chester, ever the policeman, took notes.

Mr. Lowenstein continued. "Suddenly, this thing turned in a line that would cross our wake. I looked toward Scott to see if he was seeing what I was, but he was staring straight ahead and seemed oblivious to it. When I looked back to get a better look, it had disappeared underwater. I kept my eyes fixed on the spot, but it didn't resurface. I could still see the ripples spreading out from where it had been cutting through the water. It couldn't have been my imagination.

"All of a sudden, my son yelled, 'Dad! Your line.' When I looked over, the line on my rod was being pulled out at a high rate of speed. I could hear an audible whine as the gears in the reel struggled to keep up with the outpouring line. Funny, it made the loudest sound in the early morning stillness. As I reached over to grab the rod, it was torn from the boat. After hitting the river with a splash, the rod cut through the water like a speedboat for a few moments, then disappeared beneath the surface."

"Sounds like you caught a snag," Pamela said.

"That's what Scott said." Mr. Lowenstein nodded. "If it was a snag, it must have been a big snag. What about the snake-like creature?"

"Look, sir," Pamela said. "I think you want the National Wildlife Service, not the Alton Police Department. But we'll file your concerns."

* * *

"We've got one more silly-stop before we begin real police duty, like catching speeders and all that nonsense," Pamela said to me after we had left the bank and gotten in the car.

"Pamela likes to call these human interest stories 'silly-stops,'" Chester pointed out. "The next one is a missing person."

"Missing person? How is that silly?" I asked.

"Most of them are sleeping somewhere in their car or lying behind some gin mill, or they've just had a fight and stomped off," Pamela smirked. "Correct me if I'm wrong, Chet, but I don't think we've ever had a legitimate missing person."

To that, Chester gave a big sigh. I decided it must be a hoot to work with Pamela all the time. She was bored, but so witty.

"I'd like to go," I announced.

"You heard the fair lass, Chester. Let's go."

Rachel Franklin...

We drove across town. I was a little confused as to where we were, but Pamela told me we were just to the east of the bluffs that ran along the river. Chester parked in front of a small house and we went up to the door. When it opened, I was surprised to see Rachel Franklin, the waitress from the Piasa Restaurant.

"Hi, Sara," she said, obviously confused why I was with two police officers.

"Hi, Rachel. I'm uh . . . doing a ride-along with the police this morning."

"You called about someone named"—Pamela glanced at her notepad, saving me from my long-winded explanation—"Phoebe . . . missing, ma'am?" she asked.

"Yes. Phoebe, my cat."

"Your cat?" Pamela looked at Chester, then me. "You called the police about your missing cat?"

"I'm sorry. I know I should have told the officer that when I called, but I was afraid no one would come and I don't know anyone in town and I just didn't know where to turn, I'm sorry." Rachel spilled that all out like it was one sentence, then struggled to maintain her composure, dabbing at her eyes with a tissue she clutched in her hand.

"Whoa, settle down," Pamela said. "I didn't say we wouldn't help you, but next time mention the word cat, please. It should have been in the report. We do have priorities, you know."

Rachel nodded. "I know, but Phoebe is my highest priority."

Pamela gave her an unreadable look, then asked, "May we come in?"

"Yes, I'm sorry. I'm Rachel Franklin," Rachel said as she held out her hand to Pamela.

"Officer Sweet." Pamela gripped her hand as she stepped into the house. Chester and I followed.

"Sorry for that priorities crack," continued Pamela. "Actually, I was getting sick and tired of chasing what I'm sure must be figments of people's imaginations. It'll be nice to look for something I have a reasonable chance of finding." Pamela did a quick visual scan of a well-kept living room, then smiled at Rachel. "Call me Pamela."

Chester and I exchanged glances at Pamela's apparent change of heart and interest in this missing 'person.'

Rachel explained that when she leaned out the back door of her small ranch house yesterday morning to toss out the remains of her pizza from last night, Phoebe, her Norwegian Forest cat, darted out the opening. She said it was not the first time Phoebe had gotten out, but she had always stayed in the yard and quickly returned. That morning she had gone over the fence, had not returned, and Rachel had begun to worry. She feared that maybe Phoebe had somehow gotten hurt. Worse yet, she said, with all the animal disappearances she had read about in the papers . . .

After telling her tale of woe, she sat down at the small kitchen table.

Pamela then looked Rachel up and down. "Just how old are you? Do you live here alone?"

"I'm uh . . . nineteen," she explained. "I live here with my mom. She's a nurse at the hospital and works different shifts. We don't see each other much. My dad left us a year ago. That's why we moved here." Removing her glasses, she buried her head in her hands and tried to stifle the tears that it seemed were about to erupt.

I was amazed to watch Pamela; she was so understanding and supportive. She stood behind Rachel, massaging her neck and telling her things like, "Don't worry, we'll find Phoebe."

When we left, Chester rolled his eyes.

"Not one word." Pamela glared a warning.

* * *

They immediately drove me back to the B&B and dropped me off.

"Remember, what you heard was confidential. Even though it was on the loony side," Pamela said as she opened the door for me. "At least that first one."

"Mike is here to investigate stuff like that. Can I tell him?"

Pamela looked over at Chester. "What do you think, Chet?"

"Yeah, no biggie, Sara. Tell him not to reveal his sources."

As they backed down the drive, I ran back to the Cavern.

CHAPTER 9

Cavern
Friday Noon...

Afraid to disturb Mike, I nervously stood outside and glanced repeatedly in at him. He sat at the table, studying his laptop screen. Occasionally, he seemed to stare over at something that I couldn't see. His face seemed to reflect a grim mood that caused me to hesitate, even though I had found him so approachable earlier. Now I had second thoughts. I could not believe Pamela had recommended me to help him search for this Piasa thing. Not that I regretted it. On the contrary, I needed to get out and do something, except I'd have to deal with . . . a grown man.

Finally, I summoned the courage and thought, *I've just got to do this.* I gently rapped on the glass pane.

The knock caused Mike to look up. I guess it startled him. Seeing me, he smiled and yelled, "Door's open! Come on in."

I cautiously walked in. "I'm sorry to disturb you, Mr. Kellogg, but . . ."

"I thought we were friends. If you call me Mr. Kellogg again, I'll throw you right out that door. Where have you been? I thought you knew we started early."

I nodded and took a deep breath. "Sorry, Mike. I went on a ride-along with Pamela and Chester. I thought I might learn something."

"Pamela, huh? I guess that explains the Jeep. Learn anything?"

"Just that my cousin is a stitch, but a good cop." I nervously clasped my fingers behind my back, then glanced over to where he had been staring. It was just a picture of a woman and a little girl.

"Is that your wife and daughter? Your wife's very pretty." I pushed my hands up against the small of my back to hide my sudden nervousness.

Mike reached over and turned the picture facedown on the table.

I'm sure my eyes must've grown to enormous size. *Oh boy, now I've really annoyed him . . . he probably thinks I'm a snoop.* "I'm sorry," I said. "I didn't mean anything, I . . ." I managed to stammer out. I didn't know how to talk to a man. *Why did I agree to do this?*

But he just held a hand up. "No, it's okay. I'm sorry, Sara." He looked at the back of the picture as he continued, "I just don't like to talk about it. They were killed in a car accident a couple of months back."

Inwardly, I was stunned at that news. Of all the scenarios I had run through my mind regarding what his life in Chicago must be like, that one had never surfaced. "I'm sorry, Mike."

"I know you lost your family, too," he said. "I'm sorry."

Family? If you only knew, I thought. *I miss my mom, but . . .* I forced the thoughts from my mind and spoke aloud. "I don't know why I survived," I announced. "Sometimes I think maybe it would have been better if I had perished with the others." *And not have been deposited in the care of an aunt who can ill afford to look after a teenager.*

"That's crazy," he said. "You survived for a reason. You must have something to accomplish with your life." Mike spoke the words, but the look on his face told me his mind was elsewhere. He may as well have been in Chicago.

My hands relaxed behind my back. "What do you mean?"

Mike seemed to get back to the present as he looked me in the eye. "You were spared because there is some further reason for your existence. I was left for the same reason. Like me, you don't know what it is, but unless you believe there is a path for you, you'll wander aimlessly through life feeling sorry for yourself. Here I am telling you this, and I've been wandering aimlessly the past few months. I don't know. Maybe fate deemed we meet."

I thought for a moment. *Mom always told me everything happens for a reason. Is that what he's saying?* I slipped my hands on the table and gripped the edge. "How can fate be so cruel as to take away the people we love so we can perform some task?"

"But that's what fate is," Mike answered. "Sorry, I'm not a religious person, so don't let me step on your beliefs. When bad things happen, I prefer to say it's fate. You know, it's been preordained."

How morbid, I thought as I stared over at him. *Is he saying my mom, dad and brother, and his wife and daughter all died because it was somehow planned, to leave us free to accomplish something?* I didn't like this whole line of thinking, so I tried to change the subject.

Sensing our conversation had gotten too deep for me, and remembering why I came over, I blurted out, "I don't have a camera. It was lost when the car burned. That's what I came over to tell you. All my stuff got burned. Except my CD player. Pamela said it was still plugged in my ear when she loaded me in the ambulance. I lost my other CDs, though. I just have the one that was in the player when I fell asleep. Luckily it was my favorite and hard to get . . ." I forced myself to stop talking. *Why am I nervously rambling?*

Mike laughed, "Did you think you needed your own camera to take pictures?" He got up, went into the bedroom, and returned a few seconds later with a camera case he set on the table by me. "Here, this belonged to the museum. Now, it's yours."

"I can use this one?"

"You can keep it. They replaced all of their 35mm cameras with newer digital ones, you know, that take pictures and store them on a computer chip? My boss gave me two of the older ones. I don't know what to do with one, let alone two. Now one's yours. Consider it part of your salary."

"Salary? You mean you're gonna pay me to go with you to take notes and pictures?"

Mike looked over at me with a smile. "Of course. You weren't going to do this for nothing, were you?"

I just gawked at him. "Yes, I like taking pictures. I didn't think you'd pay me to do something I love. Besides, it's a good way to get out of the house. I was going stir-crazy, sitting in my room all the time."

"Is that what you were doing last night, watching me in the early hours before dawn?"

My mouth dropped. "How did you know that?"

Mike simply smiled back.

I quickly unzipped the case to find an almost unbelievable surprise. "This is a Canon Pellix!" I almost screamed it. I had admired this camera from the 1960s and always wished I had the money to purchase one. "It has the 50mm, 1.4 lens, too."

I rummaged through the case and found it also contained a 28mm fisheye lens and a 135mm telephoto. Not to mention rolls and rolls of different speed films. "I can't accept this," I mumbled.

"Why?" he asked. "The film's good. I got it just before I left to come down here. With everyone using camera phones, I figured it would be next to impossible to buy it down here. And I got different speeds 'cause I don't know much about that stuff."

"It's not that . . . it's . . ."

"It's yours," he said firmly. "I'm glad it found a happy home. I'm not sure which way to even point the damn thing, and figuring out all of those crazy aperture settings and using a light meter is just beyond my meager capabilities. You actually know how to use that thing? If you'd prefer, I can have the museum send us down a digital one. Or you could just use your phone."

"Yes, I do know how to use it. And no, I don't want a digital. My phone went up in the fire after the accident. Thank you. This is just too much."

"Nonsense," he said. "Don't let me down. I'll take you later to get you a new phone. Part of your salary. You know, in case I need you at the spur of the moment?"

"I won't disappoint you, Mike." I tried to sound confident as I nervously shifted my weight to my other bare foot.

"Do you own any shoes, Sara? Or did they all burn in the fire too? You're not going to go into those caves barefooted."

"I normally don't like to wear shoes, but I do have sandals. Is that okay to wear in the cave?" I needed some gym shoes, but I didn't want to bother Aunt Claire for them.

"I'll take you out later for some work boots with safety toes. I don't want you to get hurt by some falling rocks. We should probably get you some kind of running shoes, too."

"I don't have any money to pay for them. I haven't even been able to replace my CDs."

"Who said anything about paying? They're also part of your salary. I've got some CDs in my car you're welcome to borrow, but most of them are by the King."

"The King?"

"Elvis. You do know who Elvis is?"

"Of course, he was my mom's favorite. You do know he's dead."

"Not his music. Well, who do *you* like? Those punk rockers? Rap? No. Wait, don't tell me. Hard metal. No, no, on second thought, you look a little bit country and a little bit rock and roll. How about Taylor Swift? Or maybe that Lavigne girl? Am I getting close?"

Inwardly, I was amused by his antics. Like Pamela, he could make me laugh. "Both Avril and Taylor are okay, but I really like Alanis."

"Ahh, Miss Morissette. I was close with Avril Lavigne."

"How is that close?"

"They're both from Canada. So, do you have all her CDs?"

"I did, but they were burned in the car fire. After this is all over, I'll get them again. I have the one that survived in my player, and Aunt Claire got me *Jagged Little Pill* in Alton. That's the only one she could find, I guess this isn't a big Alanis town." Truthfully, Aunt Claire couldn't afford to buy me more than one. It had been a coming-home-from-the-hospital gift. Not wanting to make Pamela feel obligated, I never told her about my CDs. I was impressed, though, that Mike followed singers that teens like me liked. I knew Alanis was from Ottawa, but I had no idea Avril was born in Canada too. And, unlike some of my friends, he didn't say anything about Alanis being old news.

"What do you like about her?" he probed.

This guy asks a lot of questions. Should I trust him? I looked out the window for a few seconds, then turned back. "I've never told anyone this, but I have a feeling you'd understand. I think her words speak to me. You know, like she wrote them just for me."

Mike nodded his head and pulled out a chair. "Sit."

I sat. "You think I'm crazy, don't you?" I mumbled.

Mike smiled over. "No, I think Elvis speaks to me. When I listen to the words to 'Always on My Mind,' they seem to relate to my relationship with Crystal." He paused. "No," he said, "I think it's perfectly sane."

I brightened and smiled at Mike. *Why am I always smiling at him?* "Was Crystal your wife," I asked.

He nodded.

I assumed that meant he didn't want me to go there, so I asked, "So how did you get started on this Piasa thing?"

"Long story," he said.

I looked around the room, then at the clock on the fireplace mantel. "Is there somewhere you have to be soon?" *Where did that come from? It was something Pamela would say.*

"Okay, you asked for it. What do you want to know?"

Pleased with myself, I wriggled on the chair. "First of all, you investigate strange animals. What's the last one you looked into?"

He glanced down and then up. "Beast of Exmoor in England. Someone had taken photographs that seemed to show a large black panther-like cat, suspected in the killing of many sheep."

"Did you find this cat?"

"No, but I learned many estates in England keep large cats like panthers and leopards as pets. A number of them were close to Exmoor, so I felt I was onto something when I had to return to Chicago. Then came the accident, and in the months that followed, I failed to return and follow up on the Exmoor story."

I leaned back in the chair and listened attentively. For some reason, I really wanted to hear what he had to say. I guess you'd say conquering my fear was loosening me up.

Mike continued, "Since the accident, I guess I've moped around and haven't done much of anything. My boss is a professor like Winston. His name is Paul Wiggins. Paul saw the stories about your town's earthquake, rains, cave opening up and creature sightings, and, since he knew Winston, sent me down here to offer my help. I think he was tired of my just wasting away staring out over Lake Michigan."

"That's one place I want to see again," I said. "My friends and I used to spend the summers by the lake. Are you mad you came here?"

"No, the Exmoor story will still be there when I return. I'd like to see where this leads. Maybe something strange is happening here."

I nodded, glad he had chosen to stay, as it gave me a temporary purpose in life.

"Hey, you hungry?" he asked suddenly.

I couldn't help feeling at ease in his presence. I leaned back in the chair and smiled. "I could eat. You're the boss."

"Now, that's the kind of cooperation I like," he smiled

There was a knock at the door, and Mike and I both looked over at Pamela.

"Door's open," I yelled. "Can Pamela join us?" I whispered to him.

CHAPTER 10

Piasa Restaurant

As we sat in the Piasa Restaurant, I once again felt a little self-conscious of my visible scars, especially the one above my eye. It was still a darker shade than the surrounding skin, so it stood out. I nervously twisted and turned in my seat, trying to make the scars less noticeable.

Mike seemed to know the cause of my stress. He leaned over and spoke to me in a low voice. "When someone asks you what happened, just tell them you were attacked by a great white shark while swimming at the Great Barrier Reef."

What? I'm sure he could see my eyes bug out as I listened to his words. "Isn't that in Australia? I've never been to Australia," I responded. "How does that—"

"It's a little white lie," Mike pointed out. "Don't worry, you're my assistant, so I'll back you up. It sounds so much more interesting than 'I was in a car crash.' People are impressed when you tell them that you were bitten by a shark and survived. Especially if it's a great white. It makes you into a heroine rather than a victim; you survived the sea's greatest predator."

"Do you honestly think anyone would buy that load of baloney?" asked an evidently unbelieving Pamela. "Look at her—she's just a child."

That really irritated me. I was young, yes, but hardly a child. To me, a child was younger than ten. I gave Pamela my best stern look. "I'm not a child. I'm fifteen."

"Hey, it's good to see you back in the land of the living, Sara," Pamela said. "But let's face facts. Look at you. You wouldn't make a mouthful for a shark. Besides, what would the big city boy here know about being bitten by a shark?"

Mike stared deadpan at Pamela, and in return got her bug-eyed stare. I giggled, I couldn't help myself. Pamela was just so funny. Obviously in answer to her 'what would he know' crack, Mike slowly unbuttoned the right sleeve of his shirt and rolled it up, revealing the unmistakable mark of a past bite wound on his forearm. Both Pamela and I stared at the scar.

"Wow, was that from a great white?" I gushed out.

Mike turned his deadpan look from Pamela to me. "See it worked. You thought it was a shark bite."

Pamela frowned, then smirked, "I should have known, you have no scruples. Tricking a little girl."

"I. Am. Not. A. Little. Girl," I said. "Besides, you believed him too. Maybe that's who you were referring to." I just couldn't help it. Pamela's little girl comments upset me more than she knew. "Can you please knock off those comments?"

"You are younger than me, ergo, you're a little girl," she said. "I'm sorry if that upset you, but I'll remember you're a little sensitive there." She then turned to Mike. "So what was it, your neighbor's dog?"

He first looked at me, then gave me a high five. "That was a nice comeback." He looked back to Pamela. "No, actually it was a barracuda. Shark sounds so much better, though, don't you think?"

Pamela shook her head, while I gave him a nod of agreement. Barracuda, shark, it was all the same to me—kind of exciting.

"Okay, now," Mike told me. "I was to meet with Winston this afternoon, but I got him to change the meeting to tomorrow, so we'd better get back to work. There is a lot to be done."

I looked up. "Is anyone going to tell me more of what this Piasa thing is all about? Shouldn't I know something more than that old Indian legend that Professor Moirés told me?"

"Why don't you wait until we get back to the Cavern, and I'll answer all of those questions," Mike said. "We don't want to bore the 'big' girl, do we?"

Pamela gave him a smirk and glanced at her watch, then said to me. "I've got to get to work anyway. Look, I'm off tomorrow, Sara. Would you like me to sit in on this meeting with the professor? Not that I'm interested. Just to protect your interests."

"Not if you're going to refer to me as a little girl," I said.

"I was just joshing you, Sara. Allow me my fun."

"I'm sorry, Pamela," I relented. "I'm acting like a little snob. Call me by whatever name you want."

She smiled at me, then refocused on Mike. "Maybe I can help bring Sara up to date on the Piasa? It'll probably take me a while to get to you in the morning, though."

What could I do? I smiled and nodded. I loved Pamela. Although she called me a little kid, she really never treated me like one. I knew she was just being protective of me. Between her and Mike, I thought things might stay fun and interesting. Up till now, they were doing a great job of helping me forget my situation and relieving my boredom.

Mike nodded to her and held up his hand. "Thanks, that would be great. No problem if you're gonna be late. Sara and I will meet you over at the museum. Come on, we'll get you back to your car at the Dahlgren House."

"Jeep," said Pamela, "it's a Jeep, not a car."

Mike looked at me with a 'Yikes' look and rolled his eyes as Pamela led the way out of the restaurant.

I pulled on Mike's arm, and when he leaned over, I whispered conspiratorially, "She loves her Jeep."

* * *

After I shared with him about the man at the bank's story of his fishing experience, Mike leaned back in his chair and said, "Paul mentioned a previous sighting that had taken place in Missouri of a snake-like creature supposedly ten feet long and fatter around than an anaconda." He then turned slowly around and focused on me. "Maybe it is an anaconda or a boa constrictor. I told Paul, 'Look at what's happened in Florida with Burmese pythons overrunning the swamps.' People will keep anything for a pet nowadays, but when it gets too big . . ." He trailed off in thought. So that's what Pamela was driving at yesterday with that snake remark.

"This Piasa thing, is that the Native American name?" I asked.

"Yeah, in the Illini language, Piasa supposedly translates to, '*the bird which devours men.*'" Mike shook his head, picked up his coffee and took a sip, then said, "I thought Paul was trying to pull a fast one on me."

"What do you mean?" I asked as I too took a sip of my newfound addiction.

"He and I have a deal. I do research into one of his choice of unexplained phenomenon, and then I get to do one of my own. He had picked the Beast of Exmoor, so it was my turn to pick."

"But he didn't let you?"

"No, he claimed the museum director dictated the Beast of Exmoor, said it wasn't actually his pick. When Paul gets something in his head, he's not easily swayed." Mike took a deep breath, then threw his hands up in mock surrender. "So, here I am. And you better watch the black gold or you won't be able to sleep."

"Black gold?"

"The stuff in your cup."

Late the next morning, Pamela and Chester surprised us by stopping to join us, bringing an early lunch from a local sandwich shop. I had slept late and missed breakfast, so it was much appreciated. It was the first time Mike and Chester met, and they got along immediately.

"I told Mike the stories about the guy at the bank and the lost cat," I said out loud to no one in particular.

"Well, we got another one," Chester said between bites of his sandwich. "Guy late last night, driving down Highway 100, said he saw a dead deer lying in the right lane."

"Is that the road along the river where my accident happened?" I asked.

Pamela nodded. "They call it the Great River Road. It follows the Mississippi. Anyway, to continue Chester's exciting story, which is really mine, I was getting ready to go off duty at four a.m., so I took the call. Our dispatcher had asked the guy to wait until someone came, and he did. Actually, he parked his car in the right lane with his flashers going so no one would hit him or the animal. I pulled up behind him, woke him up as he was catnapping. I know him, Jeff Tanborn."

"Jeff swore up and down there was a deer there when he called, but when I got there, there was nothing."

"Had he been drinking?" Mike asked. "It was four a.m. Who's driving around Alton at that hour?"

"Nope, he's a bartender up in Grafton at the Talbot Bar & Grill. I know him well. I've closed the place on occasion." Pamela looked over at me and wagged a polished fingernail in my face. "You tell Claire and I'll throw you in the river."

I chuckled. My cousin Pamela was a country music maven and a little wild, so it was not surprising. I knew she was bored in her job, so I could envision her dancing till dawn.

"So you think he actually saw something?" Mike asked.

Pamela was quiet for a moment, then nodded. "Yeah, I think he did. A dead deer."

"If he saw it, what happened to it?" Mike said. "Or do dead things normally get up and walk away around here?"

I could see the fire blazing in Pamela's eyes. "How should I know what happened to it? Maybe it was just stunned," she steamed. "I'm just sure that if Jeff said he saw something, he did."

"Chief says it's mass hysteria," Chester interrupted, while Mike stared over at Pamela. "We started getting those snake-thingy reports, and then all the rest just seemed to pile on. Missing dogs and cats, some big bird reports."

"Big birds?" Mike asked.

"Yeah, but it was no Piasa," Chester added. "We have eagles nesting along the river, and people are all the time calling us and saying they saw the Piasa. It's just a bald eagle, I tell 'em."

"That report this morning didn't sound like a bald eagle, Chester," Pamela said.

"What did it say, exactly?" Mike asked.

Pamela looked at Chester, who nodded. "A couple saw this bird in the early morning hours when they were biking up River Road. Said it flew across the river and landed in a tree on the Missouri side. The girl described it as big, claimed it had a wingspan of twenty feet. Said it was dark grey or dirty black. She said a bald eagle flew by, and this thing was five times its size."

"Can I talk to them?" Mike asked.

"Maybe, when they return. They called in the report on their way to go camping somewhere up north of here. They said they'd check back with us when they return."

"Thanks. By the way, did you ever find Rachel's cat?" Mike asked.

"What?" Chester said. "You too, Mike? That's all I hear from Pamela. We should do this, we should do that—"

"Shut up, Chet," Pamela ordered.

"Look, Pamela," Chet continued. "You take this stuff too much to heart. So the girl lost her cat. If you feel that strongly about it, get her a new one. Cats are a dime a dozen. I know at least three people who have litters up for adoption, and there's always the shelter. You've got to stop letting people get under your skin. You're a cop, so act like one!"

"That doesn't mean I can't be human, Chet," Pamela argued. "And I offered to get her another cat, but she wants this one back. It was a Norwegian Forest Cat, a special big cat with long hair, kind of pricey."

Chet looked to Mike, who shrugged, then he turned to his partner. "Your job is to just take the reports and turn 'em in, Pamela. Not worry about them. Next, you'll be taking her out and consoling her."

Pamela sat up in the seat. "Wow, that's a great idea, Chet. She told me she had problems making friends here. Why didn't I think of that? I knew there had to be a good reason I kept you around. Get my cell out of my purse on the floor, would you?"

Chester picked up her purse and pulled out her phone. He handed it to her while rolling his eyes. While Pamela talked on her cell, Chester got up to leave.

"I've got the afternoon to evening shift," he said.

Pamela closed her cell phone and looked over. "I left her a message. You leaving, Chet?"

"Yep, do you want me to pick you up after my shift and take you home?"

I burst out with, "We can give Pamela a ride." What was I thinking, volunteering Mike? He didn't disappoint me, though.

"Yeah," he said. "No problem."

"Are you sure?" Pamela asked.

Mike nodded. "This way, we won't be tied to a clock."

PIASA

"Okay, but don't think I'm joining this wild goose chase. I only said I'd go to the meeting at the museum. For Sara."

CHAPTER 11

Museum Meeting
Saturday Late Morning…

Later that morning, I, along with Mike and Pamela, sat in the meeting room at the Alton Museum. Winston Moirés started by introducing his two assistants, Mary Switsom and Karl Zucher.

Mary, of medium height and weight, fidgeted in her chair. I noticed she was staring at me every time I looked in her direction. She made me feel uneasy, but the feeling of dread got worse when I noticed that Karl, tall and thin with thick black hair, was glowering, off and on, in Pamela's direction. *Just what was going on?*

Winston then told his assistants, "Mike is on the staff of the Cryptozoology Museum in Chicago. He is a specialist in old legends and was available to assist us. While this is a joint venture, the Chicago museum is paying all the bills, so I will defer to Mike in areas where cost is a concern."

With a smile, he addressed Mike, "I'm not sure about taking this young lady along, though. It could be dangerous in those caves. You never know what we'll stumble across, and—"

I looked up at the obvious reference to me. *Did I have to fight for everything?*

"I was hoping you wouldn't mind my having an assistant," Mike interrupted him. "Sara is an excellent photographer. She has the approval of her guardian to accompany me."

I exhaled a sigh of relief at Mike's unexpected vote of confidence.

"I don't think we'll actually come across any real danger in those caves, Winston," Mike continued. "I told Claire I'd assume full responsibility for Sara. She won't be a burden to any of you, and if Claire trusts me—"

"Yes. Yes. You're in charge as far as the Chicago Museum end of this goes, so I'll leave that to you," said Winston. *Whew . . .*

"He meant no offense to you, Sara. He just wanted to be relieved of any responsibility," Pamela whispered softly to me.

Winston then continued, "Karl and Mary were once research assistants at the museum, so I asked for them particularly as they know the area. Karl is a geologist who has studied the bluffs, and Mary has studied the Illini Indians who inhabited these parts many years ago."

PIASA

Pamela had made me feel better, but why was he glancing over at me after every sentence? I wondered. I sneaked a peek over at Mary. *Pasta pazoole! She was still eyeballing me too.*

I tried to stay focused as Pamela leaned towards Mike, and I heard her whisper to him, "You'll notice that neither is qualified in the area of the Piasa, which is what this is supposed to be all about."

Was it my scars? I wondered self-consciously. *Am I that hideous? Maybe I can cover them up.* First, I covered the scar above my eye with one hand, and then tried to hide the one on my forearm. All I accomplished was tying myself in knots. Seeing my contortions, Pamela elbowed me to pay attention.

I struggled to maintain my composure and block their vision of my little reminders, while Mike, as an acknowledgment of Winston's remarks, bobbed his head in the general direction of Mary and Karl. They returned the gesture.

Winston continued, "Karl, did you bring the maps of the area along the river?"

I couldn't help it. It felt like everyone was looking at me, even though they weren't. Tears were welling up in my eyes.

Karl slapped his forehead with his open hand and exclaimed, "Sorry, I left them in the car. I'll run out and get them." He jumped up and left the room.

"Excuse me, let's take this opportunity to take a short break," offered Winston. "I have to return a phone call."

I could no longer control the tears as Mary broke away from staring in my direction, grabbed her cell phone and also left the room.

I struggled to harness my emotions as Mike said to Pamela, "Everyone know everyone else in this town?"

"We all went to Alton High together and then to SIU," Pamela answered while she stared at the open door. Then she gasped when she turned and saw me sitting silently with tears running down my cheeks. I wiped at my face as she got up, walked around Mike and knelt at the side of my chair.

"Tell me the truth, am I that ugly?" I asked. My eyes, I'm sure, still glistened with tears.

Pamela reached over, wrapped her arm around my shoulders and pulled me close. "What makes you say a stupid thing like that?"

"They keep staring at my scars. I must be disgusting."

"They're just concerned for your safety, that's all." Pamela tousled my hair.

I suddenly felt a huge hand grip my chin and turn my face to his. "I'm sure they are just curious; they can't possibly find you ugly. I think you're beautiful," Mike said.

Inwardly, I relished his words, thanking my instincts for making me put aside my usual apathy and talk to him. *Why couldn't my stepfather have been more like him?*

Pamela's strong arm drew me up close. "That makes two of us." Pamela then hugged me tightly. "Just relax and don't take things to heart."

Peeking over Pamela's shoulder, I saw Karl reenter the room with a large cardboard tube. Close on his heels was Mary. I reached up and wiped the remaining tears from my eyes. Within seconds, Winston also appeared, and they all retook their seats.

Pamela immediately stood up. "Excuse me, Professor, but for the record, Sara was involved in a terrible automobile accident back in February. She still has physical and mental scars from her ordeal. However, she's battling back and well on the road to recovery. This job will do a great deal for her mental health. I'd appreciate you all accepting her as she is, and please don't stare and draw attention to the physical remnants of her ordeal."

I wiped a tear away and scrunched down in my seat, slightly embarrassed at being the center of attention.

"Heavens, did she think we thought less of her because of a few scars?" Winston said, then smiled over at me. "I'm sorry if anyone offended you with their visual examination. Of course, I know who you are. I am a friend of your Aunt Claire. I was just marveling at the recovery you made; I didn't mean to offend, although I'll admit being concerned for your safety in those caves."

I nodded, while still wiping away some remaining tears. Out of the corner of my eye, I saw Mary look off in another direction. *Pasta pazoole to her.*

Later, when I thought about all this, I realized I was still afraid of people thinking I was hideous because of a few scars. In reality, as the professor had explained, they were only concerned about the slight girl getting hurt on this search for something no one thought existed. Once I realized that, I thought I acted like a child. Maybe Pamela was correct all along.

Karl noisily shook the maps out of their cardboard tube and selected one, then went to the board, tacked it up and looked to Mike. "Okay, down to business. Have you previously come across the legend of the Piasa?"

Satisfied, and grateful to Pamela for her outburst and Professor Moires for his concern, I vowed to have a good time as I settled back in my chair and listened as Mike once again pretended ignorance of the Piasa tale.

"I'm briefly acquainted with it," Mike said. "Personally, I think the artist was portraying a composite drawing of several creatures rather than an individual. More likely, the Native Americans saw a wayward condor or vulture and attached this fierce legend to it."

"That description matches similar myths in other parts of the world, though," noted Winston. "The Phoenix, the Anka, Rukh and others."

"They were always described as avian," Karl cut in. "Big birds if you will, not a creature put together with an animal erector set."

"None of these creatures could have existed," Mike replied. "If they were more dinosaur-like, they might be surviving pterosaurs. But huge, horrible birds, with sixty-foot wingspans? Come on."

Wow, this was getting interesting.

"Hold it, Mike," Karl replied. "Despite what you might see on *Jurassic Park*, pterosaurs didn't reach sixty feet, and they couldn't possibly pick up something as heavy as a man. We still don't know how the damn things even flew. If you think the legend has no basis in fact, why did you come?"

I listened as Mike answered. "Look, let's get a few things straight here before we all get off on the wrong foot. There was a petroglyph or two carved into the bluffs in this area at some long-ago time in ancient history. When were they carved? No one knows. By who? No one knows. For what reason? No one knows. Every Tom, Dick and Harry has a theory or claims they figured it out. It was the Vikings or some Chinese explorers. Poppycock. Nothing's left of the original petroglyph, so we're not likely to ever find out the truth."

Poppycock, indeed. I think Mike's actually having fun with this.

"The Indians told the early explorers the painting was there when they settled the land," Mike continued. "Some early settler later made up this cock-and-bull story about Ouatoga and the Piasa, but I don't think it happened that way. Even he later confessed to his son that he made the whole thing up."

"Remind me, who was Ouatoga?" I asked.

"Let me," answered Winston. He then summarized the story again for me, I pretended to listen attentively.

"Thanks, Professor," I said. "Which one's the petrogryph, Mike? Painted or carved?"

"Petroglyph, Sara. A petroglyph is something actually carved or chiseled into the rocks. The one here around Alton was reputed to be a petroglyph that was also painted. The paint was said to be sensitive to humidity, so at times, different parts were highly visible, while at other times they were subdued. Weather appeared to play an important part in whether you saw a vivid, colorful painting or could barely see what was there. What you have on the rocks today is a pictograph, something merely painted on the rocks."

Mike then resumed his summary to the group in general. I stole a peek at Pamela, who winked back at me. "I thought Mike didn't know that much about this," I whispered.

"So did I," Pamela whispered back.

"Unfortunately, our over-zealous forefathers blew the petroglyphs into the river to build a road," Mike continued. "None of the early drawings by Marquette survived, so, unless one of the creatures comes up and bites one of us in the behind, we'll never know what they really looked like. And, because we can no longer look at the petroglyphs, or somehow date them, we'll never know when, or by who, they were actually created."

When Mike paused, the room remained silent until he started up again. "Some think it dated back to at least 700 AD. Some say they were done by Chinese explorers. You can twist facts easily to prove your point. Politicians do it every day. Now . . . I didn't say I thought the legend had no basis in fact. I just don't believe in the creature usually described as the Piasa. Legends usually always have some basis in fact, but people tend to exaggerate. Even our Native Americans. Or in this case, a white man. As far as the size of pterosaurs"—Mike turned to Karl—"Have you not heard of *Quetzalcoatlus northropi*? A specimen they found in Texas had a wingspan of almost forty feet. I'm sure they didn't by chance find the largest of that species."

Karl ran a hand through his thick black hair as he listened.

"But I do agree, even one that size could not pick up a man," Mike confessed. "As a general rule, existing birds, except possibly *Harpia harpyja* in Central and South America, or one of its extinct relatives, can only pick up about half their weight." I thought about that as Mike smiled at Karl and said, "And I came because my boss told me to."

"Fine, how about these facts," Karl said, after a pause. "Have you heard of a teratorn? Their skeletons have turned up in places from California to New York. One found in Argentina had a wingspan of twenty-four feet."

I stole another glance at Mike, just as he looked my way and winked over at me. I waved my hand to get his attention.

"What is it, Sara?" Mike asked.

"What's this *Harpyja* bird you mentioned?" I asked.

"Harpy Eagle. The great white shark of the skies. The few that are left live in the tallest trees of the rainforests of Central and South America . . ." Mike's attention appeared to drift off.

I thought he sensed something seeming to connect.

Mike recovered his place and continued to me, "Some think that Harpies can pick up something as heavy as themselves. With claws like tigers or grizzly bears, they can hunt even fairly large mammals. They've actually been known to seize small children and pets out of yards. There are reports of them fighting off jaguars for their prey. In short, they are the premier winged predator on the planet and the largest eagle in the world. Living, that is."

Mike then smiled at Karl. "Are you saying now this creature was a teratorn? Because teratorns were nothing more than large eagles or condors."

"You painted yourself in a corner, you jerk," Pamela said softly after glancing in Karl's direction.

I'm sure I was the only one that heard that comment.

"I'm saying it, uh . . . could have been one," Karl said.

Mike's amused look returned. "The descriptions don't match. However, I'd gladly take that as an intelligent alternative. Probably much closer to actual, if the creature did exist. However, I'd estimate that bird with the twenty-four-foot wingspan weighed in at around eighty pounds. That means he could pick up about forty. Were the Illini Indians around here midgets?"

Karl scowled and became quiet.

"Mike," I asked. "Could it have been a relation to the Harpy? Then it could have picked up something that big, couldn't it?"

Mike stopped and looked at me. "Now that's thinking out of the box, Sara. I guess it's possible. There was an eagle in New Zealand that attacked and killed the giant moa, which weighed over a hundred pounds. Both are extinct now."

Winston rejoined the debate, saying in a quiet voice, "Legends abound with tales of giant birds. The interesting thing is that they sometimes contain some intriguing clues."

All eyes turned to Winston.

Mike leaned back in his chair. "How's that, Winston?"

While speaking to us all, Winston stared at Mike. "Take the thunderbird of the North American Plains, for instance. The Indians said he always came before a big storm."

Mike returned Winston's gaze. "I don't see where you're going . . ."

"For a giant bird to fly would require a lot of updrafts, no?" Winston continued.

Mike nodded.

"What precedes a big storm?" Winston added.

Mike smiled over at Winston. After appearing to think about the information, Mike replied, "Updrafts."

"Let's get back on track," Winston said after a silent moment. "Karl, why don't you review for Mike and his team what you found?"

Karl explained, "This is a map of the bluffs and surrounding area from Alton to Grafton." Karl pointed to a spot on the map. "In this area, the bluffs are close to the river, and somewhere around here is where we think the creature,"—Karl nodded to Mike and smiled—"if he existed, lived." Karl indicated a location on the map a number of miles north of Alton that was close to Grafton.

"I base that on a number of things: the various written reports of people who allegedly saw the original petroglyph, the early reports of the cave that was supposedly found, and the general layout of the bluffs. While I haven't had the time to do a thorough inspection of the area on foot, I surveyed the bluffs from my car after the quake and found a couple of new caves had opened up. There could be more, because it's kind of hard to concentrate when people are beeping their horns at you for driving so slow."

"You could have gotten your big butt out of the car and walked the path for a better look," said Mary, smiling sweetly. "That way, you could have gotten some much-needed exercise."

Karl glared at Mary and continued, ignoring her comment. "If you've driven that road, you'll know that, with the exception of the parking area under the painting, there's no place to turn off or pull over. In addition, I think the caves under the painting now deserve some renewed attention. As a result of the quake, they opened up and now extend deeper than they did before."

As Karl looked over at him, Mike quietly got up and walked over to the map.

I leaned forward in my chair to see and hear better.

Mike pointed to a spot further down on the map from where Karl was describing.

"I remember reading that there were historians," Mike said, "who thought Marquette mistakenly left the Mississippi south of Alton, down around Hartford. Here, where the Missouri River joins the Mississippi."

Winston nodded.

Mike went on, his finger tracing over the map as he spoke. "The thinking is he erroneously followed the Missouri for some length of time. That, they say, was where he made his sketch. At that time, there were drawings on the rocks up and down both rivers. Gradually, he came to realize his mistake and turned back. I understand there are bluffs along the Missouri River similar to these you're pointing out." Mike's finger continued to trace the map to an island in the Missouri River. There, he held the position and looked from Karl to Winston. "Has anyone ever checked those out?"

Clearly upset, Karl jumped up. "Jeez, Mike, can't you accept anything anyone says without raising questions? There's a piece of the blasted rock in the museum from the original painting. Do you think they were on the wrong river when they took it down?"

Mike glanced over at Karl, then replied slowly, "First of all, it's my job to question things. That's what I do. I don't think Winston wanted me to come down here and agree with everything he or you said."

Winston nodded in the affirmative.

"Second, I never said there wasn't a picture around Alton. I merely implied there could have been another one over in Missouri, and that's the one that Father Marquette saw and sketched. It's not an original idea. Some people believe it to be a logical explanation for differences in descriptions between what Marquette sketched in 1673 and others who drew or described the painting much later. You'll recall that we don't have Marquette's sketch anymore.

"In addition, there were those who didn't agree with the idea that the painting, or more correctly, the petroglyph, was put up by someone to mark the spot along the river that the creature frequented, nor by the Indians in celebration of their killing the creature.

"Third, I've seen the rock in the museum. I don't recall a longitude and latitude painted on it. However, I think you'll find that rock came from the 1925 painting of the Piasa and not the original petroglyph."

Winston again nodded his affirmation.

"Finally,"—as he spoke, Mike looked around the room at each person in turn—"I think this expedition should keep in mind what is generally acknowledged to be true. There was a petroglyph somewhere in this area that showed two separate figures. People after Marquette seemed to describe a different figure than the one Marquette sketched and wrote about. They portrayed it as big and plainly avian. Marquette recorded there were two figures, but he detailed only one, your Piasa. I think that's because he just mentally dismissed the bigger of the two carvings as he thought it nothing more than an unusually large rendering of an eagle. The other creature was fearsome and different, so he gave it his attention. Personally, I don't think he missed the boat." As he looked over to me, I smiled brightly at him. Mike gave me a quick wink, then refocused on the group.

"As long as I'm giving you my two cents, I really don't think Marquette even made that original sketch. Most think it was Jolliet, and Marquette just copied it from him. Anyway, their sketch was lost. An early visitor to the area, a German artist, Henry Lewis, supposedly did a painting of the Native Americans in their canoes on the river. In the background are the figures that Marquette supposedly depicted. I believe it's closer to the original petroglyph than what you see on the bluffs of Alton today. It shows a giant bird and just the head of a second creature.

"Much later, people wrote only about the avian one, causing us now to assume that something happened to the lower figure that Marquette described and illustrated. I think it was destroyed in the great earthquake of 1812. The thing no one can agree on is where Marquette was when he saw the petroglyphs." Mike then nodded to Karl and returned to his seat.

I couldn't help peeking around Pamela at Mike. Under the table, I slipped out of my sandals and happily waved my bare feet. This whole experience was going to be interesting.

Winston got up. "The purpose of this meeting this morning was to make sure everyone is on the same page in regards to the expedition. Who saw what, when and where in the past is not really a concern. However, I am impressed, and embarrassed, at the level of knowledge Mike possesses. He has clearly studied this mystery far more than anyone else I know, something I thought next to impossible unless you lived in this area. While Mike does not actually believe in the Piasa as we know it, he is laying that aside and will accompany us as if he did believe."

Mike nodded his agreement as Winston continued, "Karl has identified several likely spots for us to investigate, but he saw them from a distance. I asked him and Mary to check out these places for the most promising one for us to survey. He thought it was the caves under the new painting. They seem to extend north into the bluffs for quite a distance."

"Keep in mind I have not checked out the ones along Highway 100," Karl added. "But I did enter the ones under the painting and went in maybe an eighth of a mile. I didn't have any equipment, so I'm not sure if there is anything there. They may extend all the way to where the ones opened up along Highway 100."

Mike leaned back and stretched. "Anyone think of taking a look along the Missouri?" He quickly glanced over at Karl. "Just asking."

Karl shook his head in apparent disbelief. "No, we stuck to the Alton area," he responded. "As I said, I haven't had time to explore this area on the ground, let alone go along the Missouri. I only got here a week ago when I returned from working in Alaska and got the professor's message."

Winston turned his attention toward Mike. "Do you really feel there's something in that area?"

All looked to Mike.

"Yes and no, nothing specific. It was just a hunch. Let's go with Karl's plan. He's got it all laid out."

"Good," Winston smiled. "We'll meet here Monday morning at seven. We'll have the equipment ready to go by then."

Chapter 12

Visit to the Cave at Night
Saturday Evening...

Just before Mike and I were going to drive Pamela home, Chester phoned her and told her he had just gotten a call in regards to an abandoned car at the base of the Piasa painting. He wondered if we wanted to meet him there while he checked it out. Pamela didn't have to ask Mike twice. She got in the front seat and I took the rear while Mike drove.

Once we were on the road, Pamela described to us the area where we were going to meet Chester and, coincidentally, it was Professor Moires's area of search. "Highway 100," she explained, "follows the banks of the Mississippi River from Alton north to Grafton. To the east of the highway rise high rocky bluffs interspersed with vegetation and trees. In some places, the bluffs come right up to the road; in other locations, trees, shrubbery and tall weeds, sometimes quite dense, fill the area between the road and the bluffs. Got it, Sara?"

I nodded and frowned. I wasn't an imbecile.

"Why aren't you writing this down?" she asked. "Are you not Mike's assistant?"

Confused as to what she was getting at, I gave her my bug-eyed stare.

"I was the one who recommended you for the job," she said. "I can't sit back and see you screw this up. I would assume that Mike wants you to record a description of the area we're searching in, don't you think?"

We both looked to Mike, and he said, "Pamela is absolutely correct."

With a triumphant look, Pamela continued her dictation. At first I was tempted to say I had a great memory, but that would have been a lie. It was just better to swallow my pride and listen to Pamela. I pulled out the notebook Mike had given me and started writing. I tried to keep up with Pamela's description. "About a mile north of downtown Alton, the bluffs curve back away from the road for several hundred feet to form a roughly bowl-shaped area, clear of vegetation. It's used as a parking area for the large trucks of a local company. In several places, at the back of this parking area and at the north end where it meets the road, are several deep caves."

She stopped momentarily so I could catch up, writing this all down. As I scribbled down what she had said, I resisted doing something juvenile like sticking my tongue out at her smugness. After all, she did it all the time. Instead, I wanted to punch her for making me out to be some sort of slow-to-catch-on youngster in front of Mike. But in the end, I just crossed my eyes and went back to writing. She just laughed. How could I stay mad at Pamela?

Mike, oblivious to our two-year-old behavior, glanced over and then focused back on the road.

Pamela continued dictating while making various funny faces at me. Every time I snickered at her antics, Mike would look over at me like I was some kind of 'can't be serious' teenager. I thought of saying, "It's Pamela making faces!" However, I knew she'd just deny it with an innocent look, and who would Mike believe?

Pamela continued with a grin, "On the north end of the area, a cave faces parallel to the road. Above the cave, the present-day portrait of the Piasa faces the highway. Drivers leaving the downtown area of Alton, headed north on Highway 100, come around a curve and into full view of the painting. Starting in this location, and extending north for several miles along the east side of the highway, a concrete path follows the base of the bluffs and is used for biking, running or walking. People who use the trail normally park their cars in the truck lot near the Piasa painting."

Just as Pamela finished her geography lesson, we went around that curve and I saw what she meant. The painting was huge. Mike pulled his Ford Taurus into the lot and drove to the north end, where he parked behind Chester's police car. In front of it was a Volkswagen Jetta parked at the base of the Piasa painting. Mike turned off the engine and looked at the two of us.

"Am I going to have to separate the two of you, or were you just having fun?" He was obviously conscious of our antics.

We both burst out in giggles. "Sorry, Mike," I said. "I'll be good."

"Relax, Mike," Pamela chuckled. "I love this girl, but I have to needle her."

"Pamela's way of showing affection," I said.

"Anyway, I told Chester we wouldn't interfere," Pamela continued. "We'll just watch from here. He and I are connected on our cell phones, so he'll talk to us through that. I'll put it on speakerphone." Pamela then set her phone on the dash of the car.

I watched as, inside the police car, Chester reached out and adjusted his spotlight to bathe the VW in light.

"It appears empty," Chester's words blared from the cell phone into the quiet car. Chester got out of the patrol car and walked up to the Jetta, directing his handheld flashlight inside to make sure there were no occupants. "Yep, no one home," his voice filled our car.

Chester looked up and pointed his flashlight at the yawning black mouth of the cave. I could see fireflies dashing and flitting about. The sound of crickets, their chirping resonating in the night air, drifted in through Mike's open side window. As Chester walked past the front of the VW, he put his hand on the hood. "It's cold. No sounds coming from the car that might indicate fluids cooling. That means it's been here for a while."

He again flashed his light up at the caves, but I could see nothing except the fireflies and other flying bugs. Cricket noise continued to infiltrate the night air, both through Mike's open window and Chester's phone. There were no other sounds except for an occasional car that zipped along on the highway, just off to our left.

Chester walked up to the mouth of the cave and flashed his light around inside. "For as far as the light penetrates," his voice came in a whisper, "there's no sign anyone has been inside."

From somewhere, it sounded like deep inside the cave, came a strange coughing sound. "That sound is vaguely familiar," Chester said.

"Sounds like some sort of an animal," Mike replied softly. "Familiar, but its origin eludes me."

After the sound, it got deathly quiet. The crickets stopped their symphony. Chester shrugged and walked back down to the Jetta. Walking around it, he flashed his light at a bike rack on the back.

Chester finally returned to his car and called in a report with the license plate number. When he was finished, he came over to our car and stood by Mike's open window.

"Strange," he told Mike as Pamela reached over and turned her cell phone off. "It's an expensive car with a nice bike rack, so they're not likely kids. But where are they? Anyone from around here would know you can't park here overnight without a permit."

"Wait a minute, Chet," Pamela said. "Maybe it's the couple that called in their big bird report this morning. Maybe the bird flew over and picked them up and carried them off for ratting him out," she laughed.

"That's probably not far from the truth," said Chester. "The part about who the car belongs to, anyway. One of these days, some big bird is gonna carry you off, Pamela. I've got to go and do some real police work."

"Yeah, hit the Dunkin' Donuts, Chet," quipped Pamela. She was relentless.

Sunday Afternoon

It was a brilliant sunshiny day, and Mike and I had skipped breakfast and now lounged on the porch. About ten minutes into our siesta, as Mike called it,

Pamela showed up and without a word, kicked off her shoes and lay in the swing with her feet hanging over the end.

Claire came out and asked, "Who's up for lunch?"

"You really don't have to do that, Claire. I only paid you for breakfast . . ." Mike said.

"Nonsense, you hired my niece. I have to feed her anyway."

"Actually," smiled Mike, "I can do that, too."

In answer, Auntie said, "Okay, then I'm making you all a late breakfast, and since no one gave me their choice, it's pot luck." She gave Mike a quick grin and returned to the kitchen.

Mike looked to Pamela, who had lifted her legs up against the swing's chain support and silently stared at her toes, painted some shade that looked like aqua. I looked down at my toes, devoid of color. When I looked back up, Pamela was staring at me.

"It would be helpful if you were living a little closer," Mike pointed out.

Pamela turned her attention to him and frowned. "Look, I'm not working for you. I just came along yesterday because I had a few hours off and was curious and . . ." Pamela trailed off.

"And what?" pressed Mike.

"I wanted to watch out for Sara."

"You told me I was on my own," I said.

"And?" Mike stared at Pamela.

Pamela took a deep breath, swung her legs down, sat up in the swing and finished, "I had nothing better to do. There you have it, my exciting personal life in Alton."

We all turned and watched as a car pulled into the driveway and stopped. A man stepped out of the car and started up the walk. Claire came out of the door and walked down to meet him. After a few moments of conversation, she came back as the visitors left. Coming back on the porch, Claire said, "They'll have a hard time getting something in town, it's the annual Haunted House tours starting Friday. I wish I had another room to rent. I have regular customers I'm turning away."

"Oh, Claire, I'm costing you business by staying in one of your rooms," I said, knowing I was depriving her of much-needed money.

I noticed Mike lean back in his chair and furrow his brow as he apparently slipped deep into thought.

"No, don't you worry about that, dear," Claire said. "We'll get by just fine."

"What about the Grotto, Claire?" asked Mike.

"I rented it for next week. It's empty right now, but it's already Saturday, and they're coming in on Monday. At least, I hope they come. Breakfast is ready, though. Come on in and eat." Claire then went into the house.

"I just had an idea that will solve Claire's problem," announced Mike. "Sara, you can stay in the Cavern. The bedroom has a king-sized bed and there's plenty of room for us to work."

Pamela stared at Mike. "And where will you sleep?" That was exactly what I was wondering but hadn't had a chance to ask.

"My car. I'm a man of little needs."

"I can't push you out of your room!" I exclaimed. "You paid for that."

"I'm also paying your salary, so don't argue. It's settled. After we finish lunch, go and pack your things and move in. Later, we'll run over and pick you up some boots. Soon as you're settled, we need to have a planning meeting."

Dismayed, I looked over. "But . . ."

"No buts. Let's eat, then get to work."

"I gotta go," Pamela said as she slipped her shoes on and got up.

"Aren't you going to eat with us?" I asked.

"I'm not hungry. I've got the evening shift," she said as she walked quickly down the steps and left. Something, I knew, was troubling her.

* * *

In the Cavern, several hours later, Mike was hunched over his computer when I came in, carrying a large box. Sadly, it held everything I owned down here. I held out hope for still getting back to Chicago after this was over. If I was going to school here, I needed my clothes.

Mike jumped up and took the box from me and carried it into the bedroom.

I looked down at my new gym shoes. "Thanks again for buying me these, and the boots. Aunt Claire really has her hands full with the weekend coming up." I didn't want Mike to know the financial situation that Claire was in.

"Don't mention it. I told you it was part of your salary."

"Umm, Mike." I looked at Mike nervously.

"Yeah?"

"I hate to ask you for another favor, but could you take me to the doctor on Friday? I know Aunt Claire will be really busy with guests. Please don't tell her I asked, she'll be furious with me. The doctor is in Wood River, and it would really throw her further—"

"Of course, Sara. I'll make it sound like my idea. Now come here. I want to show you something. I have an additional job for you when you're not taking pictures and I'm busy."

I can't believe he said yes, I thought. *I was sure he'd say he was too busy, like my stepdad always told me when I asked for a ride.* Anxious to please, I eagerly walked over.

"I've set you up with a logon to my computer. When you get on, I want you to go on the Internet and connect to this website, strangenews.com." Mike stopped and looked back at me. "I'm assuming you are well-versed in the Internet?"

"Of course. You don't think I'm some sort of a country bumpkin, do you?" I scoffed at his question.

Mike chuckled and continued, "No, I kind of remembered that Pamela said you were a computer geek. I just wanted to make sure. You are now a registered user on the site. Your sign-in to the website and the computer are the same, Sara Williams. Your password is . . ."

"Can it be," I interrupted, "Lennore?" I was hoping he wouldn't ask me why. Emily had suggested it back home, and it would be my little bit of associating with her now. It was the name of the bright-yellow polish I always used on my nails. I remembered when I first found it at our local little drug store, Emily commented on the name and thought it was the perfect choice for me. The brand name was called Distans and consisted of many bright shades. Em found a shade of blue that was called Cosette which she always wore. My dad had noticed it right before he left on that final tour. I remember him taking my hand, and all he said was "spiffy." Then he kissed my hand. Somehow, I had to get some money and buy some polish.

Mike grinned. "Yeah, I'll change it to Lennore. Anyway, the website will verify you and let you read the news for any area you select."

"You want me to get you the news?" I frowned. *I knew it. He doesn't really trust me . . .*

"No, not quite. This website collects strange events from all over the world and attempts to classify them, if it can. If not, it just goes in as an unclassified strange happening. You enter our location, and it will return every strange or unusual happening within a set distance. Right now, I have it set for one hundred miles. Watch."

Mike showed me by entering *Alton, Illinois,* in the location. A number of events started scrolling on the screen. In a few seconds, it stopped, showing twenty-three events in the past week. "Can you handle it, Sara? Just summarize them for me."

Fascinated, I nodded and began to read.

* * *

Pamela returned later that day to the surprise of Mike and me.

"I thought you had the evening shift," Mike asked.

"So did I," she answered. "However, the chief said he had a special assignment he wanted me to start on tomorrow morning, so he sent me home. I thought I'd stop by and see if I should arrest you for terrorizing your assistant."

"Me?" I asked. "Why would—"

"She's just being her usual smart aleck self, Sara," Mike said. "Ignore the lady." I should have known it was just Pamela's wise-acre remarks. I didn't think she would shower them on Mike, though.

"What are you two up to?" Pamela asked. Her mood was better than this afternoon, but I knew something still troubled her.

"What else? Following your ridiculous legend," Mike smiled at Pamela. "How about we go out on the patio and get some fresh air?"

Moving outside, we took up residence around the table on the patio. I wanted to go back to the porch, but Mike had told me that we shouldn't just take over that prime location, as Claire had other guests and he preferred a little privacy when we were working. As the three of us settled around the table, I found it cozy. I looked over at Pamela, who was staring over at the Grotto, and it struck me. She was wearing jean shorts with a sleeveless white top. I had assumed she came right from the station, but she wouldn't have reported to work dressed like that. She had obviously taken the time to stop at her apartment and change. Why?

"Sara, what did you find out on *Strange News*?" Mike asked me when we were settled.

"Strange news?" voiced Pamela, who turned to look at him.

"Just listen," Mike said.

I looked up and tried to give them a cheery smile. Pamela had always been my favorite relative, and Mike was fast becoming a great friend even though he was older and male. Once again, I shed my shoes and happily waved bare feet under the table. I was pleased to have been assigned an important job. I decided to save what I thought he would like the best for last. "A couple of unidentified flying objects, some animal disappearances mostly. Dogs and cats, and . . ."

"Where were the animal disappearances?" asked Mike.

"I knew you'd ask me that," I smiled over at Mike. "I looked it up on the map. Out along the Missouri River mostly, just west of where it meets the Mississippi."

"The UFO reports. Did anyone provide a description?" he asked.

"A description?" I frowned, unsure of what Mike was after. I had thought he wouldn't be interested in those.

"Yes, a description. What the object looked like. Metallic? Was it disk-shaped? Did they see just a light? It's important. Did they say they actually saw something or merely hint at an unknown object?"

Slightly embarrassed at not knowing, I fidgeted in my chair, conscious of Pamela's looking over at me. However, she didn't say anything.

"It's okay, Sara," Mike continued. "I should have been more specific."

I relaxed, but was angry at myself for disappointing him. "I'm sorry, Mike. I don't remember reading about any specific object. I do recall one said it cast a huge dark shadow. The other said it blocked out the light of the moon. There were only two UFOs, both were in the early morning. But . . ." I paused dramatically, "there were some reports of a big bird."

"What about a big bird?" Mike seemed interested. I had been right.

Pamela looked over at me, then Mike. "What the heck," she chuckled, "you chasing shadows and listening to nut cases? What do all these things have to do with exploring those caves? A bunch of missing cats and dogs. Shadows in the night. Big birds that always turn out to be bald eagles. God, I'm glad I didn't take the job."

Mike fixed her with a grin. "Maybe this means nothing, and maybe everything."

Pamela gazed back at him, but kept silent.

Mike turned back to me. "Tell me everything it said about the big bird, Sara."

My good mood restored, I nodded and continued. "It wasn't the report that Chester told us about. I guess they don't have that one. This one was at the Great River Wildlife Refuge up north of here, near a town called Louisiana, Missouri. Why would you name a town after another state?" Not really expecting an answer, I looked up anyway.

Mike was looking down into the woods, and Pamela was staring at him. Noticing I had stopped, Mike looked over at me. Pamela quickly followed his lead.

I was curious about their behavior, but continued. "Anyway, someone said they saw it in the early morning hours yesterday. It took off and flew low over the river heading north. They described the bird as a dirty gray in color, with a large black beak and wings that they swore were around twenty feet in width." I searched Mike's face for any sign of excitement in my prize announcement, but he remained unreadable.

"We've got a lot of those bird sightings over at the station. Funny, how in this age of digital cameras and smartphones, no one seems to have one at these times," Pamela pointed out.

"You know," I said, "Mike gave me access to this website that monitors all strange phenomenon reports. I was baffled by why he wanted me to do this, until I went back into their files. There have been numerous reports of big birds and pet and animal disappearances in this area. Also, people report seeing this large snake-like creature at times. All since shortly after the floods last fall. They've increased since the earthquake. Was it okay that I did that, Mike? I know you didn't tell me to . . ." I guess I was trying to defend him from my cousin's remarks.

I watched as a big smile filled his face and he pointed towards me with his hand, palm up, while he grinned over at Pamela.

"Do you believe this girl?" he said. "Of course, it's okay, Sara. I'm very pleased you took it upon yourself to find out more. Now I know I've got the right assistant."

I really hadn't expected that. Inwardly, I was pleased with myself. One of my stepfather's most frequent retorts was, "Did I tell you to do that?"

"I still don't see how this is relevant to your search," Pamela interrupted my thoughts. "So a lot of pets and animals are touchy about the little aftershocks, which pop up now and then. So what? I'm sure a lot of them are roaming the hills around here enjoying their newfound freedom. Not to mention making a lot of work for me."

I couldn't help getting involved in this discussion, so I smiled at Pamela and said, "I know you're a police officer, Pamela, and you know about all these things. But I really think Mike knows what he's doing. He's the investigator."

Pamela ignored my opinion and looked over at Mike. "I don't get it. What makes you so sure you know what's going on around here? We live here; you don't. I've followed up on these reports, and the—"

Mike held up his hand, and Pamela quieted down. He got up and glanced down into the woods, then took a deep breath and spoke to her.

"My job is to investigate reports of strange animals and related phenomenon, and try to cast light on them. I expect to do my job despite any local criticisms. Sara knows who's paying the bills, and does her job. I don't mind you watching out for Sara by hanging around, but I'd appreciate you not second-guessing me all the time."

Pamela sat silently for several minutes. When she glanced over at me, I shifted my eyes from her to Mike. I didn't know who to stick up for.

Finally, Pamela stood up. "You know, I think Sara can take care of herself. She's been well trained to deal with a pompous jerk. I'm sorry I even tried to help. I'll leave and keep my opinions to myself." As Pamela turned to go, Mike grabbed her wrist in a tight grip.

"I'm sorry," he said. "I was out of line. Don't stop giving me your ideas. I'd just appreciate you not questioning my judgment. Something's going on here in Alton, and I intend to find out what it is. I don't think it has anything to do with the Piasa or any strange creatures from the past." Mike paused. "I was sent down here to assist Winston in his cave search, but it's hard to resist following up on these other stories too."

"But you're tracking animal disappearances, and you're supposed to explore some caves," Pamela said.

"As far as I'm concerned, this searching through the caves for the existence of your Piasa is a fool's errand. I'm more concerned with finding out what people are seeing today. Anyway, has it ever occurred to you they might be connected?"

Pamela's eyes narrowed. "Are you saying that something like the Piasa has returned?"

"No, of course not. I do believe there is something loose in this area capable of killing cats and dogs. But it's not the Piasa. I'm afraid that some reporter will jump to that conclusion as a way to sell some papers. That could really mess up our search. I intend to follow this and see where it leads."

For a moment, both were quiet as I looked from one to the other. Pamela looked down to where Mike still gripped her wrist.

"You're cutting off my circulation."

"Sorry," Mike said as he released her hand.

"Okay, we're square, but I'm leaving anyway. I've got to meet a friend for dinner."

As Pamela scooted her chair in, she muttered, "Wingspan of twenty feet . . ."

"Sounds outrageous, I know," said Mike. "But dirty gray, black beak and a large wingspread sounds like a particular bird I know. Just not that big, and not this far north."

"Yeah," Pamela smirked. "You and Sara can go chase this fairytale bird. I'm glad I'm through with this Mickey Mouse expedition. See you around town."

CHAPTER 13

The Caves
Monday morning...

Early the next morning, Mike and I walked over to the museum where Winston's assistants, Mary and Karl, were already loading tools and equipment into a van. Mike carried his laptop computer and a black leather case slung over his shoulder.

I had dressed in jeans with a long-sleeve, gray T-shirt, emblazoned on the front with the words, *Alanis World Tour*. Luckily, I had been wearing this, my favorite shirt, when the accident happened, otherwise it would have been lost. Now it had a few bloodstains that had failed to wash out and a small tear where my arm got caught in the door, but it was still my favorite. On my feet were my new safety boots. My camera bag hung from one shoulder, while my right hand tightly gripped the CD player. In fact, I was wearing or carrying just about all of my worldly possessions. Both Claire and Pamela, then Mike after he arrived, had repeatedly offered to take me up to Chicago to get things I could use, but the thought of facing my friends then having to move here permanently was too much. If I had to start all over in Alton, I was mentally prepared. However, I held out hope that somehow I would be able to return to my school in Chicago.

Last night, I had lain in bed awake, trying to deal with the up and down feelings I had about Mike. Except for my father, until I met Mike, most of my dealings with males, either young or old, had always been negative. Just before he came, I had come to the conclusion that from that point on, I would have as little to do with males as I could. Guys in high school were either beating me up or paying me no mind anyway, and, with my stepbrother and father now gone, well . . . I could manage just fine by myself.

"Are we almost ready to go?"

I glanced over at Winston, who was obviously in good spirits, as he boomed out those words, and came around from the front of the van.

Mary yelled to Winston while packing in her equipment, "I think we have everything!"

Karl got into the driver's seat with Winston joining him in the front. Mary got in through the sliding side door and proceeded to lounge on the rear bench seat.

PIASA

I looked at Mike, expecting him to indicate for me to go to the back of the van also. However, he surprised me by pointing to the single seat behind the driver. Sitting down, I noticed Mike was looking over a museum publication on the Piasa as he took the seat opposite me and directly behind Winston.

Karl pulled the van out onto University Avenue and drove west. Up and down the normally busy street, I stared at boarded-up businesses and for sale signs. Aunt Claire had talked about the signs of change; she said they reflected a hard economy. The spring floods and recent earthquake, I heard her telling guests, had combined to shutter many businesses.

My eyes flicked away from outside as Winston turned around and spoke to Mike. "Karl and Mary are going to set up a tent near the cave entrance. Karl prefers to stay close by the cave entrance once we start the exploration to make sure no sightseers try to enter. I didn't see any reason to argue, so I talked to the trucking company that owns the land and got their permission."

Mike gave a slight nod of agreement.

"It'll give us some security," Karl added.

Mary called from behind me, "What about the 'No Entry by Order of the Chief of Police' sign at the entrance to the caves?"

Winston held up a finger. "Good point, Mary, I called the chief and left a message for him this morning reminding him of what we planned to do. I asked him to call me back." Just then, Winston's cell phone rang. He hunched over in the front seat to hear above the noise in the van.

I put in my earbuds and was content to once again stare out the side window and listen to Alanis singing about moving on. *Yeah,* I thought, *I need to do that.*

As we passed Alton High School, it brought back the unwelcome thoughts of what I was to do with my life. I now regretted not having taken my high school in Chicago up on their offer to send down schoolwork. At the time of the accident, my only wish was that I could have died with my family. Then, thoughts of school were light-years away.

Now, I knew that when this little adventure was over, I'd have to face those realities. I realized I'd have lots of schoolwork to make up regardless of where I ended up. Claire had already been hinting about enrolling me at Alton High. While I mentally explored the possibilities of a way I could go back to school in Chicago, Alanis continued to sing in my ear about not waiting for someone to take my fears away. *Yep,* I thought, *that's me, all alone.*

I was suddenly conscious of Mike's hand waving in front of my face.

"Huh?" I asked, taking out an earbud.

"Wow, you were out of it," Mike said. "I asked when you saw her."

"Saw who?"

"Alanis. You're wearing a concert shirt."

"Oh, I've never seen her in person. I picked this up at a garage sale back home."

Mike smiled, nodded and held out a CD for me.

"What's this?" I said excitedly.

"A little present," he said. "Have you ever heard this girl?"

I took the CD from his hand and turned it over. On it was a picture of a redheaded girl, like me, in a yellow dress, with the words *A Fine Frenzy*, and, underneath that, *One Cell in the Sea.*

"Her name is Alison Sudol," Mike said. "Her group goes by the name A Fine Frenzy. Play it for yourself; she might have some words for you."

I didn't think so, to tell the truth. It looked kind of highbrow, but I stuck it in the player and turned it on. From the very beginning, she mesmerized me. Wow, I thought, this girl can sing. To me.

One of the first songs was called "You Picked Me," and as the words came out, I looked over at Mike. He seemed to know exactly what I needed. The song spoke of being difficult to reach, but being picked anyway. Is that how people saw me?

"The chief insists on having police presence with us." Winston's voice cut into my thoughts. He closed his phone and announced, "He's sent two of his officers to accompany us. They will meet us there."

Karl turned left down Highway 67, headed toward downtown Alton.

Mike moved his head closer to Winston and spoke. "I think that's a very good idea. I've had Sara tracking a number of animal disappearances in the area. There could be some sort of large carnivore around."

At the mention of my name, I pulled my earbuds off.

"Large carnivore?" Mary sneered from the back seat. "So does the big skeptic now think the Piasa is real? Even we don't go that far."

"I don't recall saying it was the Piasa," Mike replied. "I was thinking more like a mountain lion or some cat predator. It's not that unusual for a cougar to make it here to Illinois."

Winston turned in his seat to face Mike and glanced over at me. "What did you say you had this young lady doing?"

With a wisp of a smile, I eagerly volunteered, "Mike showed me how to dial into this news network on the Internet that tracks strange happenings. It's cool."

Karl turned right onto Highway 100 in downtown Alton, heading north on the Great River Road. About a mile out of town, he pulled into the trucking lot and drove to the northern end, under the Piasa painting. An Alton police car was already parked there.

I was surprised to see Pamela and Chester, both looking bored, standing outside the patrol car. "Look alive, Chester. Our big assignment is here!" Pamela hollered and elbowed him for attention, causing Chester to double over in mock pain.

As we tumbled out of the van, Chester and Pamela walked over to Mike and me.

Chester smiled at me and nodded.

Pamela finally looked over at Mike, who was standing off to the side.

"So this is the special job the chief had earmarked you for," Mike said.

"If you stop talking now, I won't pull out my gun and shoot you," Pamela said with a smile.

While we conversed, Winston watched as Karl and Mary unloaded their equipment from the van.

I glanced from Pamela to Chester, instinctively touching the scar above my eye. Pamela saw me and quickly threw in, "Hey, it's good to have battle scars. They show you've not led a pansy life." With that, Pamela showed me an ugly welt across her forearm. "Much better than some stupid tattoo. I got this from helping to pull a little girl out of a burning car."

"Me?" I asked.

Pamela nodded and elbowed Chester. "Show her yours."

Chester lifted up his head and pointed to a jagged scar along the base of his neck. "I got this breaking up a bar fight. Some drunk tried to cut my head off with a broken beer bottle. See, you're in exclusive company." Chester winked at me.

"I'm sorry, Pamela. You never told me that . . ." I stopped talking when Pamela shook her head.

"Not important," said Pamela. "It goes with the job. Small price to pay, to see you standing here."

"Mike should be in the group, too; he was bitten by that barracuda," I said.

Pamela trained an eye on Mike. "I don't know if that little bite qualifies. Do you have any others?"

Mike returned Pamela's look. "Do you want to see them all?"

"All?" I asked. "You have more than one?"

"I just told you about the barracuda. The others aren't so glamorous."

"I'd like to see, and hear, about them all," Pamela said slowly. Then she smiled at Mike.

Chester nodded his head over to where Winston, Karl and Mary stood at the cave's entrance. "Uhh, maybe we should do show and tell afterward. I think they're ready to get to work. Professor Winston might get impatient."

"Okay, later, Mike," teased Pamela. Wow, she was bold. I could never say that to a guy. Now, it was beginning to make sense. Pamela's dressing more provocative, her teasing Mike. She only did that with people she really liked. She must like him!

I followed Pamela as she headed over to the cave.

The entrance to the cave was about ten feet wide and fifteen feet high. Large and small bushes and a few small trees surrounded it. Bottles and cans and packaging materials from various parties littered the area. Inside, the cavern was more than twenty feet wide and more than twelve feet high. No, I'm not some whiz at judging distances or heights. Mike is, though, and he filled me in later. It seemed to extend like a tunnel in both directions. The floor had standing water in spots, which I assumed was from wind-blown rain as we were well above the river level. It was strewn with rock from the bluffs and more litter from late-night parties. Here, where we stood, it was lit by outside light reflected in from several additional entrances that faced different points of the compass. I could see that where we were going, there was no light.

With her hands, Pamela made a sweeping gesture to the area around the cave and then pantomimed writing. She followed that up with a crazy face at me in which she crossed her eyes and stuck out her tongue. I cracked up, drawing a look of curiosity from Winston and a smirk from Mike. Of course, with them looking, Pamela's face was all business. I pulled my little notebook out and made some notes to be entered into the computer later.

At this spot, the bluffs were separated from the river by the highway and a narrow strip of land. But from the location of the painting, the bluffs extended sharply east for several hundred feet, then meandered south for several hundred more and finally returned west to the highway along the river. The large U-shaped cutout they created was apparently kept clear of trees and brush by the trucking company. Where the bluffs started to head back toward the river, on the southeast end of the parking lot, were several more yawning cave openings.

How do I know all these boring facts? Mike had asked me to write a description of any area we go to in the journal I kept for him. I didn't want to let him down in any way. Also, Pamela had her notoriously comical way of always reminding me.

I saw Mike motion toward those other entrances as he stood behind me with Winston. "Any reason not to look in them, or are they connected with these?"

Winston looked toward the caves, then at Mike. "Karl checked them out last week. They don't seem to go anywhere; they're not connected to these. Actually, they were unchanged by the quake." Winston turned and pointed in a generally northerly direction. "These caves, however, seem to go a long way. As Karl mentioned, he went in a short distance but found nothing. They were pretty dark, so he turned back. I had told him to wait for a larger party so we wouldn't miss anything or disturb valuable evidence. While Karl is a geologist, Mary is the Native American expert. He might miss or disturb something critical to Mary."

Mike nodded in agreement. I was beginning to see why he had insisted on buying me the safety-toed boots. The caves ahead looked very dark.

* * *

Waiting to begin, Pamela and I went inside the yawning entrance and stood on some rocks in the middle of the cave. I stuffed the notebook into the back pocket of my jeans and gaped at the rock walls, my camera bag slung over one shoulder and camera in hand. My CD player dangled by the cord around my neck. I'm sure I must have looked like some kind of geek.

"After parties and stuff, lots of us from high school used to come down here and write stuff on the walls," Pamela whispered in my general direction. "Now, I'm supposed to keep the kids from doing that." We both continued to quietly read some of the messages that had been written on the walls over the years.

While searching the scribblings on the wall to the right of the entrance, I found a heart carved into the rock with the initials 'M W LOVES P S' inside the outline. I let out a happy little squeal and poked Pamela with my elbow. She reacted with a grunt.

I pointed at the heart. "This one even has your initials, Pamela."

Pamela snickered, "God, I'd forgotten Marty had done that."

"You mean it *is* you?"

"Yeah. But now I'd have to arrest him for defacing the walls. Not to mention being in here in the first place." Pamela sobered.

"Was he your boyfriend?"

"Nope, prom date."

"What happened to him?"

"Marty went east to school. Penn State, I think. I don't know what happened to him after that. Like most, he never came back. His folks moved on a couple of years ago."

"You seeing anyone now?" I asked. I checked camera angles while we talked.

Pamela shook her head. "You're kind of nosy, squirt. You have a boyfriend back in Chicago?"

PIASA

I repeated Pamela's negative headshake and said, "Maybe things will look up for you. How about Mike?" I punctuated that by pointing an elbow toward where Mike stood.

Pamela again shook her head. "No, I think we'd lock horns all the time. He's only going through the motions for his museum. I'm sure he thinks this is an episode in futility. Hey, are you trying to be a matchmaker?"

I shook my head. "I just think you're both kind of lonely and . . . I'm sorry."

Pamela put her arm around my shoulder and gave me a squeeze. "No problem. What's his story anyway? Is he married?"

"Was. His wife died," I announced. Pamela got wide-eyed at that revelation and turned to face me as I continued. "She and his daughter were killed in an auto accident."

Unbelieving, Pamela moved in close to me. "How do you know that?"

"He told me." Pamela stared over at me, then up to the mouth of the cave where Mike stood talking to Winston.

* * *

I then watched as just outside the cave, Chester helped Mary and Karl in setting up their equipment and they finished unloading the van. Karl stopped for a break and walked over to where Chester stood a few feet from me. "You know anything about a couple disappearing in this area, Chester?" he asked.

Chester nodded. "Yeah, night before last. I came and checked out a car parked here with no one around. We towed it the next morning. It's still unclaimed. We learned it belonged to a young couple who went bike riding. They had backpacks and stuff, according to their friends, so we assume they're camping somewhere. They probably didn't know you couldn't park here overnight."

"Did you check along the trail?"

"We did a visual, driving slowly all the way up to Grafton. If they were along the trail, we'd have spotted them. Naw, I think they're camping somewhere further north."

"Sara!" Mike's voice broke in on my eavesdropping. "Are you gonna use that camera or are you looking for a message from the Piasa? I don't remember it having written any love letters on the cave walls."

I moved away from Pamela and, in my new heavy boots, carefully stepped from rock to rock in Mike's direction, while holding onto the camera bag and CD player. "What would you like me to take pictures of?" I asked. I was a little taken back by his comments.

I must have annoyed him. But when I looked up at him, he was grinning.

"You have an unlimited supply of film. Get used to the camera. Take a couple of rolls for practice. I can get you lots more film. The museum is accustomed to selecting pictures out of hundreds, even thousands, taken. You never know what they'll find interesting. Get my drift?"

"You know the world has gone to digital cameras!" Pamela shouted. "It would make things much simpler."

"Yeah, it would, however—" Mike stopped when I touched his arm.

"May I?" I asked.

He nodded.

"This is the best camera in the world, Pamela. I'd rather be using it than any digital one."

"I forgot, the big city boy has you brainwashed into his methods. I'll buy you a new camera, Sara, then you can give him that one back."

"Thanks, but I don't want a new camera, this one's mine. Mike gave it to me."

"He what?"

"This is the camera I always dreamed of owning. It's complete with lenses." By this time, Pamela had moved by my side. She looked at the camera, then at Mike.

"Look," Mike said. "Before you get any crazy ideas, the museum gave it to me, and I gave it to her. It's no big deal except, apparently, to Sara."

I nodded and said, "I remember what you told me, take pictures of everything and don't forget to number them and keep a log of what's on what roll."

Mike smiled back in agreement, then turned and walked toward the outside workers.

"I think we should get started," Winston finally announced. Nods of agreement came from some; others just looked on expectantly. "Karl, why don't you and the officers lead. The rest of us will follow behind." Karl nodded, but Chester turned to Winston.

"I think it's better if Pamela and I split up," he told Winston. "I'll go up front with Karl, but Pamela should bring up the rear." Winston agreed.

Karl and Chester led the way into the caves, with Winston and Mary following close behind. I followed them, with Mike at my side, and finally, a few steps behind us, Pamela.

* * *

It was near dusk when we struggled back out of the cave under the painting. No evidence corroborating the existence of the Piasa had been found. I was starting to think Mike was right, it was a fool's errand. But I couldn't complain. For the first time in a long time, I was having fun.

"God, I need a hot shower," Pamela said.

"Second that," Chester added.

Standing at the entrance, I clicked away, taking pictures of the group and camp set up by Karl and Mary. When I finished, I moved over to where Pamela, Chester and Mike stood.

"I'm pretty doggone hungry," Mike said. "Want to get something to eat?"

Pam nudged Chester, who nodded.

"Hey, Winston," Mike called, "we're going to eat, you all want to join us?"

Winston glanced over at Mary and Karl, who shook their heads. "We want to get right on our finds, if it's all the same to you. Maybe another time." Karl and Mary disappeared into the tent they had set up earlier.

"Finds? What finds?" I asked.

"They picked up some magic rocks," Pamela joked.

Mike shrugged and looked at me. "Okay, Sara. Let's eat."

"Are you forgetting something?" I pointed out. "We don't have a car. They drove."

"Plenty of room in the back of the squad," Pamela said. "We're off duty now; we can drop you off at the B&B when we're done." With that, Pamela opened a rear door, and I gladly slid in, followed by Mike.

* * *

Taking a seat in the Piasa Restaurant, Pamela continued a conversation that had started in the car. "Look, Sara, you'll end up with a tiny scar above your left eyebrow, some little thing on your arm, and some marks on your left side and legs. Not really so bad. They'll fade with time, and you'll forget all about them."

"I'm worried about my leg."

Pamela leaned back and looked me in the eye. "You look great. You have cute little legs, honest. If it really bothers you, wear pants until the color fades. You must need some clothes, anyway. Since you won't let any of us take you home on a road trip, I'll take you shopping. My treat."

Somewhat relieved and excited by Pamela's comments and offer, I smiled briefly.

"Did you tell Mike what the chief told you?" Chester asked while waving his menu at Pamela.

"Shut up, Chet," Pamela said as she made a cutting sign across her throat.

"What?" Mike coaxed. "Come on, Officer Friendly, spill it."

"Damn you, Chet. I was waiting for the right time."

"No time like the present," Mike probed.

"Okay. The chief is getting ready to retire next year, and he doesn't want any kind of incident to upset his sterling record."

"So?" Mike asked.

Pamela twisted her napkin in her lap and stared up at the ceiling.

Chester broke the silence. "The chief said, 'I don't want that little girl to have survived that horrific accident and then get hurt looking for some stupid creature with that idiotic big city guy.' I think that's a direct quote, isn't it Pamela?"

"I still don't see—" Mike started to ask.

"I have to stay with you two as long as you're engaged in this silly search," Pamela barked. "Do you understand that?"

"Yippee!" I exclaimed. I had wanted her all along to be part of this, and now my prayers were answered.

Mike smiled and shook his head as he said, "Welcome to the team."

A young waitress hurried over. "Hi, Pamela, Chet. What'll you all . . ." She saw my visible scars and asked, "What happened to you, darling? Looks like you got all banged up."

I looked first at Pamela, and then nodded toward Mike. "I was attacked by a great white shark. Mike saved me at the last minute. He pulled my leg out of its mouth."

Mike coughed while swallowing some water and looked incredulous at my straight-faced boldness.

"Oh, my god! You poor thing."

Chester and Pamela nodded conspiratorially in support of my tale.

Now why did I do that? I thought as the waitress took our orders. Mike was right, though; the waitress promised me a free dessert.

CHAPTER 14

New Arrangements
Tuesday Morning...

The next morning, Pamela sat with Mike and me on the porch. Mike and I were in our Adirondacks while Pamela lounged on the swing.

"As long as you're gonna be in my hair all the time,"—Mike looked at Pamela—"you should get a room closer in. The museum will pay for it."

"Here's a newsflash for you," Pamela replied. "I can drive."

Mike ignored her refusal and looked to Claire, who had returned. "Do you know of anything open?"

Claire shook her head. "The weekend is booked everywhere in town. In fact, I think everyone within ten miles of Alton is filled."

"See, it's ordained that I drive," Pamela smirked.

Mike leaned back in his chair and thought for a moment, then announced, "I just had an idea that will solve everyone's problems. You can stay in the Cavern with Sara. The bedroom has a king-sized bed, and there's plenty of room for the two of you. Do you mind, Sara?"

"Mind? I'd love it."

"Then it's settled. After lunch, go and pick up what you need and move in."

Pamela looked over. "But . . . I said—"

"No buts. Let's eat and get to work."

"Wait a minute," Pamela said. "You can't just tell me what to do."

"I'll call your chief," Mike said with a grin, "and tell him you're being uncooperative."

* * *

Pamela returned later that day and stowed several bags in the bedroom. Looking over at Mike's packed bag by the door, she asked, "How was sleeping in your car last night?"

"Okay. Slept like a log."

"You said you were all stiff this morning," I pointed out.

Pamela shook her head. "Look, I'm no prude. That couch pulls out into a bed. You can sleep there. I trust you." Pamela looked over at me. "What do you think, Sara? Should he sleep in his car?"

"Nope. I already told him I thought it was stupid. But no one listens to me."

"There you have it," Pamela ended with a smile.

"Okay, if you're sure," Mike returned her smile.

Pamela turned to me. "I can't believe you had the nerve to tell that ridiculous story at the restaurant last night."

"Hey, I got a free ice cream."

"Well, don't think it'll work every time. Faith's pretty gullible."

"Sara, check the website, would you?" Mike asked.

I nodded and slid the laptop over.

"Before we start to work, can I take a shower?" Pamela asked. "You run too tight a ship; I never got to take one this morning."

"It's your cottage now, remember?" Mike answered as he picked up the phone. "You don't have to ask."

Pamela grabbed the bag she brought and went into the bathroom while Mike punched in a phone number and paced in the small kitchen.

I turned to the laptop and went on the strangenews website. There was a new article from last night. I clicked on it and read,

Car knocked off road in West Alton by flying object

Pedro Ramirez, of West Alton, reported that a large creature attacked his car last night as he drove home from the Bongo Tap and Grill in downtown, Alton, following a party for a fellow worker. Ramirez said he had worked late and afterward attended the birthday party but did not drink.

Ramirez explained, "I looked down at the clock on the dashboard and noted the time was 2:30 in the morning. My wife gets upset when I get home that late. There were no other cars around as I drove up on Oak Street, turned right onto the Clark Bridge and headed into Missouri.

"I turned up the car radio and sang along in an effort to stay awake. As I rounded the curve before Highway 94 to West Alton, I saw the shape of something large sitting in the road just beyond the edge of my headlights. Suddenly, the object seemed to leap into the sky. I slowed down and looked out the side window, but in the early morning darkness I could see nothing. I shook it off, resumed speed, and returned to singing along with the radio. Suddenly, the car lurched as something struck the roof. When I looked up, I saw moonlight shining through huge slashes in the metal."

Ramirez said the car started to fishtail down the highway and then something slammed into the side of the car, sending it careening wildly across the highway. The car tumbled down an embankment and landed right side up in the brush below. Ramirez recalls stumbling out and looking at his wrecked car and the deep gashes in his roof. When he finally looked up, he said there was nothing anywhere in the sky.

PIASA

Mike came back in as a towel-wrapped Pamela poked her head out of the bedroom.

"I'm out of the shower," Pamela said.

"Uh . . ." I said. "Mike, there's an article here—"

"In the shower, Sara, now," Pamela said. "You're like a little work-a-holic. That big guy's habits are rubbing off on you. Chill, girl. It can wait. Oh, by the way, Squirt—I can call you that, right?"

I nodded as I grabbed a towel.

"I thought you might want this." She handed me a small bag from the local drugstore. I shook out a bottle of bright-yellow nail polish.

"Lennore!" I practically squealed. "How did you know?"

"Your doctor told me you were wearing a bright-yellow polish when you were brought in. They had to remove it before you went into surgery. She remembered because her sister wore the same color."

"Thanks, Pamela." I gave her the biggest hug ever.

"We can do each other's nails before we go to bed," she said. "It's been awhile since I did that with anyone."

"I saw the cool aqua color you were wearing. It looked like Floressa from the same company."

"Yeah, well you're going to change that. I'm going this shade of red."

I looked at the bottle she handed me. It was also one of the Distan colors called Klarise.

"I'll look at the article later, Sara," Mike said as he squeezed by the two of us. "Better do as the sheriff says and hit the shower."

I giggled as Pamela stuck her tongue out at him. Could there finally be someone who could hold their own against my cousin?

* * *

That night, I was again having that dream where something terrible was chasing me when I suddenly popped awake. I sat up and looked over to where Pamela was, quietly sleeping with a half-smile on her face. I scrunched my eyes and stared at the clock on the small nightstand on Pamela's side of the bed. It read 3:17.

Outside the Cavern, through the open window, I could hear the deafening sound of crickets filling the night air. I didn't like sleeping with the window open, but last night, after I took my shower, I was exhausted. Before I went to bed, Pamela and I argued about the window and she won. There was no winning an argument with my cousin. She would inevitably play the age card. Last night she finished with, 'You know what, Sara? You're fifteen and I'm twenty-seven. Besides, if it wasn't for me your toes wouldn't be gleaming yellow. I win.' Then, she opened the window.

Shivering in the cool night air, I thought maybe tonight she wouldn't notice. I silently slipped out of bed, having decided I was cold long enough. When I reached up to close it, I saw him. Mike sat alone at the patio table, apparently deep in thought. A half-empty bottle of beer sat on the table. I knew for him, like me, sleep still came hard.

I looked down at my feet. Pamela had done a spectacular job. I left the window open and slipped quietly back into bed.

* * *

As the sun's rays streamed into the bedroom, I still pretended to sleep, but peeked as Pamela tried to shield her eyes from the bright light.

"Gotta remember to close those damn drapes tonight," she muttered. After slowly crawling out of bed, she glanced over at me. "God, how late was that girl up? She was still reading when I went off to Z-land," she kind of mumbled, and to no one in particular. She looked toward the kitchen and continued her barely audible statements. "I'd better put some coffee on; I'm sure it's somewhere in my job description."

As she padded toward the kitchen, I silently slipped out of bed and followed her. Carefully entering the kitchen, I glanced over at the pullout bed. Empty. In fact, it had already been made back up into a sofa. Or, maybe he never even slept last night. The smell of fresh coffee greeted me, but there was no sign of Mike. Pamela knocked lightly on the bathroom door. No answer. She carefully pushed it open, then shook her head.

"Get over here, Sara," she said. "Did you think you could fool me by following me around? And, just to set the record straight, I heard you get up last night to shut the window. It's a good thing you didn't, cause I'd have thrown your skinny little body outside." Pamela walked over to the front door and looked out, then glanced down. "Well, looky, looky, looky."

I moved quickly to her side. Mike was doing push-ups on the patio in front of the Cavern. Sweat cascaded from his body.

Pamela opened the door, folded her arms across her chest and leaned back against the Cavern.

Mike continued his workout routine unabated.

Finally, she called out, "My, we're an early bird. Did you get the worm?"

Mike stopped and hopped up. "I was never one for sleeping my life away. You're a cop, do you ever exercise?"

Pamela snickered, "Yeah, but I do it civilized, at a club. What's the plan today, Great Hunter?"

"That's involved. I need a cup of coffee and a shower first." Mike peeled off his sweat-soaked T-shirt and tossed it just inside the open door. He turned and once more scanned the woods below.

Pamela's eyes got huge as she stared at the back of his left shoulder.

I stuck my head around the door to look, and my still sleepy eyes followed Pamela's. I was startled awake. "What are those . . . from?" I stammered.

"Scars from bullets," Pamela explained.

Mike, at the sound of my voice, turned around. The upper left side of his chest also showed two telltale marks of what I assumed was a bullet's penetration, as well as a scar from the top of his right shoulder extending down about four inches.

"Just who in the world are you?" asked Pamela.

"I'm everything I said I was," countered Mike. "These are from other times, before the museum. They're not important."

"Like blazes they're not. Where did you get shot? Doing what? Wait a minute." Pamela walked over and carefully picked up Mike's damp T-shirt. Emblazoned across the front was 'United States Naval Academy,' while on the back it said 'Class of 1989.' Pamela dropped the shirt and looked over at Mike. "Did you go to the Naval Academy?"

Mike nodded. "Can the interrogation wait until I get a cup of coffee?"

"I'll get it," I said. I hurried back inside and over to the coffeepot, grabbed a cup and poured, while shouting over my shoulder, "Just a little cream, right, Mike?"

"Thanks, Sara. Good memory." As I got to the door, Mike walked over to the patio table and plopped down. "I don't suppose this can wait until I get a shower."

Pamela sat down across from him and shook her head.

Still in my pajamas, I slipped out with his coffee. I set it down in front of him and slid into a chair. I couldn't help it, my eyes were glued on him.

Mike looked from me to Pamela. "Okay, I went to the Naval Academy, and when I graduated in 1989, I picked Navy SEALS as my community."

"Seals? Community?" I asked. I was beginning to understand how sheltered I really was.

"Yeah," Mike explained. "There are different parts of the Navy. Surface Ships, Submarines, Navy SEALS, Aviation and Marine Corps are each referred to as a community. Navy SEALS are—"

"The premier fighting force on the planet," interrupted Pamela. "If there's a dirty, dangerous job to be done, they call in the Navy SEALS."

"Look, so I got shot a couple of times. It's really no big deal."

"No big deal?" said Pamela. "Forget that. Why did you leave the Navy? How did you come to work for a museum?"

"Why I left, I'd rather not go into. The museum? That's kind of a sweet accident. Paul Wiggins, one of the museum directors, was in Afghanistan trying to save artifacts at a museum there. The Taliban surrounded it and threatened to blow it up. I led a SEAL Team in and got Paul and the rest of his group out. My team managed to defuse the situation, but I picked up a couple of souvenirs."

"The bullet holes?" I asked.

"Yeah, the bullet holes," said Mike. "Anyway, Paul and I talked about a lot of things while we were making our way back to the good guys, and we found a common thread with unsolved mysteries and strange creatures. Paul told me his ambition was to open a museum related to cryptozoology on Chicago's lakefront. He told me to call him if I ever got out of the military. When I did, I found he had realized his goal and he had a proposition for me, and offered me this job. I took it. It's something I always wanted to do. There. You have my life story. Can I shower now?"

"No," Pamela said with a shake of her head. "Sara and I have a right to know who we're working for, don't you think? What about what happened to your wife? Family?" *Wow, was she ever bold.*

Mike shook his head and glared over at me. Why had I told Pamela that? "Wife? Let's not go there. I have no other relatives in Chicago. My mom and dad sold their home in the south suburbs and moved to southern California several years ago. There, you've heard it all, now—"

"Friends?" Pamela probed.

Mike was patient. I think about this time, I'd tell Pamela to mind her own business.

"You are nosy, aren't you?" he replied. "Outside of work, I've been pretty much alone the past few months, not that it's any of your business. I wasn't on the best of terms with my in-laws before the accident, so conversation with them since has been nonexistent. They blame me for their daughter's death. Crystal and my daughter were killed in a car accident. They were driving alone to her mother's house in early March when—"

"March?" I said. I recalled the radio report from Chicago just before my accident.

Two fatalities in the collision, a young mother and her daughter.

"Yeah," Mike said. "The car slid in a sudden snowstorm and was rammed from behind. At the wake, her parents continually suggested that my presence could possibly have avoided it."

Oh my gosh! Was it possible that they were killed just about the same time I had my accident? Maybe Mike was right about all his *Things Happen for a Reason* stuff.

"That's ridiculous," Pamela said. "How can they hold you responsible for—"

"Actually, I pretty much felt the same way. I didn't dispute it," Mike said.

"I repeat, that's ridiculous. I'm sure others must have told you so."

I nodded in agreement with Pamela's assessment. In my mind, though, I was thinking how both Mike and Pamela exhibited the same symptoms of loneliness.

"That's funny, Paul has told me the same thing on countless occasions. He urges me to stop crucifying myself over what he deemed 'an act of God,' and open up." Mike paused, looked out over the woods, and continued. "I accept negative comments from Paul about my feelings of guilt because of our long history. I'm sure others think he's cold-hearted and cruel when he gets on my case, but I know he has had only the best of intentions. Anyway, that's why I'm letting the two of you dig into my past."

"You're like a dandelion," said Pamela. "You keep pulling and pulling and there's always some more."

"You," said Mike, as he pointed to me, "get in the Cavern and put some clothes on."

"These are clothes. They're called PJ's," I pleaded.

"Sara, why are you always barefoot? Don't you have some slippers?" Mike said.

"I like being barefoot," I pouted. "I don't wear slippers."

Mike pointed to the Cavern and mouthed the words, "Get dressed."

"But I've got to take a shower first. I thought you were going in." I continued to pout.

"You've got less clothes on than anyone here, Mike," Pamela reasoned. "You go in first, then Sara. I'll wait till last. Right now, *I* need that cup of coffee."

As Mike got up to go into the Cavern, Pamela put a hand on his forearm. "Thanks for trusting us."

CHAPTER 15

New Search
Tuesday Late Morning...

Several hours later, Mike and I sat out on the patio when Pamela walked out drying her hair, a long extension cord trailing behind her.

"So how'd this all start?" Pamela asked over the whine of the hairdryer. "You know, the Naval Academy, Cryptozoology. You're the first one I've met. Cryptozoologist, that is. Well, you're the first Naval Academy guy, too . . . You know what I mean."

Mike was initially quiet, appearing to study his coffee.

"Okay, does this noise bother you?" Pamela stuck the still-whining appliance close to Mike's line of sight. Appalled at her rudeness, I waved Pamela away, but she ignored me as usual.

Mike dismissed her actions with a shake of his head and said, "I really don't know when it started; it seems like I've always been interested in . . . the sea and the creatures in it. I guess that's why pursuing them and the Navy fit so well together. Growing up, I guess you'd say I had an uncanny interest in the world's unsolved mysteries."

Pamela continued her hair drying task while she leaned up against the patio table and listened.

"One day, while I was still in high school, I was in a pinch for a paper, so I decided to use one of the unsolved mysteries, I think it was the Kraken, and my teacher loved it. I realized they presented me with a treasure trove of topics for term papers and reports. Well, they fascinated my teachers and got me the grades I needed to pursue my after high school goal."

"The Naval Academy thing?" asked Pamela.

I was interested to hear about this Naval Academy thing too, but I didn't want to butt my nose into what I hoped might be a budding romance. I knew part of Pamela's problem, other than she hated her job, was she'd found no guy in Alton that she considered dateable. Her only real male friend was Chester, but he was happily married.

"Yeah . . . the Academy . . . *thing*," Mike nodded. "Some of my friends couldn't fathom why I'd read books that weren't required for class, but mysteries and strange phenomena have always fascinated and consumed me.

I guess I inherited my desire to pursue things unexplained from my grandfather."

"Your grandfather? Was he a cryptozoologist too?" Pamela asked.

"No, Grandpa Jake was very interested in strange events and happenings of all kinds, not just animals. He accumulated a lifetime file of newspaper and magazine clippings of out-of-the-ordinary events, as well as a great library of books. When he died, he left it all to his favorite grandson, me." Mike paused, seeming to recall some sad event from his past.

"And how did you get on the Piasa?" Pamela tried to bring him back to the present.

"I came across the legend quite by accident. I never found it in a book of myths or legends; I don't think it was something that got much press. Several months after my grandfather's funeral, I dug into those old clippings of his. I came across an article from your town dating back to 1948. What caught my attention was Grandpa Jake had scribbled, '*Gotta get down to Alton one day*' on the side of the article. The clipping told of the appearance of a huge bird, described by witnesses as 'big as an airplane.' The piece quoted townspeople as saying, 'they thought the Piasa had returned.' I read the accounts and that, along with my gramps's comment, hooked me."

"You came down to fulfill a comment your grandfather made on that article?"

"Well, yeah. In a way. What particularly gripped me was that the reports were consistent in their description of the avian, and it was never reported by anyone outside of the Alton area. The clippings talked about a dozen sightings in the spring of that year, then this huge bird seemed to disappear. It was never reported again. According to the articles, some thought that it was either a wandering albatross or an Andean condor that had flown up the Mississippi and then returned south. Of course, I dismissed them back then. I thought those birds could not have been the legendary Piasa who, according to the articles, feasted on human flesh."

"So, you were a believer back then."

Mike nodded. "Back then. During my senior year in high school, I punctuated my pursuit of the Piasa by actually driving down here. The cliff painting of the creature had by this time been painted and repainted several times in various locations and finally had been replaced by a bizarre metal sculpture."

"Oh god. That monstrosity. No wonder you changed your mind. What was the town thinking back then?"

Mike smirked. "Yeah, I was unimpressed. I became convinced the town was trying to capitalize on the creature's mystery by erecting that metal anomaly."

For a few seconds, both were quiet.

"So that was a pretty wasted trip to—" Pamela said.

"Oh, it wasn't wasted," Mike interjected. "I continued to pursue the Piasa story until I graduated from high school. But I was unable to discover any reason to believe the tale was anything more than a myth. I finally relegated it to what it is, a fable, and put it out of my mind. Regardless, the trip started me on my life's path."

"Maybe you gave up on the Piasa too easily," Pamela pointed out. "It—"

"Never happened," Mike insisted. "How's your knowledge of Native American legends?"

"Well, it wasn't a major in college, but I know some."

"Have you come across the story of the *tlanuhwa* and the *uhktena?*

"Huh?"

"Sorry, those are the Native American names for them. The *tlanuhwa* were also labeled the thunderers or thunderbirds. The *uhktena* were called water panthers."

Pamela nodded. "Sure. I've heard of the thunderbird, but not your water panther. Are we talking about some kind of cat that swims?"

"No," Mike shook his head. "No one really knows what water panther referred to, except it was something that lived underwater. Usually it was never seen. Some researchers think they were actually referring to water movements like whirlpools."

"Well, they're obviously simply Native American tales," Pamela said. "Myth. Lore. Like *Hiawatha.*"

"Hmm, *Hiawatha?* You do know that was a fictional poem by Longfellow. But there really was a Hiawatha who is known for uniting the Native American people into the Iroquois Confederacy. The poem is myth, but the real Hiawatha wasn't." He paused for a moment, then continued. "I think the *tlanuhwa,* what the Indians called the thunderbird, was in fact a species of large eagle that existed back then in some more remote places of the world. Maybe it still does."

"Still does? Giant eagles? You think they're still around?"

Mike was silent. *So that's why he was so interested in that report of the big bird the other day.*

"So, you think these periodic reports of large birds are these eagles?" Pamela persisted.

"No, not all. I usually discount reports from around the country of large birds sitting in trees or swooping low over the ground and threatening people. The descriptions either resemble real birds, like the condor, vultures, even crows, or describe the witness as less than reliable. But some . . ." Mike paused and appeared deep in thought.

I recalled the report from the other day where the person took the time to call in the large bird and said she saw a bald eagle near it.

Pamela was about to say something when he continued.

"Some are thought-provoking. Reports from more remote places, like Alaska, and the mountains around Mexico and Central America, I think are worthy of investigation."

"And this water panther?" Pamela cut in. "Where does that fit into nature's little scheme? Do you think there is some kind of mysterious cat that lives in the water?"

Mike looked over at Pamela and grinned. "Do you always take things so literally?"

Pamela hunched her shoulders and pouted her lips.

I found it interesting that Pamela had dropped her little snippy act when she got to talking with Mike. I had not very often seen this side of her. I was sure now, though. She liked him. A lot.

"Actually," Mike continued, as he gazed off in the distance. "The name is a misnomer. I don't know how they translated that to panther. I think *water panther* was actually referring to a serpent-like creature reportedly seen in many lakes and rivers around that time. Sightings that have persisted down to the present day."

"Wait a minute." Pamela jumped up. "To the present day? Even the natives probably don't believe there was a shred of truth to the narratives of these two creatures. Are you sitting there and telling me that you actually believe in these fairy tales?"

"Knowing all you know, are you standing there and telling me you are so close-minded that you wouldn't believe in the Piasa if it came up and bit you in the . . . posterior?"

Pamela grinned. "*Touché.*" Pamela glanced at me as if she finally realized I was there, a witness to this exchange, then she looked back up at Mike. "I see. You were using that word because we have a little girl in our midst."

"Screw you, Pamela," I said.

She laughed and blew me a kiss. She looked back at Mike and asked, "So is that how you got into cryptozoology?"

Mike nodded.

"And I thought I was a dreamer. So, what's up for today, boss?"

"I'm trying to figure that out. I think this cave thing is a dead end. But let's eat first. We can discuss this after breakfast."

* * *

Pamela and I had just heard the newly formulated plans put forth by Mike. "Look, I'm sorry, but I have to follow my instincts. It's a waste of time to go stumbling through some dark caves that are apparently empty." He looked my way as he continued, "Besides, I can't take you into a situation where you might get hurt."

I bowed my head and stared at the floor. Aunt Claire had earlier pulled me aside and said that as soon as this job working for Mike was over, we had to start up the process of enrolling me at Alton High. I was missing a lot of school. I knew she was right, but I also knew that once I started there, I'd settle in and probably never get back to Chicago. I had hoped Mike's task would last the two weeks at least. Now he was terminating it after just one day. I shouldn't have trusted Mike. When am I going to learn? I wished there was some way I could age from fifteen to eighteen overnight. Screw college. I could just get a job and live by myself.

"I thought you had an open mind about this," Pamela ranted. "Now you're just leaving here? I thought—"

"Pamela, will you just listen?" Mike interrupted.

Pamela stopped talking immediately.

"I'm not abandoning anyone," Mike continued in a much lower voice. "That's why the museum is simply withdrawing from the search. Look, you didn't let me finish. They'll still pay the expenses for the museum here, and I told Paul I'd stick around for at least a few days to check into the missing animals and these other strange reports. Sara, are you still interested in helping?"

My head was immediately going up and down at a very fast pace. "You mean we'd still be a team?" I gasped.

"Of course. I don't know about Pamela—"

"I go where you go, sailor. The chief was specific. As long as you drag Sara around, you drag me."

Mike smiled at me. "Wait. Did you think I was going to tempt you with a mystery and then leave?"

I silently looked down. He had me pegged.

"You did, didn't you?" he answered his own question. "I thought you trusted me."

I did, I thought. *But . . .* I couldn't voice the words. I was far too embarrassed.

"Come on, finish your coffee, Pamela, and let's go get back to the Cavern. We need to come up with a plan." Mike arose, preparing to leave.

Inwardly confused with how to judge men, I got up.

Pamela continued to stare at her coffee.

Mike and I looked to Pamela and waited.

Pamela looked up at Mike. "Sorry I jumped to conclusions."

"Me too," I added.

I watched him give Pamela a comforting grin, then I shook Pamela's chair. "Come on, cousin. The adventure continues."

Pamela offered her hands to Mike, who took them and lightly pulled her to her feet.

"Thanks," she said, "for being here for Sara . . . and me. I'm sorry I doubted you."

Mike put his finger to her lips, shook his head and winked at me. "You may not think that when you're bored out of your mind."

CHAPTER 16

Haunted Houses
Tuesday Afternoon…

Once we got back to the Cavern, I recalled the earlier article on the strangenews website. "Mike, you need to look at this story on the website."

"Good," Mike said. "What have you got, Sara?"

I slid the computer over to him. Pamela stuck her head over his shoulder to read. Each stole a glance at the other as they attempted to focus on the computer screen.

"What do you think, Mike?" I think my question broke the moment.

Mike quickly refocused on the screen and silently read about the attack on Pedro Ramirez's car. "Sounds like this guy had a little too much to drink."

"But what about the roof? The scratches? Shouldn't we check that out?" I asked.

Pamela, her face inches from Mike's, turned and looked into his eyes. "Yeah, Indiana. Shouldn't we?"

"Indiana?" Mike said, narrowing his eyes.

"Yeah, Indiana Jones. Why not? You work for a museum, you solve mysteries. You're just missing the hat and the whip."

"I'm missing a lot more than that. Besides, he taught college and looked for lost treasure; he didn't work for a museum solving mysteries."

"Must you always be so precise?" Pamela asked.

A knock at the front entrance caused everyone's head to turn that way. It was Claire. Mike waved her in. "This package came for you earlier today, Mike, from your museum."

"Great. Thanks, Claire." Mike tossed the small package to me.

"You're welcome." Claire continued with a curious glance at me, then the package. "I thought you'd all like to do the Haunted House tour tonight. I get free passes, but I'm too busy to go with guests calling in for lodging this weekend. Besides, I've been on it many times."

"Hey, that sounds good," Mike said. "We can use a little diversion."

"You could use a lot of diversion," Pamela added.

Still clutching the unopened package, I smiled at Mike. "Is this for me?"

Mike nodded in my direction, while Claire handed him the three passes, waved to us all, and left.

"I can't believe you got me a present. Should I open it now?" I asked.

Mike nodded. "It's no big deal, Sara. I thought . . . just open it up."

I tore open the package and found several CDs by Alanis and another by that A Fine Frenzy girl. "Thank you, Mike."

Pamela looked on. "That was nice of you, Mike."

"It's nothing, Sara earned it."

Huh? I thought. *Could he really be that nice?*

"I'd like for you two to do a plot of all these incidents." Mike pointed to the computer screen. "You know this town, Pamela. Go back a couple of weeks and plot every dog and cat, or whatever disappearance, onto the map you brought over. Let's see if there's a pattern to them."

"Pattern?" Pamela said. "They're just animals . . ." Pamela looked over at me after I poked her to get her to stop. "What?"

"Just do it. It's easier to do what he asks, and then you find out why. Usually, the why becomes apparent while you're doing it."

Mike tousled my hair. "Now, that's my girl."

I think I blushed while Pamela gave him a sarcastic grin.

His cell phone rang, so Mike picked it up and walked out onto the patio.

"How 'bout I call them out and you plot 'em?" I suggested.

"Okay, Sara, but doesn't he get you mad with that smug confidence?"

"No, I just keep wondering when he's gonna lower the boom on me."

"Lower the boom? What are you talking about?"

"He never gets mad at me, even when I screw up. It's not normal. My stepdad would have blown his stack a dozen times with all the goof-ups I've done." I looked over at the screen. "Mark one for West Alton."

"Sara, he's not gonna lower any boom on you. Not all men are like your stepdad. From what I remember, your dad was a great guy. He helped me pick out a college. Despite my arguing with him, I still think Mike's a nice guy, like your dad. He knows you get further with sugar than with salt. By the way, you're supposed to give me an address." Pamela looked over and then made a mark on the map near West Alton.

"What did you mean by that sugar and salt thing?" I asked after glancing outside at Mike.

"He believes in letting people work out of their mistakes and learn that way. I doubt he'd ever holler at you. Mike's not the type. It's called leadership style. Your dad probably learned that in the Marines, while Mike obviously learned his in the Navy." Pamela put down the marker she had been using and gave me her full attention.

"How do you know?" I turned from the screen to Pamela.

"Chet, my partner, is like that. Believe me, I know the type. My dad is one, too."

I turned and looked out at Mike again. She was absolutely right. "You're lucky. I wish my stepdad had been like that. I still think Mike might get upset enough to holler at me, but I do see one thing about him that I like."

"What's that?"

"His quiet confidence makes me feel safe. Something I've missed having in my life the last few years. Know what I mean?"

* * *

After we finished plotting the incidents, Pamela walked out and over to Mike. "Guess what, Sherlock?"

"Do you give everyone your little pet names?"

"Only the ones she likes," I answered without thinking.

Taken aback at my revealing answer, Pamela glared at me and looked away.

I realized what I had said and looked at Mike, but he did not appear to catch my gaffe.

"Well, Indiana," came the voice of Pamela trying to cover up my boner, "you've done it again. I'm just gonna hafta start believing in you."

I handed him the map.

He was immediately drawn to the circle of incidents that, at first glance, I thought seemed to be around the town of West Alton. On second glance, I had realized the town itself was within the circle, but the incidents tended to more center around the wide expanse of the Missouri River, and in particular, an island in the river.

"What's this island?" he asked excitedly.

"I'm not sure," Pamela said. "This really large one over here is Pelican Island. I think that one is Littles Island. I don't know all their names. I'm an Illinois cop, not a Missouri one. Does this give us a place to look?"

"It sure does. We start tomorrow."

I gave Pamela a satisfied look.

"What's this one incident here, all by itself?" Mike asked.

"See, Pamela, I told you he was going to ask about that one. You owe me a dollar."

"What?" Mike asked.

"I told Pamela you were very thorough, and you would ask about that one cause it stood out. She laughed at me, so I bet her a buck."

"And that is why I picked you, over Pamela, as my assistant," Mike joked.

"I never asked to be your—" Pamela protested.

"So, what's the story on that one, *Sara*?" Mike cut her off.

"That was a strange one," I said. "We didn't think it was connected. I told you about it before, you remember when I did that ride-along? That's Rachel's cat. Pamela knows; she investigated it."

"You know," Pamela said. "Sara and I also noticed there have been a number of reports of this large bird to the north of here."

"Yeah, Sara told me about them, and I normally tend to dismiss them," Mike said. "People see a normal bird larger than a blue jay and they think it's huge. How a bird that might have a wingspan of three feet gets reported as ten, I don't understand. However, these reports don't fall into that category."

"You think there's something to them?" I asked. "The descriptions seem to be similar."

"I do," Mike nodded. "Later, though. I think we've got enough on our plate."

"What time did you want to do the tour?" Pamela asked.

"Any time after dark. We can't look at a haunted house in the daytime."

"Well, it's getting that way now," Pamela pointed out.

"Okay, lead on," Mike said. He put his arm around my shoulders and gripped me tightly. "Good job, Sara." Mike held on to me and started to guide me to the Jeep, then stopped and looked down at my feet.

"Okay, okay!" I yelled and ran back inside, returning with my new gymmers on.

Driving down the steep incline of Piasa Street, Pamela shifted the Jeep into second gear, using the engine to brake. She stopped at a red light on Broadway Street and waited to turn right. I rode shotgun, relegating Mike to the back seat. As Pamela watched for an opening in traffic, she pointed to the left and said, "Broadway is also Highway 67, Mike. If you turn left here and drive a couple of blocks down the road, then turn right, it'll take you across the Mississippi on the Clark Bridge into Missouri."

Mike looked in the distance at the structure that spanned the river.

Pamela continued to speak, "From there, it's just a few miles over to West Alton. The island is about five miles to the west of the Lewis Bridge, which spans the Missouri River."

Mike positioned himself forward in the rear seat so that his head jutted between the two of us in front. "Both aptly named, since the expedition started just south of here," he replied.

"Expedition?" I asked. "What expedition?"

Sensing a break in the traffic, Pamela turned right and shifted flawlessly into second gear.

"Near the town of Hartford, Illinois, a few miles south of Alton, the Mississippi River meets the Missouri River," Mike elaborated. "From that spot, just over two hundred years ago, a pair of undaunted explorers set out to map the area of land then recently purchased by President Thomas Jefferson. Haven't you heard of the Louisiana Purchase and Lewis and Clark?"

Pamela accelerated in second gear and then shifted into third.

I nodded. "Yeah, I had American History in freshman year. I just didn't realize they started here in Illinois." Leave it to Mike to point that out. Was there no end to what this guy knew?

"I didn't realize we were going to get a history lesson," Pamela quipped.

Disregarding Pamela, Mike continued, "Yeah, well, for various reasons, other states claimed they started here or there, but this is the spot. It really all began right down this road."

Pamela accelerated on Highway 100 and passed several huge abandoned grain storage silos that sat along the river on our left. "Okay, we're going to visit some haunted houses tonight, but what about tomorrow? Please tell me we're doing something important. Tell me you have a plan," Pamela pleaded.

For a moment we were all silent, then I asked, "What about that guy in his car? He said he was attacked by . . ."

"The police said his car rolled down into a ditch," Mike explained. "He probably got those 'lacerations' in his roof from rolling over. I'm sure that's what the cops think. He was probably out drinking, got drunk, no doubt was afraid of his wife and ran off the road. Having just wrecked the family car, he made up this outlandish story to cover his tracks. No, he was pretty far from the water. I don't think that's related to this."

"No doubt he was afraid of his wife," Pamela mimicked in a sarcastic tone. "Did you notice that little shift of blame to the woman, Sara?"

"I didn't mean to imply—" Mike tried to explain.

"He didn't mean to imply . . ." Pamela derided Mike as she turned right at a cross street and continued to meander, making rights and lefts on several streets. She finally pulled in front of a large house on a small private street. Pamela turned to Mike as she braked to a stop. Both Mike and I pitched forward from the rapid deceleration. Pamela threw the gearshift into neutral and slammed on the parking brake in a blur of motion. "This is usually an exciting house when it's haunted," she said as her door flew open.

* * *

I knew it would come up sooner or later, but I had hoped it would be later. Much, much, later. I was having such a good time, and then that little girl at the last house we visited started crying and pointing at me. I guess the scar above my eye set her off. Her parents apologized, but the damage, as far as I was concerned, was done. I couldn't help it. I tried to make light of it, but before I realized it, I had slipped into a mood similar to the one I was in right after the accident. Why was I spared? Despite what Pamela and Mike said to dispel my sudden negative disposition, I could see no future where I would be comfortable with my appearance.

Now, as we drove down an Alton street in silence. Pamela suddenly pulled up to a house and parked. "This is the Morley House," she announced. We all got out of the Jeep and, while Mike and Pamela stood looking over the dark house, I stared unseeing. I guess I was clearly agitated.

"This is supposed to be one of the scarier ones, I hear," Pamela remarked. "Jenny Dreves once wet her pants in this house. She claimed a hand touched her as she walked in an upstairs bedroom." Pamela snickered at recalling the incident, while both Mike and I stared at her.

"Sounds like fun," Mike offered with a stone-face.

"Maybe I can get a job here," I said sarcastically, and with a shake of my head, started to walk off towards the house.

"I didn't think it was right for that girl in the last house to react like that, being afraid of Sara's scars," Pamela said behind my back.

"Hey, don't worry about it. I'll talk to her," Mike replied. I pretended not to hear their exchange. They both hurried to catch up to me.

* * *

After having visited several additional houses, the situation remained the same. I was still highly disturbed over the previous incident, and I guess I dragged down any enjoyment the night would have brought to the others. Pamela drove up Piasa Street; I stared straight ahead.

Mike stirred in the back seat. "Maybe we should call it a night," he volunteered. "Somehow, I don't think we're all in the mood."

Obviously, he was referring to me. I didn't want to discuss it, so I had foiled all their attempts to draw me into conversation about it. I just couldn't shake the dire feelings running through me. Even though, I realized, I was ruining their good time.

"Besides, it's just the first night," Mike continued. "We have all the way through the weekend ahead. We can come back if we feel better about it."

"What do you think, Sara?" Pamela asked.

"Whatever. Maybe by Saturday I'll get a job haunting one, anyway."

"Head for home, Pamela," Mike said.

"No," I exclaimed. I had wanted them to have some alone time, or at least do something fun, and, now that we were doing it, I was sabotaging their good time. "Just because I'm not in the mood doesn't mean you two shouldn't be able to go ahead and do the Armstead Place. Didn't Aunt Claire say that's the best one, anyway? I'll wait in the Jeep. Honest, I'll be okay."

Pamela turned to Mike. "What do you think, Indiana?"

"Okay, we do the Armstead House and then head back. I want to talk to you when we return, though, Sara."

With that, silence descended inside the Jeep. This is it, I thought. Here's where he yells at me.

* * *

With Mike and Pamela inside the Armstead House, I sat in the Jeep parked down the street and twisted the radio dial, trying to find a station worth listening to. From across the street, an overhead street lamp poured light into the Jeep. It was very quiet.

Why did I leave my Walkman at home? Looking up and down the street, I realized there was no one else around. Still, even though I could see nothing beyond the light of the streetlamp, I felt safe parked here in a residential area of Alton.

I looked to the back seat and saw Mike's laptop. *Maybe I should do a scan on the computer. Mike would like it if I was proactive.*

Suddenly, there was a thunk of something hitting the hood of the Jeep. My initial thought was that Mike had returned, so I turned swiftly around. Sitting on the hood, staring in at me, was the biggest house cat I'd ever seen. It sat primly with all four paws tucked firmly in together, its long bushy tail curved out and up behind it, and two huge golden eyes affixed on me. While at first it scared me because of its size, I quickly realized it was just curious and didn't mean me any harm.

"Pasta pazoole," I cried. "You're the cutest thing I've ever seen." Grateful that the top was down, I slowly stood up and looked down at the cat.

The feline's eyes rose to keep me in her sight as I stood up in the Jeep. I found myself entranced with its big, golden-yellow orbs.

"That was so lame," Pamela's voice drifted over to me from down the sidewalk. "What was that supposed to be hanging in there? A shrunken head? Give me a break . . ."

At the sound of the strange voice, the cat's ears perked up. It suddenly turned, jumped off the Jeep, and streaked into the bushes on the other side of the street.

"Kitty!" I yelled. "Don't go!" I scanned the street, but the cat had vanished, nowhere to be seen.

"Hey, you okay, Sara?" Pamela called out as she and Mike approached the Jeep. "Who're you talking to?"

"There was this large cat that jumped up on the hood of your Jeep, Pamela. It was the cutest thing."

"Huge bushy tail, long-haired, silvery-colored with black stripes?" Mike asked.

"Yes! How did you know?"

"I saw her this morning out by the Piasa painting when I was explaining to Winston why we were not continuing with his cave search. If that's the cat you plotted, she must have crossed the bluffs, which means she's getting close to home."

"Let's go back," Pamela declared. "Forget the cat. I'm tired."

* * *

Fifteen minutes later, Pamela pulled the Jeep into the Dahlgren House driveway and parked back next to the Cavern. As we walked toward the door, Mike came over and put his arm around my shoulders.

"Let's sit out and talk awhile, Sara."

I sat at the table, staring down into the dark woods and awaited his wrath while Mike, after casually walking around the patio, finally sat down across from me. I was permeated with doubt about my ability to handle a lifetime of people staring and pointing. What I needed was . . .

I suddenly snapped my head up and faced him. "Do they make me look that ugly? Please don't lie to me, Mike. Be honest. You convince me they're okay and then something like this happens and . . ." Tears started to run down my cheeks. *Pasta pazoole, I didn't want to show weakness, to him of all people . . .*

Mike sat forward in his chair and I felt big hands grip mine. "Let me put it this way, Sara. Some people are insensitive, that's all. And when it's someone six years old, like that little girl, well, they can be revolting at times."

Through my waterworks, I looked him in the eye. "But I got the sense that her mom and dad were staring too. And they're not six."

"Just because people stare doesn't mean they are revolted by what they see. People are naturally curious. When they see something out of the ordinary, they sometimes stare. Remember Professor Moirés?"

"You didn't stare when you first met me."

"Let's just say I've seen, plus I've gotten, a few nicks and scrapes of my own. I know where you're coming from, but I don't let it get to me."

"Yours aren't as visible."

"No, not normally, but what was your reaction when you first saw me with my shirt off?"

I nodded. He was right. I recalled that I had at first shrunk away at the sight of the scar tissue from where he had been shot.

"Now, that little girl was probably too young for the shark tale to work, but with little kids, it's probably best you just ignore them anyway. Besides, that scar above your eye will fade with time and become unnoticeable. After a while, you'll be like me."

"Be like you? What do you mean?"

"Do you think my old wounds stop me from going to the beach? You get to where you just don't care anymore. Trust me."

From inside the Cavern, Pamela yelled with fear in her voice, "Mike! Can you come in here?" We both jumped up and hurried in. Pamela came out of the bathroom with a towel wrapped around her. Both Mike and I looked questioningly at her.

"There's a big spider in the shower. Will you get rid of it?" Pamela announced with a terrified look.

As I giggled at her, it dawned on me. He'd never raised his voice to me.

CHAPTER 17

Surprise Discovery
Wednesday Morning...

"So, our first stop is to see this car?" Pamela asked. She sat at the dining room table in the Dahlgren House, eating breakfast with Mike and me. Claire had made me French toast, my favorite, onto which I added fresh strawberries. I had secretly watched as Mike made Claire take extra money for having Pamela stay with us in The Cavern. What pleased me the most is I never had to say anything to him, he just did it on his own.

"I think that's a good start; then let's check out this area around the island," Mike replied. "Get the lay of the land, see if there's any logical explanation for the disappearance of all these poor dogs and cats."

Pamela sipped her coffee, temporarily silent. "There've been more disappearances around here than your website shows," Pamela finally revealed. "We've been told to keep them quiet. We've also had more than our share of strange reports lately. Again, we're supposed to keep them quiet, too."

"More coffee?" Mike asked.

Pamela nodded and continued. "I guess the chief's afraid of some kind of panic or people going around with guns. I told you about the motorist that reported a dead deer on Highway 100. When I went out to investigate, there was nothing. Jeff swore it was there and that while I was en route, it must have disappeared. I believe him, and there have been very few cases of roadkill found along that stretch. Normally they pick up a lot every morning from the cars all night. As I'm sure you've noticed, none of that made the papers."

"Sounds like a lot of hysterics," Mike said. "What other kind of strange reports?"

"That's just it. No one ever seems to see anything clearly. They all seem to take place in the early morning hours when it's still dark, and all that's reported are shadows or what appears to be some huge snake-like creature."

"I repeat, sounds like hysteria," Mike offered. "Where have the disappearances been?"

"Pretty much along the bluffs, but let's get back to what we're going to do now, checking out the area where that driver claimed he was attacked by the Piasa."

Mike nodded.

"I'll call Russell Samuels of the Missouri Highway Patrol. Get you an inside scoop. He might be able to help us."

"Okay, are we ready to head out?" Mike asked.

* * *

Mike and I waited as Pamela sat in her police cruiser and talked on her cell phone. She finally turned her phone off and looked up at Mike. "Russell will meet us at the gas station where they towed the vehicle. It's on 94 about a mile north of West Alton. I'll drive myself in the black-and-white because the chief wants me on call."

Mike nodded along with Pamela's statements.

"Let's hit the road," Mike said, gripping his laptop with one hand. "We don't want to keep Russell waiting. Sara, have you got the camera?"

"I'm ready," I responded, while also grabbing my CD player and new CDs.

I slid into the front passenger seat of Mike's Taurus after stowing the camera in back. I powered up the computer as Mike started the car. Kicking off my sandals, I looked over the new CDs. Elvis's voice suddenly boomed out of the car's speakers.

I nudged Mike in the arm and held up one of my CDs.

Mike's eyes narrowed as he looked at the car's CD player, then back at me.

Please? I silently mouthed the words.

Mike finally nodded.

I gave him a huge smile and ejected the Elvis CD, then inserted Alanis Morissette's *So-Called Chaos* into the player and pushed the Play button. Alanis's voice droned into the car singing about eight easy steps.

As we drove down Martin Luther King Drive, Pamela pulled her police car alongside and motioned me to lower the window.

"Hey, guys!" she hollered over. "I've got a call about a missing person up north on Antelope Lane. I've got to check it out. I'll keep in touch." She waved to Mike and me to go ahead. She then made a right turn onto Highway 100, turned on her flashing lights and accelerated.

I went back to the laptop and noticed a weather alert for our area. As Mike accelerated over the Clark Bridge, I called over from my seat, "Uh . . . Mike?"

"What is it, Sara?" he answered.

"I was checking the weather on your laptop. There's a big storm system moving in this afternoon. They're issuing severe thunderstorm and heavy rain warnings for our area."

"We'll try and wrap it up early today so we can be back before it hits," Mike said.

I continued, "Did you change the range mileage setting on the website?"

"No, it should still be at one hundred. What is it?"

"Twenty-five. I'll change it." With a couple of keystrokes, I changed the setting, bringing in a number of other reports from further outside the area. I scanned them casually, then one caused me to stop. "Oh my gosh! Mike!"

Mike turned toward me. "What?"

I couldn't believe the report or get out the words, so I turned the laptop so he could see. "Look at this one in Baytown, Illinois."

Mike slowed down and stared at the screen, then yelled, "Hang on, Sara!" He grabbed his cell phone and wheeled the Taurus into a U-turn while frantically punching keys.

"Why doesn't she answer her cell phone?" Mike said and handed it to me. "You try her," he told me. With that, he turned onto Highway 100, went flying through downtown Alton and increased speed when he came abreast of the Piasa painting. I tried Pamela several times, but she didn't answer. I got very worried.

"Keep trying her," he said.

"Do you know where she went?" I asked.

"Wasn't it a street with the name of a deer or something?" he said.

"Antelope Lane!" It came back to me. "I'll check it on the phone's GPS."

"No," he said, "keep calling her." As he drove, Mike stuck an Alton street guide under my nose. "Find Antelope Lane in here fast," he proclaimed.

"You need a GPS in your car," I replied, but instantly regretted it.

"Would you like to walk?" he asked. Luckily, the guide had an alphabetical directory, which made it quick and easy.

I checked the next street that intersected the highway and checked it against the map. Using the mileage scale, I estimated it was two miles ahead. I watched Mike's odometer, and when it got down to one mile to go, I told him we were almost there.

"Good work, Sara."

In seconds we came upon Antelope Lane and Mike turned a hard right. We went a couple of blocks. Up ahead, parked on the side of the road, was Pamela's squad car. Pamela was standing in front of it, talking to a guy. I scanned the weeds and saw it at the same time that Mike pointed it out. I'm sure that Pamela was unaware that just a short distance away, lurking in the tall grass, something was slowly creeping towards her.

PIASA

Mike pulled off the road in a hail of small stones and dust and barely stopped behind her police car. I would have sworn he was going to hit it. Mike jumped out of the car, shouting for Pamela and the guy to get down.

In that instant, the huge orange and black tiger ran out of the grass toward Pamela. The guy she was talking to turned and ran down the street. The tiger ignored him and quickly closed in on Pamela. Just when the tiger got to her, so did Mike, and he tackled her as she stood staring unbelievingly at the charging animal.

I watched as the tiger leaped over both of them and hit the side of Mike's car hard enough to dent the passenger side door. Luckily, I was still in the car, seatbelt fastened. For a moment through the glass, its eyes held mine, then it turned and ran through the brush and weeds until it got to the rocks behind the bluffs. It jumped up on a large rock and disappeared into the dense undergrowth. I was absolutely shaking from staring into those huge eyes, but I got out of the car and ran to Pamela's side, thrilled she was unhurt.

"What the Sam Hill was that?" Pamela exclaimed as she got up. "I mean, I know it was a tiger, but what is it doing here? This isn't Africa."

"Asia," Mike replied. "There are no tigers in Africa. And you're welcome."

"Yeah, thanks for getting here when you did. Wait, why are you here? I thought you guys were going to see Russell."

"I saw the article on strangenews about the escaped tiger that was missing, and we came to tell you," I said. "It was this guy's pet—"

"Hold that thought, Sara. I've got to call this in. Get some help out here."

After Pamela called for backup, I told her the story. "According to a news report, the tiger escaped from its owner when the earthquake hit. The bars on its cage were sprung and it got loose. It just disappeared, and the owner was afraid to report it because he didn't have a permit to keep it."

I paused, taking a calming breath. "When it put those huge golden eyes on me, it looked just like that cat last night, except bigger. Is there a difference between a house cat and a tiger?" I asked. "I mean, other than its size?"

"Nope," Mike said. "Except for the fact that tigers can roar and housecats purr, they're pretty much the same."

"Then why do some people—" Pamela began.

"Don't you want to hear the rest of this story, Pamela? You're always cutting me off," I said.

"Sorry, go on."

I pouted, but continued. "He's had it since it was a cub and has been putting out meat hoping to draw it back, thinking it was still in his area. When he saw some stories of missing animals down here, it dawned on him that it could be his cat, and they could just as easily be humans. So yesterday he reported it to his local police. I guess they're afraid to say anything publicly 'cause they don't want to start a panic. Someone apparently called Mike's Strange Happenings website, and tipped them off."

"Yeah, well, he might have waited too long," Pamela said. "We haven't heard a word from those campers, and now I'm up here on a missing person. And," she looked around. "Where in the world did Harry Jones go?"

"If you're talking about the guy that was standing here with you when we arrived, he ran up the street when he saw the tiger coming," Mike replied.

"Yeah, him. Harry and Candy Yates, his girlfriend, were walking down this road after their car broke down. He got way ahead of her, and after he rounded that corner up ahead, he heard what sounded like a yelp and came back. He checked all the way back to the car, but couldn't find Candy anywhere." Pamela paused, then added, "I don't understand how a tiger could roam free around here and no one see it?"

I had wondered that myself.

"Tigers are masters of stealth," Mike said. "How roam free? A more interesting question to me is when you consider that most of the missing cats, dogs and all are on the other side of that very wide river, what's he doing here?"

For a moment Pamela stared at Mike. Neither of them moved or said anything. Finally, Pamela said, "What are you saying? This cat isn't the cause of all the disappearances?"

"I just said it was interesting. You're the law, you tell me."

"Yeah, well, you're the wildlife expert, so you tell me." The two of them stared at one another until a familiar sound broke the quiet.

All three of us looked back down the road at the sound of a police car's siren. In a few seconds, a squad car rounded the bend and pulled up behind Mike's car. Out came Chester.

"Everyone okay?" he asked as he hurried up.

"Yeah," Pamela said. She quickly filled Chester in on what had transpired. While she did so, Mike walked up and down both sides of the road, studying the brush. In several places, he walked a short way into the brush and studied the undergrowth. I was confused. Should I follow him? As Pamela finished her explanation to Chester, Mike returned.

"What do you think?" Chester asked Mike.

"Take a look here," Mike replied and led us to the other side of the road.

He pointed to the weeds, which we could plainly see had been crushed to the ground.

"Look at the width of that path," he said. "Whatever made that track through these weeds had to be at least four feet wide." Mike pointed in the distance, where we could see the path extended quite a way until it seemed to end as if it went down a hill. "Notice it's not consistent. Something big came this way, then turned around and went back."

"Maybe people use this as a shortcut," Pamela pointed out.

"This isn't a path used by people, these are fresh tracks. And it wasn't your tiger. What's beyond where the tracks fall away?" Mike asked.

"The highway," Chester replied. "Then the river."

Mike then took us to the opposite side of the road, where he showed us the tiger's tracks through the brush and how they differed.

"Well, first things first," Pamela said. "We've got to find that big cat. Chet, why don't you wait for the backup. Mike and I will track this thing while it's fresh."

"Me too," I said.

"No, you stay here. It's not a place for little girls," Pamela said.

There she went with the little girl crack. Couldn't she say something like, 'It's not safe for you' or 'You're inexperienced at this stuff?' While I knew she was being protective, couldn't she have said it's no place for an untrained professional or something? I was sick and tired of being referred to as 'a little girl.' I was upset with her but didn't say a word.

"Why don't you get the shotgun out of my car?" Pamela told Mike. I silently watched as Mike went into Pamela's squad car and came out with the weapon.

"Shells?" he asked.

"In the glove box," Pamela replied.

He retrieved them and loaded the gun. They then both walked slowly through the weeded lot toward the spot where the tiger had jumped up on the rock.

I watched silently as they reached the spot and entered the thick, forested growth. Meanwhile, four more police cars arrived and the officers crowded around Chester, who explained what had happened.

"We need to split up and secure this area," Chester announced. He sent two officers to warn residents in the area to stay indoors and one to check out the track that led off in the direction of the river. The remaining officer was to accompany him following Pamela and Mike.

Chester indicated I should follow him, and we walked over to his patrol car. I waited till the others had left, then wailed, "What am I supposed to do? Wait for the tiger to return and eat me?" Pamela had told me that it was easy to manipulate Chester, so I tried this ploy to get him to take me along.

"Why don't you wait in my car?" Chester asked, looking at me while he got shells for the shotgun and loaded the weapon.

"You didn't see the size of this thing," I answered. "He'd rip the door right off and grab me. Please can I come with, Chester? I'll do whatever you say. Please?"

"Maybe that would be best," he said as he closed the door of the car.

I knew Pamela would throw a fit, but I had to see how this turned out.

"Could you show me how to use that gun you're carrying?"

"You won't need to know that," he said.

"What if something happens to you? Shouldn't I try to protect myself?"

He sighed heavily but quickly showed me how to take the safety off, then told me to just point it and shoot. Pamela was right, Chester was easily swayed. I hadn't expected to be able to convince him without him being suspicious.

However, maybe I should have stayed behind. My troubles began as soon as we started walking. There were lots of those bushes with stickers the size of olives that would attach to your clothes and hurt when they pricked your bare skin. Despite my pleas for Chester to slow down, he just told me to suck it up or go back to the cars. I was also constantly brushing up against thistle plants, which hurt worse than the stickers. To top it off, about halfway through the patch of tall weeds, I heard something slithering through the weeds ahead of us.

"Pasta pazoole," I whispered loudly. "Something just moved through that patch of clover, Chester. Can you shoot it?" I was scared.

"Pasta what?" Chester chuckled, then eyed me. "Get a grip, Sara. It was probably a big ol' grass snake. Harmless."

Harmless? I hated spiders and snakes. I looked up in an effort to gain courage and saw dark clouds billowing up from the west. At that moment came the first rumble of thunder. I remembered the forecast on the computer.

I was grateful when several minutes and ten thistle bushes later, we reached the outcrop of rock where the forested area began. It was mostly devoid of taller weeds and consisted of a lot of rock outcrops and small bushes with a sprinkle of tall trees. On our right, the ground gradually rose toward the high bluffs.

Both police officers flinched at another rumble of thunder, this time closer, as it reverberated around us. "Let's get higher up, Mark," Chester said. "You stay right behind me, Sara. If we see that cat, try to get behind a big tree or something."

I nodded, but I was more intent on finding Mike and Pamela. I had no intention of hiding behind any tree. Off to the left, and from further ahead, I could hear whispered talking. It had to be Mike and Pamela. I pointed that way and turned to Chester, but he'd apparently heard it too, for he'd already started moving in that direction.

After a few minutes, we walked into an unbelievable scene. Mike and Pamela were arguing in whispers about ten feet above us on the slope of the bluffs. About fifty feet to their left, crouched on an outcrop of rock, was the tiger, watching them. I thought they didn't see it, but Pamela apparently had. She raised the shotgun and pointed it in the tiger's direction. I watched as Mike pulled her gun up, and in the process they both slipped and came tumbling down the incline, landing at our feet. When I glanced up, I saw the big cat was loping down the rise, angling toward us. It stopped about twenty feet away and cautiously eyed us.

The first big drops of rain from the advancing storm began to pelt down, pinging off the leaves and splattering on the rocks. I picked up the shotgun that had landed by my feet and slid the safety off like Chester had shown me. The tiger sprang from his position and raced toward Pamela.

Lightning flashed from the west, followed quickly by a crash of thunder, startling both the tiger and me. More large drops of rain began to pelt down. As the big cat changed direction, I recovered, pointed the gun and pulled the trigger. The gun roared, sending a hail of buckshot exploding into the ground six inches to the left of the great cat's feet. Unprepared for the backlash of the shotgun, I was knocked backwards to the ground just as the tiger bolted past me. Chester apparently thought I had been attacked, so he rushed to my aid while the oversized drops began to pelt down all around me even more quickly.

"You didn't tell me the stupid gun was going to knock me down," I admonished Chester as he helped me up.

Relieved, Chester chuckled, "I thought the tiger got you."

A nearby rumble of thunder and flash of lightning startled everyone. Suddenly, the rain started coming down in sheets. Everyone headed deeper into the forest for some cover under the trees.

Mike looked to Pamela and Chester. "We've got some big-time problems here. Did anyone see which way that cat went?"

We all shook our heads. I had been lying on the ground, how could I see anything?

"Come on, he didn't just disappear," Mike probed.

Chester grinned at Mike. "When we came on the scene, I saw the two of you arguing and then tumble down the incline." Then he glared stonily in my direction. "I was trying to keep up with Sara, who ran ahead and picked up the gun. After she fired, I saw no tiger. It was like he disappeared."

Mike glanced at Pamela. "We did sort of get snarled up. I told you not to shoot him; there are other ways to do this."

"Screw you, Mike! Next time we do it my way!" Pamela yelled, while turning on Chester and now ignoring Mike. "What in the world were you thinking, Chester? You gave this little girl a weapon? Why did you even let her come out here away from the car?"

"Hey!" I yelled. "I. am. not. a. little. Girl!" I continued shouting, "Chester didn't give it to me. I picked it up after you dropped it. I scared the tiger away, didn't I? You two shouldn't have left me by the car in the first place. At least I wasn't standing around arguing and then ending up on my . . . bottom, when people needed help."

Pamela turned on me. "You could just as easily have killed someone, Sara. I was right in leaving you by the car, even though you may think different." She glared at Mike. "Someone had to be the adult around here."

She then whirled around and punched Chester on the arm. "And Chet, sometimes you think like a child. No offense, Sara. I'm sorry I keep calling you a little girl. It's just awkward to say teenager. I just remember how cute you were—"

"Uhh, hello!" Mike butted in. "Let's stop the blame game. I think the explosion from Sara's gun and the following rumble of thunder scared him away. Personally, I'm glad the way things turned out, although I think Pamela did the right thing in leaving Sara by the cars." He then glared at me. "You had better start obeying people in authority, otherwise, I'll fire you."

I frowned, then glared back at Mike. I could scarcely believe it. Even though Pamela and Chester had raised their voices, he still didn't yell at me.

Mike ignored my frown and continued, "But we need to know which way the tiger escaped." A vivid flash of lightning and loud booming crash nearby cut off Mike's summary.

"Uhh, should we be standing under trees in a thunderstorm?" I asked.

"Sara's right. The cars are a short way through the trees," Chester said.

I shook my head, then we all started for the police cars. "Police, and they don't know the simple rules of taking cover in a lightning storm," I mumbled, then looked up. "Haven't you guys ever watched the Weather Channel?" I added as we ran a short distance. Pamela stopped me.

"Think about that the next time you get yourself in some kind of tight spot," Pamela answered snidely. "Maybe I'll leave you to get out of your mess by yourself."

Another crash of thunder and multiple flashes of lightning cut off further conversation, as Pamela followed Chester running to the safety of the vehicles. I then noticed Mike was not with us. When I looked back, I saw that he had ascended into the rocky area where we saw the tiger and was looking for something. I ran back over to where he was.

"Mike, what are you doing? You're getting all wet. You'll get struck by lightning!"

He laughed, then turned and looked down at me. "I can't get any wetter. Get up here, my little gun-toting guardian."

I crawled up the rocks, and within seconds I was standing beside him, totally soaked.

"Why didn't you go back with the others?" he shouted over the rumblings of thunder.

I winced as the flash of lightning split the sky close by. "I wasn't looking forward to running through those weeds," I lied. In reality, I wanted to go wherever he was going. "What are you, uh, we looking for?"

"That tiger disappeared pretty quickly. I was watching him pretty closely. Had he run through the forested areas or climbed to the top of the bluffs, I would have seen him. He must have some kind of escape route or hiding place nearby."

I noticed then that Mike had the shotgun. "Uh, isn't this kind of dangerous?" I asked. "Couldn't he just pounce out on us?"

"No, I read that whole article. He's tame around people. Right now, though, he's pretty scared. I just want to find out where he is so we can come back and trap him."

We then heard the muffled growl of the tiger. It seemed to be coming from just ahead. Mike skirted a large bush and looked around. The rain was starting to let up a little. I pushed the bush partially aside and poked Mike. We both looked into a tunnel that went down into the bluffs.

"Good job, Sara," Mike said. "That's his escape route."

Then, from the depths of the tunnel, we heard a scream.

CHAPTER 18

Tunnel
Wednesday Afternoon...

Mike quickly pulled out his cell phone, I was amazed it operated, and called Pamela, telling her to send someone to where we were. "I think this tunnel comes out under the painting," he said into the phone. "Yes . . . I'll leave her here where it's safe."

He was obviously referring to me.

"Stay here, Sara," Mike said as he put away the phone. He then ducked into the tunnel. I was tired of people telling me I was a little girl, or treating me like one. Even though I was small in size, I was able to take care of myself. Pasta pazoole, I was an orphan. I had to learn to take care of myself. I was not going to be left behind, so I waited maybe twenty seconds, then followed Mike.

Although the tunnel was dark, Mike had one of those penlight flashlights, so I was able to keep him in sight. Besides, we only went a few hundred feet before he stopped. Amazingly, there was a flash that had to be from lightning, the light of which somehow danced around inside the tunnel. It was followed by the sound of thunder that also reverberated around us. At the flash of light, I was caught off guard and gave out with a loud scream like 'eeekkk!' Mike turned around and shined the little light on me.

"Sara, didn't I tell you to stay behind and—"

His whispering was interrupted by a low rumbling growl that came from a short distance ahead and off to our right. I could see that there appeared to be another cave connected to the tunnel we were in through an opening in the rock shale. That's how the lightning had flashed from outside into the tunnel. Mike turned, and in the same motion, grabbed my wrist and pulled me close up behind him.

"Don't talk," he said quietly. I could barely see a finger positioned across his lips to emphasize the point.

He pulled me along past the perpendicular cave with the tiger in it, and I saw him as I was whipped past. The big cat just watched as we silently slid by, maybe twenty feet from him. Then Mike yanked me around to the front of him—I could tell he was upset with me—and handed me the penlight while saying in a soothing voice, "You lead. I'll cover our backs, but I don't think there is any danger. We're in the tunnel that Professor Winston and his crew were exploring. They're probably up ahead or maybe have already cleared out of the tunnel. Are you scared?"

I shook my head but stayed quiet. I trusted and felt safe with him. Twenty minutes later, we walked out of the tunnel and into the caves that were under the painting of the Piasa. Standing there, talking to Professor Winston, were Pamela and Chester.

Pamela immediately started berating Mike. "You lied to me. You took Sara into that tunnel with the tiger in there. Are you nuts?"

"Pamela, STOP!" I screamed. I couldn't help it. She never gave anyone a chance to explain. That made me mad and I was yelling. "I followed him. He told me to stay there and I disobeyed him. Unless you want to adopt me, you can't tell me what to do. It's my life and I'm making my own decisions."

"Well, you're grounded, young lady. I'm older than you, and we're related, so I *can* tell you what to do."

"Stop," Mike said. "Both of you, before you say something you'll regret. Pamela is right, Sara. The bottom line is you were supposed to stay where I told you, and you didn't. You work for me, and if you disobey me again, I'll fire you. Understand?"

I nodded. "I'm sorry, Mike. I promise I'll listen to you."

Pamela grabbed me by the arm and twisted me so that I was in front of her. "You will also listen to me, Sara. I've been assigned by the chief to make sure nothing happens to you. Besides, I'm related to you! So, you must do what I say, or I'll see that you don't come out of the Cavern until this is all over. Understand?"

For a few seconds we stared at each other, then I caved. I knew she had only my safety in mind, so I hugged her and said, "I'm sorry. I will do whatever you say, but please, treat me more like an adult."

"Adult? You're a—"

Mike gripped her arm then. "I think it's time you recognized that at fifteen, Sara is turning into a young woman, not a little girl."

She shook him loose, but she stopped talking. Finally, she said, "Deal."

* * *

The rain had slowed considerably, and the lightning flashes had become less numerous by the time we reached the doctor's office in Wood River. As Pamela pulled into the parking area, Mike still talked to his boss, Paul, on the phone.

"Can you have Peter and Merle down here right away, Paul?"

"Great . . ."

"Now, do you know anyone at the St. Louis Zoo?"

Pamela nosed the Jeep into a parking space and shut off the engine.

"Call her," Mike continued, "and ask them to send some people up here . . ."

"Good . . ."

"Thanks, Paul . . ." Mike turned his cell phone off.

"Well, I guess it's all over," said Pamela. "Things will now go back to normal. I go back to work as a cop, and you go back to Chicago. You said something was killing the animals and you'd find out what, and we did. We found no evidence of the Piasa, which you said was a wild goose chase anyway, and you were correct. While the tiger's not the serpent, or whatever you anticipated, you were kind of right there too; someone had allowed their oversized pet to escape."

Mike looked over at Pamela. "Nothing's over. Things are just getting started."

"What do you . . .?" Pamela started to ask, but tapered off. Like me, she was clueless. It was like Mike was thinking in another universe.

"Let's get Sara in for her appointment," Mike answered. "It's time. Come on, Sara. Let's find out how you're doing."

* * *

An hour later, I sat quietly in the front seat of the Jeep as Pamela drove back to the Cavern. I turned around and looked at Mike, sprawled out in the small rear seat, while he talked on the phone. He had started to make himself at home back there. It was like his mobile office.

"Okay, Peter, I'll expect you around nine tonight. Safe trip." Mike turned off the cell phone and looked at my sour puss. "Who died?" he joked.

"I'm sorry. I can be such a pain," I answered. "You're right, I could have killed someone. You guys were probably right to leave me by the car."

"You scared the tiger off and kept him from possibly becoming a man-eater. Besides, you got a great checkup today. You should be happy. And I didn't leave you by the car, Pamela did."

Pamela stopped at a light and turned around. "What do you mean 'becoming a man-eater'? That tiger's already killed at least three people."

The light changed to green.

"Better move," Mike said.

Pamela turned around, slipped the Jeep into first gear, and accelerated away.

"I seriously doubt that tiger killed anybody," Mike continued. "It's probably been happily existing by eating roadkill from the highway. Tigers only become man-eaters when they've been raised that way or are starving and can't find anything to eat. This cat is not in that class. Having been a pet since it was a cub, I strongly suspect it doesn't even know how to hunt. Look how it botched chasing after us. Either way, man is not on its food chart."

"What about when he charged me? If Sara hadn't picked up the shotgun . . ." Pamela pointed out. I had the feeling it pained her to give me any credit.

"If we could replay that scene, you'd probably have found that the tiger charged you as part of a game it played. When it got to you, it would have put its paws on your shoulders and licked your face. No, I think it's been wrongly accused."

"Licked my face? When did you become such an expert?"

"I'm not, but Peter is, and he's talked with the owner. The owner told him the cat likes to stalk and charge as part of the games they play. That includes his wife, and I suspect the tiger viewed Pamela in that light. That's what its intentions likely were when Sara came on the scene."

"What about the bone that Professor Moirés said they found in the tunnel?"

"Probably the bone of some animal. Remember your missing deer? I'm certain they'll find that out when they send it to a lab. None of those people are doctors, what do they know about bones? I have two experts, Peter Gordan and Merle Decker, coming down from the museum. A team of five is coming up from the St. Louis Zoo. Our tiger hunting is officially over. They will catch the cat and that will be that."

"Why not just shoot it?" I asked. They seemed to be going through a lot of trouble to capture something that could potentially become a killer.

Mike looked seriously at me. "The great cats are rare enough without indiscriminately killing them. This creature didn't ask to be someone's pet and then be thrown into a world strange to it."

Pamela looked over at me before turning onto Lilac Street. "Cat man, remember? But he is right. We shouldn't kill it, just to kill it."

I glanced back at Mike. "God, I hope you don't protect spiders and snakes, too!"

* * *

A short while later, the three of us sat on the Cavern patio. I looked down into the woods where the trees still dripped from the soaking rain, while dark clouds overhead continued to drift past. In the distant east, the rumbles of thunder were still heard from the slow-moving storm. An occasional flash of lightning struggled to make it back out west.

"What did you mean when you said it's not over yet?" Pamela asked. "You have people coming to capture the tiger, Winston verified for us that the bone came from a deer, and you found the tiger's den. The rest of the deer bones are probably in there. The two campers showed up this morning at the station looking for their car, so what else?" She looked to Mike for answers while I got busy on the laptop.

"Take a good look at the map you used to plot the disappearances." Mike slid the map over to her.

"I don't have to look. I plotted it. So what?"

"If you still think the tiger is responsible, just how do you suppose he crossed the Mississippi River every day to feed?" Mike's attention shifted to me as I looked up.

"There are more reports today of animal disappearances in Missouri, Mike," I said. "Nothing in Illinois, except what we already know about. There is another of those large bird reports."

Mike nodded.

With a puzzled look, Pamela asked, "I don't understand. I repeat. You said in the Jeep that 'nothing's over.' What did you mean by that? Surely the search is over; nothing's been found, except some fresh bones of a deer. There was an escaped tiger, and he's evidently the blame for all of this. You said yourself you were backing out and . . ."

". . . forming my own investigation," Mike finished. "I told you. All the looking has been in the wrong place. Remember the map?" His finger tapped the map in front of her.

"Am I missing something?" Pamela looked from the map to Mike. "What are we going to . . ."

"You are thick, Pamela. I always said it could be a cougar or wolf that's moved into the area on this side of the river, but even I didn't expect a tiger." Mike again pointed to the map. "But, the area the two of you mapped out is on the other side of the river . . ." Mike paused, drawing an imaginary oval with his hand over the Missouri-side disappearances. "Sheer numbers will tell you we're dealing with another creature, one that knows how to hunt."

"What about the guy with the slashes in his car?" I asked. "He was on the other side of the river."

"I like the way this girl thinks," Mike said, drawing a smile from me. "Yeah, that's a good start, and we'll get to him . . . tomorrow. Peter and Merle will be here in a couple of hours, and we need to find out what's going on with our tiger. On this side."

"You're the boss, I guess," Pamela said. "Oh, I called Russell. There's no problem with him meeting us tomorrow. He wasn't mad you guys stood him up after I explained what happened. I still think this is kind of anti-climactic, though. We found the tiger."

"Do you have any reports of the tiger crossing the bridge and then coming back?" Mike asked.

"No, smartypants, but tigers can swim."

"Yes, but the river's current has been very strong, and I doubt he'd go over to the other side every day when he had food aplenty here. And attack a moving car, no less. No, I think we're dealing with someone else in Mother Nature's cast of characters over there," Mike pointed out.

Pamela shrugged her shoulders.

I was quiet throughout this exchange, while watching the easy way the two of them talked to one another with mutual respect. I couldn't recall ever seeing Pamela that at ease with some guy. She was always trying to prove how much smarter she was, but with him, I sensed she was struggling just to keep up.

"I'll be right back," Mike said and went into the Cavern.

Pamela looked over at me. "Hey, Tomboy! Are we okay?"

I looked up from the laptop and took a swig of water. I guess tomboy was better than little girl. A controlled gradual smile spread over my face. I never could stay mad at her. How could I? I loved her so much. "Yeah, I know you were just trying to protect me."

"That's great, but I wanted to thank you. You just might have saved my life yesterday."

"Me? I didn't do anything."

"Don't be so modest, you little shrimp. Mike told me that you spotted that item on the computer about the escaped tiger and set everything in motion. Despite what Mike thinks, if you guys didn't show up when you did, I might be pushing up daisies right now."

I smiled sheepishly. "I guess we're even, huh?" This was why I couldn't stay mad at her. Even though she liked to tease me terribly about being a little girl, every now and then she would pay me a huge compliment.

"Yeah," Pamela said. "Must be the hair, huh?" Pamela reached over and twisted my red curls between her fingers. I nodded, smiling, and likewise reached over and entwined my fingers in hers.

Mike came out and plopped in the chair. "Claire called while I was in there. She got some more tickets for the haunted house show tonight, if you want to go. You can go to some different houses this time. How about it, Sara?"

I scrunched up my face in an elaborate show of pretending to think. "Want to go, Pamela?"

"Of course. Maybe we'll see that cat again. How 'bout you, Indiana? Ready for some more scary times?" Pamela asked.

PIASA

Mike shook his head. "I've got to take a pass. Peter and Merle are coming, and we need to plot out tomorrow's course of action. You all have fun." Mike's cell phone rang.

He picked it up and, while talking, walked out toward the driveway. After standing for a few minutes, he shut his cell phone and walked back. "That was Peter. They just turned off the interstate. They should be here shortly. I should stick around."

As Pamela and I got up to leave, Pamela looked over at Mike. "You're not planning on doing anything tonight, are you?"

He shook his head, sat down and pulled over the computer. We left with a chorus of goodbyes aimed at him.

CHAPTER 19

West Alton, Illinois
Thursday Morning...

The unmistakable sound of muffled voices, coming from the outside, caused me to awaken. After looking around the dark room, I noted that Pamela was still sleeping. The voices persisted, so I stretched in bed. With the curtains drawn, it was impossible to tell what time it was. I pulled over the small alarm clock, and holding it close, saw the numbers. 5:15.

Pasta pazoole, I thought. *Who was out there? Should I wake up Pamela? Mike?*

Quietly getting out of bed, I walked over to the bedroom patio doors and carefully pulled back a small corner of the curtain. From that angle, I could see a head of curly black hair I didn't recognize. Afraid to pull back any more of the curtain without being seen, I walked quietly to the bathroom door and lightly knocked on it. There was no answer. I cautiously pushed the door open. Nothing. No one. I walked through the bathroom, stopping at the door leading into the small entranceway.

Peeking out, I could see that the pull-out sofa was made up. I slipped out into the living area, then into the kitchen, where the smell of coffee greeted me. *Pasta pazoole. Pamela was right, what woman could ever keep up with this guy? He never sleeps.*

"Do you remember that time Henry ..." Mike's voice drifted in from outside.

Relieved it was only him, I walked over to the front entrance and, like a little fool, since I was not dressed, went outside. Sitting out on the patio were Mike and two other men.

"Speaking of Henry," the man with curly black hair said to Mike. "He wanted me to tell you ..." Seeing that Mike was staring over where I stood by the door, he turned to look. "Oh, hello there."

All three men then stood and stared at me, as I was wearing very short, cotton pajama bottoms with a size-too-small T-shirt top, emblazoned with 'I Can Do Anything.' I so needed to go shopping for clothes. Not to mention my morning hair always wants to go in every known, and some unknown, direction.

"Well, good morning sunshine, little early for you to be up, isn't it?" Mike asked. By Mike's feet sat the very cat I had seen on the Jeep. It really was, in fact, the biggest cat I had ever seen.

After hurriedly ducking back in and retrieving my robe, I returned and asked, "What's going on out here at this hour?" Since when did I get so brazen? "Where did the cat come from?"

"First things first," Mike said. "This is Peter Gordan." The man with the black curly hair bowed to me. "And this is Merle Decker." Merle was short and wiry with a shock of blond, almost white, hair. Merle nodded and smiled. Merle was much younger than either Mike or Peter.

"And this," Mike said as he indicated the cat, "is Phoebe." Mike turned to Peter and Merle. "Gentlemen, this is my assistant, Sara."

"Good to see not all young women sleep till noon," Merle said.

'Young women.' I liked him already. "Your friends from the museum?" I asked.

Mike nodded. "Peter and his young assistant, Merle, are the finest trappers and explorers on any continent. We were just catching up. Sorry if we woke you, Sara."

I looked at the patio table that was strewn with beer bottles, mostly empty. "Isn't it a little early to be celebrating? Shouldn't you be getting ready to go after the tiger?" Listen to me, who was I to tell these grown men . . .

"Why should we do that?" Peter asked. "I've no desire to see St. Louis."

"St. Louis? What are you talking about? He's . . ." I was interrupted by the sound of the curtains being noisily pulled back in the bedroom. Standing, staring out on the patio in her pajamas, with red hair askew and rubbing the sleep from her eyes, was a pouting Pamela. Seeing the two strangers, her eyes grew very big. She quickly pulled the curtains closed. Within a few seconds, the curtains flew back and the door slid open. Pamela stepped out barefoot, wrapped in a robe with a hint of a smile on her face. She had hurriedly done something with her hair, and it was now pulled back in a quick ponytail. Mike introduced everyone all over again.

"There's that cute cat," Pamela said as she reached toward Phoebe. Shying away from her, Phoebe raised her tail in an arc and walked over to me. I scooped her up and put her in my lap as I sat down next to Mike. Phoebe bumped me several times with her head and then curled up in my lap.

"She likes you," Merle said. "She just marked you with her scent; you belong to her."

Pamela glanced over at the table with its cargo of empty bottles. "Someone celebrating?" she asked. "Are you even old enough to drink?" she added, looking at Merle.

"Careful, Merle, the lady is the long arm of the law," Mike grinned.

Peter laughed. "Sorry if we woke you, young lady. Mike hasn't lost his touch, though. He always could find the prettiest assistants."

Despite herself, Pamela beamed at Peter, while she seemed to ignore being classified as Mike's assistant and merely smirked over at him.

"To answer your question, Sara," Peter continued. "The tiger should be safely in the St. Louis Zoo by now, awaiting disposition. Our work here, sadly, is done."

"St. Louis?" I said. "How did he . . ."

"Our leader obviously lied to us, Sara," Pamela answered. "He and his henchmen here went after the tiger last night while we were doing the haunted house tour. I wondered what he was up to when we got home last night and found him gone."

"Actually, it was my idea," Merle said. "Once we checked the site and options, I thought that simple old Plan A was worth a shot."

"Plan A?" I asked.

"Yes. If you wanted to get a mouse to come out of a hole, what would you do?"

"Uhh, put a piece of cheese in front?"

"Exactly! I figured the tiger was pretty hungry, so we picked up a beef roast at the market, put it down at the base of the tree and waited. Ten minutes later, he came down and ate."

"Oh my gosh!" I exclaimed. "I would have freaked out."

"Well, he was just hungry. And, really, he was quite docile. Just before he finished, we hit him with a tranquilizer dart, and he was on his way to the zoo. Sorry to disappoint you both, but the fewer people involved in this, the better."

Pamela squinted over at Mike.

"If we had waited till morning," Merle continued, "he would have been impossible to coax out with all of the people around. The cat would simply have stayed put and made everything that much more complicated."

"Now you see why this man is my assistant despite his young age," Peter interjected. "He knows more about animals than even the most experienced zoo people."

"I really didn't know until Merle suggested it," Mike said as he returned Pamela's gaze. "Honest. We just came back here to get caught up on things and celebrate our good fortune."

"You're forgiven," Pamela said. "Can I get anyone coffee?"

She was greeted by a chorus of me's, including from me.

"Phoebe!" Rachel yelled as she came around the side of the Cavern and into view. As Rachel ran up to me, Phoebe lifted her head and looked from me to Rachel. She quickly bounded out of my lap and walked over to Rachel, head-bumping her several times and making excited noises.

Rachel scooped up Phoebe and hugged her tightly. "Oh my gosh, I'm so glad to see you, Phoebe," Rachel murmured, to an obviously delighted Phoebe. Everyone else stared at the tender reunion. After a few moments, Rachel tore her attention away from Phoebe and looked at the men seated around the table.

"Mike?" She beamed in recognition of him from our meeting at the restaurant. "You're the Mike that found her?"

"Guilty as charged," Mike said as he raised his hand slightly. "But actually, it was more like we found each other."

Rachel looked at me and asked, "Could you hold Phoebe for me?" I nodded. Rachel carefully deposited Phoebe back into my lap and hurried over to Mike, who stood up as she approached.

"Thank you for finding her," Rachel said. She put her hands around his neck and kissed him full on the mouth. "I could never repay you for what you've done," Rachel said as she pulled away. I'm sure my mouth was hanging open in shock at the display.

"I beg to differ," Mike said. "I think you just did."

"What the . . . ?" Merle said and looked at Peter. "We catch a tiger and get nada, he finds a pet cat and gets the reward of a lifetime."

Rachel looked embarrassed, suddenly aware she kissed Mike in front of a lot of people. However, for the first time she seemed to notice Merle. "I'm sorry," she started. "You all have no idea what Phoebe means to me. I thought I lost her, and then this morning, Mike called to tell me that he had found her."

"Would you like to join us?" Mike asked.

Rachel answered by heading straight over to an empty seat by Merle.

* * *

Peter, Merle and Rachel joined us for breakfast at the insistence of Claire.

Following breakfast, and after the dishes had been cleared, Claire joined us for coffee. I felt guilty, because somehow, I thought, I caused this additional expense for her. She sat at the head spot of the large table, while Peter and Merle, with Rachel in the middle, sat on one side. Mike, Pamela and I sat on the other side. Phoebe sat in Rachel's lap.

"I was fascinated by that piece you both did on the condors of the Andes," Claire said. "It was on the PBS station here last month." I remembered that Claire liked to watch any special that related to nature.

"I saw it, too," Rachel said. "It was terrific." Oh boy, now I felt left out. However, up until now, I hardly thought of nature.

"Thank you, Claire, Rachel," Merle said. Peter also nodded towards both women.

"What are you two up to next?" Claire asked.

"Well," Peter said. "We were supposed to be in Africa, in the Tsavo River Country, but all is on hold because of this guy." He finished with a nod toward Mike across the table.

"Are you supposed to go to Africa?" Pamela asked Mike. She just beat me to the punch.

"Just for a couple of days. I usually call the shots from the museum in Chicago. I was supposed to be assisting in the design of a new exhibit dealing with extinct cave lions, while they searched for possible caves where they supposedly lived. Some people think the lions in that part of Africa were descended from cave lions rather than plains lions. It was to be a coordinated project, now put on hold because of this little trip down the Mississippi."

"What's so special about these Tsavo lions?" I asked.

"They were two male lions who feasted on the workers building the Trans-Africa Railroad around 1910," Merle answered. "While workers were building a bridge across the Tsavo River, the two lions showed up. Nine months later, the engineer building the bridge finally killed them, but not before they had killed and eaten around a hundred and fifty natives and laborers. The natives attributed near-supernatural powers to the two, calling them *Shaitaini*, which means Devils of the Night.

"The engineer wrote a book on his duel with the lions, and in it he said they actually seemed to think one step ahead of him. He described a cave along a dried creek bed where they took some of their victims. The floor of the cave he described as *covered with bones*."

"Covered with bones? Like the Piasa," Pamela pointed out.

"Pardon?" Peter asked.

"Early pioneers in this region claimed there was a cave in the area, high up in the bluffs, and it contained the bones of many of the Piasa's victims," Pamela said. "Funny thing is, the Indians attributed god-like powers to the Piasa, too. It always appeared to be one step ahead of them."

"Well, your Piasa turned out to be a tiger," Peter scoffed. "I don't think he left any bones except for a few stray dogs and cats, and whatever else he managed to find along the highway. Although we didn't actually go up and search the den, the zoo said that from their observations, there was no evidence it had killed a human. They're supposed to come back later today and check out the den."

"Then where is Candy?" Pamela asked. "The missing hiker?"

"I'm certain it was not the tiger. If it had been, you'd have found remains. Sorry, we're not experts on the whereabouts of the local populace," Peter answered. "How about it, Merle? We need to get started. Can you tear yourself away from the young lady?"

I watched as Rachel blushed, unused to the attention she was receiving from Merle, I guessed. She slipped Merle a folded piece of paper.

"Thank you, Rachel," Merle said. "Okay, Peter, we better hit the road back to Chi-town." Peter nodded and got up.

"I'll walk out with you guys," Mike said.

Mike got up and the two explorers offered their goodbyes to us all. I watched as Merle lingered around Rachel, then he followed Mike and Peter out.

After seeing Peter and Merle off, Mike returned to the Dahlgren House dining room, just as Pamela got up from the table.

"I should get Phoebe home and feed her," Rachel said.

Rachel scooped up Phoebe, and paused to let me pet her gorgeous cat one more time.

Pamela leaned over to Mike and asked, "Are we still going to meet Russell?"

He nodded.

"You mean you still think there's something else out there?" Pamela asked.

Mike smiled and nodded again.

"Wait. You think there's another creature out there?" Rachel asked while maintaining her hold on Phoebe, who struggled to get free.

"That's what I hope to find out," Mike said.

"Are Peter and Merle going too?" Rachel asked.

Mike frowned and shook his head.

Rachel took another thoughtful glance toward Mike, then, still clutching Phoebe, walked out of the dining room.

"Are you ready to hit the road?" Mike asked me. "We'll leave as soon as Pamela is ready."

Having been awakened so early, I was dead tired, so I stretched, slowly nodded and tried to look sleepy-eyed as I asked, "Can we take a nap today?"

Mike affixed me with a withering gaze. "There is no sleeping while solving mysteries. We are meeting the Missouri Highway patrol officer in one hour. You be ready to go, or I'll go alone."

I let out a low moan. I so wanted to just go back to sleep, but I said, "I'll be ready."

* * *

An hour later, Pamela wheeled the Jeep into the gas station, where a Missouri Highway Patrol car was parked. An officer sat inside busily writing. Mike got out and walked up to the patrol car.

"Officer Samuels?" Mike asked.

"Russ," I heard him reply while opening the car door and sliding out. "Sorry, I'm just catchin' up on all the darn paperwork." Russell, powerfully built with thinning brown hair, stood eyeball-to-eyeball with six-foot Mike. Russell gripped Mike's outstretched hand.

"This is Sara Williams," Mike said, as I walked up. Russell reached for my hand while he briefly noted my visible scars.

I wanted to shrink under his gaze.

"So, you're Sara. Pamela was right, except for being a whole head shorter, you're the spittin' image of her when she was your age."

I stared up at Russell. "You knew Pamela when she was my age?"

"I should hope so; she's my niece. She didn't tell you guys that?" Mike and I shook our heads as Pamela walked up.

"Hi, Uncle Russ," Pamela said. "Uncle Russ is the reason I became a cop. He tried to talk me out of it, but . . ."

"Good thing he didn't," Mike said. Pamela squinted at Mike questioningly.

Russell then returned his gaze to me. "How're you handling the little reminders of that dreadful night?"

"Okay, I guess," I stared at the ground, not really anxious to discuss that day.

"Pamela called me the next day. She was pretty broken up about your condition. If she has a flaw, that's it: Lets victims get in her head. You can't do that in this job."

I glanced up, surprised at this revelation.

"Nonsense, Uncle Russ," Pamela pointed out. "Compassion is not a flaw."

Russell turned back to Mike. "Anyway, lot of strange things going on around here. I know the tiger may have been responsible for some of the stuff around Alton, but I'm sure he didn't swim the river or walk over the bridge every night to cause mayhem over here."

Wow, this guy sounded just like Mike.

"Pamela said you guys are tracking this stuff on your computer or something?" Russell ended with a glance from me to Mike.

"There's a website that serves as a clearinghouse for strange news reports," Mike replied. "This area of the state literally lights up with them."

"Yeah, we've been dealing with reports of large snakes or something, mostly in the river, a missing cow of all things . . ." Russell's voice drifted off.

"Did anyone describe this thing in the river?" Mike asked.

"Naw, a couple saw what they claimed were the coils of an anaconda, except it was scaly or something. Another thought it was a crocodile. 'Big one,' the guy said, 'like the one in that movie, *Lake Placid.*' He told me if one could get in a lake in Maine, why couldn't it come up the Mississippi? Some people have no concept of reality or geography."

I could tell Mike was fighting to keep a straight face.

"I think they watch a little too much *Animal Planet*," Russell continued. "There's that show *River Monsters* on it, and people here think the river is full of huge creatures. Anyway, others just said they glimpsed something large under the surface. Said it appeared snake-like, but wider. People are just on edge, Mike. When they're on edge, they see things."

Mike nodded.

"Any reports of big birds?" I asked, soliciting a glance from Mike.

"People around here are always reporting big birds. To them, a crow is a big bird. Let's go look at that car; it's around back." Russell stepped off with the rest of us in trail.

We walked in silence around to the back of the station, past what appeared to be a lifetime of used auto parts piled everywhere.

"Gotta talk to Ernie about all this junk," announced Russell to no one in particular.

The car sat by itself in a big patch of weeds. Big golden orb weaver spiders had already spun webs connecting the car to the weeds. I had seen them in a vacant lot back home where Emily and I played when we were little. My dad, my real dad, told me what they were called. Ignoring the ugly, big yellow-and-black spiders, Mike pushed through and examined the deep cuts in the roof and then the dents in the side.

Having seen the spiders, Pamela and I chose to stay in a clear area off to the side. "How can he do that?" I asked. "Look at the size of those things. They are huge. Ugh. I hate spiders."

"Ditto that," said Pamela. "Not to mention how revolting they are. We can just wait here."

"Hey," I asked. "How come I don't know Uncle Russ? Who is he to me?"

"He's an uncle on my mother's side, not dad's. You don't get down here much to know all of your relatives. I hardly recognized you when the accident happened. Luckily we share the red hair. Last time I really saw you, you were like eight years old. I was shocked when I found out this lit. . . uh, this teenaged girl I helped pull out of the burning car was my own cousin."

I watched as Russell pushed through the weeds and brushed a large garden spider off his leg. I edged closer to listen, and Pamela followed.

"What do you make of it?" he asked Mike.

"Was this guy drinking?" Mike replied.

"Yeah, he freely admitted that, but I gave him a pass. His wife would punish him far worse than I ever could. I don't think that's why he ran off the road, though. Pedro's good people. I talked to him that night, he was plenty scared." Russell picked a spider off Mike's back and set it back in the weeds. How could he even touch those things?

"Thanks," Mike said. "Did he see what it was that hit him?"

"No, he told me he saw something sitting in the road at the end of his field of vision. Before he could get close enough to make it out, '*it leaped into the sky*.' Those were his words." Russell paused to peruse the clearing where Pamela and I huddled. "What is it with women and spiders?" he asked.

Mike smiled and shook his head.

Russell continued his story. "Anyway, something then struck his roof, tearing these gashes in it. As he tried to keep his car under control, he says it struck him in the side here, and he lost it and tumbled into the ditch. By the time he got out and investigated what it was, it was gone."

"Did he hear anything?"

"Naw, but he had that blasted radio turned all the way up to keep him awake. It would've drowned out anything. Besides, between you and me, I think he's a little deaf." Mike closely examined the slashes in the roof.

While Mike and Russell examined the car, I looked at Pamela. "So, what were you like when you were my age?"

Pamela laughed. "I was a wicked little one in high school. Used to tease the boys something fierce. Know what I mean?"

I smiled and nodded.

"Uncle Russ's right, though," Pamela continued. "Except for your size, you do resemble me quite a bit when I was fifteen. Must be the family genes and the hair. We both have these thick red curls. What about you?"

"Me? What do you mean?"

"Come clean, Sara. Do you tease boys in school?"

I laughed. "I would love to be able to tease boys. But they usually don't pay much attention to me. I like it that way, because those that do notice me are usually beating up on me."

"What? They pick on girls in your school?"

I explained about how Peter hated me and how he and his friends went out of their way to harass and embarrass me.

"Well, that bonehead has gone to his reward," Pamela said. "I'll show you a few things to discourage trash like the others from thinking you're a punching bag. If you stick around here, though, you'll find the boys have more respect for women."

"Thanks, but I guess I'm not that attractive to boys anyway."

"You have a lot to learn, Sara. I only hope I'm around to see the metamorphosis. They'll come around to discovering you, be patient."

"You really think so?"

Pamela nodded.

"What's your take?" I heard Mike ask Russell, drawing my attention back to them.

Russell stared at the roof's deep indentations. "Beats me. I don't believe in no Piasa, though."

Mike grinned. "Nor do I. Did you notice this?" Mike pointed, and I strained to see without entering the weeds. It looked like there were tiny black smudges where the roof was slashed. I could see similar ones around the door.

Russell carefully examined the areas, then smirked over at Mike. "Well, I'll be. Good eye, Mike. I'll have the lab guys over here this afternoon to check it out."

"Speaking of the Piasa, though," Mike said. "Have you had any reports of large birds around here? I know Sara asked you earlier, but I mean credible reports?" I began to notice Mike kept returning to the subject of large birds.

Russell jerked his head toward Mike. "Yeah, we've had a couple, but like I said, we usually discount them."

"I do, too," Mike agreed, and I inwardly laughed. *No, you don't.*

"The thing is . . ." Russell stopped and stared at the spiders in the weeds. "Well, these were specific and reported around the same time. Both saw it the same morning and said it appeared to be a huge eagle, but it wasn't a bald eagle. They're all around here, so people oughta know what they look like. They described it as gray and black with legs like trees. Estimated its wingspan at twenty-five feet. One said it flew over his house south of here; the other saw it flying over the river."

"Which way was it going?" Mike said.

"Both said it was heading north. It was very early morning. Wait, you don't think that's connected to what we have here?"

Mike shook his head. "No, eagles don't hunt at night, and they don't attack cars. No matter how big they are. Sounds like a figment of an overworked imagination."

I started to realize that Mike, although he hid it well, got excited—if you could call his slight change of mood excited—any time the description of the eagle was given. Like it rang true of a certain eagle in his mind, and I was beginning to think I knew which one.

CHAPTER 20

A New Quest
Thursday Noon...

As Pamela drove back toward Alton, she momentarily turned and glanced at Mike in the Jeep's back seat. "Well, Indiana—or should we call him Spiderman, Sara?"

I focused my attention on Pamela and pulled out my earbud. I had been listening to *A Fine Frenzy*. "You know, Pamela, there already is an Indiana and, even though he seems to like the creepy, crawly critters, Spiderman is this wispy little guy. I was thinking we call him something like *Mississippi*." Funny, I had been thinking Mike needed a nickname when she asked me that.

"Wow! I love it, Sara." Pamela looked back at Mike. "Well, *Mississippi*, what did you find out back there?"

"I found out my two assistants are afraid of a creature—"

"I'm not your assistant," interrupted Pamela. "Let's not forget that."

"Anyway, you're both afraid of a creature way smaller than either of you, one that usually minds its own business. Everything has a place in the cosmos, and that includes spiders. The world would be overrun with bugs if it wasn't for what Sara thinks are creepy . . ."

Mike stopped his nature lecture as Pamela turned left onto Highway 67 from 94, heading back towards Illinois.

"Where are you going?" he asked.

Pamela pulled the Jeep over to the shoulder, stopped, and then turned around and faced him: "I'm headed back to Alton. Where should I be going, *Mississippi*?"

Mike pointed behind them. "Unless I'm mistaken, you said the Lewis Bridge over the Missouri River is thataway," he replied.

* * *

Twenty minutes later, Pamela parked a short distance from where the bridge crossed the river. We all got out and walked up to the base of the structure, where Pamela pointed to the west, toward some islands in the river. "Littles Island is over that way."

Mike looked up and down both sides of the river. "You didn't tell me there's no road."

Pamela gave Mike a big exaggerated smile and replied in a put-on southern accent, "Why, you all didn't ask me that, *Mississippi*!" Then she giggled while I openly laughed at her side. Mike gave us both an exasperated look.

"Let's go," he said and started walking back to the Jeep. I raced on ahead of him and jumped into the back seat. Pamela slowly got back in and looked at Mike, who appeared anxious to get moving.

"Don't say anything!" he proclaimed while sticking a finger in front of her face. "Head back to Alton. I have to find a place to rent a boat."

"Umm, can I talk?" Pamela asked.

"What?" he barked.

"My dad has a boat." She then added quietly, "*Mississippi*." I snickered loudly in the back seat.

Mike turned to me. "Is that funny to you?"

"Yes, sir," I squeaked out. Ordinarily, I would have never talked like this to someone that much older, but I was having fun and didn't want it to end. Besides, by now I knew that Mike was a good sport.

Mike looked at Pamela and shook his head. "Drive. I didn't know I was working with two comedians." As Pamela pulled on the highway, I continued to giggle in the back seat. But I caught Mike's smile as he turned away from both of us and stared out the open side window.

"My dad keeps his boat up in Godfrey," Pamela said as she drove across the Clark Bridge. "Should I head straight there?"

"Sounds like a plan to me," Mike answered. "And wow, you thought of it yourself. Impressive." He turned around and asked me, "Is that okay with you? You two didn't have shopping or something else planned, did you?"

"No," I said and nudged the back of his seat with a bare foot. "That's fine. I'd kind of like to take a little boat ride."

"Hey, kiddo," Pamela called out to me while glancing in the rearview mirror. "I haven't forgotten my promise to take you shopping for clothes. We'll go as soon as the boss here gives us some time off."

"Where we're going, all she'll need is some older clothes," Mike said.

As Pamela approached the Piasa portrait, she slowed.

I noticed several police cars parked at the base of the bluffs, below the painting.

"Mike," Pamela said, "I'm gonna stop and check this out."

"Pull in," he agreed.

Pamela wheeled into the parking area and drove up to the north end at the base of the painting. A police officer started to walk over, but was stopped by Chester. "I got it, Ron," he told him.

"What's going on here? Why all the units?" Pamela asked.

"Karl turned up missing. His car was here, so we thought that would be a good place to start looking."

"You think he went into the cave by himself?" Pamela asked Chester.

"That is the prevailing theory," Chester concurred.

"Maybe he went over to check out the tiger's den," I said.

Pamela looked back at me. "What makes you say that, Sara?"

Everyone turned and looked at me. "It was just a thought," I said. I was taken back at their reaction. "The professor told Mike he tried to escape from the tiger through there. Maybe he wanted to see what it looked like in the daytime. Maybe he dropped something. I don't know."

"It makes better sense than him going in the cave here," Chester said. "Thanks, Sara. We'll check it out. Where you all heading now?"

"*Mississippi* here wants to check out the islands in the Missouri. You know, north of 67?" Pamela said.

Chester snickered, "You giving people nicknames again, Pamela? You used to do that in school, to guys you really liked—" He quieted as Mike looked at Pamela.

Pamela hurried to change the subject, nodding in Mike's direction. "He thinks there may be new caves there." She paused, then continued. "We're going to get my dad's boat up in Grafton."

"Interesting thought. Just the three of you going?" Chester asked. Mike nodded, and Chester continued. "I was just going off shift. How about I join you? If there are caves, you shouldn't be going in alone. No telling what's in 'em. Look what we found here."

"That'll be great, Chester," I shouted from the back seat. This was like some kind of an adventure.

"How soon can you be ready?" Mike asked.

"Let me tell them to check out the den area. Then I'll go home, change and meet you up at Dave's boat dock. I'll be there before you know it . . . *Mississippi.*"

Pamela gave Mike a big smile as Chester said the nickname.

In the back seat, I giggled and buried my face in my hands in an effort to squelch the smirks.

Mike looked at all three of us and then resettled his gaze on Chester. "We'll see you then," he said. I caught his little wink, meant only for Chester.

* * *

"Wow, this is a nice ship, Pamela," I exclaimed as we walked out on the dock area. It was a lot bigger than I thought.

"Boat, Sara, it's a boat," Mike corrected me. "The big Navy haze-gray ones are ships. Little ones are boats."

"Haze-gray ones?" I asked. What was he talking about?

"Sorry, Navy ships are all painted gray," he said. "When we left port, we used to say, *Haze gray and underway.*"

"It's a Navy thing, Sara. Our leader is living in the past. Ignore him," Pamela said, then turned to Mike. "It's a Gibson 41 Sport. I think I forgot to mention it's a houseboat. Is that okay?"

"Okay? It's perfect. Is that his Boston Whaler too?"

"Yes. Some places you can't get too close to shore with this behemoth, so he uses the Whaler. Dad got this thing because he wanted to cruise down the river and explore. He loves the Mississippi. Mom was never too keen on the idea, so it's mainly gathered dust up here. He's threatened to sell it, but I guess he really doesn't want to part with it."

"Your dad know the river?"

"Is my hair red?"

"You are such a smart aleck. Think he'd want to come along?" Mike asked.

Pamela got very quiet. "Yeah, I think he's dying to be asked."

"So what are you waiting for? Go ask him." Mike ducked under the bridge roof and went down to check the interior.

I could see that Pamela was surprised by Mike's invitation. She wiped at her eyes as I walked over. "I could tell your dad wanted to go as soon as you asked him to use the boat," I said. "Think Mike knew that? He was on the phone in the Jeep, though."

Pamela shook her head and pulled out her cell phone as Chester drove up.

Mike came up from below and looked at Pamela talking on her cell. "Is that your dad?"

She nodded. "He can be here in half an hour."

"Tell him not to hurry. Having a houseboat changes things. I thought you were talking small boat, but this . . . We can stay out much longer. We need to get some supplies, food and stuff. This may take a while."

"Take your time, Dad. You'd better pack for a couple of days. See you soon." Pamela closed the phone and gave Mike a questioning look. "There can't be that many caves along the bluffs. We should be able—"

"Be prepared is the Boy Scouts' motto, and even though I'm no longer a boy scout, I still think it's an excellent way to think," Mike said. "Based on the reports I've seen, this creature seems to prefer the night or early morning hours. We need to be there at night or in the early morning. It has all the advantages at night . . . darkness, fog. By now, it knows the lay of the land. So, we may need to be there a couple of days. I'd rather be prepared to stay than have to come back and go out again. Anyone wants out, that's fine. In fact, maybe it's not such a good idea Sara going . . ."

I couldn't believe my ears. "Don't you dare say I can't go, Mike. I'm your assistant. You—"

"I should have my head examined for even thinking of taking a kid with me."

"I'm not a kid," I expounded. Why were people always saying that? "I've done a good job so far, and I haven't caused you any problems. You can't leave me behind, Mike. Please. I'll do everything you say." I looked on at him pleadingly.

As Mike bowed his head in thought, Pamela pulled him aside and I heard her loud whispering, "I'd usually be the last one to urge you to do this, but I think Sara needs you to show confidence in her. Your trust in her has turned her completely around from this mope, that Claire had no idea of how to handle, to what you see today. Really, you said yourself this is just a wild goose chase."

Mope? She actually called me that. I couldn't say anything regarding her choice of words, though, as I really wanted to go and, other than that mope crack, she appeared to be on my side. As long as I got to go, she could call me every juvenile or dirty name in the book, I'd even accept little girl.

"Maybe I should take her and leave you behind," Mike joked.

"You're not keeping me from coming," Pamela said. "It's my daddy's boat." She followed that with a Pamela trademark. She stuck her tongue out at him.

"Okay, okay, you can both go, but you have to listen to what I say. No backtalk, hear? Especially you, Sara, I'm not gonna argue with either one of you. And if this even hints at getting dangerous, I'm sending you home."

"Can I ask a question?" Pamela inquired.

"Shoot."

"If there is anything out there, I really don't think it's gonna be that hard to find. It has to be pretty big. You saw the deep slashes in that car . . ."

"Helicopter," Mike replied.

"Helicopter?" I echoed.

"From an airport up in Northern Missouri." Mike turned to Pamela. "Russell called me while you were talking with your dad at the house. Young kid borrowed his dad's 'copter to impress his girlfriend. He landed on 67, then took off again. That's what Pedro saw 'jump into the air.' It came low over his car and the skids slashed into the roof. The kid recovered it, but bumped into Pedro's car, knocked him off the road and then hightailed it for home. Didn't have his lights on, so Pedro didn't see them."

"How in the world did you track that down?" Pamela asked.

"I noticed some black paint specks embedded in the slashes of the roof. Russell had a lab crew come out, and they identified it as the type of paint used on a helicopter's skids. It didn't take Russell long to track down the chopper."

"How can you not hear a helicopter?" Pamela asked. "They're so darn loud."

"Turns out, the guy is pretty deaf."

"What's going to happen to the kid?" I asked.

"Kid violated a ton of flight rules, but amazingly he kept the thing in the air. Russell said the kid's dad was buying Pedro a brand new car."

"Now, I really don't understand why we're doing all this," said Pamela. "You caught the tiger, you explained Pedro's story, what's left?"

Mike handed her the map we created and tapped her on the head.

She looked over at me, and I reminded her of Mike's theory that something is killing a lot of animals on the other side of this river. "Remember what he told us when we made the map?"

Pamela nodded and silently took the map.

"Chester, do you think you can get a few items for this trip?" Mike asked.

"Sure, Mike. What do you need?"

Mike and Chester walked over to the parking area, where Mike began to scribble a list.

* * *

"This trip should be a good time for you to get close to Mike," I whispered to Pamela.

"Sara! Will you stop with the matchmaking? He's just lost his wife and little girl; he's not what I would call prime dating material. Anyway, he's always arguing with me."

I grinned. "Uh, I think you have that backwards. You are always arguing with him. And he's always right. Remember the tiger? Helicopter? Anyway, I only argue when he treats me like a kid."

Pamela smiled down at me and smacked me playfully on the butt. "You are a kid."

"I'll tell you what, cousin. I'll stop playing matchmaker when you stop calling me things like kid and little girl."

In answer to that, she stuck her tongue out at me. Who was the little girl?

Both Pamela and I looked to Chester as his cell phone rang. I watched his face take on a serious look while he talked. We then hurried over to where he stood with Mike, next to his car.

"Where did you find him?" Chester said into the phone. We all stood in silence while he listened. "I see. I'll tell her. Bye, Ron."

"Did they find him?" Pamela asked.

Chester looked over to Pamela. "Yes, Sara was right. He apparently was trying to get into the cave by swinging into it from the fallen tree using a rope. They think he fell and struck his head on the rocky bluffs." Chester looked down and then up. "Karl's dead."

He shook his head and leaned against the car. "That's so just like Karl. Always trying to do things alone. This is gonna be real hard on his girlfriend, Tracy. They asked me to go and tell her."

"Come on," Pamela said. "I'll go with you."

"We'll go too," Mike said.

"No." Pamela looked over at Mike. "This doesn't change things. We're still going on schedule. Let me go with Chester and talk to Tracy. We'll get the stuff on the list you gave Chester, pick up my dad and be back in a couple of hours. Is that okay?"

"Take all the time you need. Sara and I will get the boat ready." Mike's cell phone rang, and he stepped aside to answer it.

"Sara, do you need anything from the Cavern?" Pamela asked.

"My little yellow bag, my other Alanis CDs, anything else you think I'll need."

Pamela looked up at me. "Hey, you like Alanis? Me too! It's gotta be the hair."

"She's not my choice in music," Chester frowned. "I don't understand what you all see in her."

"Pay him no attention, Sara, Chet's into stuff like AC/DC. You know, uncontrolled noise. What about clothes?" Pamela asked. "No need to answer that, I know you're light there. I've got some stuff that'll fit you."

"Thanks, Pamela. You know I don't have much . . ." It was embarrassing, my wardrobe was pathetic.

"Lucky you, cause I never throw things away. I'll get you back in style."

"Thanks, Pamela, you're so thoughtful," I instinctively gave her a big hug. "I know that both you and Aunt Claire wanted to take me back up to the house in Chicago to pick some stuff up awhile back, but I couldn't bear to go. Maybe after this . . ." I also didn't want either Pamela or Aunt Claire to spend the money for gas. It was a long trip, and one I wanted to make, but gas was so expensive.

"Hey, after this, you and I can do a road trip up there," Pamela offered.

"Maybe visit Mike?" I teased. Hopefully, I'd have a way to pay for the gas by then.

"You never quit, do you?" Pamela said.

"WHAT?" Mike said. We all stopped talking at his loud exclamation.

"But why did Merle do that?" Mike continued.

"Okay, but tell him I'll kick his . . . never mind." Mike turned off the phone and stared angrily at the ground.

"Why are you going to kick Merle's backside, *Mississippi?*" Pamela asked. "Rachel wouldn't like that; she seemed sweet on the kid."

Mike glowered over at Pamela. "Chester, we need to update that list," Mike snarled.

"What do you mean, Mike?"

"We need food and stuff for three more people. Peter called our boss and convinced him that I could use a couple of bodyguards on this trip. So they're on their way back."

"Bodyguards? I thought this wasn't going to be dangerous?" Pamela said.

"I still don't think it is, but they convinced the museum of that, and now we're stuck with three more."

"But how did they even know we were going?" Pamela asked.

"That would be the third person," Mike sneered. "Your little *friend* Rachel called Merle after our post-breakfast talk. She correctly figured out on her own that I would say no, if she asked me, so she instead called Merle, and using his apparent interest in her, got him to ask me. Of course, it was news to Merle, since I didn't tell them about our search, because I knew they would want to go too. So, they called Paul."

I could see Pamela was stifling a smirk as she asked, "Do you need us to pick up some of your personal stuff?"

"Chester already offered," Mike said. "When you stop by the Cavern, let Claire know we'll be gone a day or two when you pick up my bag. Also, make sure it's okay with her that we allow Sara to come with."

I nervously bounced up and down on my toes and pulled at Pamela's arm. "You won't paint a bleak picture of this, will you?" It would be so like Aunt Claire to be protective and say no.

Pamela smiled and shook her head.

"Are you sure you don't want me to go with?" I continued. "I think Mike's in a bad mood now."

Pamela perked up. "No, someone has to stay here with *Mississippi* and get the boat ready. Don't worry, you're the last person on Earth he'd be upset with." With that, Pamela walked around Chester's Chrysler Sebring and got in. Chester slid into the driver's seat, and, as Pamela winked to both Mike and me, drove off.

CHAPTER 21

The Boat
Thursday Afternoon...

After they turned on the main highway and were out of sight, Mike looked down at me. "Pamela's right about one thing. I'm not mad at you, Sara. Come on, let's make a sailor out of you."

The water was choppy and the boat kept drifting away from the dock, leaving a wide space over water. I was a little afraid to jump at the wrong time and fall in the river. I gripped Mike's hand as I jumped from the dock to the boat.

"Just remember, Sara, the front of the boat is called the bow and the back the stern." Mike led me up some stairs, he called them a ladder, to the flying bridge, which had seating for ten people. He talked continuously, pointing out the different parts of the boat.

"You're not going to test me on this, are you?" I asked.

"No, I just thought since you're gonna steer the boat, either from up here or from inside, you'd want to know what's what. That's going to be your job on this little jaunt."

"What?" I exclaimed. "Wait. Are you telling me I get to drive this thing?"

Mike nodded.

"But I don't even have a driver's license for a car."

'You don't need a license to drive a boat. Pamela told me her dad let her drive it when she was your age. I'm sure he won't mind. It's a big river and I know you'll be careful."

"Pasta pazoole!" I screamed. "Oops, sorry, Mike."

"That's okay, Sara, it is pasta paz . . . what you said. You have to listen to Pamela's dad, though, because he'll be our guide and navigator." Mike's attention seemed to be focused across the river at the Missouri side.

While Mike silently studied the opposite shoreline, thoughts of all that had happened in the last couple of days raced through my mind. A few days ago, I had been trying to convince myself that there was a reason I had survived. Now I was involved in this unusual quest. I had always hoped my life would lead to some great adventure, could this be it? And . . . how did everything turn around so quickly?

Mike seemed to come out of his thoughts, and he grasped me by the elbow. "Let's go down below; I'll point out some stuff inside the cabin."

Once we were inside, while Mike went on about the different parts of the boat, I struggled to pay attention. I caught that the main steering was in the front, oops, the bow of the houseboat, and he called the middle of the boat amidships. Inside, he pointed out the kitchen storage and food preparation area, and I recognized the full-sized refrigerator. Behind that, in the back of the boat—Mike called it the stern—we checked out the master bedroom with a full-sized bed. On the other side, up forward, was a hide-a-bed lounge and table with chairs. Then, there was a storage area and the bathroom, but Mike called it a head. He had a different name for everything. Did we live on the same planet?

I struggled between listening to Mike's explanations and my previous thoughts of how things in my life had changed.

"What do you think of Pamela, Mike?" I ventured when Mike lapsed quiet while he examined one of the console instruments.

He looked up, seemingly annoyed. "Didn't we have this discussion a day or so ago?"

"Well, you said you didn't want to talk about it then. I thought maybe you'd want to talk about it now."

Mike stopped what he was doing and sat down on the lounge. "I guess I should have made myself clearer, Sara. I'm not over Crystal yet. I don't know that I'll ever be over her. I'm not interested in, or looking for, a mate. Is that plain enough?" he said.

Wow, now I've really done it. I had let my good mood take me into territory where I should not have gone. I turned to go.

Mike gripped my shoulder. "I didn't mean for it to come out so rough sounding. I'm not mad at you. It's just not an appropriate topic of conversation, okay?"

My eyes strayed to the pilothouse windows and I took a deep breath. *I guess that was my fault. I shouldn't have pushed him.* "Can I ask you what your wife was like? How you met her?" I knew I was pushing my luck, but Pamela had been right; he seemed to let me go wherever my questions led. At least so far. I assumed at some point he'd stop.

Mike gave me a stern gaze, then softened. "Sit," he said.

I sat next to him and waited.

Mike began slowly, "Crystal and I went to high school together, but we followed different paths, different cliques I guess you'd say today. Crystal was this popular cheerleader and always part of the in-crowd. The first three-plus years, I doubt she knew I existed, and I doubt I gave her much of a thought. I was kind of a loner, I guess, driven by something I inherited from my grandfather. I needed to find the answers to the mysteries that presented themselves, in particular those that involved strange creatures."

Mike looked down at me as I hung on his every word, then he continued. "Now that I think back on it, I guess you'd think I was kind of a. . ." He paused, like he was searching for a word.

"Geek?" I volunteered. "You were a geek?" I was conscious of my mouth being open again. Maybe I was the geek.

He smiled, reached over and pressed my lips back together with his fingers. "Did you know you stare with your mouth open? You'll catch flies that way," he joked and continued. "That wasn't the word I was searching for. I'd have said something like intense, but if that paints a picture for you, then yes, I was kind of geeky, I guess. I wasn't like far out, just driven. I was involved in school. I had to be, because of what I wanted to do afterwards. I played baseball and football, was in the honor society, other things. In short, I was involved with the things that mattered to me, and I was happy and content."

"You were the opposite of Crystal. If the two of you were so different, how did you finally get together?"

"I was trying to get there. It happened one day in my history class. I was pleading my case with the teacher, Mr. Mallory, on the existence of . . . strangely enough, it was about what we've talked about here . . ." Mike paused as he apparently realized the significance of that incident. He then continued. "It generated into a classroom discussion, but I knew the others only got involved to get Mr. Mallory off track, so they wouldn't get any homework.

"I was going with a different girl at the time, but Crystal sat right behind me. Something happened to her that day, I'm not sure I can tell you what. She even took part in the discussion. Mr. Mallory asked me about a trip I'd taken to look into the Piasa, and I told him it was a dead end."

"Like you've been telling us."

"Yeah. It was the first Crystal had heard about the Piasa, and she thought we were talking about the leaning tower in Italy. I explained the difference to her. I think it was the first time the two of us ever talked to each other directly. She gave me kind of a strange look, and Mr. Mallory started in on our lesson, so I turned back around. As class ended, she stuffed a folded piece of notebook paper in the back pocket of my jeans, then leaned in close to me. I thought she smelled like heaven. She simply said, 'Please, don't show that to anyone.' Then she slipped out of her seat and left the classroom. I didn't really think much of it at the time, and that night, I found the note when I emptied my pockets." Mike again stared across the river.

"Well? What did it say?" I asked.

Mike continued to stare out across the river as he laughed. "It said, *Meet me at Syd's at 6 o'clock.* It was the local hangout in town. The next morning, when I got to school, I went over to my locker to get the books for my morning classes. As I stood there, that heavenly smell entered my nose. I turned to find Crystal staring at me with her furrowed brows. I explained I hadn't seen her note until that night, and she simply nodded and walked away."

"She didn't tell you what she wanted?"

"Nope. She went back to her normal ways in class, ignoring me unless I was in the process of delaying class. After graduation, I went to the Academy and forgot about her. Right after plebe summer, I got—"

"Whoa. Plebe summer? What's that?"

"It's the Academy's indoctrination to the military. Very tough physically and mentally, to challenge you to succeed. Anyway, right after I got there, I got a *Dear John* letter from June, my girlfriend."

"I'm sorry I'm so stupid, Mike. What's a *Dear John* letter?"

"You're not stupid. I'm sorry, I'm hitting you with a lot of strange terms. It's a breakup letter. Most guys at the Academy got 'em shortly after they reported. The girls liked the attention of their boyfriend going into the Academy, but when it actually happened, they got lonely fast. They usually moved on. It didn't bother me that much, though.

"I struggled to maintain my academic and military grades so I'd wind up near the top of the class. I wanted to go into the SEALs, and I needed to be pretty high in class rank to get it.

"My second-class year, I—" Mike looked down at my furrowed brow. "That's junior year. I dated a female mid—uh, that's what the students are called, it's short for midshipman. Anyway, we went together for a while. We were both focused on our careers, so we easily went our own ways after graduation. Last I heard, Leslie's in line to command a ship. We were there for each other, though, and that helped get us through the very lonely times.

"After I was wounded, they sent me back home to recover. Mr. Mallory heard I was back and asked me to come in one day and speak to his class. Insisted I wear my uniform. I did, and he joked with me that even then I was able to disrupt his class.

"I stopped at Syd's afterwards for lunch. As I sat there drinking my coffee, a slightly familiar sweet smell drifted over me. I guess I had never forgotten that day with Crystal. I looked up to see her standing there. She told me at first she couldn't believe her eyes, having initially been drawn to the uniform, and then saw it was me. Another girl stood a couple of feet behind her, apparently waiting for her. Crystal asked if she could join me, and when I nodded, she told the other girl she'd be back to the office a little late.

"After the girl left, Crystal told me it took long enough for me to show up. I knew she meant the note. We talked. She had been married and divorced, now worked for a real estate office. Wanted to know all about me since high school. Asked how long I was home, then she asked me out."

"She asked you out? Look at you." Mike looked away, and I knew I had embarrassed him. "Sorry, Mike. Continue. I'll try not to interrupt."

"That's okay, you can interrupt. Anyway, one thing led to another, and we fell madly in love. She told me outright, though, that she couldn't stand to be alone and wanted to end our relationship if I stayed in the Navy.

"So I went to see Paul at the museum, and he offered me this job. A month later, I retired from the Navy. Six months later, Crystal and I got married. I felt on top of the world. I not only had the job I always wanted, but I had the most beautiful woman in the world as my wife. But she showed another side after we were married. Argumentative, manipulative. Very attached to her mother. I got her to move up to the north side of Chicago to be away from her parents. They moved to Brookfield, which was fairly close."

Mike looked down and shook his head. "I don't know why I loved her so much, because she was always arguing with me. At first, I thought it was just over all the wedding plans. And she was so close to her mom, always did stuff with her. After the wedding, it just continued. Again, I thought after we had Allison, she'd settle down into our own life."

Mike paused as we both watched an eagle fly over the boat and land in a nearby tree.

"Did things change then?" I asked.

He shook his head. "No, it just continued. She insisted Allison had to go to a pediatrician in Oak Park that her mother picked out. Crystal had to grocery shop by her mom in Brookfield. It started to come to the surface and unravel about the time the accident happened. She wanted to visit her mom, and I had a lot of work to do on a new exhibit. I asked her for two hours; she said a lot of mean things and stalked out with Allison. If I had only gone with her, I'd still be in Chicago." Mike again paused.

I sat silently. Inwardly I felt special that he had entrusted me with his story, but guilty because, while I was happy that Mike had come and rescued me from my misery, he had endured such sorrow in the loss of his wife and daughter. But he did appear to genuinely believe it was meant to be and, ever since he had told me that, I believed it too.

Finally, I said softly, "What happened to things being preordained? Remember, you told me that we were probably supposed to accomplish something and . . ."

"You are the clever little one turning my words back on me. Okay, but let's just drop the matchmaking thing, okay?"

I nodded. "I understand, but I was just thinking."

"I know I'll regret this, but what were you thinking?"

"Your wife, minus the mother fixation, sounds a lot like Pamela." I giggled, jumped up and ran as Mike looked for something to throw.

* * *

While we waited for Pamela and Chester to return, I looked over at Mike studying charts of the river. It was a glorious sunshiny day outside, and I hadn't felt this good in months.

"Everything set?" I asked.

He looked up. "Yep. We just need our supplies and the rest of the crew. Thanks for all of the help, Sara. You'll make a fine sailor."

"This is the first time I've really been on a boat. Is this what you did in the Navy?"

Mike thought for a moment. "You are full of questions, aren't you?"

"I'm sorry, I was just curious."

"Let's walk, Sara." He led the way out of the cabin and down to the stern of the boat. He looked out over the river, then indicated a spot and sat dangling his legs over the side. I happily kicked off my shoes and sat next to him, my feet swinging over the water.

"Navy SEALs don't spend much time on boats or ships, as the big ones are called. I did some sailing at the Academy, and we'll just forget the rest for now."

"So is this Academy like a special school or something?"

"Yes and no. It's the Navy and Marines four-year college, except you wear a uniform and live on the campus that we call the Yard. It's very regimented and military-oriented."

"Sounds kinda dismal. Why'd you go there?"

Mike's eyes narrowed as he peered out over the Mississippi and downriver. "I always wanted to go to the Academy as far back as I could remember. There was never any other choice for me. Worst time of my life, outside the past six months, was sweating out the appointment."

"Appointment? What do you mean?" I snuggled in close to him as a cool breeze blew over the water from the west.

"You getting cold? I told you that you could—"

"I'm okay. Can I just snuggle in by you? I used to do this all the time with my dad in those few times he was home."

Mike put his arm around me and pulled me in close. "Do you miss your family?"

I nodded as I recalled my mom, and how she always stuck up for me. Tears started to roll down my cheeks.

"Growing up is hard enough, Sara," Mike observed. "It's so much harder when you've been dealt the blow you have. You're a brave girl, and it's been wonderful getting to know you."

"Hey, where is everybody?" yelled Pamela, as Chester's car pulled up alongside the boat. "Can we get some help?"

I wiped at my eyes and jumped up, the mood broken, and ran forward to the car. As Pamela stepped out of the Chrysler Sebring, I noted that her tight knit top showed every curve, while khaki shorts accentuated her slender waist and shapely legs.

"Wow, Pamela, you look terrific. Maybe I should change." Not that I could come close to matching looks like hers. But I would be more comfortable.

"I thought you might feel that way, so I brought along some extra stuff. Hope it fits. You're so small, though." Pamela tossed a bag to me. "So was I, in high school, and lucky for you, I never throw things away."

"I'll take those and put them below," I offered.

"Wait, Sara," Mike said as he came up behind me and laid a hand on my shoulder. "Can you and Chet handle stowing all this stuff, Pamela?"

"Sure, Mike. Did you remember something else?"

"Can I borrow your Jeep?"

"Sure, what's up?"

"I told Peter I'd pick up Rachel at the library, to save time. They won't be here for another two hours." Mike looked Pamela up and down. "Are you going like that?"

"Naw, I just wear this to run errands around town. I've got a similar one in white for sailing, though." As Mike furrowed his brow, Pamela laughed. "Just pulling your chain, Mike. Don't worry, I'll change to something more appropriate." I could tell she really enjoyed needling him.

"Did you need me to do something, Mike?" I asked.

"Yes, come ride along with me."

"Sure," I said.

CHAPTER 22

On the Way
Thursday Late Afternoon…

Mike and I sat in the Jeep at a red light. I was crushed as he had just dropped the bomb on me. He'd decided it was too unsafe to take me.

"You okay?" Mike asked.

I wiped at my eyes again. It was so embarrassing, crying in front of him all the time. "No, I'm not," I said. "I'm miserable, but it's my problem, not yours. You obviously don't trust me, otherwise you wouldn't be leaving me behind. Maybe you never did."

"Look, I just thought it over and decided it's just too dangerous, that's all. We don't know what we'll find out there, and I can't be watching you and running an expedition at the same time. It has nothing to do with trust. You have to understand that."

Why was everyone treating me like I was eight years old? I understood his reasoning, though. After all, I was not his responsibility, and Aunt Claire would undoubtedly agree with him. I knew it was useless to argue with Mike. "I understand that you don't want me along. I don't want to talk about it anymore. Can you just take me back to the Cavern?"

"After I pick up Rachel and drop her off at the boat. I'm sorry, you've had enough pain in your life already."

I failed to see how not taking me was avoiding my pain. I was heartbroken.

* * *

Thirty silent minutes later, Mike pulled into the shopping mall that contained the library, the agreed-on pickup point for Rachel. As he looked for a place to park, I saw a familiar figure standing by the entrance.

"Rachel is by the curb," I said. There was no sense in arguing. I was out of ideas. My only chance, I thought, was to appeal to Pamela to talk to Mike.

He swung the Jeep around and pulled up to the curb. With a big smile, Rachel bounded over and got in. However, Mike's stoic look caused her smile to quickly melt away. Whatever had put him in this mood? I wondered.

169

"I'm sorry, Mike," Rachel said. "I should have directly asked you, I know. I feel terrible for going behind your back. I was just so afraid you'd laugh at me and say no." Looking up, she noted his determined look had not changed. "I shouldn't have done it. You don't have to take me . . ." Rachel opened the door and started to slide out. She was stopped when his hand reached out and firmly gripped her shoulder.

"Stay in the car, Rachel."

"But, I—"

"Why?" Mike asked. "Why do you want to go?"

Rachel swung her feet back into the Jeep, closed the door and nervously smoothed her sundress. "My mom and I moved here from St. Paul, after I graduated from high school last year. My mom explained that we would just be moving down the river a ways. And I had Phoebe. I tried to get a job here, at the local library, then the museum, but there was nothing. So I started the waitress job. It's okay, just not what I had hoped for. I guess I need to go to college."

"That's not answering my question. Why do you want to go?" Mike asked. "First Sara here, now you."

Rachel turned and saw me scrunched up in the small back seat. "Hi, Sara. I'm so sorry. I didn't even know you were there."

"I wish I wasn't," I said. "You have someone championing for you to go. I'm outta luck."

"I repeat," Mike said to Rachel. "Why?"

Rachel tugged at her sundress, trying to pull it over her knees. "I think for similar reasons that you came here, except I believe the Piasa was a very large eagle, like the one that's been reported around here lately."

"Interesting," Mike said. "So you're a closet Piasa believer?"

"Partly. I'm interested in what you do, cryptozoology. I really wanted a job with the museum, but I couldn't get one. I took the waitress job to save for college. my Mom can't afford to send me."

Mike nodded and asked, "Are you sorry you came here?"

Rachel nodded, then shook her head. "I know no one in Alton, and my efforts to meet anyone have proven futile, except for Pamela. I was beginning to think my mom and I really made a mistake in coming here. It really resonated with me when I lost Phoebe. Then, you showed up at the restaurant. Talking about the Piasa."

That's all I needed to hear about this town: there's no one here.

"After I left the bed and breakfast this morning," Rachel said. "It dawned on me. I was on the fringes of this great search. It seemed like my one chance in life to live a great adventure. I read about them all the time. I didn't have any idea of how to contact you, so I called Merle for your number. He didn't know about your plans and . . . well, one thing led to another, and he asked me if I wanted to go along. I'm sorry. I didn't mean to go over your head." Rachel again pulled at the hem of the short dress.

"Let's take you home," Mike said.

Rachel nodded and looked out the side window. I could see her profile. Tears of disappointment began to sprout. What a rat he was. First he burst my bubble, now hers.

"Directions?" Mike asked as he pulled out of the parking area.

"Turn right," Rachel managed to say, obviously trying not to show her misery.

"You'll need to change out of that dress and into something more adventure-oriented," Mike commented.

My eyes riveted on the back of his head.

Rachel's head popped up. "What? You mean . . ."

"I'm taking you home to pick up your stuff," Mike answered. "This isn't a romantic novel that we'll be involved in here. You won't get to stand on the deck, with that little smock all torn and tattered, waiting to get rescued."

I couldn't believe my ears. He was letting her go but not me? She was only a few years older than me.

Mike paused as Rachel's smile grew. "Don't look so happy," he continued. "Hopefully, you'll not be bored out of your mind."

"Thanks, Mike. You won't regret it." Rachel turned and beamed a smile at me. "What about Sara? Why won't you let her go?"

"I can't watch her and run an expedition. I'm not a baby—"

"You call me a baby one more time and I'm going to jump out of this Jeep while it's moving. There's no way you can stop me and drive, *MR. KELLOGG!*" I said loudly.

Mike quickly pulled over to the side of the road and stopped. He turned around and faced me. "Look here, Sara, I don't deserve that. I apologize for saying that. I was wrong, it was a slip of the tongue. But I'm right about not taking you. I—"

"How about if I keep an eye on Sara?" Rachel said. "She and I will be companions. We'll stay out of your way, and you won't have to worry about us."

Mike sighed, then looked down at the rear floor and saw my bare feet. "Where are your shoes, Sara? When that boat leaves the dock, you'd better have some kind of shoes on those feet." With that, he turned back around and drove on.

I couldn't believe it. In fact, I was moved to tears. "Thank you, Mike. Thanks, Rachel."

She turned around and winked.

PIASA

Two hours later, with the arrival of Peter and Merle, we departed. Illuminated by dying rays of sunshine, and with me unbelievably driving it, the houseboat cruised south down the Mississippi River.

Mike climbed up on the flying bridge and stood by Pamela and me. Pamela had changed into a khaki, long-sleeved shirt and jeans. I had dressed similarly in jeans and a dark-blue shirt that Pamela had brought for me. The jeans fit great, but the shirt sleeves were a little long and it was baggy. But to me, it was new stuff, and she again promised to take me shopping for clothes after our trip was over. I couldn't believe all of the things she had already done for me.

"How are we doing, ladies?" Mike asked.

"Good, Captain," Pamela laughed.

"According to the chart, we should turn into the Missouri shortly," I said. "I'll probably need Dave then." By now, I was happy that the sleeves were too long. As the evening progressed, it got cooler, and I was able to keep my hands warm in the excess sleeves.

"Where'd you learn to drive a boat so well?" Dave said as he came up from behind.

I beamed at the unexpected compliment. "Mike showed me."

"She's a natural," Mike said.

"Okay, Sara. Ease up. We're coming up to the Missouri here," Dave said.

When Dave relieved me for a break, I checked on what was going on inside the cabin. Peter, Merle and Rachel sat talking on the pull-out couch, while Mike sat at the table. He had powered up his computer and was searching the latest news on the Strange Happenings website. I walked over and stood next to the table with my arms folded and silently watched. True to her word, Rachel broke away from Merle and came over next to me. Mike finally looked up and saw her.

"I hope you're still not upset that we horned in on your monster hunt, Mike," Merle called over.

"Nah, I'm sorry I gave Rachel such a hard time," Mike answered with a smile to her. "I should have told you two right after we loaded that tiger. I don't know what I was thinking, 'cause this might be even more than the sum of us can handle." I guess at that point, he noticed me standing there. "You need me, Sara?"

I shook my head. "No, I just wanted to know if there's anything I can do for you. You don't know how much this means to me, getting to go with. I'm sorry for any mean things I said."

"Stop thanking me, Sara. Don't forget, though, if it gets dangerous, you're going back." With that, he looked back at Rachel. "You too!"

Dave then stuck his head down and yelled loudly, "Sara, Mike, we're at the island!"

Mike, I and the others came up on deck to join Dave. Merle and Rachel sat out of the way. Peter stood quietly next to Mike. I took over the driving so that Dave could answer any questions that anyone might have.

Looking ahead in the dim twilight, I saw a large island with a smaller one on the left. The river at this point divided around Littles Island, with the main part of it flowing to the left and a smaller branch flowing to the right. Part of the right branch appeared to then flow further to the north. The land to the right side of the river was marshy and Dave said it was uninhabited; it was floodplain for the river, with numerous levees dotting the landscape. In the distance, off to the right of the larger island, rose a number of bluffs reminiscent of those around Alton. Already, plumes of fog hung low over the islands and surrounding areas.

Mike pointed to the larger of the two islands. "Let's steer to the starboard of that one, Sara, and keep going upriver on the branch off to the right. I'm interested in taking a look around those bluffs that are surrounded by the river." Peter quietly nodded his agreement.

Dave looked over. "Bluffs surrounded by the river? I don't remember any bluffs—" He squinted off to the right and finally pulled a pair of glasses out of his shirt pocket and put them on. He stared in the direction of Mike's pointing.

"Heck, that must be new since the floods last fall, or the earthquake, Mike. I'm sure those bluffs were surrounded by land, not water. Sara, throttle up and steer to starboard of Littles Island. Do you know which direction is starboard?"

I smirked at Dave. "Starboard's right and port is left. The easy way to remember is, both port and left have four letters. Anything else you'd like to know . . . Dave?"

Dave and Mike both laughed. "I'm amazed Mike taught you so much in so short a time."

"She's a very smart girl," Mike said. That made me feel better, but I still wished people would stop intimating that I was a child. I mean I was young, but not that young.

I watched Mike as he took in the sun sinking rapidly in the west. Wisps of fog now floated above the water in a number of places. He turned to Peter and said, "We've only got a short amount of time until it gets really dark. I think we should call it a day." Peter nodded his approval.

"Dave, why don't we stop to the lee of Littles Island somewhere and settle in for the night. Let's all get something to eat," Mike advised. "I assigned myself as cook tonight. I could use a helper, though."

Pamela jumped up and volunteered, and they walked back to the ladder. I turned and looked in time to see Mike showing her the way below with an exaggerated wave of his hand.

* * *

It was getting dark when, following Dave's instructions, I throttled down after easing the boat as close to the island as possible. At first, I was afraid I'd run it aground, but Dave talked calmly and made me feel at ease. He never gave me the sense that he thought I was too young. I reveled in his confidence. The fog had thickened, and now rivaled the dark in opaqueness. The sound of crickets was deafening as Dave proceeded to anchor the boat both fore and aft. Looking off to the right, I barely made out the new channel of the river that meandered off to the northwest and into a wall of wispy fog. The tops of the bluffs, surrounded by water and barely illuminated from the western sky, were all that was visible in that same general direction.

"Come and get it, or I'll throw it away," Mike yelled from below.

"Go ahead, Sara," Dave said. "I want to take a bearing on the bluffs from here while I still can."

"Okay," I replied, then prepared to go below. "Is there gonna be a pretty moon tonight?"

Dave looked at a three-quarter moon barely visible in the rapidly foggy and darkening sky. "Certainly looks like it, but with the rain just to the north of us and all this fog around us, we'll probably not see a thing." We both looked up at a flash of lightning to the far north. "Tomorrow it's supposed to rain here. Good job today, Sara. You can drive my boat anytime."

"Thanks, Dave. You are a great teacher. I would work with you anytime. It was fun. Don't stay too long or you'll miss out," I added.

* * *

Following the after-meal cleanup, we all gathered inside the cabin. Merle, Rachel, Dave and I sat at the table while Pamela and Chester sat on the pull-out lounge. Mike leaned back against the kitchen cabinets. Peter sat up by the inside steering.

"Did you get a hold of Russell?" Mike, first to speak, asked Pamela.

She nodded. "Yes. Uncle Russ said he'd be by as soon as he can finagle the equipment. I told him where we are."

"What equipment?" Chester asked. That's what I wanted to ask.

Mike stared at the floor a minute, then looked up and nodded to Pamela. "Night vision goggles, a couple of flare guns, additional sleeping bags and some binoculars for the daytime," Pamela replied.

Pamela then spoke to us all. "Uncle Russ's suggestion. Since we don't know what we're up against, I also asked that he come along. He can't until tomorrow, though, when he's off duty. He'll drop the stuff by tonight. Mike and Russ felt it would be best if we operated as three teams."

Mike then took over explaining what he called our method of operation. "Several of the sightings have taken place at night, but most were in the early morning hours. It leads me to believe that whatever this is operates at night but returns in the morning to wherever it lives. I think that's here, somewhere in and around these bluffs.

"I feel the best chance of finding, observing and photographing it would be at night or in the early morning. That means we have to adapt to its schedule. So, I've made up three teams. One will operate in the nighttime hours, one in the early morning and one during the day.

"Against my better judgment, I dragged Sara into this, which I now regret. I have not included her or Rachel. They will stay on the boat. First sign of danger, though, I'm sending you both home, Sara." As I got up to argue, Mike waved me down. "No arguments. My mind is made up. Rachel said she would help keep an eye on Sara, but I shouldn't have transferred that responsibility."

Pamela moved over to my side as I fought the disappointment that rose in my heart. I glanced up at Pamela with glistening eyes.

"A responsibility?" I whispered. "Is that all he always thinks of me?"

"He didn't mean it like that," Pamela whispered back. "He's got a lot on his mind. I'm sure this is somehow connected to his loss of his own family. Let's just hope it doesn't come to that."

I shook my head and said quietly, "How could I have expected anything more? That's what my stepdad would have said."

"Your stepdad may have said those words, but he wouldn't mean them," Pamela said. "I think Mike really cares about your safety. More than you know. Besides, if it was up to me, you wouldn't be here in the first place."

"Ahoy there, is anyone up?" came a voice from outside and down on the water.

Mike, joined by Pamela and me, walked outside and looked back over the water at a speedboat. It had come out of the fog and pulled alongside. Mike waved down to Russell, as Pamela yelled, "Uncle Russ! Throw me a line."

After Pamela secured his small boat to ours, Russell handed up the equipment to her. "Remember, you need to take care of this stuff, or my butt's in a sling."

"You bet, Uncle Russ. When are you coming tomorrow?"

"Not sure, but don't worry, I'll find you. Take care of my baby, Mike."

Pamela's eyes narrowed. "Hey, you got that wrong, Uncle Russ. You should be telling me to take care of him."

Russell smiled and waved as Pamela cast off the line. "Pamela?" Russell added.

Pamela looked over at him.

"Call me if you need me. Remember."

Pamela nodded. "I will, I promise." As he drifted away, he restarted the motor and then, while accelerating, he did a one-eighty and sped away downriver and into the foggy night.

We watched until he faded away into the slate-gray darkness. The way I felt then, I should have just gone with him.

I stood off out of sight as Pamela tugged on Mike's arm.

"Why did you make that awful responsibility crack regarding Sara?" she hissed. "You task her with a job and then seem to imply she's a big bother. You embarrassed her something awful. That was uncalled for."

"I . . . didn't mean . . . it was just a statement, like . . . Well, someone has to keep an eye on her. I told Claire I'd take charge of her. That makes her my . . . responsibility, so—"

"You should learn that some things are better left unsaid. You could have just not even mentioned sending her back and left it at that. This all may be nothing. You built her confidence up and then knocked her down. It's just as bad as me calling her a little girl. You just used a more grown-up term, hiding behind responsibility. There was no reason to belittle her like that."

"I'm sorry, you're right. I'll talk to her. Let's get back inside, though, and finish our planning."

I silently watched as Mike started back inside, then I turned and looked up at the sky. Stars of the Milky Way blinked back at me as he ducked into the boat. Terribly disappointed and angry at him, I waited a minute or so, then went back in.

With the added equipment safely stowed, Mike resumed the meeting. "My team, that's Pamela and me, will do the early morning shift. The second team, operating at nighttime, is Peter and Merle. Chester and Russell, when he gets here tomorrow, are the daytime team."

"Sara, you'll continue to drive the boat. Dave, you're the guide and navigator, and Rachel, you're along for the ride."

At least he didn't take that away from me.

"How about I'm mission chronicler?" Rachel asked.

"Okay, that sounds good. We'll take turns cooking," Mike continued. "Pamela and I did tonight, Sara and Peter have breakfast. Rachel and Merle will take lunch tomorrow. We have enough supplies for another night, and then we'll have to reassess."

"What about sleeping?" Merle asked.

"That's Pamela's forte. I'll let her handle that."

"It's dad's boat, so I insisted he take the bed," Pamela interjected. "The guys are sleeping inside and the women have the flying bridge. I think Chet and I brought enough sleeping bags." Pamela began a quiet count.

"Good idea," Mike said. "Finally . . . We need a watch. This creature seems to prefer night or early morning. There's not much we can do at night, even with the night vision goggles. With the floods and quake, the land here's been in an uproar. While we're safe on the boat, it's not safe to go walking out there on terrain we know nothing about, in the middle of the night.

"Tonight, we can do nothing more than observe. Hopefully, we'll spot something. If we're really lucky, we'll find out where he calls home. It's now eleven. I'll take the watch from now to three. Pamela, you have it from three to five. Peter and Merle have done a lot of driving, so I'm giving them the night off. Chester also just got off a long on-duty spell, so he's getting a pass. The rest of you sleep, we need you all fresh at five. That's breakfast. We're underway at five-thirty. Our best chance to catch sight of it should be then."

I had half expected him to ask me if assigning me to breakfast was okay. I was itching to respond. I could handle cooking eggs and getting up at the crack of dawn. But he never asked.

CHAPTER 23

Night Watch
Thursday Night…

I had picked the back of the flying bridge deck as my spot for the night, but I was still upset about that responsibility crack and couldn't sleep. Rachel chose a spot by me and went right to sleep. Opening Auntie's cell phone—she had insisted that I take it with—I managed to make out the time as shortly after midnight. I could see Mike down at the stern as he leaned on the rail and stared out over the water. In the dim light and fog, his eyes carefully searched the shoreline and then in the direction we had come from earlier. There had been several large splashing sounds, but I had no idea where they originated. Each time I heard one, I saw Mike anxiously searching the water. That seemed plainly fruitless as the fog had set in, but every now and then, it seemed to clear somewhat. Earlier, I had also overheard Dave describing something to him he had seen while taking the compass readings. Mike told him not to tell the rest of us until they were sure what it was. With all this mystery going on, I knew Mike was determined to send Rachel and me back as soon as possible. Probably right after breakfast.

A noise from up near the bow seemed to put him on alert. He made his way around the bridge, and I sat up and watched as he squinted into the dark night. After I saw him return to the stern, I stood up. This, I reckoned, was my only chance to find out why he was treating me like I was a huge liability. I wiped at the tears that kept appearing on my cheeks, pulled my yellow robe tightly around me and padded over to the rear ladder.

Before I could take one step down, he looked up. "Sara?"

I glanced over at the sound of his voice. I'm sure he could plainly see I had been crying.

"What is it, Sara? Are you okay? Is—" he asked as I came down the ladder and over by him.

"I'm fine," I said quickly, with a little edge to my voice. As I wiped my eyes with the sleeve of my robe, I said, "I just couldn't sleep. I won't bother you and I'll be quiet. I just want to sit up for a while. Or am I breaking one of your precious rules? Could you please just leave me be? I won't bother you." While I had been planning to just plainly ask him why he was treating

179

me as if I was much younger, at the last second I chickened out and just gave him smart aleck answers.

"I don't think that's such a good idea. Tomorrow will be here pretty quick, and I need you in top physical shape to drive this boat. Try to get some sleep." He paused, then continued, "Is this about what I said? That you were a responsibility?"

I nodded. "But that's okay, you're probably right. Why should you trust me, when no one else does? I . . . um . . ." Even though he was giving me the perfect opening, I was still hesitant to explain myself.

"Come sit a minute, Sara." Apparently, he knew that I was struggling with something.

I tugged the robe tighter around myself and watched as Mike drug the large container that contained the life vests over.

Mike first scanned the water, then indicated a spot for me to sit.

"Thanks." I instantly plopped down next to him and dangled my feet over the side.

"Before you say anything," Mike said. "I just want you to know that I do trust you. Why do you think I'm letting you drive the boat? You must understand, though, that I'm only concerned for your safety, and, though you may hate the word, I don't take responsibility lightly. Your aunt put her trust in me, not anyone who I might choose. I won't allow myself to put you in a position where you could get hurt, and I won't pass that determination on to others. That does not make you a burden in my eyes. A burden is thrust upon you. I choose to take you along willingly. If that makes you angry with me, then I have to accept that."

I nodded.

"Now, what is it that's really bothering you, Sara?"

Briefly, my self-disturbance continued. Finally, I said, "Do you see me as a . . . child?"

"That was a poor choice of words on your cousin's part. No, I don't. You are a budding young woman. However, I promised your aunt that I would keep you safe. If you translate that into my thinking you a juvenile, I'm sorry."

From a distance came a loud splash, then stillness.

"What was that?" I asked.

"Probably a big catfish rolling over," he said.

"You're lying. Is that part of keeping me safe?"

He gave me a good-natured smirk. "Yeah, I don't know what it is. Maybe what we're searching for. See? I trust you."

"Yeah, but I had to challenge you."

"The important thing is I didn't lie to you, I just tried to mislead you. Okay?"

I just couldn't help myself. I smiled. The realization had hit me: he would do anything to protect me even if it meant I would hate him for it.

"Get back to sleep," he said.

After a moment of silence, I nodded. "You going to be okay?"

He pulled me up close and whispered, "Yeah, I'll be fine. Go get some sleep."

I silently motioned with a finger for him to bend down. When he did so, I kissed him on the cheek. I don't know why I did it; I guess it was because he was keeping me safe. I turned and ran back up to the flying bridge and my sleeping bag.

When I looked back down, Mike touched his cheek and looked back up toward me for a long moment, then picked up the night vision goggles and resumed scanning the shoreline.

I lay back in the sleeping bag and contemplated my situation. *Now, why the heck did you do that? You're supposed to be mad at him.* However, deep down, I knew that what he said made perfect sense.

Anyway, in a few days it would be over, I would be back in the B&B with Aunt Claire, and Mike would go back to his home in Chicago. Not that that was good, but with all that had happened to bring me out of my period of self-pity, thoughts of returning to my home in Chicago and my old friends had resurfaced.

Another splash from somewhere out in the water drew my attention. Then it was quiet. I slipped back into my musings. At least I was not as self-conscious about my scars now. Mike had convinced me that looks weren't everything, and I was beginning to realize that my scars were not what made me Sara. The people that stared didn't know who I was, and now, thanks to him, I felt I would be able to handle the curious glances.

As I twisted and turned in my sleeping bag, I kept thinking, *I've got to get to sleep, I don't want to let everyone down tomorrow.* After a moment of stillness, I rolled over again and peeked down to the stern of the boat. Mike was looking out with his goggles at the shore.

* * *

Two hours later, I was still awake, staring at 2:35 on Claire's cell phone. Mike had gone up to the bow of the boat and back several times, and now his feet hung down over the stern. He looked down at his watch and probably knew it was not only Saturday, but close to time to wake up Pamela. I watched with partially closed eyes, lest he catch me, as he scanned the riverbank and surrounding area once more with the night vision goggles.

I rolled on my back and looked up. While the fog hung close to the water, it did nothing to block out the star-filled night. In this desolate area of the state, away from the lights of towns and cities, the sight of a myriad of stars was magnificent. I had never seen this view in Chicago.

"Brilliant, aren't they?" Mike said. He had obviously crept up and caught me with my eyes open. "Did you think I was fooled by your pretending to sleep act?" Oops, not so obviously. "Come on. As long as you're awake, you may as well keep me company until Pamela relieves me. Then you better go to sleep."

I smiled and jumped up, grabbed my robe and followed him down the ladder. I sat down on the stern and dipped my feet in the water. My yellow nails, as I swirled them in the water, seemed to catch rays of the moon and reflect them back at me.

"They're a grand sight," he said, looking up. "I can recall similar sights from my times at sea. Out on the open water at night, the stars stretch from horizon to horizon in an astonishing display. A pity most people never get to see them."

"I keep hearing those splashes," I said. "Have you seen anything?"

"Yes, a friend of mine, a nosy teenaged little miss, who likes to spy on me."

That he called me nosy was not lost on me. "You're gonna have to teach me how you do that," I said. "You see and hear everything." Truth be told, I was kind of sticking my nose into everything.

He just smiled at me, then looked out over the water and said, "What makes that big a splash at night?" I knew he was wondering more to himself, and not expecting me to answer.

"What do you think it is?" came a voice from behind us. We both turned to see Rachel standing over us. "Can I join you two?" she added.

"Is no one sleeping tonight?" Mike said. "Sit down." He moved over, and Rachel sat down next to me, also draping her feet over the side. Her black toenails were a contrast to my yellow ones. She pulled her pink robe around her slim frame. I pulled mine up around my knees so it wouldn't get wet. "What is it about you women that you can't get to sleep?" Mike asked.

Rachel affixed him with her half-smile. "I'm the mission scribe. I can't do that asleep. Besides, I told you I would stick to Sara like glue. This is everyday stuff to you, but, like Sara, I'm super excited to be a part of this. Like her, I don't want to miss anything."

That, I realized, was it in a nutshell. Rachel was good at expressing things I felt. I looked back over at Rachel as she continued.

"No, seriously, I was sleeping, off and on anyway, but the splashes woke me up. I repeat, what you think is making those noises?"

"Probably a big catfish rolling on the surface," he told her that same lie he told me.

"Beeswax. Come on, Mike. I'm not fifteen."

"Hey," I said. "What does that mean? I am fifteen, but I didn't buy that baloney either."

"Sorry, Sara, no offense," Rachel said. "Look, Mike, this is new to Sara, but I know a lot about animals. Especially cryptid ones. Do you think it's the Piasa?"

"You know I don't believe in the legendary Piasa," he countered. "I believe there are sound reasons and explanations for everything."

"What about some type of enormous eagle?" Rachel challenged him.

"Come on, Rachel. We both know that eagles hunt by sight, during the daytime, not at night. Besides, all the fish eagles I know of are small compared to the ones that eat mammals. Last I heard, the bald eagle belonged in the fish eagle family."

"You come on, Mike. You're trying to twist what's happening to put us at ease. I think you believe there may be some kind of unknown creature out there."

"Unknown to Alton, Illinois, yes. But probably not unknown to science."

Rachel looked down at me and then at Mike. "Whatever. I just wanted to thank you, Mike, for taking me along. Even though you are sending Sara and me back. I understand your motivation." Rachel started to get up, but Mike grabbed her wrist, forcing her to stay seated.

"You know," he said. "If you were right, and I don't think you are, it could have been very dangerous. You must have an idea of what such a creature would be capable of. Why?"

"Did I come?"

Mike nodded.

Rachel looked out over the water for a few seconds and then turned back to Mike. "I wanted to experience at least one expedition in my lifetime. When my efforts to land a museum job proved futile, I was resigned to that never happening for me. Of course, everyone wants that great adventure, but few ever come face to face with it. After taking the waitress job, I was willing to give it up, though. At least I had a job, and not everyone can even say that.

"Then you came into the restaurant and talked about those reports. I could almost feel the adventure that oozed from you. Anyway, I don't think the creature is that dangerous right now, because it's just developing."

A huge splash sounded from out over the river.

"You're hallucinating. Get back to sleep," Mike advised.

"Yes, sir," Rachel quipped with a hint of a smile.

"And I'd better wake up Pamela," Mike finished with a glance at me.

"Do you think she'll be okay? I sense the hallucination, or whatever it is, is close with all of that splashing we've heard. It's hunting the river, isn't it?" Rachel said.

I felt a sudden nip at the bottom of my foot and something that felt kind of scaly swished past my toes. I tore my feet out of the water and jumped up, shaking the one that had been nipped.

"Sara, what's wrong?" Mike asked.

I turned to him. "I think something bit my foot. I'm not sure what it was, but it felt scaly like a snake." As I stood there shivering, Mike picked up the night goggles and slipped them on. He knelt and leaned over the stern, scanning the water in all directions. He looked up and shook his head.

"I didn't imagine it. It was real, I tell you," I stammered.

He got up and walked over.

"Sit down," he said. "Where did you feel it?" I raised my left foot. He gripped my ankle and looked at the underside of my foot. I could see a tiny rivulet of dark liquid dripping down from the ball.

"Is that . . . blood?" I said.

He leaned in and touched the liquid, then tasted it with his tongue. He looked up at me. "It's blood," he said. "It doesn't appear to be a puncture wound like a bite. Maybe something scratched you. It could have been a snake, but I doubt it. Probably just a fish. Those yellow toenails probably acted like a lure that some old catfish couldn't resist. Or maybe you scraped the side of the boat when you pulled your foot up. Don't worry, you won't die. I'll take you to the doctor when we get back just in case."

My eyes grew big, but he was probably right. I saw no mark like I imagined fangs would leave. "What if it was poisonous?" I questioned.

Mike looked over. "I've seen snake bites before, Sara. That was a scratch. Even if it was a snake that swam past your foot, it didn't bite you."

Unconvinced, I nodded.

"Even if it was a snake's scales, they aren't poisonous. However, I think that maybe you just scratched it on the side of the boat pulling your foot out of the water. We're fine."

"YOU think? WE'RE fine?" I admonished. "I'm the one who got bit."

Mike looked over at me in disbelief. "It stopped bleeding, but if you want a band-aid on it, there's a first aid kit in the cabin." He started to get up.

"What is all the commotion?" Pamela walked up while rubbing her eyes. "People are trying to sleep."

Mike sat back down and shook his head. "What are you doing up?" he barked.

Pamela rapidly blinked her eyes in a gesture of awakening and looked over at Mike. "I'm up to relieve you, remember?" she replied as she yawned.

"Sara thinks something brushed or bit her foot in the water, and it was bleeding a little. She thinks it might have been a snake. I think she scratched it on something."

"Well, despite all this excitement, I'm going back to sleep," Rachel said, getting up and quietly padding back up to the flying bridge in her bare feet.

Mike looked at me and pointed to the flying bridge. "You too. Get back to sleep. Now."

"Yes, sir," I squeaked as I got up.

He gave me a look and I headed for the ladder.

Pamela turned to go also, but stopped when Mike said, "Where you going, Pamela? It's your watch, remember?"

"Oh," she recovered and said in a loud whisper, "sorry, I almost forgot."

"Forgot, huh? Are you gonna stand watch like that?"

Pamela looked down and realized she was wearing a halter-top and shorts. She ran up to the upper bridge and slipped on jeans over the shorts and pulled on a sweatshirt, then hurried back down. I rolled on my side and listened.

"See or hear anything?" she asked.

"No," I heard him say. Does that man ever give anyone the right answer? I watched as he handed her the night vision goggles. "Do a sweep and then take them off. Keep a sharp eye and ear out. Do you have your nine mil?"

"My what?"

"Your gun, Pamela, do you have your gun?"

"Oh, I left it by the sleeping bag. I'll go get it."

Pamela was this perfect cop who made Chester look like a bumbler, yet she could do little right around Mike. Why was that? I wondered.

"Sit down. I'll bring it down before I go to sleep," he said. "You probably won't need it anyway." Pamela sat down next to Mike and hung her bare feet down over the side, swirling the water with her pink toes.

"Feet. Out of the water," Mike said. She complied so quickly I stuck the pillow over my mouth to suppress the giggles. After a moment of silent watching, I saw Pamela shiver. Mike looked down at her as she wrapped her arms around herself.

"Look," he said. "I suggest you keep your feet out of the water. One incident is all I can take tonight."

"Sorry." She wrapped her arms around her legs in an apparent effort to stay warm. "I . . . never mind." I knew she was itching to make a smart remark, but realizing he was still probably upset by the incident with me, I guess she decided to forego needling him.

"Be right back," he said and got up. I pretended to sleep as Mike came up the ladder and grabbed Pamela's sleeping bag. "Go to sleep, Sara," he said as he went by me. "You too," he said to Rachel, whose face I couldn't see. I heard him going down the ladder and opened my eyes to see him throw the now fully opened sleeping bag around Pamela.

"It's his training," Rachel said to me as she flipped over and faced me. "I heard you ask him how he knew things. Pamela told me he was a Navy SEAL. They are trained to study everything around them. That's why they are so good at what they do."

"Can I ask you a question?" I said.

"Sure, anything, Sara."

"Why are your nails painted black? Seems kind of dismal."

Rachel kind of chuckled. "It's from my Goth phase when I was younger. Back in high school, I wore black everything for awhile. Drove my mom crazy. She kept insisting that's why no one would hire me when we moved here. I guess she was right, because the restaurant was the first place I tried after I ditched the Goth look. They hired me on the spot."

She looked down at her feet and raised one to expose the color. "I wouldn't give up the nail color, though. It's my little act of rebellion. I think that bright yellow you wear is from the same line as mine."

"It's called Lennore," I said.

"Yep, it is. Mine's called Margaux. We're like buds now."

"I have an idea," I said to Rachel. "We'll talk at breakfast."

"Okay, Sara. Let's get some sleep before he catches us again."

"Right." I looked from Rachel down to Pamela, who had looked up at Mike, obviously touched by his gesture, as he sat back down beside her.

"Thanks," she said.

"You're violating the rules for a sentry," Mike said. "You should be alert at all times. Hard to do, looking so comfortable."

"I won't tell if you don't, Captain," Pamela said softly.

"Keep a sharp eye out."

A loud splash from a little way up the river, but out of sight in the wisps of fog, caused Mike and Pamela to look in that direction. After continued splashing, there was what sounded like heavy rain falling. It sounded like something lifted up out of the water, then fell heavily down. That was followed by several loud, blood-curdling screeches.

When I looked back down, Pamela and Mike were still staring in the direction of the sounds.

I quietly scooched closer to the ladder, planning to spy on Mike and Pamela, when I bumped my pillow. It slid noiselessly down the side of the raised deck on the port side. I looked down at it lying on the main deck, then glanced out over the water.

PIASA

A short distance away, illuminated by moonlight from a break in the fog, something glided up and out onto the surface of the bluff shoreline. At its widest part, it looked about three feet across and roughly twenty-five feet long. Because its width was relatively the same throughout its body, it appeared snake-like, although a snake of that size would be colossal. A rough body appearance gave the illusion of scales, but I could tell it was merely wrinkled skin.

The head, set at the end of a long neck, reminded me of a dragon, about three feet long and eighteen inches wide. Its eyes were raised much like an alligator's. When it moved over the ground, it looked much like a snake, apparently using its body plating to grip the surface and skim it along. I got a glimpse of the large creature as moonlight reflected off its teeth, which protruded out the side of its closed mouth.

When I realized it was staring straight back at me, I screamed.

Pamela and Mike heard me and hurried over.

Reaching me first, Pamela asked, "What is it, Sara, what did you see?"

"Something terrible," I managed to croak out. "It was big and, and . . . it went up on the bluffs there." Pamela looked in the direction I was pointing. It was now gone.

"What?" Mike asked as he came over. "What did she see?"

I simply shook my head.

"I think she saw our Piasa," Pamela said.

CHAPTER 24

New Plans
Friday Morning...

The first thing the next morning, Mike informed everyone of my sighting.

"What?" Dave asked. "Where in the world could this thing have come from?"

We were assembled for breakfast in the cabin of the boat. I was still upset. After what I saw, I was sure Mike was sending me and Rachel back.

"I don't know," Mike replied. "I wrote a paper a long time ago, while I was in high school, espousing the theory that what early explorers reported as lake monsters in the big lakes and rivers were related to sea monsters that were reported in the oceans. Of course, by now even I thought they had all disappeared. This thing . . . is what I'd expect of one that was a baby."

"Baby?" said Pamela. "Lake monsters? Come on. Are you trying to pull our legs?"

"I hope I'm wrong. Some people who claimed to have seen it initially thought it was an alligator or crocodile. Sara described something way larger. Whatever it is, we'll find the answer in those bluffs. Until we see it close up, we lump all our experiences together. This thing appears to have no problems in either environment. I had Pamela call—"

There was a loud bumping noise outside, as if something had struck our boat. I jumped; I was terrified. I saw Rachel's face also clouded in fear.

"Hey! Is there anyone home?" Russell's voice called.

"Uncle Russ," Pamela yelled. "The cavalry has arrived." Pamela ran out on deck, then quickly stuck her head back in and yelled, "Someone watch those eggs!"

"I've got them," Rachel said as she hurried over to the electric stove. "Better make some more coffee, Sara."

Russell walked in dressed in fatigue pants with a casual shirt and carrying a rifle. He was met with a chorus of greetings.

"Not sure I know everyone," he said.

Mike moved over and introduced Peter and Merle. "They're also from the museum—"

"Hey," Russell interrupted. "I recognize them from some television specials on the Discovery Channel."

"Guilty as charged," Peter said. "I hope we didn't bore you."

"No, you guys are quite good. Not like some of those yokels on the Animal Planet who seem to want to throw their face and personality at you rather than their subject," Russell replied.

"The young lady," Mike jumped into a lapse, "is Rachel Franklin, who you should know because she works at—"

"The Piasa Restaurant," Russell said.

"Yes, I remember you," Rachel said.

Pamela smiled over at Russell. "Coffee, Uncle Russ?"

"I'd love a cup."

"Russell likes it black," Rachel added.

"And breakfast! I'm cooking," Pamela added.

I saw Mike frown at the weapon Russell carried.

Russell also saw Mike's frown and immediately veered over his way. "You were right to call me, Mike, even if it turns out to be a wild goose chase."

"What is the weapon for?" Mike asked as he looked over at Pamela, who stood by Chet.

"I thought—" she started.

"I don't want this creature hurt," Mike snapped. "We don't even know what it is or where it came from. Its value to science could be immeasurable. I won't have any part of going after it with weapons. My plan was to observe and identify it. Maybe get a picture. Anyone with different ideas—"

"I'm sorry," Pamela said. "I just thought we have a lot of civilians on this expedition, and I didn't want any of them to get hurt."

"Yeah, well, we're going to take care of that this morning. Sara and Rachel are going back with you, Pamela, in the Boston Whaler."

I turned quickly around from making the coffee and put my small frame in front of Mike. "Please, Mike, we're a team." It was my last try to convince him, he was so stubborn.

"I'm sorry, Sara. I promised your Aunt Claire there would be no danger. Obviously, that is no longer the case. You know I talked to you about this last night. Peter, Merle and I are trained to deal with this type of situation. I can't tell the police what to do, but I ask they not accompany me with any type of weapons."

"If you send them back, Mike, I'll agree to put the weapon aside and follow your orders," Russell said. Chester also nodded his agreement.

I fought back the tears and tried to get out of the cabin. Pamela grabbed me by the back of my jeans and held me there.

"I agree they should go back, but I'm not going anywhere," Pamela said to Mike.

"Relax, Pamela," Mike said. "I just need you to take them back, and then you can rejoin us."

"I think we can find our own way back," I said as Rachel turned and walked out.

I wriggled free of Pamela's grasp and went and sat with Rachel up on the flying bridge, glumly staring out over the water.

After a few minutes, Mike came up and sat next to me. "I suppose you're not talking to me?" he said.

I continued to pout and switched my gaze to the stark cliffs of the island. Finally, I looked at him. "I understand. I don't agree, but I do realize you're doing it for my own good. I wish I was eighteen so people would stop doing things for my own good."

Mike looked to Rachel. "You okay with this?"

"You mean you taking away my one great adventure? I think that thing is the Piasa. What did you think? I was going to be happy?"

"I'm sorry. This won't be your only chance at that big adventure. You'll have more, hopefully tamer ones. Come on in, you two. We'll get you on your way after breakfast."

As Mike got up and led the way, Rachel and I looked to one another and smiled. Before he had joined us, we had devised a plan.

* * *

After breakfast, everyone was still gathered inside the cabin and we all listened as Mike tried to summarize the situation. "Sara saw something last night, something big. I think it resides somewhere in those isolated bluffs. Don't ask me what it is, I don't know for sure. Rachel thinks it's the Piasa. If it is anything unusual, I lean towards the offspring of a lake serpent, but maybe they are one and the same. It could also be something more conventional." Mike shook his head. "I don't know. But, for simplicity sake, let's just go along with Rachel and call it the Piasa."

The rest of them looked on soberly, and at first, no one spoke.

"Pamela told me about your lake serpent theory. Is that what you really think this thing is?" Russell asked.

Mike nodded. "I originally suspected a mountain lion or wolf, but with these water sightings, that leaves them out. I then looked for something that can go on land and in the water, like a large snake or alligator, maybe a crocodile. But, from what's been reported and what Sara saw, it doesn't appear to be one of those."

"What I saw looked kind of like a huge dragon that swims," I said. "I just saw part of it last night when it glided up on the bluff shore. For something so big, it moved real fast. I didn't see its whole head, I was too busy staring at its teeth."

Mike looked down at his watch. "Okay, it's six-thirty. Let's get Sara and Rachel on their way, and then we'll break into teams and see what we can find."

* * *

After the Boston Whaler had been lowered into the water, Dave quickly showed me how to drive it.

"Call when you get back," Mike said. He had come down in the boat too.

When Mike rose to get out of the boat, I stood up, suddenly causing the boat to rock precariously in the water. Mike turned and grabbed my arm to steady me. I put my arms around him and hugged him. Something told me he wasn't going to make it through this expedition without some additional scars.

"Be careful," I whispered. "Please." Then I broke free and sat back down, facing forward.

After Mike got out of the boat, Rachel got in, I put the boat in gear, and it pulled away from the larger craft. Rachel waved to Merle, but I stared straight ahead and did not look back. I didn't want anyone to see the tears already running down my cheeks.

* * *

When we got to the Lewis Bridge, I pulled the whaler under the structure and let the boat idle. "How long do you think we should wait?" I asked. We both couldn't help looking up under the bridge where numerous birds, Rachel said they were swallows, had made nests.

Rachel looked down at her watch. "How about ten minutes?" she said. "We need to be running our motor while they are running theirs, or they might hear us. Are you sure you want to do this? Mike might get pretty sore if he discovers us following them."

"I'm sure. You said yourself it's the adventure of a lifetime. Why should we miss out because they want to be extra careful?" I looked to the weeds along the shore where those orb-weaver spiders had taken residence. They were like all over this place.

"I was thinking, though," Rachel answered slowly. "Why don't we instead go and explore that cave while they're searching here? Maybe we can find out what made Karl go back."

"Wow, that's a great idea. If we don't find anything, we can come back here and find them."

"Okay, but Mike told you to call him when you got back. How are you going to handle that?"

"With this." I smiled and pulled my aunt's cell phone out of my bag. "Aunt Claire insisted I call her once a day."

* * *

We ended up sitting there for hours. First I couldn't restart the boat's motor, then we argued about what to do when I finally did get it started. There was only about an hour of daylight left, so Rachel wanted to forget it all and just go home while I insisted we continue with our plan to explore the cave.

I eventually convinced her, but our delay under the bridge proved costly. It was already getting dark when the storm system suddenly overtook us. As our small boat plowed through the wind-whipped waters of the river, lightning flashed all around and the reverberation of thunder seemed constant. Rain pelted down continuously, sometimes horizontally, stinging our faces. We could barely see.

"Where the heck are we?" Rachel shouted.

I was trying desperately to remember the clues as Mike had instructed me. "We're coming up on the Mississippi ahead," I answered. At least I hoped we were. "I'll have to steer to port!" I yelled. "That's left."

"I know which way is port!" Rachel yelled back. "Do you think I'm stupid?"

The smart aleck way she said that made me angrier, so I made the turn sharp, sending the small boat careening wildly to the left as we entered the Mississippi River and causing the choppy waves to splash into the boat.

Rachel, totally soaked in the small open craft, turned to me. "You did that on purpose, you little snot. When we get back on land, I'm gonna kick your skinny little butt."

"You and what army?" I said. I guess I was very bold, talking to someone older, someone who could indeed easily kick my butt. After all, she had a few inches and probably a few pounds on me. But I was mad, as she had suggested this alternate plan. We were both shouting at each other, not only because we were both upset and uncomfortably wet, but we needed to yell in order to be heard over the roar of the boat's motor, the wind and the storm.

A bright flash of lightning nearby lit up the river and was followed almost immediately by a crash of thunder. Another lightning bolt cut through the sky nearby, and the intensity of the pouring rain seemed to increase. Now, I was more than simply mad. I was terrified.

Rachel grabbed me by the shoulder and pointed towards shore. "Hug the shoreline as best you can," she hollered above the sound of wind and rain. She paused at a loud crash of thunder. "The last thing we need is to take a lightning strike sitting in the middle of the river. Pull ashore when you get to that cave. There we can get out of this weather, at least."

I nodded, my hair plastered to my face by the heavy rain, my T-shirt stuck to my thin body. To top it all off, I was very cold. "This was a stupid idea," I said loudly.

Rachel wouldn't even look at me, she just shook her head and stared out on the black river. I quieted down as I realized that we would, unless the storm sunk us, soon get to shore, and then she might make good on her promise to hurt me. Why rile her up even more?

I angled the boat northeast taking it upriver, but also toward shore. "Which way are you going?" Rachel screamed while attempting to keep her eyes open in the blinding rain.

Another flash of lightning and the rain intensified even further.

"How the heck am I supposed to know?" I answered, shouting over the storm noise. "I'm just going to shore here."

I dodged a log floating in the river, causing Rachel to lose her footing and fall. She landed on her butt in the bottom of the boat, splashing water everywhere. I reached out to her with a hand that she grabbed, the wisp of a smile forming on her face. As I tried to pull her back to her feet, a flash of lightning hit a tree just to our right, releasing a shower of sparks accompanied by a tremendous clatter. Small pieces of wood rained down on the boat. I reacted by dodging the boat away from it, causing Rachel to fall again, this time dragging me down with her while steering us back out into the river. She again landed on her bottom and I fell on top of her.

"You drive a boat like a little girl," Rachel chuckled. She brushed a lock of her brownish hair out of her eyes. Streams of water ran down her face.

"In case you haven't noticed," I said, "I am a little girl." Yeah, I had to admit it, she was right. "At least, I'm younger than you."

"Not by much," she said.

"Four years," I answered. "That's a lot."

"Actually, I'm only seventeen, Sara."

"You lied?"

"I'm tired of lying," she said. "The restaurant owner said he'd only hire me if I was over eighteen, so I blurted out I was nineteen. Everyone always said I had developed early and looked older. We needed the money, and it was my last hope. You won't tell anyone, will you?"

"No." I smiled back. "You didn't finish high school? "

"No, in fact that's one of the reasons we moved here. I was an outcast in high school, probably because of my Goth ways. Mom convinced me to give it up and suggested the fresh start. I have a year to go, but I'm studying for my GED. One of the teachers fixed it up for me."

"So do you really know a lot about the Piasa? Animals?"

"I watch a lot of nature shows on TV. The Piasa? I toured the museum when I first got here when the Piasa exhibit was up. One of the reasons the old guy who runs it wouldn't hire me was I was only seventeen."

"What about Merle?"

"I told Merle the truth. Can't have a relationship built on false goods. He understood perfectly. He's only twenty-one, so we're in the ball park. I really like him and we agreed to think about a long distance relationship. If I don't drown out here on the river, first."

For some reason, Rachel's confession broke the tension between us, and we both started giggling. Through stifled laughter, she added, "You'd better check our direction before we run into something."

I got up, and this time pulled her to her feet.

"We're almost there!" I yelled. "We're passing the painting. Or where I think it is. I still can't see a thing. It's got to be just up the way here."

I pointed. "Look for a huge fallen tree leaning up against the bluffs. Pamela said it got uprooted in the earthquake." The rain had let up momentarily, and I hoped we located the cave before it restarted.

"I don't know. How will we get up to the opening?" Rachel asked. I could tell she was continuing to have second thoughts.

"The tree, you dope. Mike said that Karl must have somehow climbed up the tree. If he could do it, so can we."

"Yeah, but Karl fell out of it and got himself killed."

"Maybe what he found was so spectacular, he didn't pay attention to what he was doing. Anyway, I'm sure the two of us little girls can handle it."

Rachel chuckled at that while I urged myself to believe it.

"Is that it? Right up ahead?" Rachel asked.

"Yep, that's it," I said. Was she really going to beat me up? "Are you still mad at me?" I asked, fearful of her answer.

Rachel, wet to the skin and with a drop of water poised on her nose ready to plunge to earth, looked over at me. "Sara, you look like someone dumped a bucket, no, make that a barrel, of water over you."

"I couldn't look any worse than you," I said. There I go, probably riling her up even more.

For a moment we were silent as I pointed the craft to a spot just to the north of where the tree was, and we gently glided onto a muddy beach in the drizzle. After we gingerly stepped on shore, Rachel gripped both of my shoulders and looked me in the eye. *Here it comes, she's gonna clean my clock.*

"You're a feisty little wench," she said. "I like that. Don't you ever change, Sara. I love you just the way you are. I think I've finally found a true friend." Then she hugged me.

PIASA

I hugged her back.

CHAPTER 25

The Cave
Friday Night...

Standing at the base of the fallen tree, we stared up into the branches.

"Wow, it's a long way up there," Rachel noted, pulling me out of my shock.

I couldn't let her know I was afraid. Mike always seemed so calm in emergencies, and I wanted to be like him. What would he do?

"You scared?" I asked. "Want me to go up first and check it out?" In truth, I was probably even more petrified.

"No, I'm not scared," Rachel snipped. "After all, it was my idea. Besides, I can't let you go up there alone."

When lightning flashed to the west and thunder reverberated around us a few seconds later, I jumped and Rachel shrieked.

"Here comes another round of storms," Rachel stated the obvious.

"Let's hurry and get up into the cave before we get soaked," I yelled.

"Before we get soaked?" Rachel said. "In case you don't realize it, you're standing in a puddle of water that you created."

* * *

Three-quarters of the way up the tree, I stopped momentarily and clung to a large branch. From just below me, I had heard Rachel's fearful voice. "Oh no, Sara. We're so high up."

I glanced down and saw her face, a mask of terror. "Rachel! Don't you know not to look down?"

"Too late," she said. "Did I mention I'm afraid of heights?"

"Take a deep breath." It took all the willpower I had to pretend calmness.

She looked up at me. "Well, if a skinny little kid like you can do it, so can I."

"You're like the pot calling the kettle black," I chuckled. "What do you weigh, like a hundred pounds?"

Rachel smiled. "A hundred and ten, and I'm a whole head taller than you."

"And a whole lot dumber," I said, pleased that she seemed to relax when we traded insults. Now, if I could only do the same.

197

"That does it," she said. "When we get in that cave, I'm giving you the spanking you've got coming . . . you . . . little . . . girl."

"Yeah, well, at the rate you're moving, I have nothing to fear." Trading banter with Rachel was exhilarating. Here was an older girl who accepted me for who I was and treated me as an equal. While she teased of beating me up, I realized she never meant it. It was all just good-natured ribbing. And for some reason, I liked when she called me a little girl. I guess we were kindred spirits. She was right, I too had found a friend.

As we closed in on the entrance, lightning flashed close by, followed immediately by the clash of thunder. The rain had returned.

"Move, Sara. We need to get out of this tree. I must have been crazy to follow you."

"This is your great adventure, remember?" I mocked.

Perched near the top of the tree, I gauged the distance to the cave, which was several feet to my right. "I think I can jump into it," I said.

"Are you crazy?" Rachel said. "What if you miss? You'll end up like Karl."

"It's only a couple of feet, but I've got these stupid flip-flops on. I should have worn my boots."

"Oh my god, you climbed this tree wearing flip-flops? What are you? Part monkey?"

A bright flash of lightning to the north and the boom of thunder ended the chitchat, and I suddenly made up my mind. I reached down and removed one of my sandals and tossed it into the cave. Taking off the second one, I casually flipped it just as a gust of wind slammed into the tree, causing the flip-flop to hit the lip of the cave and spiral down to the ground far below.

"Pasta pazoole, that's not good!" I exclaimed. "Now I'll have to go barefoot."

"What did you just say?" Rachel said. "Who taught you something like that?"

I looked over at Rachel. "I made it up. I use that instead of swearing, but it's the same thing. Did that dispel my little girl image for you? In fact, maybe it's you who is the little girl."

"If I wasn't afraid I'd fall out of this tree, I'd slap your face." Rachel clutched the large branch she squatted on as another squall buffeted the tree. "Maybe this wasn't such a good idea. We should go back."

The pelting rain increased in intensity, while strong bursts of wind lashed the tree, moving it closer to the cave. I had to do something before Rachel decided to chuck it and climb down, plus get myself out of this situation now, before I let on how scared I really was.

"No," I said with more conviction than I felt, "that's the defeatist words of a little girl." Then, seeing my opportunity, I jumped.

I landed near the edge of the cave and for a moment teetered precariously on slippery mud, then forced myself to fall into it. As I fell, my ankle twisted under me, causing me to scream in pain as I hit the cave floor. I looked up into the cave, but could see little.

"Sara!" Rachel hollered. "Are you okay?"

"I think I twisted my ankle. It's dark in here."

"It's dark in there? You're in a cave, you little ninny. What did you expect? Electric lights and a rock band?"

"Are you coming, Miss Smarty Pants?" I said with as much iciness as I could muster. Inside, despite the pain in my ankle, I was relieved to have finally done something of which I could be proud.

"Yes . . . No . . . I'm petrified out here," Rachel cried. "I'm afraid I'll miss and fall. I want you to call Mike right now and tell him where we're at and ask him to send help. A fire truck with one of those long ladders would be nice."

I stuck my head out of the cave and looked at Rachel holding onto the tree branch. All she needed, I reasoned, was a little negative encouragement. As a blast of wind-driven rain lashed my face, I bowed my head, peered back at her and yelled, "You're in no position to tell me what to do, you little teen-aged coward. After all, this was your pasta pazoole idea anyway."

"Stop with that pasta pazoole stuff. Have I told you lately that you can be a smart-mouthed little wench?" she shouted.

"Pasta pazoole on you," I said. "It's a free country."

Despite our precarious situation, we both started laughing. I realized then that maybe staying in Alton wouldn't be so bad. After sharing this ordeal, I knew Rachel and I would remain friends. That is, if we survived. If we were going to do that, I needed to get her out of the tree and into the cave.

"Come on, Rachel. You can do it. I'll grab you when you jump." *Yeah, how are you going to do that with a throbbing ankle and barefoot, standing in slippery mud?*

"I can't. I'm afraid!" she cried. I could share her feeling of dread. If not for Mike, I would never have been able to push my fright aside and accomplish this feat.

High winds continued to pummel the tree. With the absence of my weight and the constant battering of winds out of the northwest, the top of the tree began to slide along the bluff, closer to the cave. As the branch with Rachel appeared to settle near the cave entrance, I screamed again, above the wind and rain, "So, a little girl can do something you can't do! You are a coward!"

PIASA

I'm sure she realized she was in a perilous position and knew, as I did, that the wind could cause the leaning tree to fall at any time. I think the coward comment riled her because, finally, Rachel looked at me. And as the wind momentarily subsided, she jumped.

Rachel slammed into me and the two of us tumbled to the cave floor. I ended up under Rachel and let out a loud yelp as we hit some debris strewn about the entrance.

"Oh, I'm sorry, Sara, are you okay? Did the 'coward' cause you to twist your ankle some more?"

"No, it's not my ankle, it's my butt. I fell on something sharp." Reaching down, I pulled the item from under me, but in the darkness of the cave I could not make out what it was. "It feels like ..." A flash of lightning illuminated the cave, and I could plainly see I was holding a piece of old bone.

"Did that come out of your bony little behind?" Rachel asked.

"If you don't shut up," I said. "I'll shove this up your cowardly butt."

For a moment we stared at one another. Then, at the same time, we reached out and hugged.

"I'm sorry I called you a coward," I said.

"I'm sorry I caused you more pain," she replied.

We laughed at each other, then looked to the inside of the dark cave and waited. In seconds, another lightning flash lit up the cave. The floor was covered with bones.

"Look, the Piasa must have existed," Rachel said. "Where else would all of these bones have come from?"

We moved further into the cave and surveyed the floor with each lightning flash. "This must have been what Karl saw when he came in here to escape the tiger," I said as I stared in awe.

"How did they all even get in here to escape?" Rachel asked.

"They all didn't escape through here. Karl just entered it, but either the tiger scared him or he saw that there was no way down. Then he and the others went down the tunnel to where the painting is. There's an opening in back somewhere. The next flash should show it to us." As I said the words, a bolt of lightning crashed over the river and illuminated the cave and back wall.

"There!" I pointed out the oval-shaped opening that was barely big enough to fit through.

"Looks kind of small," Rachel noted.

"Yeah, when Mike and I ran past it, I glanced through it and saw the tiger. Karl must have gotten up to it before the tiger came back, and Karl saw the bones. The tiger then scared him off, but Karl came back the next day and climbed the tree as we did. Once they caught the cat, of course," I said.

Suddenly a cell phone started ringing. At first we both jumped, then I relaxed after hearing the unexpected sound. I looked towards the entrance where I had unknowingly dropped it. Padding over in my bare feet, I was careful not to step on sharp bones.

I picked it up, and when I opened it, I saw Mike's cell phone number displayed as the caller. "It's Mike," I whispered. "He must be checking up on us. I can't answer it. What would I tell him?" After several more rings, the phone was quiet.

"What'll we do, Rachel? Mike's gonna be really angry. Maybe I should call him back and tell him—"

From outside came the rustling of branches. I looked up to a large creature peering into the cave from the tree. I immediately recognized it as the one I had seen last night. As I stood frozen in terror, he opened his mouth, revealing those razor-sharp teeth.

I screamed. Rachel screamed also as she looked up and saw the menace we faced. We tried to back up slowly toward the rear of the cave while still keeping the nightmarish intruder in sight. I suddenly stepped on something pointed and yelped as the jagged ends of a bone punctured my bare foot. I tried in vain to find a level spot and yet move quickly. I kept stepping on sharp splinters of bone that pierced my bare feet. Oblivious to my screams of pain, Rachel pulled me along.

We watched as the serpent-like beast slowly slithered into the cave. In a flash of lightning, its head swiveled toward Rachel and me. Huge eyes glared at us. Then a deafening crash of thunder caused it to turn quickly and look back toward the opening.

Rachel pulled me close.

"What is that thing?" I asked in a low voice.

"I think it's the Piasa," Rachel whispered back. "Apparently, we're in his home."

The creature stared out of the cave for several seconds, then pulled the remainder of its body into the opening, twisting itself like a snake. As we tried to carefully move backwards, it turned swiftly and stared intently at our position. Slowly, like the yawn of a cat, it opened its mouth, revealing rows of pointed teeth. Then it quickly closed its mouth.

Frightened by its sudden movement, I turned and fell. Another sharpened splinter of partially-fossilized bone pierced my left thigh. Rachel pulled me up as I screamed in pain and, oblivious of what the scattered bones were doing to my bare feet, she yanked me quickly to the rear of the cave. I was aware of a tremendous pain in my thigh, and I knew my feet were bleeding profusely from deep cuts caused by the splintered bones, but I hurried as best I could as I was pulled around the cave. By feeling around the rear wall of the cave, Rachel found the opening. She quickly pushed me through it and joined me in the long tunnel.

My head swimming in pain, I looked through the opening as a flash of lightning illuminated the cave. I saw the creature look right then left, as if suddenly aware that its prey had disappeared.

I started to whimper from the pain, but was stopped by Rachel's hand that covered my mouth, her fingers tightly gripping my cheek. I struggled briefly, then relaxed.

Rachel leaned in close until her lips were practically inside my ear. "Stop struggling and don't say a single word," she said. "You've got to suck the pain up. Our lives depend on it. Nod if you think you can do that, and I'll release you."

I nodded slowly. When she removed her hand from my mouth, I leaned over and likewise whispered in her ear. "You have to do something, Rache. My feet are bleeding and the pain is so intense."

"You may have a bigger problem than the pain, sweetie," she whispered.

"What?" I mouthed, rather than spoke, the words during a flash of lightning.

"If you don't get a heck of an infection from those old bones, it'll be a miracle. We have to get you to a doctor quickly. I'll try to bandage them the best I can."

We were still both soaking wet, and decided the best chance for me to avoid further complications of an infection from the clothes we wore was to use mine. Besides, I had a halter top under the long-sleeve denim shirt I had been wearing, so Rachel tore my shirt up and made bandages for both of my feet and my thigh. She had to work between lightning flashes, as that was the only time she could see anything. Although she tried to be careful, I winced and squealed softly when she had to pull them tight in an effort to stop the bleeding.

Despite her care, I was in tremendous pain. It was like the accident all over again. I was continually forcing thoughts of 'more scars' out of my head. I already had those from the accident, now I would add more from these puncture wounds and the cuts on my feet. At least those were on the bottoms of my feet, and who ever looks at the bottom of their feet?

When she finished, Rachel dragged me along in the pitch-black passage behind the cave. The plan was for us to try to get out by way of the cave under the Piasa painting. We figured, in the total darkness and with my injuries, it would take us about two hours. Now, I blinked my eyes and tried to focus, to no avail. I felt a lot of pain in my feet and thigh, and my body was going through a series of spasms. The sudden sound of rolling thunder caused me to turn my head back in the direction of the opening we had just come through. I could barely make out the small hole.

Then, lightning flashed in from outside, and in its effort to penetrate the darkness of the cave, it provided enough light for me to see that the Piasa was busy smashing away with its body at the back wall. Soon, it would widen the opening enough to fit through. I tried to squint into the ebony tunnel ahead, but could see nothing. Another flash of lightning and the clatter of thunder caused the creature to again temporarily stop its efforts and pull its long neck back through the opening. Now I could hear the rain pelting off trees and rocks outside. How wonderful it would be to let the rain wash the dirt and blood from my feet so that I could see the extent they were cut up. I began to wonder if I would ever feel the rain or see the outside again.

Resisting the urge to cry, I watched as the Piasa, apparently recovering from the unwelcome noise of the thunder, pushed a part of its larger body through the widened opening. In the dying illumination from a lightning flash, it lunged up the tunnel at us, displaying its hideous curved fangs accompanied by a loud hissing shriek when it came up short. It apparently terrified Rachel as well as me, for she turned in the inky blackness and ran, dragging me behind.

Suddenly, I heard a 'thunk' sound. Rachel let go of me and I heard a soft thud. I quickly realized that Rachel had run into the cave wall where the passage angled off to the right. I figured this all out by crawling around the cave floor. From behind me came the sounds of the Piasa, scraping away, busily trying to widen the tunnel opening.

I sat down on the cave floor and felt around in the dark for Rachel's head. Finding it, I pulled her still form up close and cradled her head in my lap. Ignoring the pain from the wound in my thigh and my cut-up feet, I implored her to wake up.

"Rachel, come on, I can't do this alone," I cried. Remembering Rachel's glasses, I felt for them and instead found her face wet and sticky. Touching it and putting my finger to my lips, I immediately realized it was blood.

Panicky, I tried to get up, but became dizzy and settled back down. "Rachel, please wake up. We've got to . . ." I began to feel very weak. Once again, I implored the unconscious Rachel to help me, but to no avail. It was only a matter of time until the creature got through the opening and came over to finish the job. My feet were a mass of pain, and everywhere I touched on my leg was blood. My thigh continued to burn terribly. I pictured the infection spreading through my body like the venom of a snake.

Collapsing on top of the unconscious Rachel, I realized I would have a hard time walking on the debris-littered tunnel floor even if I could see where I was going. In the total blackness of the cavern, it would be near impossible to find my way out. While I had been able to feel Rachel's pulse, I knew that I would not be able to count on any help from the out-like-a-light waitress.

Another burst of lightning showed the creature, with its mouth of razor-like teeth, coldly staring at me. After giving me a prolonged hiss, it quickly went back to work enlarging the opening.

At the depths of my despair, and ready to curl up and cry, I remembered something Mike had told me in one of our discussions. Words, he said, he lived by. "When you feel you can't go any further, it's time to start getting down to business." Buoyed by his words, I got to my feet and attempted to lift Rachel up and carry her. The pain, however, drove me back down. I sat there and whimpered.

Out of the corner of my eye, I noticed the creature had stopped flaying away at the wall and was staring back toward the cave opening, as if listening to something. Pulling its head back through the opening, it returned to the cave. I strained to hear, but in the confines of the tunnel, I couldn't hear anything from the outside except for the sound of the wind and heavy rain.

Suddenly a flash of lightning, followed by the roll of thunder, illuminated the cave and tunnel. Noting that it was much brighter than before, I looked toward the opening and was surprised to see that the serpentine nightmare had not returned. It had, however, widened the opening considerably. I realized the creature could now almost fit through.

Suddenly, the beast's head poked back through the breach and gazed at me. Despite all my vows to be brave, I whimpered loudly and started to cry. At that point, I was sure I was going to die.

The creature, after having resumed its attempt to crawl through the opening toward us, stopped at what sounded like a motorboat engine. It turned back, and I could hear it slithering toward the cave mouth and the noise.

Seeing the Piasa leave, I decided to take a chance and crawled to the opening. I could still hear the faint sound of a boat motor and saw that the creature had some difficulty maneuvering in the close confines of the cave. Clearly in the water it was formidable, but on the ground it was at a disadvantage. I knew, though, that this was just delaying the inevitable. Someone had probably pulled into shore to get out of the storm. They would leave, it would return and . . . I quickly crawled back to Rachel's side.

I was again startled when I heard what sounded like a gunshot. It was followed by a terrific hissing and screeching by the creature, which sounded kind of far away. Had it left? Was someone out there? Maybe a police car was driving by and saw the creature at the mouth of the cave. Maybe it wasn't connected at all.

PIASA

I thought about trying to yell to whoever fired the shot, but I was unable to do much more than sob loudly. I tried to stand up, but the pain from my cut-up feet, despite the makeshift bandages, drove me back down to my knees. I again thought of crawling towards the cave opening, but found it harder to move. My thigh throbbed terribly. I began to worry I'd lose my leg. Then I thought, *Wait, what makes you think you'll even be alive in the morning?*

CHAPTER 26

Hope for Rescue
Friday Night...

"Sara! Rachel! If you can hear me, go into the tunnel at the rear of the cave. The creature is too big to get in there. I'll get you out somehow. Crawl to the back of the cave. Go into the tunnel, now."

Those barely audible words, despite the sounds of the storm and my location in the tunnel behind the cave, somehow drifted back to me. I knew it wasn't my imagination. I couldn't believe I was hearing Mike's voice.

I wondered why the creature, who'd almost finished widening the hole, had not returned. Now I could envision Mike face to face with this thing. In a calm moment from the storm, I heard the hissing shriek of the serpentine monster. From its intensity, it sounded far away, and I dared to hope it had left the cave.

Overcoming my initial fear that it would suddenly appear and attack me, I tried to stand. But my legs and feet screamed in protest. *I'll have to crawl.* I gently laid Rachel's head on the tunnel floor and turned toward the opening, barely visible in the light from the storm.

A sudden flare of lightning illuminated the immediate area, and I pulled myself along to the breach. I hesitated to move beyond the entrance to the cave, waiting instead for the next lightning burst.

When it came, I struggled to crawl, searching with my throbbing toes for places to leverage my small frame so I could move forward. I used lightning flashes to see what was on the floor ahead of me. After each one, I stopped and relaxed, waiting for the next display. They came quickly. While the bleeding of my thigh and feet appeared to have stopped, I was afraid the strain of movement would reopen the wounds.

A sudden loud shriek of the creature decided for me. By its volume, I knew it had left the cave. I had to know what was going on outside. In desperation, I began to crawl faster. As my feet searched for a toehold, I felt them sliding off whatever I leveraged myself on. Reaching down to my aching thigh, I could feel the fresh blood oozing.

As I reached near the mouth of the cave, lightning lit it up again. I looked forward and gasped. Lying right in front of me was a skull. I knew it was human.

PIASA

Once again, Mike's voice yelled out our names and told us to seek the tunnel behind the cave. In answer, the creature howled back at him.

I could not believe my ears. That *was* Mike. He was close by. But how could that be? How could he possibly know where we were, and how did he find us?

With a concerted effort, and ignoring the bleeding, I pushed and pulled myself to the mouth of the cave and put my head out into the rain and wind. Nothing had ever felt so good, I thought, as water droplets splashed on my face and in my hair. I almost burst out crying, it made me so happy. Suddenly the rain, which had been coming down in a torrent, slowed down.

Looking over into the tree, I saw the creature wheel around, its massive head hovering above the serpent-like body, while loudly hissing and staring down at . . . Mike. At that moment, the creature let out a piercing shriek and lunged in his direction. When it was ten feet from him, it stopped and stared motionless, seeming to await his next move.

I watched as Mike wiped the rainwater from his eyes. I knew he was at a disadvantage to the thing that was now fixated on him. Mike suddenly faked going to his right, then quickly turned and jumped for a branch higher and to his left.

My heart stopped as Mike grabbed the branch, swung and leaped to another across from it. The Piasa missed getting him while snapping off several smaller branches from where he had just departed. Mike was probably running out of tricks to fool the creature. Once more it crashed through the smaller branches and eyed him. From Mike's position, it was still at least twenty feet up to the cave and me. After that last exchange of movements, though, at least the Piasa was now below him.

At that point, it dawned on me. Would Mike have come alone?

I scanned the ground, and in a flash of lightning made out what looked like someone off to the left behind some bushes. Seeing similar bushes off to the right, I hoped there was someone there as well.

Knowing Mike needed help, I took a deep breath and hoped my voice could carry to whoever was there. "It can't move as well on the ground!" I screamed as loud as I could. "Make it come down to the ground!"

At the sound of my voice, Mike looked up and shouted at me. "Sara! Thank God you're okay. Get away from the entrance!"

The serpentine creature also eyed me and then started to slowly move up.

I tried to wiggle out of the rain and back into and away from the mouth of the cave, but found it was more difficult than crawling forward. My toes searched for a place to anchor me so I could wriggle back.

Suddenly there was the sound of several shots being fired. The Piasa let out a hideous shriek.

When I finally managed to get back to the cave opening and look out, I saw that the creature had apparently forgotten me and Mike in the tree, and was now quickly moving down the tree toward the ground below. Standing at the base of the tree, her revolver pointing up, was Pamela.

Mike again screamed for me to get away from the entrance.

Poised just above the ground, the creature looked up at the sound of Mike's voice. It immediately seemed to recall its former mission and started slithering back up.

"Oh no!" Pamela screamed. "Mike, watch out!" She fired another round at the creature in an attempt to lure it back to her. The Piasa looked back and hissed, but kept coming up the tree.

At that instant, a bolt of lightning struck the leaning tree, and it erupted in a shower of sparks and caught fire. The point of impact was about ten feet below Mike, who held fast, but precariously, to the top part of the tree.

Amidst a loud cracking noise, the bottom forty feet of the tree, with the creature in the middle of it, swayed unsteadily, then fell away to the ground.

Mike braced himself, expecting the top to also fall, but was surprised, as I was, that it held. Looking off to my right, I saw the branches from the crown were wedged in between some rocks in the bluffs above. I looked down at the Piasa, which had launched itself out of the tree when it crashed down.

While it stared at the fallen tree, I saw Russell run out from behind the bushes and fire several more shots at the creature. Again, the ear-shattering shrieking and hissing, and the creature drove toward Russell.

Mike turned and continued his climb toward the cave.

I watched as the Piasa attempted to lunge for Russell, but Pamela and Chester stepped out of the bushes and each fired at the creature.

The Piasa looked from Russell to Pamela to Chester and shrieked and hissed loudly while wheeling around in a half-circle. I almost felt sorry for it.

I looked back to Mike, who was ignoring the cracking and creaking sounds of the tree above him as he vaulted up the branches. I hoped he would make it up and into the cave while the group below kept the creature busy.

When he reached a position two feet below the cave entrance, the tree began to slide down, then stopped. Mike froze. I, as well as he, knew that too much movement would cause the tree to come completely loose from the rocks and plunge to the earth below.

As I looked into the branches, I couldn't believe my eyes—a rope! I cautiously reached over and gripped the cord. Slowly and carefully, I untied it from the branch that it had been attached to and searched the cave for somewhere to fasten it while making a noose with the end.

Spotting a small spire of rock that jutted out from the floor, I carefully looped the rope over and cinched it. Crawling to the lip of the cave, I tossed the rope down to Mike, who grabbed it and pulled it tight.

When I looked back down to the ground, I saw that the Piasa was unable to decide which prey to attack first. Then, the creature slithered toward Russell. It moved quicker than it did in the cave as it tried to head off Russell's retreat by moving diagonally at him.

Russell stopped and aimed at it, but the Piasa darted towards him. The sudden movement startled Russell, causing him to drop his weapon as he backed away. The Piasa raised its head high.

With a loud crack, the top of the tree pulled free from the rocks and slid down the bluffs. As the tree fell, Mike swung clear on the rope and quickly rappelled upward toward me and the cave.

As the Piasa prepared to strike Russell, the top of the tree landed with a resounding crash next to it. The clatter of the falling tree startled the creature and stole its attention away from its intended victim.

That allowed Russell the few precious seconds he needed to scoop up his gun and run into the bushes and relative safety.

I looked down into the smiling face of Mike, who was now just a foot below me.

Out of the corner of my eye, I caught movement below and watched as Chester stepped from the bushes to its far right and fired several shots at the creature. It turned and shrieked at Chester's disappearing figure. Then Pamela drew the creature's attention with a well-aimed volley that seemed to enrage it even more. It turned toward her.

"Now!" Pamela screamed, and Peter came scrambling from the bushes to the right of the creature and pulled on something. He had what looked like a black rock in his hand. With a deft toss, the projectile landed close to the Piasa's middle.

Momentarily shocked by what was tossed at it by its intended prey, the Piasa backed away, its head hovering ten feet above the object. The thing exploded, sending pieces of metal flying in all directions, including up into the Piasa. It reacted by squealing loudly. I heard pieces slashing through the bushes and saw leaves and branches flying.

I watched in horror as both Peter and Pamela fell backward, apparently hit by the jagged, flying pieces of whatever Peter had thrown at it.

After instinctively ducking when the object exploded, Mike remained about a foot below the cave entrance. He put his foot into a crevice and looked up towards the cave, now about eight inches above him. He finally pulled himself up to the level of the entrance and looked in.

I had backed up and was lying facing him, just back of the lip of the cave, in a great deal of pain, but I managed a smile. In a flash of lightning, Mike looked around the cave. I knew he was looking for some sign of Rachel.

"She's in the back tunnel, Mike," I said. "She's hurt bad."

Below, I could still hear the creature shrieking its anger and defiance at the prey that had hurt it. Several more shots rang out from the ground below, indicating the creature had not given up the fight.

Mike gripped the lip of rock at the entrance, and with great effort, pulled himself up and onto the floor of the cave.

Looking down, he withdrew a revolver from his belt and took careful aim at the Piasa below. Mike fired shots until the gun clicked on empty.

I could hear lots of flopping noises and shrieks and wails from the creature.

Mike threw the weapon down, gently picked me up and staggered toward the back of the cave.

I could hear loud hissing behind us. When I looked up, I saw the Piasa appear on the edge of the entrance and pull itself in. Blood oozed from several of the creature's wounds.

Mike plowed straight ahead in the dark cave. I was not sure if he was headed in the right direction. I envisioned him running smack into a wall. Luckily, a sudden flash of lightning from a new approaching storm weakly illuminated the back wall, and he saw the opening at the rear of the cave. I was horrified to see how big the opening was now.

"It's been trying to get to us," I said. "I think it can almost fit through now, but I couldn't leave Rachel behind."

With a hiss, the creature slowly plodded after us. Mike clutched me close and ducked through the opening into the tunnel. He turned and, in a sudden timely flash from the storm, I saw Rachel on the floor about twenty feet away.

The sound of movement behind us told me the Piasa was getting close. But Mike ducked down and quickly covered the distance even as the creature came partly through the hole and darted for him. He shielded me from the Piasa with his body. I turned and looked up. It was unable to reach us, its main body still too large to fit through the opening.

Mike slowly crawled forward while holding me tightly to him. As he turned to check on the Piasa's position, the dim glow from a sudden new flash of lightning revealed the creature was attempting to break through the remainder of the cavity.

He seemed calm as he carried me the rest of the way down the passage to where Rachel lay, barely visible even in the almost continuous lightning flashes. Setting me down, he then stumbled back and stared toward the rear wall of the cave and the Piasa.

When the next lightning bolt dimly illuminated the cave, I saw to my shock that it had resumed widening the hole. In seconds it would surely be able to get completely through. A sudden boom of thunder followed the lightning flash and caused the Piasa to instinctively pull its long neck from the hole and look back toward the cave's entrance.

It all happened so fast. I couldn't believe Mike's reactions. He reached under his shirt and extracted what I recognized as one of the black rocks that Peter threw at the creature. Pulling out something that apparently activated it, he moved forward a few feet and tossed it toward the hole in the cave wall, trying to get it through the crevice and under the Piasa before its head returned to block the opening. Just as the lobbed 'rock' reached the hole, the creature turned to continue its assault on the wall. The black 'rock' bounced off the long neck and back through the breach, falling onto the floor at the base of the opening. On our side.

I knew Mike had no time to retrieve it and throw it again, so I fully expected for the thing to explode and for all of us to die. Mike turned and raced back to where he had deposited me and fell on top of me and Rachel, attempting to shield our small bodies from the impending blast.

The Piasa hissed loudly, then I heard scraping noises. I assumed it was trying to pull back into the cave.

There was a tremendous explosion that lifted me off the floor of the cave despite Mike being on top of me. It was deafening. As I listened to the sounds of rocks and stuff clattering around the cave walls, I was surprised to realize I was still alive.

CHAPTER 27

Trapped
Later Friday Night...

"Mike," I whispered. "Are you okay?" I feared he had taken the brunt of the explosion to protect me and Rachel. My words sounded funny to me because, I realized, my ears were ringing at the same time. There was no sound from Mike, so I carefully wriggled myself out from under him.

I felt around and discovered he was absolutely covered in dirt, rock and debris. I was amazed to find he was still alive. I felt blood flowing on the back of his shirt from somewhere, but after a few minutes, he stirred and sat up. The ringing in my ears was subsiding, and I realized Mike was not only okay, but was talking to me.

". . . Don't worry, Sara, I'll get you both out of here."

"But you're hurt too. And what about the creature?"

"The good part is the cave is sealed off now, so it can't get to us. Don't worry about me. It's just a little cut."

"But you're bleeding," I said.

"Scratch," he insisted. To him, I realized, everything was like a nick.

"Do you think the creature is dead?"

"No, I doubt it. It escaped the full force of the blast. However, it's not our problem now."

"Yeah, well, now we're in perpetual darkness," I said. "I can actually feel the thick dust in the air. We must be breathing this stuff. That can't be good."

"That's the bad part. However, it's just local to here. As soon as we get a little way down the tunnel, the air will be clearer."

"It's so quiet," I whispered to Mike. "It's like I've gone deaf."

"We're just cut off from the sounds of the storm outside," Mike said. "Outside, the lightning is still sizzling and thunder cracking, but we can neither see, nor hear, evidence of either."

"What was that thing you threw at it? Some kind of bomb?"

"Hand grenade," he said. "A metal case filled with explosives. When it explodes, it throws out jagged pieces of metal. Luckily, neither you or Rachel got hit by any."

"Yeah, but you did."

"Scratch."

"Where did you get those things?"

"Russel brought them. Just the two of them. He collected them off some kid at the high school. Kid didn't even know what they were. Said his uncle brought them back from the Gulf War."

After a few minutes of me crawling and Mike carrying Rachel, the air was definitely clearer. The absence of the storm's noise made me want to freak out, because I knew that meant we were sealed in. With the cave entrance to the tunnel now blocked, and both Rachel and me so injured, the only way for Mike to get us out was by going the mile or so back down the tunnel to the parking area under the painting of the Piasa. In the darkest of dark. With Rachel unconscious and me unable to walk, it was hopeless. But Mike remained calm.

"Wait," I said. "What about going the other way to the tiger's secret entrance behind the bush. Wasn't that shorter?"

"I checked," he said. "Blocked by the explosion. Besides, if we go this way, once I get you two to the cave's entrance, I can make it down to the highway and get us help."

"Give it to me straight, Mike. Are we gonna get out of here?"

"Of course we will," he said. "Remember what I told you."

"You mean when the going gets tough, the tough get going?"

"Yup," he said.

Despite his words, I was sure I was going to die. The realization came to me that even if the dust was settled elsewhere in the tunnel, it was pitch black. We would be completely disoriented in the unlit cavern.

I felt Mike's hand on my shoulder. He gave it a small squeeze and said. "Trust me. Are you still bleeding?"

"Yes," I said. My voice sounded small and frantic in comparison to his cool and composed manner. "I fell when that thing came into the cave, and a bone stuck pretty deep into my thigh. My feet got all cut up when I ran across all the old bones in the cave trying to get away. My leg and feet are bleeding, and they hurt real bad." I quieted a moment as a sob I didn't want him to hear came out. "Rachel bandaged them up but then she ran smack into the wall and her face is all bloody. Will she die?"

"She has a good pulse, nice and steady. You've got to keep it together. The problem is I can't see a thing. How did your feet get all cut up? Weren't you wearing the boots?"

"No, I had my sandals on, but I lost one. You know I like to go barefooted. I'm sorry, Mike. I'm so much trouble, and I don't listen to you when I should." I was on the verge of losing it.

"Don't worry, it's a life lesson. I'll get you out of here. Can you walk?"

After a short pause, I answered, "No, but I can crawl."

214

"Look, Sara, you're both small, but I can't carry you both and feel ahead to make sure I don't walk smack into a rock. You're about the same size, so I'm going to take Rachel's shoes off and have you put them on. You should be able to walk slowly then. I know it'll still hurt, but your cuts shouldn't get any worse and we'll leave it to the doctors to sort out. Are you willing?"

He waited, so darn patient and relaxed. I'm sure he knew, from the sounds I was making, that I was getting my initial panic under control and regaining my courage. I finally said softly, "I'll try walking even if they don't fit. Rachel wrapped some makeshift bandages on my feet."

"Well, let's hope the shoes fit over them. In the meantime, try to keep from breathing this dust in." He found Rachel's feet and removed one shoe. "Lucky for you, she's wearing tennis shoes. They'll give you some support and cut down on your pain. Put your right foot up toward the sound of my voice, Sara."

I put my foot up in his direction, and he found it and gripped my ankle. As he did so, surprisingly, I chuckled.

"What's so funny?" he asked. "I'm glad you see humor in our situation. That's good, don't think about bad things."

"I was thinking of last night. When I thought I got bit and I cried like a baby. Now look at the scratches."

Mike chuckled and carefully slid his hand down the bottom of my bloodied foot. "I'm just trying to remove any small pebbles stuck to it," he said. "Tell me if I touch a particularly painful spot."

"No," I said. "It's okay."

He then slipped the shoe on and found it was only a half-inch or so too big.

"How's that fit, too loose?"

"I have really small feet, Mike. But the bandages take up some of the slack. I think it'll be okay," I apologized.

"You're doing fine, don't tense up," Mike said. His words soothed me.

"Let me get her other shoe off. Put up your other foot." He quickly recovered Rachel's other shoe, then carefully checked my other foot for stray pebbles and put it on.

"Try standing up," he advised.

I carefully stood up and tested my feet. Pain was still there, but it was more bearable. "It'll be okay. Just take care of Rachel. Don't worry about me. I still can't believe you found us. How did you know—"

"We'll get to that later."

"I'm sorry for disobeying you, Mike. We just—"

"It's okay, Sara. Don't worry, we'll get out of this. Try to stay right behind me." From the sounds I heard, I knew that Mike had picked up Rachel. "You ready?"

"Yes." I gripped the back of his belt as we started up the dark passage.

I fought the urge to cry as I stumbled along behind Mike. I had told him the shoes from Rachel helped, but the pain was getting worse as we stumbled forward down the black abyss. Each step caused me to wince and pray that Mike would stop and take a break. Several times I stubbed my toe on outcroppings of rock, and I'd scream out loud. Each time, Mike would stop and talk soothingly to me.

I tried to put the pain out of my mind, choosing instead to dwell on the miracle of him coming back, and not only finding us, but risking his life to protect Rachel and me. How could I have given him such a hard time previously? I realized that Pamela was right, not all guys were created equal. He was not in the same mold as my stepfather or brother, or any of the guys at my high school for that matter. But just how special was he? Will it be possible to find some guy my age, but like him, when I was ready to get serious about dating? Who was I kidding? How would I find someone, anyone, when I was all scarred up?

Something to ask Pamela about, I thought.

As I bounced off another outcrop of rock, I remembered where I was. What was I thinking? I'll never even see Pamela again.

A half-hour later, Mike reeled back, after yet again walking into the wall of the cave.

In the darkness of the underground chamber, I knew he had a hard time walking while also carrying Rachel and looking after me dragging along behind him. I'm sure he knew I was at the end of my rope. I could tell even he began to tire from the effort, and I realized his wound must be sapping what remained of his strength. I was acutely aware that our situation was getting very grave.

Although Mike said she still had a weak pulse, Rachel had not stirred. Mike estimated it would still take another hour, based on our present speed, till we got out of the cave. I didn't have an hour. I don't think I had two minutes left in me.

If only we could see where we were going.

Completely spent, I tugged at his belt.

"Are you okay, Sara? You've been awfully quiet."

"Can we stop a minute, Mike? Is Rachel going to be all right?"

"I hope so, Sara, I hope so. I wish I could see her face to determine the extent of her injury, but I don't want to take a chance of damaging anything by pawing at it in the dark. I'm impressed at how brave you've been. How is your leg?"

"Just a few more scars, I guess. My thigh seems to be stiff. It still hurts real bad."

"Is it still bleeding?"

"No, it stopped, and I'm trying to walk very carefully so I don't start it up again."

While he talked to me, Rachel stirred in his arms and moaned, then whispered, "What happened? Sara?"

"It's Mike, Rachel, try not to talk. We're in the cave. Don't worry, we'll get out of here."

"What happened? Where's Sara?"

"Sara is right here with us. You ran face-first into a wall, and I assume you have at least a concussion. Your face is cut up, but I can't see it in the dark," Mike advised.

"Are we gonna get out?" she whispered. With a start she seemed to remember and whispered, "That creature . . . is it?"

"Gone, we hope. We'll make it, Rachel; we'll make it. Do you feel any pain?"

"Under my eyes and I've got a terrible headache. I think I'm gonna . . . pass out."

"I can't see to do anything with your injuries. Hang in there, Rachel." Mike again started forward. I knew I couldn't last long, but I didn't want to tell him. He had enough to worry about.

From up ahead, I thought I saw a diffused light . . . then nothing. Then, as Mike felt his way around a corner, someone shone a flashlight on him, then me.

"Mike, Sara, thank God. Is Rachel okay?" Pamela asked.

"Barely," Mike replied. "You're an angel. How are the others?"

Pamela looked over at him. "Russell and Chester are taking Peter to the hospital. He caught some of that shrapnel from the grenade he tossed at it. I think he'll be okay. Let's have a look at Sara and Rachel."

Illuminated by Pamela's light, I looked over, wiped the tears of joy from my face and tried to smile. "Hi, Pamela . . . can't believe . . . you came. I saw you get hit by that blast also."

Pamela bent over and gently tossed my dust-caked hair with her hand. "Nothing to write home about, just a scratch. Us reds have to stick together."

Mike carefully set Rachel down. "Sara's thigh got punctured by something and her feet got badly cut up when she ran across the bones in that cave. I'm afraid of an infection from all that was in there. We put Rachel's shoes on her feet, so she could walk. I don't think we want to take them off. Let's leave that for the doctors."

Pamela nodded in agreement as Mike continued, "I haven't been able to see Rachel. She ran into the wall and got a concussion. Her face is bleeding . . ." Mike stopped talking when Pamela trained the light on Rachel's face.

With a sigh of relief, Pamela said, "It was her glasses. They must have dug into the skin under her eyes. How about you, Mike? Any wounds from the explosion?"

"I think I caught a piece of shrapnel in my back, but it's okay."

"Turn around, big guy." As Mike did so, Pamela quickly checked his back. "You have a hole in the back of your shirt," Pamela said. "Stay turned around."

Pamela examined his back closer and continued, "Well, it looks like you have a hunk of shrapnel or something lodged in you too. It looks like it stopped bleeding, so I won't pull it out and start it up again. You really feel okay?"

"Yeah, never better. You lead and I'll carry Rachel and Sara. Sara, you grab me around my neck and wrap your legs around me."

"I'm okay," I lied. "I can shuffle behind you. I don't want to be a burden."

"Nonsense to both of you," Pamela said. "I'll carry Sara. No sense in her little feet taking any more punishment than necessary. Grab me around the neck and wrap your legs around, Sara."

"But I can—"

"Do it!"

I immediately gripped my arms around Pamela's neck, and we started forward.

"Your leg's bleeding, Pamela," I said.

"It's just a scratch." What was it with both of them? Everything was 'just a scratch.'

With me holding Pamela's light to guide us, we reached the entrance to the caves below the Piasa painting a short time later. Coming out in a steady rain, I was grateful to see several ambulances and a sea of police cars.

Paramedics carefully took Rachel and loaded her onto a stretcher. When they took me from Pamela, I asked, "Can I please just stand in the rain for a minute? It feels wonderful." The rain caused small valleys in the caked dust and grime that covered my entire body.

"Enough, Sara," Pamela said and nodded to the paramedics. As one of them gently helped me inside the vehicle, Pamela pushed Mike forward into the ambulance with me and pointed out his back to one of the paramedics.

PIASA

"She's cut too," I told the paramedic who was treating me. "Don't let her get away."

. He immediately looked over at the wound on Pamela's leg and told a policeman to make sure she was put in the other ambulance with Rachel. Then I passed out.

Chapter 28

Alton Hospital
Saturday Morning…

When I awoke, one look at my surroundings told me I was once again at the Alton Hospital. But, I was happy to have thus far survived. Mike appeared asleep in a chair on one side of me and Pamela on the other. I closed my eyes when I heard footsteps just outside.

"Good morning, Dr. Smart," Pamela said.

"What's the bottom line, Doctor?" Mike asked.

"We've cleaned the wounds pretty thoroughly, and I'm sure we've arrested any potential infection," Dr. Smart said. "The puncture in her thigh caused her to lose a lot of blood, but it'll cause no permanent damage. She's on antibiotics, so we just wait and see how she responds."

"How about her feet?" Pamela asked.

"They were pretty nasty cuts. However, despite them being a little tender for a while, we should be able to let her go home in a day or so. She is one tough girl."

After the doctor left, it was relatively quiet for a minute or two.

"Did you hear what you wanted to hear, Sara?" Mike asked.

I peeked out and saw both Pamela and Mike staring down at me.

"I told you she was faking," Mike said to Pamela.

"Do you like have some kind of a sixth sense?" I asked.

He moved over to the side of my bed and grinned down. "I saw the smile when she said you were tough."

I smiled back up. "Hi, Mike," I said quietly. "Hi, Pamela."

As Mike reached back and pulled over a chair, Pamela sat next to me on the bed and said, "Hi, Sara. How you doing?"

I scrunched up my face as I asked, "How did they look?"

Mike looked at me quizzically. "What?" he asked.

"My feet. They must look pretty bad."

Mike looked down toward the base of the bed at my bandaged feet. "I didn't think so, but I'm not a doctor. Anyway, the cuts were on the bottom of your feet. Who looks at the bottom of their feet?"

"I do," I said. "I can put my toes in my mouth. Now I'll have more scars."

"Yeah," Pamela said. "But Dr. Smart said the puncture wound will close up nice and tight and be barely visible. She also said you're becoming a regular patient. And that you must be incredibly brave."

I then brightened up. "I can tell people I was bitten by the Piasa. That's even better than a great white shark."

"The Piasa, huh?" Pamela said.

"Yeah, that's what Rachel told me. She says it has to be the Piasa. But I know Mike thinks it's his lake serpent thing. Which do you think it could be, Pamela?"

"Well, they could both be right," Pamela said with a glance at Mike.

"How is Rachel doing?" I asked.

"Good," she said. "She has those cuts under her eyes from her glasses which are not serious. They took her down for some test on her head, but they think it was just a concussion."

"I'm willing to bet they find it empty," Mike said. "For that matter, maybe they should take Sara down for tests on her head. I think I already know the result of that, too—empty." Mike paused as I narrowed my eyes, then he smiled over at me. "What made the two of you go into that cave? I thought we had a deal. You were supposed to go back and . . . Say, whose lamebrained idea was it, anyway?"

"Rachel's, but I'm guilty too. I thought it was a great idea." I paused as I studied Mike's stony face. "At the time, anyway. How were we supposed to know . . ." I trailed off as Mike's expression did not change.

"Are you mad at me?" I finally croaked out the words.

Mike's stony face gradually dissolved into a grin. "How can I stay mad at my assistant?"

I happily scrunched up my face after realizing he was just needling me. "Thanks, that makes me feel better. Anyway, the pain is going away."

"The doctor told us you had been very lucky that you were cut the way you were," Pamela said. "She said if some of those slices were closer to your toes, you could have lost them."

For a short period we were all quiet.

"Did you kill it?" I whispered.

Mike bowed his head and then looked at Pamela. "We don't know. Pamela and I are taking a boat out, along with Peter and Merle, to check for any sign of where it had its den. Pamela was the last one to see it, and she saw it dive into the river. They're dragging the site for it, but I don't think they'll find anything. The current is just too swift. No telling where it could end up. If, in fact, it actually died." Mike noticed my eyes were at half-mast. I was in need of sleep but would not admit it. I didn't want them to leave.

PIASA

As I fought the darkness closing in, I quietly asked, "You're hoping it didn't die, aren't you?" Mike nodded and I continued. "I should be driving the boat. Can you handle things without me?"

Mike smiled down. "I'll try, partner. Get some sleep." He and Pamela turned to go.

"Mike," I whispered. "Thank you. I knew you'd come for me. But you didn't tell me how you knew we were in . . ." With that, I guess I drifted off to sleep.

I awoke sometime later after thrashing around in the grips of a nightmare. Sweat beaded on my forehead as I recalled I was trying to grab onto Mike as he stepped into what I perceived was a trap. From somewhere, I heard a knocking sound.

I tried to place it and . . . sat up in bed with a start. Sweat was rolling down my face as I stared at two men standing in the doorway to my room. One was distinguished and older with graying light brown hair. The other looked very young. Actually, he couldn't be much older than me, maybe eighteen. The younger one gawked back at me with his mouth hanging open. For a second, no one spoke as the three of us stared at one another.

Finally, the older man asked. "Young lady, are you Sara Williams?"

I looked over at him. "Yes, yes, I am. Who are you?"

"I'm Professor Paul Wiggins, Miss Williams, a friend of Mike's from the museum. This is Fernando Elkins, he also works for the museum." At the sound of his name, Fernando recovered from his apparent discomfort and followed Professor Wiggins into the room. He continued to gaze, but close-mouthed, over at me.

"I'm pleased to meet you, Professor Wiggins," I said nervously, then looked over at Fernando. "Hello, Fernando." Sweating profusely, I probably looked a sight.

"Where is Mike?" Professor Wiggins asked.

I snapped my gaze from Fernando and affixed a steely glare on the professor. "He went to find out if the Piasa is dead or still alive."

Professor Wiggins walked all the way into the room and looked intently at me. "I thought the creature was dead," he said.

"I think Mike needs to see a body," I replied.

Coming up from behind the professor and Fernando, Rachel peeked in with a huge grin, held up her hand and waved just her four fingers while holding her wrist steady. On her raccoon-like face—she still had two black eyes from her crashing into the cave wall—was a big smile. "Sara! You're sitting up. Are you feeling better?"

"Rachel! I'm feeling much better. Are you going home?" I asked.

She nodded. "My mom's taking me. She gets off shift shortly."

At the mention of her name, the professor turned to her. "Rachel? Are you Rachel Franklin?" he asked. Rachel bobbed her head. The professor held out his hand to her. "I am Paul Wiggins. This is Fernando Elkins."

I was confused. What were they doing here?

Rachel reached out and took his hand while smiling to Fernando. The professor lightly squeezed her hand and, while still holding it, looked squarely at her. "Mike works for me, Miss Franklin, and upon his recommendation, I wish to discuss something with you."

He finally released her hand and glanced over at me. "I think Miss Williams should get some rest, however."

At the mention of my name, I struggled to dispel the exhaustion he apparently saw painted on my face. "Would you accompany me to the cafeteria?" the professor asked Rachel.

Rachel, with a perplexed look on her face, stepped out into the hallway. The professor looked over at me and said to Fernando. "On second thought, why don't you stay and keep Sara company? I'll be back shortly."

Fernando turned and smiled as the professor, gripping Rachel's arm as if he was afraid she would run off, left the room.

"Is it okay?" Fernando asked.

I gave him a shy grin. He was cute.

I watched quietly as Fernando nervously fidgeted at the side of my bed. I wasn't very good with guys near my age, and they usually ignored me anyway. I was uneasy with his presence. I'm sure he'd rather have gone with the professor. Finally, I asked, "So, what do you do at the museum?"

"I'm a guard normally, but I was asked to drive the professor here."

"Wow, exciting. Do you know Mike well?"

"No, I've never met him. I only just started. It's really not that exciting, I mainly spend my time trying to keep teenagers in line."

"Teenagers? Like me? Like you?"

He shook his head. "Sorry. That must have sounded stupid. I don't talk to pretty girls much."

That was a first. A boy saying I was pretty. "Me? Pretty? I've got a lot of scars."

He paused, and I noticed him staring towards my bandaged feet. "Did you get hurt bad?" he asked.

"I don't know. They haven't told me much." I reached for a glass of water, causing my leg to come out from beneath the sheets. He saw the scar from the auto accident and the heavy bandage on my thigh.

"Did it do that too?" he asked.

"Yes and no," I said. "It did this one." I pointed to my bandaged thigh. Pointing to the scar from the auto accident, I said, "I was bitten by a great . . ." I paused as the little white lie words seemed caught in my throat. Heck, I couldn't tell him that. Finally, I looked down and said, "I was also in an auto accident. Like I said, I've got a lot of scars. Do you still think I'm pretty?"

"You're beautiful," he said.

* * *

"He offered me a job!" Rachel practically screamed the words at me as she ran into my room. "Professor Wiggins is giving me a job with the museum in Chicago. Isn't that great?"

"Wow," I said. "That's great, Rachel." So much for having a friend down here in Alton. I was happy for her, though. She deserved a break from somewhere.

"Come, Fernando," the professor said. "Mike finally answered his phone, and I must meet with him before we drive back to the city. It was a pleasure to meet you, Miss Williams."

"Sara," I said. "My name is Sara."

He smiled. "You've been around Mike too long." He turned to Rachel and said, "Don't forget next week, Friday. Come up to the museum, and I will introduce you around. Then you can return here and get started."

"Return here?" I said. "You're coming back?"

"Yes. I'm to work with Mike on an exhibit about the creature here."

"Mike's coming back too?" I asked.

"No," the professor said. "He's too busy with other projects. He'll just oversee this from the museum."

"We're going to re-excavate that cave of bones," Rachel said excitedly. "I have to gather all of the stories from this area, and of course the bluffs area where the creature came from needs to be explored. All of this will be my job. Do you want to help?"

"Yes, I'd love to." I would really rather be joining my friends in Chicago, but I couldn't tell Rachel that. However, I wasn't looking forward to going to Alton High.

"Don't forget to keep an open mind," the professor said to Rachel. "I hope you have learned that from Mike."

"I've learned a lot of things from Mike," Rachel said. "But that's not one of them. He didn't believe in the Piasa. I did."

"Piasa? You think this creature was the Piasa?" the professor said.

"Why yes, what else could it be?" Rachel said.

"Correct me if I'm wrong, but didn't your Piasa have wings?

225

"Well, uh . . . yes, but maybe they—"

"Does Mike agree with you?"

"Well, no. Mike thinks it's some kind of lake serpent."

The professor laughed. "But it is, Rachel, that's exactly what it is. Didn't you know that?" The professor still chuckled as he and Fernando left.

"They know," Rachel said.

"Know what?" I asked.

"That I'm only seventeen. Mike told the professor, but said he'd vouch for my capabilities. My mom told him when they brought me in. He came and saw me and said he'd still hire me as long as I finished high school. He then wants me to go to college. The job with the museum is part-time, so I can still keep my job at the restaurant. We can be a team, Sara."

Chapter 29

What Was It?
Sunday Afternoon...

The following afternoon, Mike walked into my hospital room while Rachel was sitting in a chair, keeping me company.

"Mike," Rachel said. "Thank you. Professor Wiggins said you recommended me for this job. I don't know how to thank you enough. "

"You earned that job, despite your little cave exploration shenanigan. In fact, that may have helped get you the job. No thanks are necessary. Don't forget our agreement. How are you doing, Sara?"

"Okay," I lied. Oh, physically I was alright, and I knew I'd get better, but I wished he could stay here in Alton. "How soon are you going back?"

"I was originally trying to get on the road tomorrow afternoon. I just need to wrap up a few things. But now I think it'll be a few days."

"Did you see it?" Rachel urged.

"See what?" Mike asked.

"The eagle. Pamela said you two could find no trace of the Piasa, uh, I mean lake serpent."

Mike laughed. "Paul straightened you out on that, huh? Who knows, though, they could be one and the same."

"But back to the eagle. Pamela said she thought you considered that the real Piasa. Is that right? Could that have been the Piasa?"

"I don't know, Rachel, it's just my theory. The bird described around here matches the harpy eagle, except for the enormous size. The harpy has a distinguished crest that could be what the painting on the cliff tried to show. The huge claws shown on his feet . . ." Mike paused. "But the lake serpent had a crest too. Who knows? Depends on your point of view."

"What do you think, Mike?" I asked. "Did the thing die when the cave exploded? Is it buried in the rubble?"

"No. Pamela saw it come down the cliff after the explosion, and it went back into the river. She and I have searched up and down the river for miles. Nothing. Maybe it's dead . . . we just don't know."

"You never told me how you found Rachel and me. How did you even know I was in trouble?"

Mike gave both of us a stern look. "When you failed to phone me, I called Claire. She said you never showed up. That was our deal, remember? You were to call me?"

I nodded sheepishly.

"Pamela called the station and asked them to look for the boat. One of the patrol cars reported it ashore at the cave location. Plus, Rachel's mother called her in as missing. It didn't take a mental giant to figure out what you two were up to. We traced Claire's cell phone, that you had luckily left on, to the cliffs."

"Sorry, Mike," I said.

"Are you going to pursue the big bird reports?" Rachel said.

"Pursue? The bird is gone. Last I heard, there was a report from Lacrosse, Wisconsin, of an unusually large bird. What's to pursue?"

"Which one do you really think matches the legend of the Piasa?" Rachel asked.

"You'll remember there were two petroglyphs. A large eagle and what resembled the lake serpent," Mike pointed out.

"That's not answering my ques—"

"What did the Native Americans say Piasa meant, Rachel?"

"The bird that devours men."

"That's your answer."

Rachel smiled. "Thanks. I feel I won a small victory."

* * *

Two days later, in the late afternoon twilight, I sat outside the Cavern with Mike. It was still a little hard to walk on my feet and my thigh ached, but it was good to be home. Despite Dr. Smart's order not to walk, I was able to by perching up on my toes. Mike gave in to my insistence and let me continue to stay in the Cavern. In fact, he paid Aunt Claire for two months' rent on the Cavern so that I would have a place of my own. He was leaving the next day for Chicago.

We sat in silence while he quietly nursed a bottle of beer. The air was clean and clear following the two days of heavy rains. Remnants of the slow-moving storm had by now curved northeast and lashed central Illinois while grinding toward the east coast. Mike and I listened to the sounds of insects buzzing around and small creatures scurrying in the night.

"Knock, knock," came a female voice from behind us.

I turned to see Pamela, in uniform, looking around the corner of the cottage.

"I just got off. Gotta 'nother of those beers?"

"You bet, sit down. I'll get you one," I said.

"No," Pamela said. "Sit on your keister. I'll get them, Sara. On second thought, is it okay if I borrow Mike to talk to for a few minutes?"

"Sure," I said. I didn't need a piano to fall on me. I knew she wanted to be alone with him. "I'll go read my book."

I tottered in on my toes while Pamela quickly grabbed a six-pack from the fridge. As she left the Cavern, I told her to just yell if they needed refills. Luckily the kitchen window was open, so I sat up against the outside wall, making sure my head was below the window so they couldn't see or hear me, and listened.

First of all, Mike and Pamela talked over the happenings of the last few days. I could tell Pamela started to relax after having two beers, and despite her protests, Mike quickly opened and gave her another. With a giggle, she took the beer and quickly drank half of it. I know cause I peeked.

I could tell she had something on her mind, but Mike failed to pick up on her uneasiness. In that way he was just like any guy.

As Pamela took what looked like a final swig of her beer, Mike looked at her intently. I had by now found a comfortable position where I could not only hear what they were saying but see them. At first I felt guilty, but then I knew that if I asked Pamela what they talked about, she'd say, 'Nothing.'

Mike suddenly asked her, "What kind of job are you looking for?"

Pamela set the empty bottle next to the two she had previously finished and looked down at her watch. "Well, keep in mind this is coming from a girl who never has more than two beers and just now sucked her third dry and is contemplating a fourth. Also, I haven't gotten more than four hours sleep in the past three days. All from hanging around you." Pamela paused.

"I'll still like to hear your plans, no matter what," Mike replied. "You are the most amazing woman I've ever met." He slurred some of the words.

Pamela giggled. "You know we should just end this before we say something we shouldn't. We're both quite drunk and . . ."

NO, keep talking, I thought.

"You're not that drunk and neither am I." Mike sobered. "What do you want to do?"

"No, I guess I'm really not. I was trying to excuse myself from your question." Pamela's face took on a serious grimace. "Look, Mike, I like my kind of work, but there's no future here for me. I feel funny telling you all of this. We talked about it when we were searching the shoreline south of St Louis the other day." Mike nodded along as Pamela spoke. When he noticed she had stopped, he looked up.

"Have you thought of getting a job where you'd have more opportunity?" he asked.

Pamela shook her head. "Enough of my problems," she said. "What are you doing when you get back?"

"As soon as I get back, I've got to go to England and then Africa. Follow up on other projects, you know. Another beer?"

"You are a piece of work." Pamela snickered, then snorted. "I'd better get home and to sleep—"

"What do you mean, piece of work?"

Pamela stared at Mike quietly. "I've gotta go." She shakily got up.

"So what *do* you work for, Pamela? In that boat, you told me it wasn't money. What drives you on?"

Pamela eyed Mike questioningly. She sat back down and shook her head. "I've really gotta go," she whispered softly. Mike reached over and gripped her hands.

"You're in no condition to drive," Mike pointed out. "You ought to know that, you're a cop. Stay here, you can trust me."

"No, I don't trust myself, and I'm not gonna force you out of your bed on your last night here."

"It's Sara's bed. Besides, I'm fine sleeping anywhere."

Pamela stared over at Mike, looked away and said, "Look, Mike. In case you haven't picked up on the clues, I'm having trouble sleeping after all that's been going on. That's why I went to work. I'm not as tough as you might think. With all that's happened . . . I'm not going to sleep anyway . . ." she trailed off. "Chet and Uncle Russ were right. I let my job get to me too much. I'm working tomorrow, and then they're letting me take leave for a month or so." Pamela bowed her head and stared down.

Mike got up and pulled her up to her feet and said, "Let's go inside. Maybe we can work something out."

Pamela affixed Mike with a sleepy stare. Mike leaned down and kissed her softly as her arms wrapped around his neck. They quietly hung on each other until Pamela backed away.

"I like how you work things out," she said as she attempted to pull him toward the Cavern.

Mike stood his ground, forcing her back. "What," he insisted, "drives you on?"

Pamela gave him a coy smile and asked, "What's the last thing you came up here for?"

Quickly, I hopped into the bedroom as they came in through the kitchen door.

Mike and Pamela came into the bedroom, and Mike looked down on me as I pretended to read my book. "Hear what you wanted to?" he asked.

"Huh?" I said, pretending to not understand his inference.

He picked the book out of my hands and showed me the cover. It was Pamela's book, a steamy romance novel that I had grabbed by mistake.

"You are so busted, girl," Pamela giggled. "I won't tell Claire you were reading this smut if you do me a favor."

"What?" I said.

"Sleep on the roll-out tonight and don't come into this room."

"Deal," I smiled.

CHAPTER 30

Going Home
Wednesday Morning...

Late the next morning, I awoke from a nightmare in which I was being chased by the lake serpent. The creature had just seized me in its mouth when I awoke with a start because I had heard . . . What?

"Hey, sleepyhead, it's about time you got up. You're throwing me way behind schedule," Mike said from the foot of the roll-out bed.

"Mike!" I said softly. "How long have you been standing there?"

"Long enough to count the cuts and scratches on the bottoms of your feet," he answered.

I looked down to see my unbandaged feet sticking out from the sheets. I immediately noticed I needed a fresh coat of yellow polish on my nails.

"Thirty-seven," Mike said.

"Huh?" I asked. I'm sure I had that clueless, puzzled look on my face.

"Cuts and scratches. How ya feeling?"

"Pretty good. I tried walking around a little this morning, after I got up for the bathroom. I found this way to switch from my toes to my heels without much pain. I didn't peek on you guys. I promise."

Mike just laughed. "We were probably already having breakfast at the house," he said. "Pamela had an early shift."

"She's gone already?"

He nodded. "How's the leg?"

"It's kind of stiff, but it's working okay. I'm supposed to go back today and have it checked out. I forgot to tell Aunt Claire."

"I'll do it," said Mike.

"You'll tell Aunt Claire?"

"No, I'll take you."

"I thought you had to leave today."

"Someone talked me into staying another day. I'll catch the blazes from Paul, but I'm used to that. Besides, if we get done early enough, I can still hit the road later."

* * *

Mike stood by the side of his car with my doctor while two nurses maneuvered me out of the wheelchair and onto the front seat of his car. I was a little embarrassed, as I had fallen asleep waiting for the doctor. I had slept through my doctor's final checkup and had missed seeing Pamela, who had apparently stopped by and painted my nails.

"Okay," Mike said. "I need to get out on the road. I'm kinda anxious to get back to the Windy City. But first, let's get you over to your Aunt Claire's."

As I settled onto the front passenger seat, I winced a little as my lightly bandaged feet, fresh from poking and prodding by Dr. Smart, touched the floor of the car.

"Goodbye, Sara." The chorus came from the nurses as they left. Dr. Smart lingered temporarily, and I leaned my head out of the window and listened to her final instructions while Mike went around to the driver's side and got in.

"Don't forget, Sara, no walking, no hiking, no exercise, no nothing until you get the okay. I'll see you in a couple of days and we'll get those stitches out. We'll have you back on your feet in no time."

I gave her my brightest smile at that good news. I never told her about my ability to walk using just my toes. I knew she'd order me to stop and Mike would see to it I followed her orders. Besides, they were my feet, and what she didn't know . . .

"I especially don't want to hear you were walking on your toes, Sara. You can start that in about a week."

I assumed that Pamela had ratted me out.

When the doctor walked away, Mike started the car. Elvis popped on, singing "Viva Las Vegas."

I frowned and gave Mike my best pout.

Mike reached over and pressed the skip-to-the-next-CD button. Alanis sang about "Eight Easy Steps."

I instantly smiled and looked over at him. "You put that in for me?"

Mike nodded and pulled out of the hospital parking lot.

I punched the skip button to my favorite, number six, "Precious Illusions." Alanis began singing about someone rescuing her.

I relaxed as I listened to Alanis's special words to me and looked out the side window. All morning I had told myself I would be brave when Mike left. I so envied him going to Chicago. I had so wanted to return to Magnolia High and my friends. Maybe when I was older . . .

Coming up on University Avenue, Mike made a left turn and accelerated. After looking at his watch, I noticed his frown. I watched as he stepped on the gas, I knew he was as anxious to leave Alton as I was for him to stay.

I slipped my bandaged feet up on the dash. Looking up, I could see my exposed toes and the numerous cuts and scratches on them reflected in the windshield, but now I was oblivious of them.

"Put your feet down," Mike said. "If for some reason the airbag deployed, it would crush your legs and seriously injure you."

Knowing he was surely right, I silently put my feet down and returned my gaze out the side window as I mouthed the words of Alanis's song.

As Mike zipped by the next cross street, an Alton police car turned on its flashing lights and pulled out behind him. Mike glided over to the side of the road and looked over at me.

I grinned at him. "You had to pick up a souvenir, didn't you?"

Mike shook his head.

The police officer walked up to the car and stuck her head down. "Going kind of fast . . . Mike! Sara!"

I let out a shriek. "Pamela!"

"How are you, Sara?" Pamela asked.

"Great. The stitches come out and the bandages come off for good in a couple of days. Thanks for coming to the hospital and doing my nails."

"I didn't come to the hospital and do your nails. I've been at work since four this morning," Pamela replied.

"But if you didn't do them, who did?" I asked. "Mike?"

"I brought it for you to do, but you were sleeping. I was going to ask the nurses to do it but they seemed too busy and, since I used to do Crystal's, it wasn't like I was a greenhorn. Did I do okay? Mike said.

"So you must have snitched I was walking on my toes, too."

Mike grinned and looked down at his watch. "So, do I get a speeding ticket or what, Pamela?"

Pamela sucked in her breath and a strange look crossed her face.

"You okay, Pamela?" Mike asked.

Pamela nodded. "Yeah, I'm okay. I just recalled something in a dream and I got a sudden chill. No ticket, Mike. I was just about to call it quits for the day when you zipped by. Sorry, I didn't recognize the car."

Mike winked up at her, then asked, "We're headed over to Claire's. Follow us."

"Sure," Pamela said, then glanced over as I put my feet up on the edge of the seat and fanned my toes. Contented, I grinned back at her while twirling my hair between fingers.

"God, we are a lot alike," Pamela said to me. "We even have the same habits."

* * *

Mike pulled into the driveway of the Dahlgren House with Pamela behind him in the patrol car. After parking, she came over and helped me out of the car. Together we walked up to the front door that Claire held open and we all sat down at the dining room table.

"Wait a minute. I almost forgot." Pamela hurried back outside.

"Can you stay for lunch, Mike? It's all ready," Claire asked.

"Mike? Can you stay?" I asked eagerly, anxious to delay his departure as much as possible.

Mike looked at his watch and grudgingly nodded his agreement as Pamela returned. She reached over and handed me a CD case.

I took the case and screamed, "My Alanis CD case! Where did you find it?"

"Funny thing. While they were dragging the river at the spot I saw the creature dive in, I sat down on the bank and found it wedged in between two rocks. Then it dawned on me that the cave was located across the highway from the spot where you had the accident. The case must have been lying there all this time. In all the excitement, I forgot to give it to you before."

"I hope you're planning on staying for lunch, Pamela," Claire asked.

Pamela smiled sweetly at me, then Mike. "Of course. I wouldn't miss this for the world."

I raised my eyebrows at Pamela's response, but said nothing. I wondered what had happened between them last night after I went to sleep. I also knew, though, that it was none of my business. Looking over at Mike, I asked, "I've been meaning to ask you, you said someone asked you to stay another day. Who was that?"

"That was me, Sara," Pamela replied. "I asked Mike to stay. I wasn't sure if I could get off in time to get everything done. I'm going on a month's leave from the department, and I had a proposition for him that we needed to work out."

I looked from Mike to Pamela as a questioning look formed on my face. "I don't understand . . ." I said.

"Mike will explain it all to you. I've got to turn in the patrol car and get back to my place so I'll be ready."

"Ready for what?" I asked.

Pamela smiled. "I think Mike should tell you." Pamela got up and waved over to Claire and left. I looked at Mike questioningly.

"Eat your lunch," Mike announced. "I promised Paul I'd be in at work tomorrow. By the time we load your stuff in the car and meet up with Pamela and help her with her stuff . . ."

I stared open-mouthed at him. "Load my stuff? Meet up with Pamela? Load her stuff?"

Claire walked over in front of me and folded her hands. "It's not that I'm getting sick of having you around, I just know you wouldn't be happy at Alton High. When Mike told me he lived close to Magnolia, I approached him about you staying with him during the school year."

Mike continued, "Obviously, everyone thought it was a great idea, but I thought it really might get tongues wagging in my neighborhood. I don't care what people think about me, but I was not going to put you in a position where people thought . . . well, thought less of you for living with some old guy. Then Pamela suggested that she come up with us and she'll stay with you during the week in your parents' house. I suggested that you both come by me on the weekends. When I'm in town, that is."

By now, I'm sure tears were carving streaks down my cheeks as Claire moved behind me and hugged me tight.

"I thought . . . What about the doctor?" I stammered out, still stunned at this news. *Why was I concerned with that?*

"I'll bring you down to see the doc, but she also gave me a copy of your records so that they could take care of you in Chicago if need be. I'll take you in right away for a checkup so there won't be any problems."

"What about Pamela's job?" I said, while trying to stifle my instinct to cry at this happy turn of events.

"Pamela needed to get away for a while. She's gonna stay in Chicago while she sorts out what she wants to do," Mike elaborated. "She'll be with you should the need arise. By the end of that time, I might be able to handle things with you on my own. Of course, your Aunt Claire is always willing to take you back for any length of time should all else fail. I already called and started the ball rolling on getting you enrolled in high school for the fall. Pamela and your friends are going to tutor you on what you missed. You've got to get well, 'cause I may need an assistant on my trips. You know, to keep notes and take pictures."

I wiped away the tears and looked up. "Me? You want me?"

"You're the best assistant I ever had. We might go to the Tsavo River country in Africa to search for some cave lion's den when you're on break from school. Unless you've got some other plans. Then I'll have to hire someone locally, I guess."

I tried to get up, but stopped when Mike walked over. He knelt next to me as I wrapped my arms around him.

"You were right," I exclaimed through my tears while hugging him fiercely.

Mike looked at me quizzically.

"We both had things to accomplish in our lives," I added.

EPILOGUE

Chicago, Illinois
Saturday...

The following weekend, as I contentedly sat in a chair in Mike's kitchen on Saturday morning, he slid his laptop over to me. It was on the strangenews website, and the article headline said:

Pilot almost collides with huge bird

A bush pilot flying near Canada's Kluane Wildlife Sanctuary in the Yukon Territory said he almost collided with a huge bird that was as big as his aircraft. He described a bird that was gray and black with huge talons and a wingspan approaching 25 feet. Reports of this bird have persisted in the Territory for a week.

"Wow," I said and slid the computer back over to Mike. He depressed some keys and slid it back over. This article said:

Fisherman sights Sea Monster in Gulf of Mexico

The captain of a shrimp boat reported that he saw a strange creature yesterday while returning to Galveston Bay. The 25-year veteran fisherman said he was still thirty miles out in the gulf when a serpent-like creature surfaced about a hundred yards from his vessel. The captain described it as fifty feet long and having a visible protuberance on its large head, similar to antlers on a deer. He said the creature then sounded and he did not see it again.

I looked up to Mike just as Pamela slid into the kitchen and looked first at Mike, then to me.

"Mornin,' Sara," she said.

"Hi, Pamela."

She then moved over to Mike and poked him with a finger. Mike turned in his chair, and Pamela plopped herself in his lap.

"Hey, my little baby girl," she said to me.

I looked up. She had started calling me her little baby girl ever since we got to Chicago. For some unknown reason, I loved it.

"Uh, don't you have a book to read upstairs?" Pamela asked.

The Temporary End.

239

ACKNOWLEDGMENTS

Thanks to Calee Allen for her terrific job of editing and telling me where I was off base. And to Zora Knauf for her usual stellar job of formatting.

This is a third edition of the novel, *PIASA*. The original printing was in late 2010/early 2011. The second edition in 2017 contained a few editing changes and corrections and was rewritten to eliminate any undesirable language. This, he final one has been professionally edited and some scenes slightly changed (for further explanation see the Author Notes).

Piasa is a work of fiction. Names, characters, places and incidents are the products of the author's imagination or are used fictitiously and are not to be construed as real. Any resemblance to actual events, locales, organizations, or persons, living or dead, is entirely coincidental.

However, wherever possible, I presented the actual legend of the Piasa as I researched it, but as with any tale of long ago, there are surely differences of opinion. Since my original novel, *Piasa*, was published additional theories have been put forth regarding who created the original Piasa image. I ignored them in the second edition and also here as no one really knows the origin of the petroglyph. While Alton, Illinois, is an actual city, I have taken liberties in my story to construe the landscape to fit my novel. I have depicted the site and image of the Piasa reproduction as it was when I visited it in 2002. In a 2010 visit, I found that the site no longer resembles one which inspires mystery as it did earlier. Rather, it had been remade into a sterile image with paved parking area and sealed off cave openings. It has since further been transformed into a park. Additionally, the image reproduced on the cliff today is supposedly based on Marquette's diary description as the original image was lost to progress. It should be noted that some believe the image painted today is the product of a later colonist's imagination. Henry Lewis' book *The Valley of the Mississippi,* was based on what Lewis saw on the bluffs in the late 1840's and is considered by many as a more accurate portrayal of what Marquette was describing. Lewis's sketch also showed the second figure which Marquette ignored.

Cryptozoology is a real science but, to my knowledge, is not embraced by the 'scientific community' and is relegated to paranormal. The harpy eagle, tiger and lions are real creatures that fall under the umbrella of Zoology. All other creatures mentioned in the book are actual cryptids. Lake serpents were widely reported during the early years of the fledgling United States and by Native Americans. Many such creatures are still reported today in various glacial lakes of North America. Native American legends of the tlanuhwa and the uhktena, the Thunderbird and Water Panther, are a part of many tribe's lore.

Your comments are welcome on my website, www.michaelkott.com or on my Goodreads author page.